GIANT KILLER

GIANT KILLER

Vernon Tom Hyman

Richard Marek Publishers
New York

Library of Congress Cataloging in Publication Data

Hyman, Vernon Tom.
  Giant killer.

  I. Title.
PS3558.Y49G5   813'.54   80-29124

ISBN 0-399-90099-3

Printed in the United States of America

To Bern and Tom,
who made it possible

CONTENTS

Politics have no relation to morals

—Niccolò Machiavelli, *Discourses
on the First Ten Books of Livy*

PROLOGUE

Rio Dulce, July 1984

Carmelita watched the gringo through the wooden louvers of the door. The damp heat of midday poured through the slats into the shade of the kitchen, and she could feel it on her face and smell the perfume of flowers and rotting jungle vegetation borne on the humid currents. Rivulets of sweat trickled down her arms and the valley between her breasts, braless under her cheap cotton shift. Despite the heat, the draft chilled her wet skin, and she hugged her arms and shivered.

The gringo was lounging at the outdoor bar by the boat dock, drinking rum and quinine water from a plastic glass. He wore dirty chino shorts, canvas sneakers with no laces, and a frayed straw hat with a sun-bleached cloth band that said "Nassau, the Bahamas" on it. The hat's brim was tipped forward, hiding his long nose and his glass eye and the prominent ridge of bone behind his eyebrows that gave him, with his long-waisted, wiry frame, something of the appearance of a rat.

Carmelita had been alone at the Pension Izabal with the gringo since the supply boat last came upriver three weeks ago. She had said her rosary every day for all those days, and prayed every night to the Blessed Virgin Mary to forgive her for the mortal sin she knew she must commit.

Yesterday she had fashioned some pom incense in the shape of a heart and burned it secretly in the jungle, to propitiate Yum Cimil, the Maya Lord of Death, and she had prayed also to Kukulcan to guide her hand in the terrible trial that lay ahead.

Today she would kill the gringo.

The Pension Izabal—her prison—lay in a remote southern corner of Guatemala's El Peten, clinging like a parasite to the banks of the Rio Dulce, thirty miles upstream from the coastal city of Puerto Barrios, and a mile downstream from the jungle lake called Izabal. There was no access to the *pension* by road, and its facilities consisted entirely of a ramshackle collection of four thatch-roofed, screen-windowed shacks, clustered around an empty concrete swimming pool, and a concrete-block main building with a kitchen, dining room, and a back room for Carmelita, who comprised the *pension*'s entire staff.

The dock—a narrow plank wharf long enough to berth four boats—served the *pension* as a kind of open-air main entrance and lobby. The back end of the dock had been elaborated into a crude outdoor bar with a thatched roof, supported by four tall posts to keep off the rain and sun. Both dock and bar were decked out with strings of red and green Christmas-tree lights, the kind that blinked on and off. Many of the bulbs were missing from the sockets. The remainder blinked through the long, claustrophobic jungle evenings every night until midnight, when Carmelita shut off the gasoline generator.

The patrons of the Pension Izabal were mostly rich Americans who came to fish the Atlantic reefs off Belize and along the Quintana Roo. A few came for other reasons—for escape, offbeat adventure, or simply by mistake.

Now, during the height of the rainy season, no one came at all. The only craft at the dock was the *pension*'s own *canoa*, a native dugout cut square across the stern and fitted with an ancient five-horsepower outboard.

A year ago, the gringo had arrived to manage the *pension*, and Carmelita's life of routine hardships was abruptly plunged into an ordeal of terror. The gringo held her a virtual prisoner, and like a sadistic master with a pet, his lust for torment grew with its practice. Carmelita, a mestizo from the jungle village of Poptun, bore his outrages with an Indian's stoicism, because there was no other choice. Her brother Abolardo would have killed the gringo for her, but he was far away in Belize City.

Twice she had tried to escape in the *canoa*. The first time the gringo caught her because she failed to start the outboard motor. The second time she managed to get the motor started but ran the *canoa* aground a mile downstream. The gringo came down the jungle path along the river, found her, and dragged her back and tied her to the stove in the kitchen.

That evening he returned to the kitchen, drunk, and raped her, punching her repeatedly in the face and stomach, until she passed out. He slapped her awake, cursing her in English, and then drew out his machete and teased the blade across her flesh repeatedly, bathing her in her own blood. She spit in his face, finally, and he retaliated with the machete. With one savage, calculated blow, he chopped the toes from her left foot.

After that night the gringo kept the spark plug for the outboard in his pocket, and when the supply boat came, he locked her in her room behind the kitchen.

Carmelita's plan was simple. When he passed out from the rum—as he did nearly every afternoon—she would walk up and plunge the big bone-handled kitchen knife into his back with all of her strength. Then she would remove the spark plug for the *canoa* from his pocket—she must not forget that—and roll him off the dock and into the river. No one would find him until he had floated miles downstream, and no one would care when they did.

The gringo was toying with a scorpion he had captured, slashing the machete blade repeatedly into the wood of the bar, barely missing the scorpion's head. When he tired of the game, he brought the machete down hard and neatly severed it from its pincers. The insect, alive but defenseless, darted off the edge of the bar and scrambled through a wide crack in the dock flooring. The gringo flipped the machete after it, embedding the point in the plank floor, and laughed. He drained his glass of rum, and moments later his head bumped gently onto his arms and he slept.

Carmelita watched from the door, barely daring to breathe. When she was certain that he was asleep, she inched open the drawer in the kitchen table and pulled out the long knife, and crept outside, clutching it tightly against her dress. At the edge of the dock she hesitated, mesmerized by the gringo's proximity, terrified that she might not be able to strike.

Her hesitation saved his life.

The throb of an engine broke the stillness. Carmelita came out of her trance and looked downriver, straining her eyes to penetrate the haze. A large twin-engine diesel hove into view, thumping through the murky waters at high speed, pennants on her flying bridge whipping in the breeze. The big boat cut throttle fifty yards below the *pension*'s dock and idled past. When Carmelita realized that it intended to stop, she retreated in panic to the kitchen.

The boat came about upriver, issued a double blast from her air horn, and angled across the current toward the dock. The gringo stirred and raised his head unsteadily. When the boat had closed to within thirty feet, she reversed engines briefly, then let the current carry her toward the dock at a crawl. The bow nudged the pilings, and a black deckhand in a bright purple shirt and dirty white trousers jumped to the dock, catching lines thrown to him from the bow and stern and quickly securing them.

A second black jumped to the dock after him; both took up posts at separate ends of the boat and waited, standing with a lazy insolence that belied their alertness. Large bulges under their gaudy shirts indicated pistols. Half a dozen other men crowded the boat's fantail, brandishing rifles and whispering to each other in a subdued excitement.

An older man—tall, thick-chested, and Caucasian, too carefully dressed to be a vacationing fisherman—emerged from the cluster of deckhands and stared across at the gringo. The big man wore a sailing cap at a jaunty angle and aviator sunglasses that disguised his face, but there was no missing the expression of disgust as he took in the scene before him.

From behind the kitchen-door slats Carmelita could feel the tension as the gringo and the man on the boat appraised each other. At length the tall man spoke.

"Cyclops?"

The gringo nodded, and tilted the empty glass to his lips, to catch any final drops.

"We got a job for you," the tall man said. "Kind of an emergency."

The gringo smiled and raised his glass in the boat's direction, as if offering it a toast. A moment later the glass was arcing through the air. It missed the tall man's cap by a few inches and bounced on the wooden deck behind him. No one moved, but the clicks of a dozen safety catches were as audible as crickets in the jungle.

The gringo laughed. "What kinda job?" he asked.

"Your kind of job."

The gringo rocked his head slowly back and forth a few times, as if trying to make out the faces on the boat.

"Big?" he asked.

"Yeah," the tall man replied. "Big." He motioned to the two blacks waiting on the dock with their pistols drawn, and they started to move toward the gringo, to escort him on board.

"The biggest," the tall man said, to no one in particular. "The goddamned biggest."

The Cyclades, August 1984

Demetrios clutched the envelope to his chest and trudged up the path to the master's private spot, overlooking the sea. Every day after breakfast, the master retreated to this hill to sit in his "outdoor temple," as he called it—a flat piece of marble that once formed part of the lintel of a real temple in the classical age—and watch the ships cross the blue-and-gold Aegean far below. Sometimes he sat for hours, barely moving, his eyes fixed on the horizon. Demetrios disliked to interrupt the master during these meditations, but this time he had no choice.

The master was the wisest man Demetrios had ever known. He understood everything, even the hearts of men. At least Demetrios believed that he did, but Demetrios' judgment was based on narrow experience. He was the son of an orchard keeper, and he knew almost nothing of the world. He had been to Athens only once, when he was a young man.

The master was his employer, but he was also his friend and teacher. He told wonderful stories in his eloquent Greek, and Demetrios often tried to memorize them, so he could try them out on his friends in the village. Demetrios knew of no one whose Greek was so learned, so precise. And Greek was not even the master's native tongue. No one knew what that was. Demetrios had asked him many times, but the master always evaded him. The master did not like to talk about his past.

Demetrios knew also that the master was dying. He did not show it, but Demetrios knew it just the same. It puzzled him, that the master had come here, to this tiny island, to spend the last days of his life just watching the sea. Every time he asked the master about it, he got a different answer. Once the master had replied, "This is the island where Homer came to die. What greater recommendation do I need?" Another time he had said, "All the world is right here. I do not need to go anywhere ever again."

But the strangest answer the master ever gave was this one: "I do what a chameleon likes to do. Sit all day in the sun."

"Why a chameleon, *levendi*?" Demetrios had asked.

"Because that's what I am, Demetrios. That's my name."

Demetrios reached the top of the first rise and paused to catch his breath. From here he could see Plakalos Monastery and the ruins of the Crispo castle, sights as familiar to him as the tiny streets of the village. Beyond, the sea shimmered in the sun.

When he neared the master's spot, the master turned to face him, hearing his approach over the stones on the path. His thin face was smooth and deeply tanned, like the supple leather of the wine *bottas* they sold in the shops in the village.

Demetrios bit his lip. "I'm sorry, *levendi*. The man came to the village by special boat and walked to your house. I would not let him come here, but I had to promise him to take you this. He waits at your house now. He said he must know that you have read it before he leaves."

The master took the envelope from Demetrios. He began working open the edges, peeling back the wax seal carefully from the paper, so that he would not tear it. Demetrios stood several feet away, pretending to be looking out at the sea, but watching the master out of the corner of his eyes. No one had ever brought a message to him before. No one had ever come to visit him.

The master extracted three pages from the envelope, opened them and read them, his face impassive. After what seemed like a long time, he looked over at Demetrios and smiled.

"Tell the messenger that I have read the letter, so that he may be on his way. Then get our boat ready. Tomorrow you will have to take me to Santorini, so I can catch the midday ferry to Piraeus."

"You are leaving Ios." Demetrios said it more as a statement than a question.

The master folded the sheets of paper carefully back into their envelope. "Yes, for a little while. You must take care of everything here for me until I come back. Let me stay here another hour, and then I'll come down to dinner."

Demetrios nodded, and turned to descend the path. Inside, he felt a profound anger at the messenger and his message. He knew the master would not be back.

I
The Game

1

Jay Thompson had slept poorly, and the fatigue left him feeling vulnerable. Much of the night he had lain awake in his room at the Hay-Adams, rehearsing for this morning's encounter with Roland. Now, when he needed to be at his absolute best—charming, persuasive, quick-thinking, and firm-talking—his head buzzed, his eyes burned, and his mouth felt as if he had eaten glue for breakfast. He gazed glassy-eyed out of the cab window as it moved past a line of high-school students gathering at the north gate for a tour of the White House. It was a gloomy day, with a cold wind that had people on the street grabbing for their hats.

Thompson let his head fall back against the upholstery and struggled to focus his energies on his mission, but his brain kept losing the picture, leaving him with a standby image of the back of the cabby's fat neck and head framed in the windshield. He saw a detached view of himself, too: tall, thin, mid-thirties, with an arrogant jaw and pointed nose he didn't like and straight brown hair cut by an expensive barber to hide the corners of a receding brow. In his soft blue shirt, carefully fitted blue pinstripe suit, and glovelike Italian shoes, he looked sleek and prosperous, an upper-middle-class professional bent on an important errand.

Looks were deceiving. He felt like a disheveled bum hiding under his own skin. His absurdly expensive attaché case, glowing with its rich cowhide patina on the seat next to him, looked alien and intimidating. It was a gift from Gloria four years ago, to remind him—or more likely to remind herself—that he was a successful executive in a glamorous business.

Thompson closed his eyes and tried to shut out the self-doubts that assailed him. He knew he faced a major test in his professional life, one that could affect his career dramatically. A moment of truth. Even in the supposedly civilized trade of book publishing, they came, every now and then. He had to be up for it.

Money and prestige were at stake. Particularly money. Thompson kept repeating the sum to himself, over and over, his tired brain stuck on the phrase like a turntable needle on a record scratch: one million dollars . . . one million dollars . . . one million dollars.

It was the sum advanced by his publishing house, J. P. Marwick and Sons, to Allen G. Roland, former director of the CIA, for his memoirs.

One million dollars. More than he could earn in twenty years.

Every major publisher in New York had been after Roland, so it was considered a great coup for Thompson to have landed him. Roland had been discretion itself throughout his entire military and intelligence career. Keeping his mouth shut, he once told an interviewer, was easier than lying, and a lot safer. His laconic style had often exasperated Congress and the media, and had prompted a wag in the Carter administration to dub him "Old Zipper Lips," an inspired nickname, because the rows of deep vertical lines around Roland's tight lips did indeed suggest a zipper.

But then John Douglas Mills, a conservative Republican senator from Texas, became President of the United States. With the nation upset and angry about energy costs, unemployment and inflation, Mills was swept into office by an unprecedented landslide, winning a majority in all fifty states.

And Mills didn't waste any time turning his mandate loose against the Washington bureaucracy. As it happened, Roland's head was the first to roll. Mills fired him on his second day in office and replaced him with an old Army buddy, General William Ward, a political crony with no experience in government and a mediocre military record. Washington insiders were not surprised, because Roland had made the mistake of unzipping his lips just once during the election campaign, characterizing Mills's proposal to deport all the country's illegal aliens back to Mexico as "stupid and dangerous." The remark, made off-the-cuff in answer to a reporter's question, made headlines. The Mills camp was furious.

Roland accepted his firing as inevitable, but Mills was in a vindictive mood and wanted to punish him further. He arranged for General Ward, his new DCI, to appear before the Senate Oversight Committee and level charges of financial dishonesty against Roland and his management of the agency. Roland was subjected to weeks of humiliating public grilling by the committee, forced into the impossible position of trying to defend both the agency and his career without being able to reveal the classified information that would refute the charges against him.

He emerged from the hearings a ruined man, his career at an end and his reputation in tatters. The experience made him bitter, and he began telling close friends that he intended to write his memoirs, hinting that he had some stories to tell.

No one doubted that. Roland's knowledge of the secret workings of over four decades of United States foreign policy and that of its allies and opponents was encyclopedic. Publishers, smelling a best-seller, began to court him avidly, and Roland did not discourage their overtures. In fact, he hired himself a literary agent and put his memoirs up for sale. Thompson had risked his company's million dollars (of which Roland so far had received half) on the bet that Roland, to restore his own reputation, would drag out some spectacular skeletons from the government's closet.

Thompson had had a difficult time persuading old Sam Marwick, the head of the house, to back his gamble. The house was rich, thanks to the backlist of prominent authors Marwick's father had left behind, but Sam was a notoriously tight-fisted publisher. He had little use for political memoirs in general, and Allen Roland in particular.

Marwick had danced up and down in his office, calling Roland's agent, Max Feldman, a pirate for demanding so much money.

"Over a dozen best-sellers came out of Watergate," Thompson had said. "Dirty linen is expensive, Sam."

Marwick relented when Thompson put his job on the line, but he warned him that if Roland failed to deliver the expected blockbuster, his job would be on the line anyway.

That was two years ago. Last week Thompson had received the first draft of the memoir, and he was still reeling from the shock. There was no dirty linen at all. None.

The manuscript covered the already known facts of his life—his work for naval intelligence during World War Two, his recruitment into the wartime OSS by "Wild Bill" Donovan, and his early years with the CIA under Allen Dulles. In stolid, bland prose, Roland plowed dutifully through his entire career, touching base along the way with all the well-worn CIA events—Guatemala, Lebanon, the U-2 affair, Iran, the Dominican Republic, the Bay of Pigs, the Kennedy assassination, Vietnam, Chile, Watergate, the Church hearings. He included the usual cast of characters and said the customary things, leavening his account with a dose of solemn philosophizing on the role of an intelligence service in a democracy, some self-congratulations for rebuilding the agency from the shambles of the late seventies, and some mild criticisms directed at some of his predecessors. President Mills, the man who had ended his career and contributed largely to the destruction of his reputation, was not even mentioned.

And that was it. No revelations, nothing not already on the public record. A flat, bland memoir. It wasn't next year's best-seller, and it certainly wasn't worth a million dollars.

Thompson knew that he was in deep trouble. He had saved manuscripts before, but this one demanded an entire change of attitude on the part of the author. He called Roland's agent, Max Feldman, first, and informed him that he considered the memoir to be an unmitigated disaster. Unless Max could persuade Roland to spill his guts, Thompson warned, J. P. Marwick and Sons would be forced to cancel the contract.

Max promised to help, and with his eye no doubt nervously focused on his own ten percent of that million, he arranged for Roland to meet Thompson in Washington to discuss revising the manuscript. Thompson intended to attack on two fronts. First, he would soften Roland up to the idea of a truly confessional autobiography. Second, he would persuade Roland to take on a collaborator.

The collaborator Thompson had in mind was a young journalist, Harriet Mitchell, who worked in the Washington office of the New York *Times*. Thompson knew that Mitchell, an aggressive and skilled interviewer, could pry things out of Roland that the old master spy didn't even know that he knew. She was a formidable investigative reporter, as many public personalities had learned—to their considerable chagrin. "After Maxine Cheshire interviewed me," a former cabinet member once told a friend, "I wanted to kill her. But after Harriet Mitchell got through with me, I wanted to kill myself."

The taxi turned onto Reservoir Road in Georgetown, Roland's street. Thompson watched the town houses slide by, and he thought about the money again, and his own future, and began lining up the arguments he would employ to turn the situation around: This is a unique opportunity, Mr. Roland, for you to set the record straight on a score of controversial matters. . . . You owe the public, whom you served so well all these years, the truth as you really saw it. . . . You owe posterity an accurate account of your participation in some of the greatest events of this century. . . . Surely you would not want your version of history, the real version, to die with you? . . . Etc., etc. It all sounded pretty phony. Roland would probably laugh at him.

But being persuasive was a major part of Thompson's job, and it had been his experience that shameless flattery of Very Important People usually worked.

Thompson noticed that he was chewing his fingernails. He slapped his hand down onto his lap in disgust and took a deep breath. The cab stopped in front of 225, and Thompson got out, pretending to be full of bounce and enthusiasm, but mocking himself inwardly. The book editor as salesman, he thought, with his sample case of flatteries, clever small talk, pertinent anecdotes, reassurances, cajoleries, admonitions, historical perspectives, carrots and sticks.

The front door of Roland's town house was high and intimidating, with a matched pair of giant brass carriage lamps flanking it, like bodyguards. Thompson found the buzzer, with its discreet nameplate, *A. G. Roland*, in gold script, leaned on it, and waited nervously.

The street was almost deserted at two in the afternoon. The only human beings in sight were two young children playing on the front steps of the house next door. One, a delicate dark-haired child of about five, was sitting in a small red wagon and trying to persuade the other child, of about the same age, with blond curls, to pull the wagon. His thin voice was vexed and impatient: "I have a *very, very* important meeting to attend. I *must* get there at *once*. And you promised to be my chauffeur, so you *have* to take me!"

The blond curls shook her head vigorously. "No, I don't!"

"Yes, you do!" Firm, insistent.

"No, I don't!" Adamant.

"Yes, you do!" A shrill scream.

Thompson watched their game. Five minutes, and still no answer. Thompson could hear the bell ringing inside, so he knew that it was functioning. He remembered that Roland had a housekeeper, but perhaps this was her afternoon off. He rang again, pressing the buzzer insistently.

The children next door had fallen silent and were watching him with curiosity. Thompson cleared his throat, feeling suddenly like an intruder in the neighborhood.

"Did you children see Mr. Roland leave here?" he asked them.

They shook their heads in unison, and the girl spoke up. "I'm *quite* certain that no one left while *we* were here."

Thompson muttered a thank-you and started to bang on the door, feeling uncomfortable. It seemed like such an aggressive act, pounding on someone's dwelling—come on out! I know you're in there!—as if to beat the house and its occupants into submission. In this instance, the house surrendered immediately. The door swung open from the force of his first knock, and Thompson stepped back, startled.

After a thoughtful pause he ventured into the foyer, a dark wood-paneled vestibule with a small, new-looking oriental rug on the floor. Just inside the door, under an ornate gilded mirror, sat a massive side table that had probably never borne the weight of anything heavier than a calling card. Beyond, a dim hallway stretched back past a staircase to a closed door at the rear of the house. A faint odor of pipe tobacco—something harsh, with a lot of Turkish Sobrahnie in it—hung in the air. The place felt stuffy.

Thompson called out Roland's name. His voice cracked a little, and the words came out louder than he had intended. There was no answer. He called several times, and then peeked into the front rooms to see if anyone was hiding there. Some spy, Thompson thought. Can't keep a rendezvous in his own house, and forgets to lock his own front door.

Thompson came to the closed door at the end of the corridor and knocked politely. No response. He paused, tormented by a momentary indecision, and then opened it. The room beyond was obviously Roland's study, quite different in feel and appearance from the expensively overdecorated front parlors. It was dusty and book-lined, with a fireplace full of ashes, a well-used burgundy carpet, a couple of high-backed Queen Anne armchairs, and a large campaign desk, appropriately spilling over with papers and books. Two old sailing prints hung on the wall behind the desk, and sitting on the ledge of a large casement window was an ancient brass telescope on a wooden tripod.

Allen G. Roland was also in the room, hanging by a length of nylon rope from what had once been a ceiling fixture for a chandelier. He hung suspended about a foot from the floor, rotating slowly, like a pendulum on an unwound clock, exhausting the last fractions of energy from the mainspring. Near him, kicked over on its side, was a step stool.

The rope around his neck was tied like an authentic hangman's noose, with about nine inches coiled in back of the knot. Roland's head was twisted sharply to one side, his face an angry purple, and his eyes stared at a point somewhere near the far corner of the ceiling. He wore an expensive charcoal-gray pinstripe suit with a white shirt and a red tie with a small black pattern on it—dressed, it appeared, for an important occasion. He had removed his shoes and placed them neatly by the desk. His feet, dangling in their black stockings, looked very small.

Thompson stood there, disbelief slowly crumbling under the weight of horrible reality. Finally he stumbled from the room and made his way to a window in the front parlor. He clutched the windowpane, its surface unnaturally cool and slippery under his fingers, and stared out at the two children, still playing their innocent game on the lawn next door.

He tried to think what to do. His mind was racing out of control, spinning in a chaotic jumble of emotions just short of panic. His pulse was pounding, and he felt dizzy. He kept swallowing to keep from gagging. "God damn you, Allen Roland," he groaned. "God damn you!"

2

With four Scotches, Thompson began to feel a welcome sensation of numbness. He wondered, as he did from time to time, if he was becoming an alcoholic. It was an occupational hazard—endless business lunches and dinner parties for authors, all made tolerable by booze. Now Roland's death had given him the most compelling excuse to drink he had had in years.

Harriet Mitchell sat beside him, drinking white-wine spritzers. They were squeezed into a small table against the side wall in the Old Ebbitt, the ancient bar and grill on F Street. A dense cloud cover of pipe and cigarette smoke had reduced visibility in the narrow room considerably, and the noise from the young singles crowded several deep at the bar forced them to lean close together to hear each other. They had met once before, briefly, at a cocktail party in Washington, and had instantly adopted a familiar manner with each other.

Harriet was a striking woman of about thirty, with a round face, large brown eyes, and silky brown hair that fell in a wave across her forehead. Her lower lip protruded slightly, enough to give her a perpetually pouting expression, which fit her spiky personality. She was outspoken and quick-witted, and a shade too aggressive for Thompson's taste, but the Scotches were rapidly changing his taste.

Thompson had called her about a hour after discovering Roland's body to tell her she was out of a ghost-writing job. In the panic and confusion of the moment, it hadn't even occurred to him that Roland's suicide was a front-page news story. Harriet, however, jumped instantly into action, and after three hours of intense scrambling—picking Thompson's brain, talking to the police, to the Public Information office of the CIA, to President Mills's press secretary, Jared Scott, and to several former members of the CIA who had worked with Roland—she had filed a story for the paper in time for the next day's edition. It would run on page one.

"This is a strange line," Thompson said, holding up the computer carbon of the story she had brought with her. " 'Although the White House refused to speculate on the reasons for Roland's suicide, press secretary Jared Scott indicated that close friends of the former director had noticed that he had been in a state of severe depression since his dismissal as CIA chief.' Who were the close friends?"

Harriet shook her head. "He wouldn't say. If Roland had any close friends, Scott certainly doesn't know them. That's just Scott being patronizing and insufferable, as usual."

Thompson thought for a moment, then rattled the ice cubes in his glass in the direction of the waitress. "He must have been depressed about something else. He was fired over three and a half years ago, after all."

Harriet arched an eyebrow. "Are you going to tell me you think he killed himself because he was seriously ill?"

Thompson blushed. "It occurred to me."

"No. I called Bethesda Naval Hospital. He had a checkup two months ago. Aside from his war wounds, a recurrent hiatus hernia, and an allergy to milk products, he couldn't have been healthier."

The waitress arrived with a new round of drinks. Harriet looked Thompson in the eye, brushing her hair where it fell past her cheek with a slow, habitual nervous gesture. "I have a better explanation for his death."

"What's that?"

"Somebody killed him."

He glanced up at her.

"That's paranoid."

Harriet pulled up her handbag from beside her chair and began rummaging through it. It was an enormous leather sack, bulging with what appeared to be the contents of an entire medicine chest. She eventually ferreted out what she was looking for and handed it across to Thompson. It was a clipping, three paragraphs long, from the New York *Times*, dated October 23, 1983.

"I came across it in the files this afternoon while checking some facts in my story. I couldn't use it, but I thought it was interesting."

LIBERAL LEADER ASSASSINATED IN GUATEMALA

(*Guatemala City, Guatemala, Oct 23:*) Dr. Jorge Villa Santiago, a leader of the liberal opposition party here, was found hanged yesterday afternoon in his home in an outlying section of the city. Suicide was immediately ruled out because the victim's hands were bound. Dr. Villa Santiago was an outspoken critic of Guatemalan President Gomez, and also of the United States, which he has frequently accused in the past of using CIA personnel to keep President Gomez in power.

Dr. Villa Santiago, 63, had been a member of the leftist government of Jacobo Arbenz, overthrown in a military coup in 1957. It is generally acknowledged that the CIA played a major role in that coup.

A spokesman for President Gomez denied any government responsibility for the opposition leader's death. Dr. Villa Santiago is the latest casualty in a rash of political assassinations in this country in the past year. Twenty-seven deaths and eight disappearances are attributed to a right-wing terrorist group called the White Hand, which supports the present regime. Dr. Villa Santiago is the third such victim to be found hanged.

Thompson folded the clipping and handed it back to Harriet.

"Nobody hanged Allen Roland."

"What makes you so sure?"

Thompson thought about it. "Well, other than the fact that his hands were not bound, there was the kitchen stool."

"Not very persuasive."

"But what assassin would go to all the trouble of stringing him up in his own house and risk getting caught?"

"To make it look like a suicide, of course."

"Okay. But why would anyone want to kill him?"

Harriet laughed out loud.

"What the hell is so funny about that?" Thompson demanded.

"I'm sorry. I guess it just sounded so naive. I don't *know* anybody who had a reason to kill him. But I imagine in his line of work he collected a few enemies—the kind who know how to kill. Don't you think?"

Thompson sighed. Winning arguments with Harriet was probably very difficult. "I'm not a fan of political conspiracies. It usually involves reading meaning into meaningless connections. I know a guy who thinks there's something very significant in the fact that John Kennedy, Bobby Kennedy, Martin Luther King, and Mary Jo Kopechne all had last names that began with a K."

"Well, maybe there is."

"What? A gang of killers who hate the letter K?"

Harriet stabbed Thompson's hand with the tip of a swizzle stick. "But CIA people get killed all the time! Why not Roland? Someone was paying back an old score. Or maybe Roland knew something incriminating about someone."

Thompson took the stick away from her. "If he did, he certainly neglected to include it in his manuscript. And CIA people don't get killed all the time, except in novels. Now who's being naive?"

Harriet slumped back in her chair. "Okay. Let's change the subject," she said. "Can I ask you a personal question?"

Thompson flinched instinctively and heard himself saying "Sure" in a guarded voice. Harriet Mitchell was famous for catching her subjects off guard with sudden "personal questions."

"Don't you ever eat?"

Thompson laughed, relieved and disappointed at the same time.

"The last thing I had to eat was a cheese Danish at ten-thirty this morning," she said. "And I'm *not* on a diet."

The waitress was found, hamburgers ordered, and Harriet made a trip to the ladies' room. Thompson watched her as she maneuvered between the tables. Her navy-blue dress had the perfect drape of expensive cloth, and hung closely around a pair of long and well-shaped legs. She walked fast for a woman, a tomboyish, defiant stride that called attention to what Thompson noticed was an exceptionally well-shaped rear end.

A portly, red-faced man with beetling white eyebrows sitting with a party of three young women raised a fat hand in her direction as she passed by his table. He aimed it toward her thigh, but she deftly angled out of reach, shook an admonishing finger at him, and brushed on by. Thompson heard his wheezy laugh.

"That was Senator MacNair," she explained when she returned, pulling her chair up to the table with some vigor. "Republican, New Hampshire. Friend of the President. Friend of Big Oil. Friend of nuclear energy. And an enemy of the people. Those simpering females are members of his staff. A captive audience."

MacNair looked over at Harriet, and she flashed a smile at him. The senator smiled back absently and refocused his attention on his admiring employees. Thompson noticed that MacNair's hand, the one that had grabbed for Harriet, was now under the table, firmly attached to the thigh of the girl on his left.

"He tried to get me fired from the *Times* after I wrote a series exposing some of his friends in New Hampshire who were operating a heating-oil kickback racket. He's a corrupt old Neanderthal, and about as public-spirited as Count Dracula."

Thompson watched Harriet's mouth as she talked. It was a wide, delicious-looking mouth, and her lips made exaggerated movements to emphasize her words. "He seems pretty friendly," he said, hearing a tinge of jealousy in his voice that surprised him.

"The old coot will make a pass at anything that moves."

The hamburgers came, and the two of them fell silent, concentrating on their food. Thompson wondered what possibilities the evening contained. They weren't exactly out on a date, although it had begun to seem like one. And tomorrow he was supposed to be back in his office in New York to face the dismal aftermath of Roland's suicide. It seemed disrespectful of Roland's memory to be drinking and having a good time, but he felt impelled in that direction, to escape the unpleasant image of the poor man hanging from the ceiling of his study.

He watched Senator MacNair. Two of the girls got up and left, and the third, on whose thigh MacNair still maintained a heavy grip, seemed prepared to stay. MacNair's voice diminished from its former bawdy wheeze to a low, intimate rumble. His big paw began a slow rubbing motion on her crotch. Moving in for the kill. Thompson thought of grabbing Harriet in the same manner. He was almost drunk enough to try it. What would she do? Yell? Punch him in the mouth? Or just slap his hand away?

"Do you think I'm as sexy as she is?"

Thompson looked at Harriet, toying with that errant strand of hair again. Personal-question time for real now.

"Who?"

"The girl with MacNair. The one you're watching."

"I'm sorry. I didn't know that it was so obvious."

"Well?"

"Almost."

"Very funny. Are you married?"

"Formerly."

"Why did she leave you?"

"What makes you so sure *she* left *me*?"

Harriet picked up her spritzer glass, took a sip, and measured him with her big eyes. "Just a good guess. You're not the type to walk out yourself. You might have wanted to leave, but you would have hated the confrontation more."

"I'm beginning to think you're something of a smart-ass."

She smiled. "So I'm right, you see?"

"More or less. But I'm not going to let you provoke me into any major confession. I'm too drunk and it's too boring and complicated, like most of my life."

"Now you're being stuffy—and patronizing."

Thompson frowned. "Give me a break. It's been a rotten day."

"Are you very inhibited?" Thompson stared at her angrily. Harriet seemed pleased at his reaction. "You seem inhibited to me," she added.

"Maybe if I slapped you in the face it might change your mind," he replied.

"It might," she admitted. "But I just don't think I'm your type."

"Really? What is my type, then?"

"I don't know. Big-busted blonds, probably. The dumb, compliant kind."

"That's because the sassy ones with brown eyes and unruly hair scare me to death."

They looked at each other for a long, serious moment, and then broke out laughing. Harriet reached over and squeezed Thompson's hand, then pulled her handbag onto her lap and extracted half a dozen plastic pill bottles from its depths. She removed a pill from each one, swallowed the whole handful with her wine, and dropped the bottles back into the bag.

Thompson watched, fascinated. "Now can I ask *you* a personal question?"

"No cause for alarm," she said. "They're just vitamins."

"So many?"

"C and E, and B-complex and iron. If I don't take them, I get colds."

"But what are all those other bottles?"

Harriet looked embarrassed. "Well, there's APC, Chlor-Trimeton, Maalox, Valium, Coricidin, Dexamyl, Darvon, Nytol, aspirin, codeine, and a few other things."

"Wow."

"I like to be prepared."

"I'll say."

"All right, so I'm a bit of a pill freak. I'm neurotic, and you're inhibited." Harriet stole a glance at her wristwatch. "Let's go to bed," she said.

Thompson gulped.

"Well, why not, for heaven's sake? I hate all that courtship stuff. I'm too busy to wait until the fourth date, or whatever. And you look like the fourth-date type to me." She cast her eyes down at her empty glass. "It must be all those spritzers," she confessed in a low voice. "I don't usually behave this way. I just feel incredibly horny."

Thompson signaled the waitress for the check.

In the taxi Harriet leaned into him and they embraced around a wet, passionate kiss. Thompson slipped his hand beneath the navy-blue dress and up along the underside of Harriet's smooth bare thigh. The velvety warmness was electrifying, and the sensation of Harriet's fingers grazing the front of his pants gave him an instant, throbbing erection.

Minutes later, they walked from the cab to her apartment on the second floor of an old brownstone off Dupont Circle. Harriet seemed subdued, and at the door she became nervous and embarrassed. She pressed a hand gently against Thompson's shirtfront, and lowered her eyes.

"Listen, Jay." Her voice was soft, regretful. "I have to be up for a story on the Conway campaign. It's been a very long and tough day for both of us, and you have to be in New York tomorrow morning. It's way past midnight. We're both exhausted."

His erotic haze evaporated swiftly. "That's true, but . . ."

Harriet looked distressed. "I'm sorry, really. I like you and I want to be honest. I was feeling a little high and I got carried away. I mean, I would still like to, but the wine's given me a headache and I suddenly feel very tired. . . . Dammit, I always say the wrong thing."

Thompson felt manipulated. "You really like to call the shots, don't you?"

Harriet's voice hardened a little. "Don't be silly. I'm just being practical."

"You're just being a tease."

Harriet shook her head in exasperation. "Now you're acting like a spoiled baby! Good night!"

She slammed her apartment door in his face so hard it rattled the lighting fixture in the corridor ceiling. Thompson stood staring idiotically at the tidy black plastic plate beneath the peephole on her door that spelled out *H. Mitchell* in white letters. It was the second nameplate he remembered staring at that day.

Suddenly Harriet was at the door again, tears streaming down her face. She grabbed his arm and pulled him inside, quickly locking the door behind them. Thompson's head was reeling—no woman changes her mind that fast!

The narrow foyer immediately inside the door opened directly into a living room containing a tastefully eclectic mixture of new and old furnishings, set off with thick rugs, colorful pillows, black-and-white prints, and a lot of books.

But presently it was a shambles. Lamps were smashed, books ripped apart, records pulled out of their slipcases, the contents of desk and table drawers strewn about and walked on, pillows slashed open, furniture fabric torn apart, and in one place, the wallpaper had even been partially stripped from the wall.

In the bedroom, the depredations continued. The bed had been pulled apart and the mattress slashed down the middle from top to bottom. Two empty suitcases lay open on the floor, on top of clothes which had been yanked from the closets and scattered about among a debris of boxes, papers, letters, shoes, panties, belts, bras, and stockings. A small television set on the dresser, and a portable typewriter and tape recorder on a small desk—the normal booty of the burglar—were untouched.

"Is anything missing?" Thompson asked.

"I don't think so. The jewelry box wasn't opened . . . and I don't have any silver."

They stood together by the edge of the bed, and Harriet, still crying, started to laugh at the same time. Thompson put his arm around her, and she rested her cheek against his chest, struggling to regain her composure.

"Maybe I'd better stay," he said.

She nodded.

3

On the thirtieth floor of 150 East Fiftieth Street, the floor that housed the editorial offices of J. P. Marwick and Sons, Publishers, Thompson emerged from the elevator, feeling like a dead plant. It was past eleven in the morning, and the receptionist, a middle-aged lady of rigid standards who had the infuriating habit of looking at her wristwatch whenever Thompson came in, did so now as he walked past. He made a mental note to himself that he must do something about getting her promoted to some job out in the company's warehouse in New Jersey. She'd love it there with the time clocks.

"Mr. Thompson," she said as he pushed on the heavy mahogany door leading to the editorial area, "Mr. Marwick would like to see you immediately." The severity of her tone told him she expected Marwick was going to chastise him for getting to work late. She didn't read the newspapers.

"Thank you, Grace." He tried a smile but managed only to bare his teeth at her. He pushed through the door and headed unsteadily toward his office, hoping he could make it to the relative safety of his desk before anyone spotted him. His head was splitting from a hangover, and the accumulated loss of two nights' sleep was affecting his vision and his coordination. He and Harriet had stayed up for most of the night, straightening up the apartment and drinking up the two bottles of wine in her refrigerator. Finally, near dawn, they had fallen asleep on top of the bed, fully clothed. Somehow, Thompson had made the nine-A.M. shuttle to New York.

Outside his office, his assistant, Kate, was fighting a losing battle to keep pace with the phone. All three buttons were flashing, and as soon as she hung up on one line, it rang again immediately. She cupped her hand over the mouthpiece when she saw him.

"Thank God you're back! All hell is breaking loose. Here!"

She thrust a stack of telephone message slips in his hand, with a note from her on top.

"Don't tell anyone I'm here," he said, and ducked into his office, shutting the door behind him. He collapsed into his big leather chair and took a deep breath, promising himself that somehow he would get to bed by eight o'clock, even if the planet was invaded from outer space. He looked at Kate's note:

> You've had calls this morning from **CBS, NBC, ABC**, channels 5, 9, 11 (not necessarily in that order), and from the **AP, UPI**, the New York *Times*, the Washington *Post, Daily News*, **L.A.** *Times, Newsday, Newsweek*, and *Time* magazine. Also from the **FBI**. The rest of calls are the routine hysterics from authors, agents, etc. They're all on the slips. And Mr. Marwick has called *eight* times! He's frantic. You'd better see him right away.
>
> Poor Mr. Roland. What a terrible thing for him to do!

Thompson smiled. Even the New York *Times*. He supposed they didn't yet know that their crack investigative reporter in Washington had already pumped him dry. He threw the stack of slips on the desk and struggled back to his feet, deciding he'd better expend his fading energies coping with Sam Marwick.

When Marwick's secretary saw Thompson, she looked so relieved Thompson thought she was going to collapse at her desk. She told him to go right in. "He's in a terrible temper," she whispered.

Thompson nodded his thanks. "So am I, Margaret." He pushed open Marwick's door and walked directly to the chair in front of Marwick's desk, and sat down.

Sam Marwick pretended to be engrossed in the contents of a file folder, and he focused on Thompson slowly. He appeared exceptionally calm, Thompson noticed, and that was a bad sign. Marwick was the sort of curmudgeon who enforced his will routinely with temper tantrums. When he was really enraged, he affected an arctic tranquillity.

He studied Thompson over his half-frame glasses for a few moments, then removed them and directed his gaze out the window. "I've been in here since eight o'clock this morning, Jay, taking calls from every damned news agency in the Western world. And when I haven't been doing that, I've been looking for you. In fact, I've been looking for you since last night, when I first heard about Roland's suicide."

Marwick had a rude habit of staring at people. He did that to Thompson now, fixing his agate-hard blue eyes on him like a cat measuring its prey. "I've left messages at your hotel in Washington," he continued, "both last night and this morning. They claim that you never came in last night. I called you at home in the city last night and this morning. No answer."

Thompson nodded, trying to meet his stare.

"Now, you'd think, Jay, that given the situation, a responsible person might at least have had the courtesy—and that's all I'm talking about, Jay, I'm not even talking about brains—but the courtesy, to have called me sometime yesterday, or early today at least, to let me know what the hell was going on. And maybe be around to help me handle the situation."

Thompson sighed wearily. "I thought there was no need to bother you until I got back from Washington. That was this morning, an hour ago. And I had no idea the press was going to make such a fuss."

Marwick raised his voice a notch. "I'm not talking about the damn press, Jay. I'm talking about money. We've had to make some decisions."

"What decisions?"

"We're suing the estate of Allen Roland to get back that five hundred thousand dollars."

Thompson's mouth fell open. "Jesus! How about waiting until the body is cold? Feldman's a reasonable man."

Marwick swiveled around in his chair. "It might interest you to know that I had a conversation with Max Feldman just an hour ago, while you were still missing in action. Not only does Feldman not intend to return the half-million, he expects us to pay him the *other* half."

Thompson thought about that. "On the basis that Roland turned in a complete manuscript?"

"That's right."

"And revises are no longer possible."

Marwick nodded. "It's take it or leave it."

"Don't jump the gun. Roland's death may make the book very popular. It's great publicity. Why not stall Feldman for a few weeks? Maybe we can renegotiate a lower advance."

Marwick turned back, and most of the anger drained out of his voice. "No, we can't do that. We've both read the manuscript and we both know that it's not what we paid for. It's weak as hell. You admitted it. Hell, he didn't even bother to get it professionally typed! I've never seen such a sloppy manuscript. There are typos and overstrikes on every page! Anyway, with Roland dead, we have no way of improving it. Controversy won't do us a damned bit of good, because by the time we could get the book out—five months from now at the earliest—nobody would remember or give a damn. If we were talking about twenty-five thousand dollars, or even fifty thousand, that would be one thing. But Feldman will never come down to that level. Even at half a million you know as well as I do that you have to sell a hell of a lot of books to make your money back. If this ends up in a lawsuit—as I intend it to—I want to make sure that our reaction to the manuscript is unambiguous. We have to reject it now, emphatically. If we wait, Feldman will have an argument against us."

Marwick stood up and walked to the window, his signal that the conversation was over. "The matter's out of our hands, anyway."

Thompson didn't like the sound of that. "What do you mean, out of our hands?"

"The FBI was here this morning. They're conducting an investigation into Roland's death. A direct order from the President, they said. They confiscated all copies of the manuscript and the correspondence. I told your secretary—what's her name, Kate—to give the bastards everything they wanted and get them out of the building."

Thompson stood up. "You gave them my files?"

"The files belong to the company, not you."

"You didn't have to do that! How about our lawyer, didn't you—"

Marwick waved his hand, as if to shoo the subject and Thompson both away. "Yes, I checked with our lawyer, and his advice was to give them everything they wanted. We're talking about the FBI, Jay, and the death of a former director of the CIA."

Thompson felt his face burning. "Have you ever heard of the First Amendment? We have every right to that material! And if our lawyer told you otherwise, he ought to be fired for incompetence! You didn't have to hand over anything to some jerk from the feds just because he walked in here and demanded it. And why wasn't I even asked about it?"

Marwick smiled, a nasty grin that said he was about to have the last word. "I'd have asked you about it, Jay, if I had been able to find you."

Thompson stormed out of the office and retreated toward the men's room to compose himself. The desire to crawl into a dark hole somewhere and go to sleep was positively overwhelming. He leaned on the sink and contemplated his white face in the mirror. The skin seemed to sag visibly, and the shadows under his eyes were taking on a deep purple hue, as if someone had punched him.

He reached into his pocket for his comb and pulled out a wad of paper, a stack of phone messages from the Hay-Adams's front desk that he'd hastily stuffed into the pocket and forgotten about when he checked out of the hotel that morning. Three were urgent requests to call Sam Marwick's office, one was from Kate, one was from Harriet Mitchell from early yesterday afternoon, and one wasn't even meant for him at all. It said:

> 11A.M. Tues.
> Virginia Smith
> The key and the directions
> are in the sleeper.
> Be careful.

Thompson puzzled over it for a moment, wondering why the sender hadn't left his name, then crumpled it up with the rest and threw them in the paper-towel receptacle. Virginia Smith would just have to find her key and her directions on her own.

Thompson spent several minutes throwing cold water on his face and combing his hair carefully, making sure the receding hairline on the left side was adequately hidden. Then he straightened his tie, brushed off his shoulders, and marched out to start returning the phone calls.

4

"Get off the goddamned telephone, Skip," Dave Rapoport shouted, "and let's get on with it!"

Skip Lawrenson, Democratic presidential candidate Harrison Conway's media adviser, stuck a finger in his free ear to shut out Rapoport and the other voices in the room and continued talking on the telephone.

"He should have been born a mutant," Howie Jackson said, to no one in particular, "with ears and mouth shaped like a receiver, a push-button face, and a cord sticking out his ass!"

"I heard that," Lawrenson replied in his Kentucky drawl. "Fuck you."

"Okay, okay, guys!" Harrison Conway shouted, clapping his hands together. "Let's get down to business!"

Conway was sitting on a big sofa in his suite at Washington's Madison Hotel, surrounded by his five principal campaign strategists and advisers—David Rapoport, his campaign manager; Buzz Reilly, Helen Swanson, Howie Jackson, and Skip Lawrenson.

Harriet Mitchell sat on a chair near the back of the room, yawning from lack of sleep. She had covered the Conway campaign on and off for the *Times* during the year and was on close terms with everyone in the room. This morning, however, the story she was after had nothing to do with Conway. She was waiting impatiently for a chance to speak to Skip Lawrenson. The meeting was an important planning session and it was typical of Conway that he didn't in the least object to Harriet's presence. He made a fetish of openness, of never having anything to hide.

Conway was considered the political heir of Adlai Stevenson. An intellectual, a member of the liberal establishment, he had served two terms as governor of Illinois, and had been ambassador to the UN. But the similarity with Stevenson ended about there. Conway loved the rough-and-tumble of politics and he was equally at home with farmers, factory workers, housewives, and college presidents. In fact, he loved to talk so much that he was hard to stop. He had a habit of turning simple greetings into major addresses. His Republican opponent, President John Douglas Mills, frequently used a quote from Churchill on him: "Conway can compress the greatest number of words into the smallest amount of thought of any man alive."

Conway was talkative, but he was as smart as any figure in national politics. Behind his common-man affability was a masterful political operator who combined the practical with the idealistic, who thought out his positions on the issues and stuck with them. And believed in them. Even his foes would agree that Harrison Conway was a man of integrity and compassion.

His political style and substance were less Stevenson and more Hubert Humphrey. He was the down-to-earth populist, ever ebullient and optimistic, a man who believed devoutly in God, country, and the democratic process, and never tired of bragging about it.

The latest campaign polls, showing Conway increasing his lead over Mills nationwide to five points, had put him and his staff in a euphoric mood, and the meeting was having a hard time getting started. The subject was Texas, President Mills's home state, rated a toss-up in the polls.

"There's a big Hispanic population down there," Howie Jackson said, "They could follow the pattern of California, and upset the conservative, anti-Mexican sentiment in Dallas-Fort Worth, the Houston suburbs, and the panhandle. But right now we're not reaching enough of the Hispanic vote."

"I just screened some new commercials this morning," Lawrenson interjected. "We've got a really great one in Spanish, now. Let's blow more bread on a media blitz down there. We could hit San Antonio, Laredo, Austin, El Paso, Brownsville, and the rest of downstate with a lot more Spanish radio and TV spots. If we can pump up the Spanish vote to forty percent, we could offset north and west Texas and carry the state."

Conway nodded. "I agree with Skip. What's our budget situation?"

"Well," Jackson replied, "we'd have to cut back air time from some other area. But that could be done. If New Jersey is going twelve percent for us, we shouldn't spend another dime up there."

"We can find the money," Lawrenson agreed. "I'd buy heavily into local Spanish-language radio. We can stretch our bucks because it's very cheap time. And there's not a Mexican alive who doesn't listen to the radio."

"I think TV and radio commercials are a terrific idea," Helen Swanson added. "But let's not stop there. Mr. Conway, you're scheduled in Texas for all day on Monday, the twenty-ninth, and half a day Tuesday. Why don't we add some more stops in south Texas? They'll give us good press and TV coverage down there. You'll draw big Hispanic crowds and get the message across in person. Big impact, low cost."

"Good idea," Conway said. "What's our Tuesday schedule now?"

After a flurry of searching through the mounds of notebooks, files, newspapers, and clutter of coffeecups on the two tables jammed against the back wall, Buzz Reilly found the schedule and read off a list of stops, beginning Tuesday morning with a breakfast with local labor leaders in Austin, and ending Tuesday afternoon with a rally at the new customs building in Laredo.

"That rally sounds interesting," Rapoport said. "What's that all about?"

"It's a protest rally," Reilly explained. "The government opened a huge new customs installation there last year—part of Mills's program to seal the border. The new complex down there looks like a Maginot Line. They even have a prison—twenty detention cells for illegal aliens. Our local organizers think it's the perfect symbol of Mills's bankrupt policies vis-à-vis Mexico—and I think they're right. They plan on drawing a huge crowd to block the border traffic and demonstrate against the administration's Mexican policy. So Harrison is scheduled to address the rally at three o'clock. It's a tailor-made Hispanic vote-getter, I'd say."

The room murmured in agreement.

Conway played devil's advocate for a moment: "Will we be drawn into anything ugly? I don't want to see a repeat of that El Paso tragedy."

Conway was referring to the riot at the border near El Paso, where an angry crowd of Mexicans on the other side of the border began throwing rocks at the border patrol when they arrested two illegals trying to slip across. One of the Mexicans broke free, and while trying to get back to the other side, was shot at and killed by the officer chasing him. That started a rampage. Three more died, including one immigration officer. The affair created enormous tensions along the border, and provoked another public condemnation of the U.S. by Mexico. The Mills administration reacted to the crisis by beefing up the border patrol.

"They promise a peaceful event," Reilly said.

"I'll hold you to it, Buzz," Conway replied.

After the meeting, Skip Lawrenson plunked himself into a chair beside Harriet. "Christ, I'm exhausted already," he muttered, "and the day isn't half over."

"I don't feel a bit sorry for you," Harriet said. "Did you get anything for me?"

Lawrenson nodded. He pulled a folded slip of paper from his pants pocket and handed it to her.

"You're gonna owe me big for this," he said, looking solemn. "I really compromised myself for this information. I wish to hell I'd never told you I had a friend at Bethesda Naval Hospital. I'll probably have to marry her now!"

"You poor dear. I'll have to have attribution."

Lawrenson looked stricken. "Attribution my ass! If that information turns up in the *Times* with my name attached to it—or anything that even *hints* at how you got it—I'll personally break every bone in your gorgeous body. I mean it, Harriet. This is strictly NFA. It's a lead. Where it takes you is your business. Frankly, it scares me. I'm glad I'm a media adviser, not a reporter. I've got to run!"

Harriet nodded and watched Lawrenson disappear into the adjacent room of the suite, where another scheduling conference had already begun.

Harriet opened the piece of paper. It was a short note. The information on it stunned her.

Harriet squeezed through the throng at the door of the White House press-briefing room and elbowed her way toward two friends, Harry Simons from the New York *Post*, and John Danziger, the regular *Times*

White House correspondent. The room, whose floor covered a swimming pool installed for FDR, had been converted by President Nixon into a small auditorium for press briefings, and today there was standing room only.

President Mills rarely held press conferences. And when he did, he chose small spaces. In the light of the recent polls showing a new drop in his popularity, the event was expected to produce some news.

Since his landslide victory in 1980, President Mills's popularity had been eroding steadily. The decline could be traced to many sources. During the first three years of his presidency he had alienated much of the women's vote by his outspoken attacks on the Equal Rights Amendment, still languishing short of the needed number of states for passage. He had alienated organized labor by some presidential strike-busting; and he had alienated the minorities by strong stands against busing, urban renewal, and increases in the welfare and education budgets.

And his four years in office had seen the price of home heating oil rise to $2.50 a gallon, gasoline to $3.00, and the average cost of a new house to over one hundred thousand. Food prices had shot up seventy-five percent, unemployment was hovering at nine percent, and the inflation rate, after the severe recession of 1982, was rocketing along at twenty-three percent a year.

But Mills's biggest problem was Mexico. As a result of his tough policy on illegal aliens, relations with that country stood at their lowest ebb since the Mexican War. The border with Mexico—from the Texas Gulf to the Pacific Ocean—had been shut as tight as the Iron Curtain, and the flood of illegal immigrants stopped cold. At the same time, a nationwide federal program of mass deportation, called Operation Clean Sweep, had, in four years, hunted down and expelled nearly a million Mexicans and Latin Americans. The border reinforcement and the deportations had cost the government over three billion dollars and had put Mexico on the brink of severing diplomatic relations with the United States. The Mills administration could have weathered that setback domestically, but Mexico went further. It expropriated the assets of American businesses in Mexico and turned off the oil and gas spigots. To make the retaliation hurt all the more, in 1982 Mexico discovered major new oil fields in the Gulf of Mexico, giving it the largest proven gas and oil reserves in the world.

Despite these humiliations, Mills still had the support of conservative elements of the Republican party, blue-collar workers, the farmers, the military, and large segments of Big Business, who approved of his lavish military budgets, his scuttling of the SALT treaties, and his generally tough foreign policy. And with their support had come a lot of money and a lock on the GOP nomination, even though many Republicans were unhappy with Mills and privately expected a Republican defeat on November 6.

The Democratic standard-bearer, Harrison Conway, wasn't offering very many compelling solutions to the terrible problems the country faced, but he was well-liked and trusted, and the public seemed increasingly in a mood to back away from the abrasive, wheeler-dealer tough guy and embrace the safer, more predictable Conway.

Throughout the entire campaign Mills had remained stubbornly confident of victory, doing battle with the media as they heaped increasing criticism on his performance in office. Mills was a fighter—a gutsy, resourceful politician—and the press, knowing his penchant for drama, waited with some suspense to see what Mills might yet pull to turn the tide of the election back in his favor.

John Danziger nudged Harriet's arm. "Here we go," he said.

Presidential press secretary Jared Scott stepped up to the small speaker's stand, waited for quiet, and then spoke: "Ladies and gentlemen, the President of the United States."

A Secret Service man opened a door on the right side of the room near the platform, and President John Mills strode in, looking relaxed and confident.

He was a tall, beefy man, and affected a rough, down-home Texas style that belied his shrewdness and sophistication. His trademarks were his homely humor and a very forceful, intimidating speaking style. "He's got John Connally's head and Lyndon Johnson's balls," an old Texas political rival once said of him. "But he's a much bigger prick than either of them."

Mills ran a hand over his balding pate and grinned at the gathering, pausing for dramatic effect as he surveyed the faces in the room.

"I'm pleased to see," he said slowly, "that my popularity with the fourth estate remains as high as ever."

This drew a polite laugh. Mills then disappointed them by saying that he had no prepared statement. He threw the floor open to questions.

Over the sea of hands and the babble of "Mr. President!", Mills let his finger fall on Shirley Garrity of the Associated Press.

"Mr. President," she said, "Roosevelt Rains of the Urban League was quoted yesterday as saying, 'President Mills's administration has been a sick joke, an affront to the ideals of responsible government and moral leadership.' Do you have any reply to that?"

President Mills winced visibly and drew a big laugh. "I don't think any reply is necessary. Mr. Rains seems to be suffering from progressive delusions of grandeur. He used to claim only to know what was wrong with our cities. Now he thinks he knows what's wrong with the whole country."

Mills seemed to sense that his put-down of Rains didn't go over well. "Mr. Rains reminds me of my old friend Harry Pearson, a state representative from Amarillo, years ago," the President added. "Harry was honest but a little naive. During the Vietnam war Harry decided he was going to run for the United States Congress, seeing as how the country was going to hell without his help. So he called a press conference down there at the capitol in Austin, to announce for the race. One reporter asked him, 'Harry, what do you think of the international crisis?' Well, Harry looked this man right in the eye and said, 'Son, I'm sorry to hear those fellas are in trouble. They make a hell of a good pickup truck!' "

When the laugh died, Mills recognized Douglas Davies, the CBS correspondent:

"Mr. President, Harrison Conway, your opponent, said in a speech in Columbus, Ohio, last night that, and I quote: 'In my opinion, the President's mishandling of our relationship with Mexico adds up to the single worst blunder of any President in this century.' How would you answer that charge?"

Mills gazed at the ceiling for a moment, then back toward the far end of the auditorium. He was controlling his temper.

"I'd say he's one mad Democrat." Laughter. ". . . and I'm just happy as the devil to see him holding a strong opinion about something for a change."

Mills's disapproval of Harrison Conway went deeper than partisan politics. He considered his liberal ideals fuzzy-headed, and he was thoroughly convinced that Conway was too weak and ineffectual a man to govern the country.

But what was really disturbing Mills was the Mexican issue. Conway had latched on to it and made it the chief issue of the campaign. At every stop he hammered away at Mills's failures with Mexico, and every week Mills slipped further in the polls. Nothing Mills did seemed to reverse the trend. In the beginning, when Conway was just discovering how good an issue Mexico was, Mills had defended his record doggedly. When that didn't seem to work, Mills had counterattacked Conway vehemently. So vehemently that Mills's campaign aides had had to beg him to tone down the attacks.

Harriet realized that the session might end before she got her chance to ask her question. Fortunately press secretary Scott always made certain that the *Times* was heard, so Mills's finger finally pointed in her direction.

She stood up, trembling. "Mr. President . . ."

She heard her voice ring out. She was conscious of the President's hard eyes bearing down on her. No matter how tough and seasoned one became as a reporter, confronting the President of the United States in public was always a terrifying moment. For several seconds she was unable to continue, the wording of her question having totally fled her mind. The crowd of journalists turned to look, wondering at the sudden silence.

"Mr. President," she repeated, recovering her poise. "Do you have any statement to make on the investigation under way concerning the death of Allen Roland, former director of the CIA?"

Mills glared at her. This was not a welcome question.

"I have none," he said evenly. "When the investigation is complete, a report will be issued. Naturally, when anyone takes his own life it's a personal tragedy . . . for family and friends."

Mills quickly pointed to another reporter on the other side of the room. Harriet raised her voice at once. "I'm not finished with my question, Mr. President!"

Mills's eyes came back to Harriet, flashing with anger. The room stilled with expectation.

"I have it from a reliable source," she said, her voice quavering, "that Mr. Roland was tortured and killed."

The air seemed to leave the room, the void of silence disturbed only by the distant clatter of a teletype machine in the outside room. Mills stared at her, a look of bafflement—or fear—apparent on his stony features.

"By God," he said in a low voice, "I can see I'm in trouble with the New York *Times*. I know they want to retire me from office. I didn't know they wanted to make a fool out of me as well!"

Nervous laughter fluttered across the room. No one's hand came up for another question. Jared Scott, with a matador's sense of timing, stepped swiftly in front of the cluster of microphones.

"Thank you, Mr. President!"

Mills ducked immediately into the corridor that led back to the Oval Office, Secret Service closing ranks behind him, and the crowd of reporters began a stampede toward Harriet Mitchell. Simons, the *Post* reporter, looked at her, his face registering amused disbelief.

"I think I've got the *Post*'s afternoon headline," he said. " 'Reporter tells Prez: You lie!' "

5

Wednesday night, October 24

Max Feldman walked east along Fifty-seventh Street. He took long and rapid strides, his trim, muscular frame bent slightly forward, hands plunged into the pants pockets of his suit. It was past midnight and he had been enjoying drinks at the Russian Tea Room with some old friends from the theater. It had been a warm and comfortable interlude, but the afterglow faded with every step he took, and his anger came surging back.

Sam Marwick had made him mad as hell. He'd known Sam for almost thirty-five years—ever since Max had first started his literary agency. He had known Sam's father, J. P., who had founded the publishing house. Father and son, they were both tough bastards, but good publishers, and Max had always respected them. He thought that Sam lacked his father's vision and taste, but he was a smart businessman in an age when running a publishing house defied the laws of financial gravity. Max and Sam had had their disagreements over the years, but somehow they always managed to patch things up and continue doing business with each other. At least until now.

Max could excuse—even understand—Sam's resistance to paying out the remaining half-million. He'd expected that. That's why he hadn't wasted any time putting pressure on him. But for Marwick to demand the first half-million back, and to demand it the day after Roland's suicide—that was outrageous. "Sam," Max had told him on the phone, "your father would be ashamed of you. You know that, don't you? Your father would be ashamed!"

Max reached the corner of Fifty-seventh and Madison, in front of his office building. He looked at his watch: twelve-thirty. He should be home, he thought, but he felt restless and frustrated, and decided a little work might help calm him down.

He rang the night man's buzzer and waited for the old man to make his way to the heavy brass door and unlock it. After several minutes Max became impatient and tugged on the handle. To his surprise, the door was unlocked. He went in, locked it from the inside, and looked around the lobby for some sign of the night man. Nobody appeared to be on duty. This fueled Max's anger even more, and riding up alone on the elevator, he began plotting his strategy against Marwick.

He knew the manuscript wasn't worth a million dollars, and with Roland no longer around to follow Thompson's suggestions for revising it, it would never be worth a million. He would have been willing to negotiate a lower advance from Sam, but Sam had infuriated him with his threat of a lawsuit. Well, two could play that game. Max would slap Marwick with a suit of his own, for full payment of the advance. He'd get Sam in court and make him defend the publisher's acceptance clause in the standard author's contract.

Stepping off the elevator on the twenty-ninth floor, Max remembered that he had left his copies of Roland's manuscript in the file cabinet behind his desk. He had better lock them up in the office safe, he decided. The FBI had called him that afternoon, with some bureaucratic nonsense about confiscating all of the copies of the memoir. Max had told them to get lost.

He fiddled impatiently with his key case, looking for the key that unlocked the Medeco cylinder he had installed after a break-in last year. He had hated giving up the old brownstone on East Sixty-fourth Street. It had housed the office since the late forties, and he had always felt safe there. But the agency had just gotten too big for the space. He had three full agents now, and another nine people on the payroll. And at sixty-three, he had no intention of retiring for a long, long time. Physically he was as robust as a young man. He still put in ten hours of work every day and another hour of hard exercise: squash, tennis, or his favorite, judo—something he had become expert in as a Ranger in World War II. He never had cause to use it during the war, but it had once saved his life in Central Park, when a mugger attacked him with a switchblade.

He inserted the key in the lock and discovered that this door was unlocked also.

Inside, in the dark outer vestibule of the suite, he saw a crack of light shining from beneath the door to his inner office. He stepped silently up to it and listened. The cleaning lady had gone home long ago, and no one else in the office ever worked this late.

Whoever was inside, Max decided, would never win any prizes for stealth. He could plainly hear the clatter of a file drawer banging open.

Jay Thompson was back in Allen Roland's study in Georgetown. The room was bathed in blinding white light from banks of floodlights overhead, and dozens of thick serpentine black cables crisscrossed the floor. Roland was still there, swinging from his hangman's noose, his face caked with layers of ghastly white makeup. His eyes were shut but he seemed to be alive, talking in a low monotone. Thompson, alone in the room with him, could not understand his words.

The walls around them were entirely glass, and jostling, angry faces crowded several deep around the outside. Hands and fists banged on the glass until Thompson was sure that it would shatter, and muffled voices shouted at him to open the door. He looked around, but there didn't seem to be a door. The room felt intensely hot, and the din from outside was so loud Thompson could feel the floor vibrate. Roland's corpse continued to drone on unintelligibly; then abruptly it yelled something audible above the noise: "They found out! They found out!"

"Found out what?" Thompson wanted to know, but Roland didn't answer. The faces outside the glass walls leered at him and squashed their noses against the glass, the way children do. Harriet's head became visible in the crowd, her face contorted with shock, as if she were witnessing some dreadful calamity.

. Thompson saw that Roland's feet were missing. His body terminated in a pair of pressed trouser cuffs, with nothing sticking out the bottom. Roland's shoes sat in a far corner of the room, and the missing feet were still in them, the bare ankles protruding from them like a macabre set of shoe trees.

"Virginia Smith," Roland said.

The room was becoming unbearably hot, and Thompson wanted desperately to flee, but looking down, he saw that his own feet were also missing. Then the glass walls shattered with a thundering crash, and in the whirl of wind and heat and noise, he began to faint.

He woke in his bedroom, to the sound of a low moan that he realized was his own. The bedside light was on, shining in his face, and he was still dressed, his clothes twisted around him as if someone had been wringing him out like a wet sock.

He had come home at seven, turned on the news, and fallen asleep immediately. The clock-radio now said one o'clock, and the television set was showing an old horror film.

He pushed himself up from the bed, turned off the set, and removed his clothes. He dumped them on a chair and staggered to the kitchen to find something to slake his thirst.

Feeling drugged and listless, he returned to the bedroom with a cold bottle of beer and sat down on the edge of the bed and sipped it. The nightmare had deposited a residue of anxiety that clung to the fringes of his consciousness. Instead of evaporating, it started to grow as Thompson recalled the events of the day. After his argument with Marwick, the press had asked a thousand questions, most of them inane. He had thought about resigning, and almost went back to Marwick's office to tell him to go to hell. Kate had talked him out of it. Beyond the immediate satisfaction it would bring, the idea didn't really appeal to him very much anyway. Marwick, with no sons and one daughter who hated both her father and his business, had promised Thompson that he would make him publisher when he retired.

Thompson looked at the telephone on the bedside table, next to an unread stack of manuscripts. He wondered if he dared call Harriet at this hour. For the first time since Gloria had left, he felt profoundly lonely.

His eyes returned to the telephone. The receiver sat in its cradle backwards, so that the cord crossed over in front of the set. Gloria had always hung up the phone that way. It was one of those many minor irritants in their marriage. He was neat and she was messy, and whenever she hung up the phone backwards, he would always pick it up and turn it around, so the cord hung neatly in place on the left side of the phone. He never hung up the receiver that way himself.

But it was that way now.

He stared at it, trying to remember when anyone had last been in the apartment. The cleaning lady, six days ago. But clearly someone had used the phone since yesterday, when he left the apartment to go to Washington. If it had happened earlier, he would have noticed. Thompson found it hard to push his mind forward to cope with the implications. He looked carefully around the room. Everything was in perfect order. He opened the drawers in the captain's chest where he stored his underwear and shirts. Nothing disturbed. He checked the two closets, and the drawers in the night tables on each side of the bed. One of the drawers contained an expensive watch he no longer wore, and a set of gold cufflinks. They were still there.

Thompson searched through the entire apartment—bedroom, living room, study, kitchen, and bath. He found no evidence that anything had been disturbed, and nothing at all was missing. He inspected the front door closely. It bore absolutely no sign that anyone had broken in.

But he was sure that someone had. He could almost feel it, as if the unknown intruder had left some subtle trace, some after-scent, below the level of the five human senses to detect, but detectable nevertheless. Thompson cursed his paranoia, but there was no harmless explanation for the phone. No one else—not even the building superintendent—had the keys to the apartment. But someone had used the phone. The shambles of Harriet's apartment swam vividly back into his memory.

Thompson sat and sipped his beer and tried to puzzle it out. Something was wrong. Some indefinable menace was abroad, whose nature he could not perceive.

Max Feldman crouched at the door and listened. He heard one filing cabinet drawer slam closed and the rattle of another drawer being yanked open. Max's anger, accumulating steadily since the afternoon, finally boiled over.

He pushed the door open with a powerful shove and crashed into the room, halting in the middle to orient himself to the intruder.

The burglar, bent over the filing cabinet behind Max's big mahogany desk, looked up, surprised, and squinted his one good eye at Max, as if he doubted what it was seeing.

Max brought his arms up, crossed like a pair of scissors, palm edges outward, and advanced on his target, concentrating on the spot on his neck he intended to hit. He registered a brief image of the man—thin, deeply tanned, with a narrow face and long nose, lips stretched apart, teeth bared like a snarling dog's.

Max took a deep breath and lunged forward, bringing his arm down in a rapid chopping motion. His blow struck the intruder's shoulder at a glancing angle, and Max saw his hand, gripped hard by the wrist, plunging toward the floor, pulled by a strength far greater than his own.

A knee smashed with brutal force against his face, breaking his nose and knocking his false teeth deep back into his throat, choking off his wind. A bone-snapping blow at the base of his neck followed, and Max crumpled silently to the carpet, his nose and mouth pouring a bright and clashing shade of red blood into the subdued peach-cream hues of the deep-pile carpet.

Three minutes later he was dead.

6

Thursday morning, October 25

It was nearly ten o'clock when Thompson surfaced from a fitful slumber. He awoke disoriented and panicky, clutching the thick down pillow in his fists and bolting upright from the bed. The room was hot, the sun filtering brightly through the curtains. He had closed and locked the window late last night, even though it was ten stories up the face of an eighteen-story building, and no one but a human fly could possibly break in that way. It was an atavistic impulse; fear of the unknown.

The clock-radio had gone on at eight and was still playing, broadcasting yesterday's basketball scores. The telephone receiver rested innocently in its cradle, with the cord on the left side, just as Thompson had repositioned it.

The phone was ringing, and he realized that it had been ringing—had indeed awakened him. He reached from the bed to answer it, and heard a strained, trembling voice on the other end. It was Kate, his assistant.

"My God!" she said. "When are you coming in?"

"I overslept. Sorry. What's the matter?"

"Mr. Marwick wants to see you."

"What does the old bastard want now?"

"It's about Max Feldman," she said. "He's dead. Last night." She sniffled and drew a deep breath. Thompson asked her to repeat what she had just said. "Mr. Marwick is worried that it might have been because of Roland," she added. "You know, they argued about the contract."

"What happened?"

"He jumped out his office window."

Thompson muttered a string of swear words under his breath. Things were falling apart, and he hadn't a clue as to why. Two suicides and two searched apartments within forty-eight hours. Did Roland's manuscript carry some supernatural curse? Was it bizarre coincidence? He doubted it. Deep down in his gut he knew they were connected. It was alarming. Extremely alarming.

Kate was still talking to him about Max Feldman. He remembered that she adored him. She had met him only once or twice, but in the course of daily business they had chatted briefly on the phone many times, and Feldman was unfailingly polite and warmhearted—one of the few in the business who treated her like an adult. He had been her favorite among all the agents Thompson dealt with. For that matter, he had been Thompson's favorite, too.

Thompson realized that he had no intention of going to work. "I'm not coming in, Kate," he said. "Tell Marwick I'll call him when I can."

"He'll be furious."

"Make up one of your good excuses. You don't know where I am or when I'll be back. And don't give anyone my home number. Just hold the fort for me."

Kate sighed. "Okay. What are you going to do?"

"Take a trip."

"You can't say where?"

"I'll tell you when I get back."

"Tomorrow?"

"Probably," he replied. "Just stonewall everybody for me in the meantime. I'll get you an extra week off as a bribe."

Kate tried to sound more cheerful. "I'll get that from you in writing. And if these phones don't stop ringing, I'll be the next suicide."

"Any of them important? Did Harriet Mitchell call?"

"No, she didn't. Mostly press and magazine people. And your poor neglected authors. They've all called. The phone is ringing now. Hold on."

Kate was back in a minute. "That one was from Washington. A Mr. Klimentov. Do you know him?"

"Never heard of him. Did he say what he wanted?"

"Just that he had some important information for you, but he wouldn't say about what. You can call him at—"

"Save it. He's probably another Russian dissident trying to sell his memoirs. I seem to attract a lot of those. I'll call you back later if I can."

He hung up and dialed Harriet Mitchell's number at the *Times* in Washington. She answered on the first ring, sounding harassed.

"It's me—Jay."

"It's about time! Why do you have an unlisted number, you silly man? I just called your office and your damned secretary wouldn't give it to me!"

"Probably because you called her a secretary. She's an editorial assistant. She's just trying to protect me."

Harriet's voice softened a fraction. "Yeah, yeah, I know all about that 'editorial-assistant' stuff. Big title, small salary. She's your secretary. Anyway, I was right about Roland."

Harriet's habit of quick *segues* threw him. "What about him?"

"He didn't kill himself."

"How do you know that?"

"I got someone to steal a look at the Navy medical examiner's report. It's classified. No one is supposed to see it, so I'm in real trouble with the White House. The report says that he was tortured."

Thompson bit his lip. The alarms were getting louder. He told Harriet about Feldman's death and about the FBI confiscating Roland's manuscripts and correspondence from his office. He left out his suspicions about his phone and apartment. They seemed suddenly trivial.

"Do you think they're connected?" Harriet asked.

"They must be."

"Then maybe Feldman wasn't a suicide either."

"That's what I'm thinking. Will the *Times* let you come up here and check into it?"

"I'll have to make a fuss. They'll want to put a New York reporter on it."

"Convince them."

"I will."

"I'm counting on it, because I need a favor from you—today if possible. Remember the photocopy of Roland's manuscript I gave you to read when I first asked you about ghosting the book with him?"

"Yes?"

"Do you still have it?"

"I think so."

"Where? In your apartment?"

"No. It should be right here in my desk. Wait a sec."

Thompson held his breath.

"Yes, it's here."

"Thank God. Don't let it out of your sight. It's the only copy we have. Bring it to New York with you when you come. As soon as possible."

"What are you thinking?"

"I can't tell you yet, I'm following a wild hunch. But I need the manuscript."

"Remember, I have an exclusive on anything you find out. Where shall I meet you?"

"Where your plane lands—at the La Guardia shuttle gate."

"That's intriguing."

"I'm taking a flight from La Guardia to Hanover."

"Germany?"

"New Hampshire."

Harriet was puzzled. "A college reunion?"

"Sort of. I'm going to see an old professor of mine."

7

The common room on the third floor of Sanborn House was got up to resemble somebody's idea of Elizabethan England. There were wide-board floors, leaded glass windows, a big fireplace, a low-beamed ceiling, and a large solid plank table in the middle, stacked with what looked to Thompson like the same copies of *Antaeus, Sewanee Review,* and *Poetry Magazine* that he had pored over with such reverence when he was a student there fifteen years ago. The ambience was a little pretentious, Thompson supposed, but it was wonderfully comforting, and he had always loved the place.

He knocked on the heavy door at the far corner of the room and waited. After a short pause it opened and the compact form of Thomas Owen Kirkpatrick Smith stood before him, dressed in baggy brown corduroys and a gray sweater pulled over a white tennis shirt, his smooth tanned face framed in a halo of fluffy white hair.

Smith nodded and smiled broadly, causing wrinkles to break out dramatically around his eyes—those sharp blue-green eyes that had seen so much.

Smith shook Thompson's hand warmly, ushered him into his cluttered office, and sat him down in a cracked leather armchair by a window with a magnificent view of the campus. Smith retreated behind his desk, a scarred old oaken relic awash with loose papers, manuscripts, books, and letters, wheeled out a metal typing chair with a small adjustable back and big round castors, and pulled it up near the window, next to Thompson.

"At my age," he said, "I find those big soft swivel chairs with the tilting backs are only good for sleeping in."

Smith was nearly seventy, and although formally retired from the English department, he still held an office and the title of professor emeritus. He was the author of several highly respected volumes of criticism, one brilliant book about chess, and he remained compulsively active—lecturing, writing, counseling students. The role of the wise old professor seemed to suit him in his declining years. It was a safe harbor after a life of storm and tragedy.

Like Allen Roland, Smith had served in the OSS and the CIA, and had established a reputation as a genius at cryptanalysis, the arcane art of code-breaking. But both his career and his psyche were permanently crippled by a double misfortune in 1954. Deeply depressed by the death of his first wife in an auto accident, he had allowed himself to get drunk one night in a bar in West Berlin. In that state, he let slip a small secret to the wrong confidant. The consequences were devastating. A network of eighteen spies, each recruited by him personally, was rolled up in East Germany overnight. All eighteen were executed.

Smith never fully recovered his emotional equilibrium. There followed years of depression, heavy drinking, and a tendency to seek out increasingly dangerous assignments, to take unnecessary risks. Through it all he remained brilliant, but his close friends, especially Allen Roland, finally persuaded him to retire from the CIA before it killed him.

He remarried, divorced, and remarried again. Through his third and present wife he found his way into teaching. The academic life bored him, but it held his more self-destructive tendencies in check. He had written eloquently about all these matters in his autobiography, *A Life in the Dark*, which Thompson had published. The book had made him something of a celebrity, a role that both pleased and embarrassed him.

In gratitude, he had helped Thompson acquire Roland's memoirs. Smith's word had tipped the balance in Thompson's favor in the brisk competition for the book.

After a few minutes of small talk, Smith reached across and put a hand on Thompson's shoulder. "You didn't travel all the way to Hanover to hear me tell you how I'm getting along in my retirement. What happened to Allen Roland?"

Smith listened, sitting still as a stone, while Thompson narrated the events of the past forty-eight hours—his finding Roland dead, the break-in at Harriet's apartment, the FBI taking the manuscripts and correspondence, the presumed search of his own apartment, and Max Feldman's death. He went through his recital carefully and in detail, hoping Smith might somehow endow it all with meaning.

"Finally," Thompson said, "Harriet Mitchell talked to someone at Bethesda Naval Hospital who was involved in Roland's autopsy, or at least saw the report. It indicated that Roland had been tortured. She didn't tell me what the signs were. The report's been classified, so she was lucky to find out that much."

Smith nodded, a look of pain shadowing his face. "I didn't imagine for a minute that Allen had killed himself, even when I read Miss Mitchell's account in the *Times* yesterday. He was a devout Catholic, for one thing. For another, he didn't have the personality for it. He was a fighter who thrived on adversity. Despair was not a word in his vocabulary."

"What about Feldman?"

"He may have been thrown out that window. Victim of a crude form of political assassination called defenestration. It's never been very popular anywhere except in Czechoslovakia, for some odd reason. Jan Masaryk met his end that way in 1948. It has obvious advantages. It requires no weapons—just a window on a high floor—and it looks like a suicide. These people, whoever they are, may have feared that Feldman knew something because of his connection with Roland, something that they didn't want him to know. So they silenced him. Or he may have walked in on them while they were searching his office for something—perhaps copies of the manuscript."

Smith said it all rather matter-of-factly, as if he were discussing a scene from a Sherlock Holmes story. Thompson looked out Smith's window and tried to imagine what it must have been like for Max, struggling alone against unknown killers late at night, twenty-nine stories above the street. Smith's window, only three floors up, conveyed little dread Autumn sunshine was pouring in, and from the path below he could hear the boisterous voices of students.

"But why, professor?" Thompson asked. "What are these people after? I swear to God there's not a damn thing in that manuscript that anyone would even want to *sue* about, much less kill for. And I ought to know. I've been through it a dozen times; when I found Roland, I was on my way to badger him to get him to put just that kind of stuff in. We gave him a whopping advance, and my job is now on the line because there *isn't* anything controversial in it."

Smith stroked his chin thoughtfully. Thompson had the sinking feeling that the old man was equally at a loss; the whole business didn't make a bit of sense to him, either.

"It's a puzzle, no doubt about that," Smith replied. "And I'm afraid you really haven't given me very much to go on." He cast his eyes down at the attaché case Thompson had brought with him. "I hope you didn't lose *all* the copies of Allen's manuscript?" Smith raised his eyebrows to punctuate the question.

Thompson smiled. "No, professor, I managed to save a copy for you."

Thompson retrieved the case, opened it, extracted a large manila envelope, and gave it to Smith. Smith weighed it in his hand, as if he might pass judgment on its contents from its heft alone.

"I have an idea," he said. "I've got a meeting with a group of students in about ten minutes. Something about the Dartmouth Indian symbol again—our favorite local controversy. It'll take an hour or more, I'm afraid. So let me take this home after the meeting, read it, and then you come over and join me for dinner. Ellen is away visiting relatives in Ohio, but I still know how to cook an exceptional fillet of sole."

Smith stuffed the manuscript into a capacious green canvas bag, already straining at the seams with books and magazines, and slung it over his shoulder. "Cheer up, Jay. There may be something in here after all," he said, patting the canvas. "I'll see what I can find. Come on over at six-thirty. You remember the place—eleven Hanover Terrace."

The group shuffled noiselessly through the cavernous reading room on the ground floor of Baker Library, gazing in awe at the murals of Mexican painter Clemente Orozco that covered the walls. The painter had attempted an ambitious pictorial history of mankind, and the scenes depicted, in garish colors and primitively drawn figures, a distinctly anticapitalistic view of man's progress: greedy bankers sitting on stacks of gold, generals surveying mounds of skeletons, a Christ brandishing an ax. The viewers were parents of students, mostly, and tourists visiting the campus. The murals and their Marxist message left them a little stunned and confused.

The one-eyed man in their midst, with his ill-fitting wash-and-wear suit and his obvious lack of interest in the work of Clemente Orozco, blended uncomfortably into the group. When the crowd reached the far end of the lobby, he separated from it and moved off in the direction of the public telephone booth by the stairwell. Propping himself against the booth's folded glass door, he examined the directory until he found the inevitably long column of Smiths. His finger traveled slowly down the column and stopped at "Smith, T.O.K."

He slid the directory back onto the shelf, seated himself on the small metal bench inside the booth, closed the glass door, and fumbled in his suit pants pocket until he had extracted a coin and a small silver whistle about three inches long and not much fatter than a straw.

He examined the whistle closely in the dim light, turning it over several times, and finally stuck one end in his mouth and dialed the number, pausing carefully between each digit. When he had dialed the last digit, and before the phone on the other end of the line had a chance to ring, he blew a single high-pitched note into the mouthpiece.

Then he sat back and waited, receiver pressed between ear and shoulder, his thick fingers toying patiently with the whistle.

8

Thursday afternoon, October 25

Madame Regine's apartment was on the third floor of an elegant town house on the Boulevard Raspail. A fitting compromise, the Chameleon thought, as he studied the imposing exterior—a graystone from the Empire period, with its high windows looking suitably aristocratic behind their tidy second-story balconies. It had the dignity and grandeur of the town houses along the great avenues of the Sixteenth Arrondissement, but its location, on the Left Bank, near Boulevard St.-Germain and the raffish attractions of the Latin Quarter, paid appropriate homage to the bohemian ancestry of the woman's profession.

Madame Regine was an astrologer.

Her story was well-known. A Romanian Gypsy from Transylvania, she had miraculously escaped Hitler's concentration camps and come to Paris as a refugee at the end of World War II. She had survived the early years in postwar France in classic Gypsy style—telling fortunes, reading palms and tea leaves, holding séances, and bilking customers with a variety of con games from the ancient, inexhaustible Gypsy repertoire.

But she possessed a special gift that set her apart. Gradually word of her uncanny abilities as an astrologer began to spread throughout Paris, always a fertile field for the occult, and then throughout Europe. By the 1970's Madame Regine was something of an international celebrity, sought after by the rich and powerful from every part of the world.

Madame Regine did more than read horoscopes for the jet set. She consulted the stars to determine the destinies of nations and the men and women who led them. And she had made some astonishing predictions: she had accurately forecast the return of De Gaulle in 1958, the building of the Berlin Wall, the Cuban missile crisis, the assassinations of both the Kennedys, and Nixon's downfall. Political leaders, heads of state, and royalty from dozens of countries sought her advice and predictions on a regular basis. Few, of course, would admit it publicly.

A popular notion was abroad in Paris that Madame Regine was more sorcerer than seer, that she was really a secret practitioner of witchcraft, who took an active supernatural hand in actually causing the events she predicted. Some of her supposedly more enlightened clients certainly seemed to believe her possessed of godlike omnipotence. National elections in Europe and the United States inevitably sent emmissaries scurrying to the Boulevard Raspail with cash tributes in hopes Madame Regine would influence the heavens on their behalf. They had made her a rich woman.

The Chameleon mounted the two flights of marble stairs to the third floor and rang the bell. A plump middle-aged Haitian dressed in an uncomfortably tight black French maid's uniform met him at the door and ushered him in.

Madame's quarters were tasteful and luxurious, showing no hint of the arcana of her trade. The walls, in fact, were hung with paintings by Picasso, Miró, Mondrian, and Léger, and by several lesser-known impressionists. Her polished teak bookshelves were equally impressive. The Chameleon's practiced eye caught many rare editions—in French, German, Italian, and Spanish.

Madame Regine met the Chameleon in her parlor, a high-ceilinged, light-flooded room whose windows overlooked the wide boulevard below. She rose from a divan and held out her hand. The Chameleon blinked in wonderment. She was extraordinarily small—no more than 140 centimeters, he judged—and her close-fitting black floor-length gown further emphasized her doll-like size. He took her hand—incredibly tiny and delicate—and pressed it against his closed lips.

Madame waved the Chameleon to a chair, a smile enlivening her face, which appeared much larger, proportionately, than the rest of her. It was a dark, ageless, and sensual face, with broad lips and enormous black eyes. A creature unlike the rest of us, he thought. Exceptional. Probably psychic. He had known such people. As a young boy, he remembered them. They came to the Valley of the Kings to prey on the tourists.

"Monsieur . . . Markham, I believe. Welcome. My English is only passable. I apologize." Her voice was throaty and low.

"No need, madame. We may speak French."

"But you are my guest!" she protested in English.

"But you are the formidable one," he replied in French. "Small in size, I see, but great in stature. I owe you the respect of speaking your tongue."

Madame Regine laughed, a low brittle chuckle that caused tiny wrinkles to radiate to the corners of her face. "Very well, my gallant one. Your French is obviously serviceable. As good as your native English, as far as I can tell. So I will permit you to indulge me."

What would she have thought, he wondered, if he had spoken to her in her true native tongue, Romany? Or if she knew that he spoke forty other languages, and that his native tongue was Egyptian Arabic, not English. But be careful, he advised himself. Her perceptions are remarkably keen. It was probably a mistake for him to display his fluency in French. Singularly un-American.

The Chameleon lowered himself into a Queen Anne chair across from the divan, and the maid appeared and offered refreshments. He accepted tea.

"I thought Americans detested tea," Madame exclaimed.

"We are learning," the Chameleon replied. My second mistake, he thought.

"Your credentials are impressive, Mr. Markham," Madame began, cutting directly to the point. "I'm very curious to know why you've come."

He waved a hand dismissively. "I fear I will disappoint you, then. A routine mission on behalf of a rich and influential client, that's all." He emphasized the word "rich."

Madame Regine laughed. "I have heard of these 'routine missions' before. Then I know disaster is impending!"

The Chameleon forced a laugh. "No, nothing like that this time. It's simply that I represent an individual who would like to seek your advice—"

Madame interrupted. "I do not give advice, m'sieur. I read only what is written in the stars."

He nodded, slightly annoyed by the woman's grand manner. "Of course. I am not educated in such matters, so you must forgive me. I merely seek to learn if a consultation for my client would be advisable. He's a very important figure in the United States, and he never commits himself to any course of action without examining every fact and ramification beforehand. I am, alas, often responsible for this 'fact-finding,' as he calls it, on his behalf."

Madame Regine's face looked stormy. "So! You wish for character references? Recommendations? Is that it?"

The Chameleon nodded. "As a necessary first step," he said apologetically. "A formality, of course. Once that is out of the way, then I'm sure we can arrange for a . . . profitable consultation here in Paris very soon."

The Chameleon expected that money would be her weak spot. But he detected no particular response. Instead, her dark Gypsy eyes were boring in on him, harsh as laser beams, and he felt the edges of his confidence beginning to melt. For one of the few times in his extraordinary career, the Chameleon suspected that he was overmatched.

"Your client would like recommendations from some of my clients, is that it?"

"Yes, madame. American clients. And the more important they are, the easier it will be for me to persuade him to seek your counsel."

Madame Regine continued to stare at the Chameleon for a few moments longer; then abruptly her mood of graciousness vanished. The tiny woman stood up and waved her arms in the air.

"You are a fraud!" she yelled. "I don't know who you are, but you are not who you say! You have insulted me!"

"I beg your pardon!" The Chameleon strove to push indignation into his tone.

"You are here under false pretenses! Do not deny it! I insist that you leave, or I shall call the police!"

He stood up, unnerved by the woman's sudden attack. He had seriously underestimated her.

"You are quite right, madame," he said, his voice firm and reasonable. "And I apologize. I've misled you. You must forgive me. I have compelling reasons to ask what I ask. Reasons I cannot share with you. I'm most sincerely sorry to have insulted your intelligence and intruded on your goodwill."

The woman seemed somewhat mollified. She was curious about him now, he sensed.

"You're only sorry that you couldn't deceive me!" she retorted, but much of the anger had faded from her voice.

The Chameleon nodded. "I admit that I underestimated you. What gave me away?"

Madame Regine was not revealing trade secrets. "There was no one aspect in particular. You are an excellent *poseur*, very practiced. But you should have remembered that my people are also very practiced. One quickly recognizes a familiar act!"

"I simply had no choice but to try, madame. I'm frankly desperate for certain information." And if you can read my mind, the Chameleon said to himself, you will see that I am willing to pay handsomely for it.

"Your name is not Markham," she said.

"No."

"But you will not tell me who you really are?"

The Chameleon shook his head. "In truth, I would just give you another false name. You can tell far more about me with your own astonishing powers than my real name would convey."

Madame smiled uncertainly. The flattery was not totally lost on her, but her suspicions remained.

"I look into your eyes," she said, "and I see they have no bottoms to them. The more one knows about you, I suspect, the less one knows. But I can judge many things about you. You are a strong man mentally, but physically you are ill. You are a man without beliefs, without family or community. You have traveled much, and you have traveled alone." Madame's voice became suddenly harsh: "You are also, I regret to say, a man of violence."

The Chameleon did not dispute her characterizations. He decided to press his point. "I am bent on a mission of great importance. I did not welcome it, but it has fallen to me to carry it out. I will not profit from it; indeed, it will likely cause me considerable grief. I cannot say that it will not involve violence, but I assure you the ends will be justified by any means necessary to achieve them. My chances of success are remarkably slim, even so. I came to you on an intuition. I thought there was some chance you might provide me with a vital clue."

Madame Regine sat back down on her divan and stared out one of the French windows. The Chameleon remained standing, waiting for her response.

"I cannot reveal the names of any of my clients," she said at last. "It is not *done!* No matter what reasons you might have. It is a confidence I keep, without condition. My name, my entire reputation, depend on it. I cannot risk all that for a favor to a stranger. If my clients wish to reveal their association with me, that is of course their own affair—I don't object. It brings me new clients. But many of my clients are people of great public responsibility. They would be ridiculed for their association with an astrologist."

The Chameleon shrugged in disappointment. "I understand, madame. I am sorry to have troubled you."

He had underestimated her again, he thought. She was not as greedy as he had expected. She was rich, after all, and could afford to take the long view—protecting her reputation for discretion where it counted most.

The Chameleon turned and headed for the doorway. The Haitian maid was waiting with his briefcase and cane. Madame Regine followed him a few steps and then spoke. "Wait."

He turned back.

"I am also a clairvoyant, you know."

"Yes?"

Madame smiled. "I think you are in for a very hard time these next few days."

The damned woman, he thought. First she refuses to cooperate, now she wants to tell my fortune. "What else do you see?" he asked.

A shrewd look crossed her face, tightening the edges of her lips. "I do not give free consultations, m'sieur."

He saw her intentions and smiled. This was her way of accepting the bribe. "Nor would I expect you to. What is your fee?"

"In this unusual circumstance, whatever you feel is appropriate."

The Chameleon withdrew a wallet from his inside coat pocket and produced a stack of American dollars. He counted out twenty hundred-dollar bills and laid them on the three-legged Louis Quatorze table near the doorway. Madame Regine followed the stack with her eyes, obviously trying to assess its total.

"Two thousand dollars, madame."

She smiled benignly. "Sit down, m'sieur."

The Chameleon returned to his chair and the maid brought him another cup of tea. He wondered what his sum of dollars was going to buy. She had to be impressed with his generosity.

Madame sat silently for several minutes, collecting her thoughts. "I see that death is near you," she said at last, "and near to others. Death . . . and blood, deep and running in many directions. . . . There is a battle of giants. . . . And rivers of blood.

"Giants?"

"Yes . . . and giant killers."

"How many?"

"I do not know."

"Who are they?"

Madame Regine smiled savagely. "I do not know!"

He studied her face. It was impassive, closed.

"Is that all?"

"Yes."

The maid brought him his cane and briefcase. The stack of hundred-dollar bills had disappeared from the table. The damned woman has tricked me, he thought. Conned me out of my money!

The maid opened one of the tall double doors into the outer hallway, and the Chameleon turned to say good-bye.

"A privilege to meet you, madame."

"A privilege to meet *you*, m'sieur."

Their eyes met. He felt no anger. She had won their little game. He deserved the defeat. One still learns, even in middle age.

"If you're going back to the United States, Monsieur Markham," she said, her tone suddenly light and chatty, "you must say hello to Senator MacNair for me! A dear friend!"

The Chameleon raised an eyebrow. "Senator MacNair?"

"Yes. Albert MacNair. From *New Hampshire*." She pronounced the name of the state carefully, in English. "A charming man!"

The Chameleon looked at the small woman thoughtfully, a thin smile beginning to bend his lips. It was serendipity, not astrology, that he had always believed in. His faith was paying off again.

"Thank you, madame," he replied warmly. "Thank you! I shall certainly give him your best!"

9

Thursday evening, October 25

After dinner, Smith and Thompson took their cups of coffee to a small study in the back of Smith's house. A beautiful fireplace, faced with travertine, took up most of one wall, a long desk situated between two low windows most of another, and the remaining areas were lined with books.

"Would you like a brandy, Jay?"

Thompson accepted. Smith handed it to him in a rather ceremonious fashion, as if presenting him with a well-deserved reward. Or was it a gesture of consolation?

They sat on small sofas facing each other across a butler's table and swirled their drinks in silence. Smith had not mentioned the manuscript once all through dinner. Thompson could not remember when he had ever seen Smith so reticent.

Smith went to a humidor, retrieved a cigar from it, and carefully unwrapped it. He offered one to Thompson, who refused.

"Ellen hates me to smoke them," Smith said. "So I usually don't in the house. But one right now, with that brandy, is irresistible." He puffed extravagantly for half a minute until the cigar was properly fired up.

"Well, Jay, you're absolutely right," he said at last. "There's not a damn thing I can find in that memoir that's not already public information. I'm especially baffled, because Allen knew enough to embarrass every administration back to Eisenhower. Many things he'd confided to me are not in here. He must have lost his nerve."

Thompson nodded, disappointment sweeping over him. He'd expected too much of Smith. He was brilliant, but he wasn't clairvoyant, after all.

"And yet," Smith continued, "I'm convinced from what you've told me that somebody thinks that Roland has hidden something very important somewhere, and they're desperate to find it, and determined to keep it from falling to someone else. I thought at first that it might be hidden in the manuscript itself, but obviously it's not. And obviously they've already seen the manuscript and reached the same conclusion themselves."

Thompson looked up, startled. "How do you know that?"

"I doubt that the FBI agent who stopped by your office was genuine. The Bureau just doesn't operate that way. It cannot legally confiscate documents without a court order, and that takes time. Somebody simply posed as an FBI agent to get the material. And failing to find what they were after in that material, they continued the search—Feldman's office, Miss Mitchell's apartment, your apartment."

"Well, then, they've recovered everything—from Roland, from Feldman, and from my office. That includes all the correspondence and every copy of the manuscript, except this one, which Harriet had in her desk at the *Times*. Maybe that's all they want."

Smith inhaled and blew a plume of smoke into the air. "Perhaps they want to destroy all the material related to his book—for some reason we haven't yet discovered—but I think they are still looking for something, something they expected to be in the manuscript that wasn't. And whoever they are, they are skilled and determined."

"Do you have any idea who?"

Smith threw up his hands. "There are too many possibilities. Any number of Communist governments might fear that Allen planned to expose something detrimental to them. But then Israel and several of the Arab states—Pakistan, Iran, Syria, and Libya, just to name four obvious ones—might have similar fears. And then there's Cuba. And quite a few other Latin-American governments not above this sort of thing. Mexico comes immediately to mind. Relations with them have become exceedingly hostile, thanks to President Mills's bull-headed xenophobia. Since the shutting of the border to illegal immigration two years ago, and the forced repatriation of over a million Mexicans, Mexico has been spying on the U.S. regularly. Perhaps they were after Allen. About all I'd rule out are our European allies, and only because I don't believe they'd resort to killing in such a situation."

"What about an American enemy?" Thompson asked.

Smith rubbed his earlobe between thumb and forefinger. "Possible, but unlikely. The CIA and FBI might still be tempted to bend the law here and there, when they thought they could get away with it, but this kind of savagery is not their style. Whom does that leave? The Mafia? Always a possibility, I guess. But I can't imagine what Roland could know that would concern them."

"Couldn't it be a crank? Or an embittered ex-employee? Somebody with a grudge against Roland, or fearful that Roland was about to expose him in some way?"

Smith shook his head. "No, I don't think so. Because I don't think one man could kill two people, search two apartments, a house, and an office in two cities 250 miles apart in two days. It's a team, I believe, but as to its identity, I don't have a clue."

He retrieved the bottle of brandy and refilled both glasses. Thompson realized that they had come to a dead end. He sipped the brandy and gazed at the rows of books and framed documents on the walls—dozens of honorary degrees and awards in several languages, each with the professor's name on it. The laurels of an exceptional life.

The professor's name triggered a connection in his brain. "This is probably nothing," he said, "but I might as well mention it. I had a strange phone message left for me at the Hay-Adams in Washington. I picked it up with a batch of others when I checked out, and I was in such a hurry, I didn't read it until yesterday. As it turned out, it wasn't even addressed to me."

Smith glanced at him. "Do you still have it?"

"No. I threw it away."

"Do you remember the message?"

"Yes, I think so. Let's see . . . 'Virginia Smith . . . the key . . . and the directions . . . are in the sleeper.' I think that was it. Something very close to that. And then it said, 'Be careful.' That was all. The sender didn't leave a name. I assumed it was a mistake. The desk clerk just left me somebody else's message."

Smith took up a pad and pencil from the desk and asked Thompson to repeat the message so he could write it down. He studied it for a long time, not saying anything. Gradually a smile broke over his features, and turned into a gentle laugh. "You are a most dramatic storyteller," he said. "Saving the punchline for last."

"What do you mean?"

"That discarded message was from Allen Roland. Leave it to that clever old fox to think of it."

Thompson was bewildered. "How's that again?"

"He must have called you between the time you left the hotel and arrived at his house. He knew he was in some kind of danger. When he called you and found you weren't in, he had to think of something quickly, because he must have known that he didn't have much time."

Thompson was more puzzled than ever. "You figured that out from that phone message?"

Smith went over to the small desk under the window and brought the manuscript back to the coffee table between them. "Roland has left you a coded message somewhere in this manuscript. I'm certain of it. I'll explain."

Smith handed Thompson the pad on which he had copied his telephone message:

Virginia Smith.
The key and the directions
are in the sleeper.
Be careful.

Below that, Smith had rewritten the first line:

Viginère. Smith.

"Viginère," Smith explained, "is a code, named after its inventor, Blaise de Viginère, a sixteenth-century cryptographer. Ironically, his original system is much more difficult to break into than the one his name is associated with, which is a debased form of the original. But that's the one that has rescued him from obscurity, and I assume that Roland used that version here."

Smith dropped his cigar in the ashtray and continued his explanation.

"It's called the Viginère Tableau, and it's based on a table, or *tableau*, of multiple alphabets. A simple, monoalphabetic code, one that uses a direct substitution, like a 'p' for an 'e' can be quickly broken into by anyone if the message is long enough, based just on letter frequency—the number of times different letters appear in English usage. But by using the polyalphabetic substitution system of the *tableau*, the same letter in the message, or plain text, as it's called, will never appear as the same letter in the cipher text."

Thompson nodded uncertainly. "I'm with you—more or less."

"Now, the *tableau* uses a key that both the sender and receiver have to know. It's usually a short phrase that can be easily remembered. I take it that the key here is the phrase 'the sleeper,' and that the message itself—the 'directions'—is in the chapter called 'The Sleeper'—the one that deals with various cases of moles or sleepers who infiltrated opposition governments."

Thompson stared with astonishment at the pad on which Smith had magically transformed his phone message. "And the 'Smith' here is you!"

The professor smiled modestly. "Well, he knew I would help you, of course."

"But, my God, I came within a whisker of blowing the whole thing! I threw the slip away and forgot all about it!"

"Yes, it was a close call. It was understandable but unfortunate that the clerk at the hotel misunderstood or misinterpreted the key word—Viginère. Roland must have been in a terrible hurry at that point, and the mistake was such a natural one. The astonishing thing is, though, that Allen devised a message whose meaning only you—with my help—would be able to interpret. Extraordinary."

Thompson was still grappling with the implausibility of the message. "Are you sure, professor? Where *is* the message?"

Smith nodded. "That's the question, of course. Let's see if I can find a code book that has a Viginère Tableau in it first. That'll save us the nuisance of having to type it out from scratch."

Smith searched among the titles on his bookshelves, extracting and replacing volumes until he found the one he needed.

"This is it," he said, blowing the dust off and returning with it to the table. "This volume dates from the thirties, and Viginère's elegant old ciphers have been out of use for a lot longer than that."

Smith opened the manuscript, charged with renewed energy and enthusiasm, and tipped the shade on the floor lamp near the table so that it would shine directly on the pages of the manuscript.

"Bring that chair in the corner over here beside me, Jay, and let's see if we can find it."

Smith leafed slowly through the pages of the chapter called "The Sleeper," while Thompson watched, his eyes fixed on the photocopy of Roland's discouragingly bland and familiar memoir with a new anticipation, as if they were the leaves of a rare and forbidden document.

"There are potentially dozens of ways and thousands of places to hide a message in a manuscript of this size," Smith began, turning the pages. "There are various kinds of invisible ink, requiring heat or certain chemicals to make them reappear. And of course there's the famous microdot—a photographed document reduced to the size of a typewritten period, and glued on a page in the place of one. It's even possible to record sound on electromagnetically treated paper, so that one can lift a spoken message from the page and play it back like a tape from a recorder. Laser technology makes it possible to imprint and uncover a message by light alone—like a very sophisticated form of photography. Computer techniques allow you to scatter a message throughout the pages of a manuscript in such a way that it could only be found and deciphered by another computer programmed to the same code. The methods get more exotic every year."

Thompson shook his head. "It sounds like we have an enormous task ahead of us."

Smith laughed. "No, I don't think so. Many things are *possible*. But I'm operating on a set of assumptions. First, in keeping with the character of such an old cipher, I'm guessing Allen has used an appropriately contemporaneous method to hide the message. The message has to be short, and Allen had to be able to get it down quickly. And he had to expect we could find it easily, once we knew it was there. I'm further assuming that the message is right here in this chapter, entitled 'The Sleeper.' Since he used those words as the key for the code, economy of effort would dictate that he also use them to denote the place in which he has hidden his message. I'm looking for something fairly obvious—the first or last letters on a page, or a paragraph, or a line, or a word. Easy stuff, really. But safe. Without the key, the wrong party would be hard put to break the code, even if he found it."

Smith examined the pages of "The Sleeper" chapter carefully, one at a time, holding each page up to the light, examining the back side, and scribbling long lines of letters in a notebook.

Thompson refilled their brandy glasses and paced the room, surveying the bookshelves, reading the many framed awards. Minutes stretched into a half-hour. Feeling he was more a distraction than a help, Thompson picked out a book from the shelves and sat quietly on the sofa reading it, leaving Smith to concentrate undisturbed.

An hour later Thompson looked over to see that Smith had given up on "The Sleeper" chapter and was examining the other pages in the 560-page tome. Not a promising sign, he thought.

Several hours later Smith threw the pad and pencil on the table in defeat. Damn! I can't find it," he said, uttering a sigh of profound dejection. "I *know* it's here, but I just can't find it!"

Thompson closed his book and nodded in bleak resignation. "Well, I'm sorry to have put you through all this. You can't continue all night. Perhaps tomorrow . . ."

Smith didn't hear him. His mind was working furiously, unable to abide the frustration he felt. "I'm missing something," he muttered, more to himself than Thompson. "Something simple. I must try to put myself inside Roland's head."

He gulped some brandy and began turning the pages of "The Sleeper" chapter again, looking for an idea. Suddenly he stopped, picked up one page, and examined it closely, holding it near the light.

"Wait," he said. Thompson looked at him. He was holding the page scant inches from his eyes, his expression intense.

"Yes!" he cried. "I have it. Look!"

Thompson jumped up and returned to the chair beside Smith. Smith was tapping the page with his fingernail, shaking with excitement.

"Here, you see!" he said. "At the bottom of this page there's an extra two lines of typing that have been struck over, as if he had simply mistyped something! But if you look carefully at the letters beneath the overstrikes, you'll see that they don't form any words!"

Thompson looked at the lines:

ӾӾӾӾӼ̵ӾӾ̵Ӿ

Ӿ̵Ӿ

"I see it," he said, "but I don't get it."

Smith grinned in triumph. "Ah, but don't you see, Jay. If they don't form any words, why did he type them? Surely not to exercise his fingers!"

Thompson nodded, catching Smith's excitement. "Both simple and ingenious."

Smith agreed. "Beautifully simple. And I almost missed it. Typical of Allen. Sometimes he's *too* clever."

Thompson almost corrected Smith's tense, but bit his tongue in time.

Smith pulled over the code book, opened to a page containing a solid block of alphabets:

```
  — a b c d e f g h i j k l m n o p q r s t u v w x y z
A — A B C D E F G H I J K L M N O P Q R S T U V W X Y Z
B — B C D E F G H I J K L M N O P Q R S T U V W X Y Z A
C — C D E F G H I J K L M N O P Q R S T U V W X Y Z A B
D — D E F G H I J K L M N O P Q R S T U V W X Y Z A B C
E — E F G H I J K L M N O P Q R S T U V W X Y Z A B C D
F — F G H I J K L M N O P Q R S T U V W X Y Z A B C D E
G — G H I J K L M N O P Q R S T U V W X Y Z A B C D E F
H — H I J K L M N O P Q R S T U V W X Y Z A B C D E F G
I — I J K L M N O P Q R S T U V W X Y Z A B C D E F G H
J — J K L M N O P Q R S T U V W X Y Z A B C D E F G H I
K — K L M N O P Q R S T U V W X Y Z A B C D E F G H I J
L — L M N O P Q R S T U V W X Y Z A B C D E F G H I J K
M — M N O P Q R S T U V W X Y Z A B C D E F G H I J K L
N — N O P Q R S T U V W X Y Z A B C D E F G H I J K L M
O — O P Q R S T U V W X Y Z A B C D E F G H I J K L M N
P — P Q R S T U V W X Y Z A B C D E F G H I J K L M N O
Q — Q R S T U V W X Y Z A B C D E F G H I J K L M N O P
R — R S T U V W X Y Z A B C D E F G H I J K L M N O P Q
S — S T U V W X Y Z A B C D E F G H I J K L M N O P Q R
T — T U V W X Y Z A B C D E F G H I J K L M N O P Q R S
U — U V W X Y Z A B C D E F G H I J K L M N O P Q R S T
V — V W X Y Z A B C D E F G H I J K L M N O P Q R S T U
W — W X Y Z A B C D E F G H I J K L M N O P Q R S T U V
X — X Y Z A B C D E F G H I J K L M N O P Q R S T U V W
Y — Y Z A B C D E F G H I J K L M N O P Q R S T U V W X
Z — Z A B C D E F G H I J K L M N O P Q R S T U V W X Y
```

"Now we copy out these two rows of overstruck letters . . ."

Carefully Smith examined the letters underneath the x's at the bottom of Roland's manuscript page and copied them in a steady, neat hand onto a yellow legal pad:

svhalgjxpvbugwwpeghfhyelxmhspvubvydsvgczvvydorxumebzj

vlrktvfnzfmemqesimhrlhsvildhyilperpqzesmgy

"Now we copy the key over them, thus."

thesleeperthesleeperthesleeperthesleeperthesleeperthe

svhalgjxpvbugwwpeghfhyclxmhspvubvydsvgczvvydorxumebzj

sleeperthesleeperthesleeperthesleeperthesl

vlrktvfnzfmemqesimhrlhsvildhyilperpqzesmgy

"Now we move down this vertical column on the left side of the *tableau* until we find the first letter of the key, a 't.' Then we follow the horizontal row across from that 't' until we find the 's,' the first letter of the cipher. From that 's' we follow up the column to the top row, and that gives us the first letter of the text—a 'z.' "

Smith printed the 'z' neatly beneath the 't' and the 's' and continued on. In less than two minutes he had the entire message decoded. He inserted slashes between the words and put the pad on the table, where both stared at it for some time:

zodiac/file/in/cellar/door/at/middleburg/sorry/
i/couldnt/finish/
dangerous/but/important/worth/more/than/a/million

Thompson collapsed back into the chair and finished off the brandy in one gulp. He felt a mixture of fatigue and depression, and the beginnings of a headache. "What kind of insane game is this?" he asked. "Roland seems to have set up a posthumous treasure hunt. What does he mean, 'in the door'?"

Smith looked in the direction of the door leading from the study. "All the doors in this house are solid, because it's an old place. But most new doors are hollow-core—a wooden frame with sheets of plywood glued to each side to make a sandwich. Not a bad place to hide something, really. Like most good hiding places, it's right out there in the open, where it's apt to be overlooked. Just as I missed the code under the overstrikes."

"Wouldn't you have to cut a hole in the door, and wouldn't that be hard to disguise?"

"Not at all. One removes the door from its hinges and cuts an opening through the bottom. It can't be detected without removing the door again, something anyone searching a house is unlikely to think to do—or to bother."

"And Middleburg, I suppose, is where Roland's weekend house is located, out in Virginia?"

"Yes, it must be that."

"And 'Zodiac.' What does that mean?"

"I'm guessing, but it's most likely a code name. It may be Allen's own appellation for some project or individual. Or it may be the name of a secret operation, used by those involved in it."

Thompson looked at his fingernails. Over the last two days they had been bitten to the quick. "Now what?" he asked.

Smith removed his glasses. "I'm not sure what to advise you, Jay. I knew Allen Roland for a long time—ever since World War Two, when we both worked for Bill Donovan. He was the toughest man in a tough, dirty trade. He survived as long as he did because he was enormously resourceful and intelligent. But on his way to the top he saw a great deal, was privy to many things it's better not to know. Allen was, perhaps above all else, a repository of important secrets. Twice before during his career it almost cost him his life."

Smith paused, remembering something. Once he even saved the life of an assassin hired to kill him. It was during the war, in southern France. He was driving on the Grande Corniche between Nice and Monaco, on his way to a secret meeting with an emissary from Admiral Canaris. Another car attempted to push him off the cliff. They caught bumpers, and the would-be assassin lost control of his vehicle and smashed into a cliff abutment. Allen pulled him from his car before it exploded. The man was an Egyptian, working for the Germans. Instead of killing him, Allen persuaded him on the spot to become a double agent. He never revealed the man's identity, but he told me, some time ago, that he had used him successfully many times during his years at the CIA. The man became, in a sense, Allen's personal secret weapon, willing and able to do almost anything for him. He owed him his life, you see. A kind of honor among thieves, I suppose."

Thompson shook his head. "Nothing about that in his manuscript."

"No."

Smith sighed, and for a moment it looked to Thompson as if he were on the verge of tears. He fought off the gloom that had descended on him by tearing off the top two or three pages of the legal pad bearing Roland's decoded message and lighting the edges of them with a wooden match. When they were ablaze, he carried them to the fireplace and threw them in.

"I suppose," Smith said, watching the flames, "that Allen found out one secret too many. Whatever it is, this 'Zodiac,' it must be an earth-shaker."

Smith added the page from the pad with Thompson's "Virginia Smith" message on it to the fire and sat back down again. "It was a secret he apparently intended to reveal, but I don't know why. He wasn't a particularly moral man, so I doubt that it was a matter of conscience that moved him to tell you the location of the file. There must be a more compelling reason."

Smith's remark chilled him. What more compelling reason? "You mean a threat to national security—that kind of thing?"

Smith nodded. "Possibly. Whatever it is, some party found out that he knew about it, and suspected he might reveal it. To prevent that, they decided to steal whatever evidence he had and then kill him. But he outsmarted them. He hid the evidence and devised an ingenious way to pass it on in an emergency."

Smith pressed thumb and forefinger into the corners of his eyes and pondered the situation in silence.

"And so they are still looking for it," he continued after a moment. "I assume, along with the places we already know they've searched, they've also been through the house at Middleburg. And perhaps they even found the file in the door, though I doubt it. They would have looked there first, and if they had found it, they would not have bothered with you and Mitchell and Feldman. So they must still be looking for it."

Smith drained off the dregs in his brandy glass and looked at Thompson again, those steady blue-green eyes examining him compassionately.

"In fact," Smith concluded, "they must now believe that you have it."

Thompson tried to sound offhand, but he had trouble clearing his throat. He felt as if he was being told he had contracted a terminal illness. "And now that we've deciphered Roland's note, I guess that, in a manner of speaking, I do have it. Or at least know where it is."

"Yes. You and I are the only ones who know."

"Should I go to the police?"

Smith shook his head. "What can they do, really? The deaths appear to be suicides, and your apartment break-in can't be proved. And they won't touch that FBI business at your office. I doubt they would help at all."

"They'd think I was paranoid."

"Probably they would, yes."

Thompson felt like screaming. Why couldn't Smith help him? Who else could he turn to?

"Why did Roland pick *me*, for God's sake?"

"I don't know. But it disturbs me—beyond the fact that you're now unfairly caught up in something about which you know nothing. Allen must have felt isolated and desperate, unable to trust more obvious sources of help."

Smith stood up and paced the short distance between the coffee table and the window. "You must be very careful, Jay. Your apartment is almost certainly bugged. There are dozens of simple, quick ways to do it, and if someone took the trouble to break into your apartment, he would certainly take the trouble to plant a listening device of some kind. It's information they're looking for, after all, not manuscripts."

Smith tugged on an earlobe and gazed into the now dark fireplace. "The misplaced telephone receiver suggests they may have left a harmonica bug. It's quick to install and very effective. One unscrews the mouthpiece cover, takes out the standard diaphragm, and replaces it with another one that has the bug built into it. It's an ingenious device. Someone simply has to dial your number—from any telephone in the world—and blow a note on a special whistle just before it starts to ring. The whistled note prevents the phone from ringing, but turns it on, so it becomes in effect a microphone, picking up all conversation in the room. It monitors your telephone calls as well."

Thompson pressed his temples with the heels of his palms. The headache was on full force, now. Brandy and tension. A bad combination.

"I'm thinking of staying with a friend in Washington for a while."

"If you mean Miss Mitchell," Smith warned, "I don't think that's very wise. You'll be exposing her to the same danger you're in. You had better avoid seeing her for a while."

"What the hell should I do?"

Smith thought for a moment before answering. "Take a vacation from work. Leave New York City. Go somewhere you're not known. In a few weeks, things will change. These people are in a hurry."

Smith paused. "Of course, if you could get the file from Middleburg, that might tell us what you're up against. And suggest a way to fight it. I'd do what I could from here to help you, of course. . . ."

Smith let the thought trail off. He suddenly looked old and tired. Thompson felt guilty for having dropped such a difficult problem in his lap. As bad as it was, it was still his problem, not Smith's. He had no right to drag him into it. He could see that Smith wanted him to go after the file, but knew it would be dangerous. And knew that he couldn't help him very much if he got into serious trouble.

The room had become stuffy with the smell of stale cigar smoke and brandy. Thompson noted that it was nearly four o'clock in the morning. He felt chilled and fatigued, his mind prey to unsettling fantasies.

Smith was piling Roland's manuscript back into a neat stack.

"Do you think my life is in danger?" Thompson asked him.

"Yes."

Smith said it flatly, a simple admission of fact.

10

Paco found what he was looking for. It was parked in front of the Hotel Principal, on Calle Bolivar, a narrow back street that ran between Avenidas Madero and 16 de Septiembre. *Hijo de puta*, he thought, it had taken him all day just to find one! He watched it for nearly fifteen minutes from the other side of the street, strolling casually up and down the block to make certain that no one was watching him. Occasionally he stopped to gaze in one of the lighted store windows near the corner of Madero, to admire the rich displays of cassette recorders, color TV's, radios, digital watches, stereo sets, and hand calculators. In his head he had already spent several times over the thousand pesos they were going to pay him.

It was eleven-thirty. The shops were closed and the street was deserted. The Hotel Principal, a small one-star establishment, was quiet. Paco patted the tools tucked into his belt under his vinyl jacket and crossed the street, walking fast.

He had stolen many automobiles in his five years in Mexico City—Cadillacs, Mercedeses, BMW's, Peugeots, Porsches, Volvos, Corvettes—but no one had ever asked him to grab a Toyota Land Cruiser.

Jeeps were valuable, but they were just not in demand in the auto-theft circuit. At first he wasn't even sure what one looked like. He had had to pose as a buyer at the Toyota dealership on the Reforma just so he could check out the nature and location of the jeep's windows, door locks, and ignition slot.

Paco approached the driver's-side door, facing away from the curb, and pulled from under his jacket a small flat bar of tempered steel, sharpened like a chisel at one end and curved like a miniature crowbar at the other. The steel bar was not an ordinary tool of his trade; he had determined that he needed it specifically for the Land Cruiser. He slipped the blade of the crowbar end underneath the narrow lip of the door's edge, just below the key cylinder. One hard pry pulled the lip back, exposing the narrow crack between the door and the doorframe.

He turned the bar around and worked the chisel end into the locking mechanism, partly visible in the crack. One hard push in the right spot snapped the locking claw off the post, and the door popped open.

Paco had been counting the seconds, something that he did automatically. Fifteen. Not bad for an unfamiliar vehicle, but much slower than his average.

In an instant he was in the driver's seat, with the door shut after him. From his belt he produced an eighteen-inch-long metal pipe with a screw-threaded tip and a heavy steel sleeve that slid the pipe's length. Called a slam-hammer, it was used by auto-repair shops for pulling dents. Car thieves had found another use for it.

Paco jammed the screw end of the device into the ignition-key slot and twisted it several hard turns, causing the screw to bite into the soft metal of the key slot and firmly wedge itself inside. He slammed the sleeve back against the pipe's rear flange rapidly and forcefully. After about six bangs, the entire key cylinder lifted free of its housing, leaving behind a neat round hole with exposed electrical contact points sitting in the bottom. Paco dropped the slam-hammer and reached into his belt for his third tool—a simple screwdriver with a rubber-covered handle.

He slipped the screwdriver into the hole and twisted it around until it formed a bridge across the contact points. He was rewarded with the sound of the ignition firing into life.

Paco cruised carefully to the corner of Madero and Bolivar, and turned right toward the Zocalo. In a couple of minutes he would be on the highway north, to the city of Pachuca, an hour and a half away.

The euphoria of his success began to fade on the lonely road, when he reflected that the customers wanted not just one, but two Land Cruisers. Both had to be identical 1983 models, and both had to be delivered by Saturday, October 27. He was going to have to find another of the damned jeeps tomorrow before he would see any of that one thousand pesos.

11

Friday afternoon, October 26

Thompson waited impatiently in the back of the theater for his eyes to adjust from Washington's midday sun to the darkness inside. When he could at last make out the aisle, he moved cautiously toward the front, counting the rows as his feet crunched noisily over loose popcorn and candy wrappers. At number fifteen he paused, squinted along the row to his left, and saw the dim, shadowy outlines of Harriet Mitchell, slumped down in the stygian gloom, her head barely level with the seat back. He sidestepped along the row and settled hesitantly into the seat next to her. Most of the seat's stuffing had been removed through a large tear in the plastic upholstery and the seat itself slanted forward at a dangerous angle, threatening to dump him on the floor. An oppressive odor hung in the air, composed of stale cigarette smoke, urine, and a cloyingly sweet industrial deodorizer.

"What took you so long?" Harriet whispered. "I've been in this creepy joint for hours, fending off the perverts."

Thompson looked around. About five people were in the theater, each separated from the others by a wide circle of empty seats.

"Well, you seem to have driven most of them away."

Harriet pulled Thompson's hand onto her lap and squeezed it hard. He leaned over and kissed her in back of the ear. She had gone to some trouble to appear inconspicuous—wearing faded blue jeans, a loose dark pullover sweater, and a floppy hat that partially hid her face.

"This is the first one of these films I've ever seen," she whispered. "Unbelievable! It's called *The Spy Who Came in the Cold.* The plot is not very sophisticated, but the closeups are wonderful!"

Thompson looked up at the screen. It showed a man in a trench coat standing on a dark balcony, peering in a window and lazily stroking an erect and unusually large penis. The camera cut to the scene he was watching—a man wearing a vaguely Russian-looking army tunic, and nude from the waist down, cavorting with two young women in garter-belts and high heels. As the camera cut back and forth, the trench-coated man worked himself into a masturbatory frenzy while the three in the room began changing positions with accelerating frequency, as if competing in some gymnastic routine. Occasionally the camera zoomed in very tight, and the screen would fill with awesome ten-foot penises and cavelike, gaping mouths and vaginas. Pubic hair turned into bramble bushes and pimples into anthills. The erotic impact was considerably compromised by the poor lighting and color control, which rendered the sexual organs in angry shades of reddish-purple; and by the soundtrack, out of synch with the voices and made nearly inaudible by a loud background hum.

"Next time, let me pick the rendezvous," Thompson said. "This is giving pornography a bad name."

Harriet giggled, then squirmed around in her seat to face him. "Tell me what happened," she said. "What did you find out from Smith?"

Thompson told her, finishing his whispered account with Smith's warning to him that his life was in danger. Harriet squeezed his arm and rested her head against his shoulder and for a long time said nothing.

"Are you really worried?" she finally asked.

Thompson nodded. "And scared. I'm jumping at shadows."

Harriet pulled her leather bag from the adjoining seat and began fumbling through it in the dim blue light. She found a folded white envelope and pressed it into Thompson's hand.

"You can stay at Herb Franklin's apartment. It's just across the river in Alexandria. Near the Rosslyn metro stop. Herb's leaving on assignment for the *Times* in the Middle East, and he'll be gone at least a month. There are two keys inside—lobby door and apartment door. And the address is on a slip of paper inside. You can stay there as long as you like."

Thompson fingered the envelope uncertainly for a moment, then slipped it into his shirt pocket. The significance of the moment was not lost on him. Overnight he had become a fugitive. He also found himself wondering who this Herb was, that she could get the keys to his apartment so easily.

Harriet pulled on Thompson's arm and leaned close to his ear. "I want to go with you!"

"To Herb's apartment?"

"To Middleburg!"

Thompson turned to stare at her. He was startled at the intensity of her voice.

"Forget it."

"I will not forget it!" she hissed. "You're taking me with you!"

"I'm not taking you with me because I'm not going!"

Harriet seemed genuinely shocked. "You have to go! Are you crazy?"

"I'm not crazy. That's why I'm not going."

Harriet squirmed angrily in her seat. Thompson could hear her cursing under her breath.

"Before you burst with frustration," he said, "let me tell you what I'm going to do. I've had eight sleepless hours since Hanover to think it out. As soon as we leave this theater, I'm going to Ninth and D streets to the FBI. I'm going to tell them the whole story—everything—and let *them* worry about it."

"Jay. Listen to me!" Harriet was no longer whispering.

"We're getting involved in something way over our heads," he went on. "Whoever these jokers are who want Roland's papers, they're professionals. They kill."

"We *have* to pursue it, Jay!"

A slurred male voice from the back of the theater made itself heard: "Shaddap down there!"

Harriet lowered her voice, but raised her insistence. "Even if the FBI believes your story, by the time they get around to checking out the door in Middleburg, the file will be gone!"

Thompson felt exasperated. He hadn't expected this reaction from her. "Listen, I know you're thinking that it might be a great career boost for you to break this story, whatever it is, in the *Times*, but believe me, all you'll get out of this is killed! We don't know what went on in Roland's life, so we can't judge the nature of the threat. I'm no fan of the FBI, but they're better at catching killers than I am. So let's let them do it. You can still follow the story, after all. From a safe distance."

Harriet pulled on Thompson's arm again. "Jay, you're not listening to me! When the FBI gets there, the file will be gone!"

"Why?"

Harriet dropped her voice to a barely audible whisper. "Because even if these people don't catch up with you, they'll still find out where the file is . . . from Professor Smith."

"How will they know Smith knows?"

"Because you told me over the phone you were going to Hanover to see an old professor of yours."

"So?"

"Our phones are bugged, you told me. So they probably followed you to Hanover."

Harriet let the message sink in, then offered her solution: "We can get the file tonight, then take it to the FBI tomorrow. Then you'll have something tangible that will help you convince them, and I'll have something for a story."

He hated to admit it to himself, but she was thinking more clearly than he was. Still, going after the file was dangerous.

"You're manipulating me."

"Then you'll go?"

"I didn't say that."

After a long pause Harriet threw in her clincher. "Then I'll go alone. I mean it, too."

Thompson crossed his arms and sighed. "In that case, you go right ahead."

Harriet slammed herself down in her seat and kicked the seat back in front of her hard with both feet. Another angry silence fell, punctuated at length by what sounded to Thompson like a sniffle. He looked out of the corner of his eye and saw that Harriet was crying.

She wiped tears from the corner of her eyes with her sweater sleeve, grabbed her big bag from the seat next to her, and made motions to leave. Thompson suspected that she really was impulsive enough to carry through on her threat—especially since he had just goaded her by calling her bluff. He hated the idea of going to Middleburg, but he couldn't possibly let her go out there alone. He stood up and followed her down the row of seats and up the aisle toward the exit.

"Okay," he said, "You win."

II
The Chase

12

Professor Thomas Smith felt the presence of a shadow.

After seeing Thompson off, he had returned to his study in the back of the house, cracked open a window to let in the autumn air, and sat down to prepare his notes for a lecture that evening. The subject, "Robert Frost and the Nature Metaphor," was a popular old standby that he had been delivering in essentially the same form for years, and now it bored him intensely, and he found it next to impossible to bring his renowned powers of concentration to bear on the material. His mind kept returning to Roland's strange message.

Smith's eye was drawn to a gray squirrel loping along the far edge of the backyard. When the squirrel crossed a pool of dappled shade cast by an oak tree, Smith's mind was seized by a painful memory.

He was sitting on a bench in Montsouris Park in Paris on another early afternoon in October—the fall of 1943, nine months before the Allied invasion—waiting for a man named Reynard, his contact in the French Resistance. The park was empty and Reynard was late for the rendez-vous, already ten minutes past the agreed-upon meeting time. Smith was about to leave when he saw Reynard coming along the path under the tall park oaks. He was walking fast, almost running. Smith remembered the play of light and shade on his features as he approached, and the vivid, jarring image of two men in the uniforms of the Vichy police suddenly appearing in the shadows of the path behind him. They opened fire. Reynard looked like a man in convulsions, legs and arms dancing and jerking out of control as dozens of bullets slammed into him. As quickly as they had materialized, the assassins disappeared from the path and Reynard staggered forward for a few steps, then collapsed in a bloody pile not a hundred feet from Smith's bench.

Smith felt real terror at that moment. What move would not give him away? To remain sitting there would be absurd and unnatural, as much a giveaway as jumping up and running off. He needed to make a convincing display of innocence and surprise, and he needed to do it immediately, without calculation.

He resorted to the simple trick of imagining that he was an innocent bystander, and acted spontaneously out of that mind set. He stood up, called for help in French, then hurried over to Reynard's shattered body, forcing his mind to regard the young patriot as a total stranger. After Smith felt he had made a suitable fuss, he ran off purposefully, affecting an attitude he hoped looked like a man going to summon help. As soon as he was safely out of the park, he made his way on foot across Paris to the working-class district of Neuilly, and went into hiding.

The memory of the murder haunted him for a long time. Had the Vichy police waited just a few seconds longer, they would have caught Reynard and Smith together, and Smith, too, would have died. Thank God it had not been the Gestapo. They would have waited.

But the memory came back to him now for another reason. Smith recalled Reynard telling him, a week before his murder, that he thought he was going to die. "I feel the shadow on me, Tommy," he had said. It was a popular expression in the underground then.

Smith recognized the feeling. He felt the shadow now.

The sense of it was so strong, so palpable, that he could not ignore it, could not drive it away. He put aside his lecture material and sat thinking for a few moments, trying to locate the proximate cause of his premonition, marveling all the while how real it was, like something supernatural clinging to his soul.

On an inspired impulse he picked up the telephone receiver and unscrewed the mouthpiece. Cradled within the threaded Bakelite cover sat the expected diaphragm, a perforated metal-and-plastic disk little bigger than a silver dollar in diameter and about a quarter of an inch in thickness.

Attached magnetically to the back surface of the diaphragm was something that did not belong there—a small round piggyback device, silver in color and no larger than a stack of three dimes.

The harmonica bug.

Smith carefully replaced the diaphragm and screwed the mouthpiece back onto the receiver, leaving the bug untouched, and walked over to the window. The squirrel had vanished, leaving the lawn still in the shadows of the oak. The main thing now, he knew, was to think clearly, to resist panic.

His espionage days were long behind him, but Smith felt the old reflexes returning. Thompson must have told someone—probably Harriet Mitchell—that he was coming to see me, Smith reasoned, and the other side picked it up on the bug in one of their telephones and then followed him here. Well, Thompson was an innocent in these matters, after all. How could he have been expected to know that he was putting someone else's life in danger? Even so, Smith mused, the other side had moved with incredible speed.

He was contaminated now, in the red zone, and there was no time to brood about how it had happened or what the consequences were likely to be.

Whoever put the harmonica bug in his telephone must still be nearby, Smith assumed. Nearby and waiting. If he was going to defend himself, he had to act at once.

He decided on an unusual course of action.

He unlocked a bookcase cabinet in the study and took from it a heavy ebony case containing a rare Persian chess set, its pieces carved in ivory and black onyx, its board alternating squares of jade and banded alabaster set in a rose-marble base. The set, over a thousand years old, was a gift from the Shah of Iran in 1953, a private expression of thanks for his help in restoring him to the throne.

He set the heavy stone board on the coffee table and positioned the pieces, the opposing ranks of ancient foot soldiers arranged facing each other across the board, and behind them the rooks, knights, and sages, flanking the intricately carved masterpieces of the set, the Shah and the firzán, or minister, now called the queen. Once they were in place, Smith did not move a piece, but sat in deep contemplation, his eyes fixed on the polished jade and alabaster squares, replaying in his mind a game he had once played to a draw against the great Cuban chess master Capablanca. He could still remember each move, as he could recall the entire play of hundreds of games, and he played it out in his mind's eye as a mental exercise to prepare his memory for the rigorous effort he planned to subject it to in the next hours.

When he was satisfied that he was ready, he picked up a pad and pencil and focused his powers of total recall on the night just past. He slumped, trancelike, back against the sofa, and began replaying in his head, word for word, the entire late evening's conversation with Thompson. Now that he knew that someone else had overheard it, he needed to know exactly what had been overheard.

The crucial area was the conversation about the coded message:

"Now we copy out these two rows of overstruck letters. . . . Now we copy the key over them, thus. . . . Now we move down this vertical column on the left side of the tableau *until we find the first letter of the key, a 't.' Then we follow the horizontal row across from that 't' until we find the 's,' the first letter of the cipher. . . ."*

Smith's recall was approaching the critical exchanges, and his extraordinary concentration caused his eyelids to flutter and his hands to tremble.

"What kind of insane game is this? . . . Roland seems to have set up a posthumous treasure hunt. What does he mean, 'in the door'?" . . . "All the doors in this house are solid, because it's an old place. But most new doors are hollow-core—a wooden frame with sheets of plywood glued to each side to make a sandwich. Not a bad place to hide something, really. Like most good hiding places, it's right out there in the open, where it's apt to be overlooked. Just as I missed the code under the over-strikes." . . . "Wouldn't you have to cut a hole in the door, and wouldn't that be hard to disguise?" . . . "Not at all. One removes the door from its hinges and cuts an opening through the bottom. It can't be detected without removing the door again, something anyone searching a house in unlikely to think to do—or to bother." . . . "And Middleburg, I suppose, is where Roland's weekend house is located, out in Virginia?"

Smith raced his memory through the rest of the evening's conversation like a tape recorder on fast forward, and satisfied at length that he had remembered everything, he broke out of the trance and moved from the sofa to the desk, to begin the next, more difficult exercise—formulating a plan of counterattack.

He listed the facts as he knew them, jotting them down on a notepad, as the first stage in developing a solution. They were grim and unpromising:

Roland kept secret file about X
X learned about file
X wants file
(NB: the party after file not nec. X. Could be Y, who wants what Roland has on X. But same consequences ensue.)
X killed Roland and Feldman trying to find it
X searched Roland's house in G'town, M'burg, agent's office, Mitchell's and Thompson's apts.
X took material from Thompson's office
X bugged Thompson, Mitchell (not certain), now me
X learned from bug that file is in door in M'burg house
But doesn't know *which* door, because word "cellar" not repeated aloud last nite
But X knows that Thompson and I *do* know exactly which door
X (or Y) has three options:
1. tear apart all doors in M'burg house—time-consuming
2. extract exact location from Thompson—have to find him first
3. Extract location from me

Yes, of course, Smith thought. X's best bet by far. And his certain first choice. Extract location from me. And X knows right where I am.

13

Friday afternoon, October 26

Jay Thompson wandered south through the afternoon crowd on Fifteenth Street, looking for the Metro station and wondering what to do with himself until six, when Harriet would meet him in Rosslyn with a borrowed car for the trip to Middleburg.

The idea of breaking into a murdered man's house to get a few pieces of paper that someone else was willing to kill for terrified him. If Harriet had not challenged him, made it appear a test of his bravery, he would never have agreed to go. But now that he was committed, he rationalized other reasons for going. Risking some danger now was preferable to enduring a case of chronic anxiety. And the file might really solve the whole business; once he put it in the hands of the FBI, he could end this bad dream and go back to work. And since he had apparently put Smith's life in danger as well, he was especially obliged to make the effort.

Thompson turned east along G Street, and thought halfheartedly of finding a men's clothing store. His attaché case, now doubling as an overnight bag, had nothing in it but a shaving kit and dirty underwear. He wandered on for several blocks, until he spotted a large pylon rising up from the sidewalk on the southeast corner of G and Thirteenth streets. The Metro Center, his destination. He stood across the street and gazed at it, debating whether to board it or continue looking for a men's store. He was not eager to get to Rosslyn, to cage himself up and wait for the evening, but he had nothing else to do, and feared wandering around out in the open. Throngs of pedestrians, purposeful and hurrying, swept by him in both directions, enhancing his sense of aimlessness.

He remembered a game he used to play as a child, when his mother took him into town shopping with her. To overcome the boredom of following her around through all those dumb stores, he would single out the most sinister-looking stranger he could find and pretend he was an evil character sent out to capture him. A pirate, a Martian, a barbarian, a Nazi—whatever met his fancy. Thompson would entertain himself ducking through a store's aisles and displays, ahead of the stranger's path, trying to elude his sight.

To his astonishment, he realized that he had subsconsciously picked out such a man again—a nondescript individual in a tan polyester suit, wearing a hat and holding a cheap black vinyl briefcase. The man was window-shopping behind Thompson, half a block away. Thompson had noticed him earlier because he seemed to be moving out of step with the sidewalk traffic, strolling idly, like a tourist.

Thompson felt foolish for suspecting the man. It was childish, like his game. The stranger was probably a salesman with an hour to kill between appointments. Or, judging from his garb, a lobbyist for the synthetic-fabrics industry, waiting to nail some congressman. But Thompson was in a paranoid mood.

When the light changed, he dashed across to the southeast corner of G and Thirteenth and through the entrance to the Metro station. A short escalator took him down to the turnstiles, and there he stopped to study the wall map to get his bearings. The Washington Metro was a relatively complicated system, and Thompson had not used it for some time. He scanned the map impatiently to find his destination. It indicated Rosslyn as the fourth stop on the Blue Line from Metro Center, in the direction of National Airport. He dropped two quarters into the slot on the Farecard Vendor and received a small rectangle of paper with the number fifty printed on it. At the turnstiles, he inserted the card in a slot, watched as the turnstile swallowed the card, canceled the fifty-cent figure, and coughed it up a second later from another slot. He snatched the card up and walked on down two more short escalators to a large tunnel intersection, and followed the arrows pointing to the Blue Line, on the left.

A train was just pulling in as he reached the platform. It came to a noiseless stop, the doors slid open, and Thompson stepped on and sat in the seat nearest the door. He surveyed the sparsely populated car, and saw to his satisfaction that the man in the tan suit was not there. He was certain he had moved deliberately enough so that anyone following him would have no trouble keeping pace.

Of course he knew the man wasn't following him; it was a useful exercise, that was all. Just in case.

The train whooshed smoothly on, making its way to McPherson Square, Farragut West, Foggy Bottom, and under the Potomac River to Rosslyn, a former slum across from Theodore Roosevelt Island that in recent years had become a community for low-level bureaucrats and middle-class tradespeople. Thompson stepped out onto the platform and found the escalator to the surface.

He was astonished at its length. It ascended upward at a steep angle through an enormous arched tunnel with a futuristic waffled surface to a height the equivalent of a ten-story building. Passengers near the top appeared to be riding a stairway to the heavens, shrinking slowly into infinity. Four sets of stairs rose through the mammoth tunnel, two on each side of a glass-enclosed elevator shaft that shot up from the platform, passed the escalator at the midpoint of its run, and disappeared through the ceiling high overhead.

Thompson watched the elevator car begin to ascend rapidly up through the glass shaft. The escalator step he stood on reached the juncture of stairs and shaft at the same instant as the elevator car, and Thompson's gaze was drawn to the car's interior. One man was inside, wearing a tan suit and hat and carrying a vinyl briefcase. For a split second his eyes locked onto Thompson's and then the elevator had ascended past, to rise out of sight through the tunnel ceiling.

The back of Thompson's neck prickled and his palms were suddenly wet.

The man *was* following him.

At street level the escalator gave out onto an enclosed exit area with big floor-length windows that allowed a view of the sidewalks and the line of storefronts across the street. Thompson stopped near the exit turnstile and tried to locate the elevator door, but could not find it.

He fumbled for his fare card, inserted it into the slot in the turnstile, and was about to push through when he saw the man through the windows, standing under a store marquee across the street. Thompson ducked down behind the turnstile to watch him. After a short wait, the man turned and walked slowly along the sidewalk, his eyes fixed on the station exit.

Thompson could not understand how the man had gotten outside the station so quickly until he noticed the square bronze-colored toll-booth-like structure sticking up from the sidewalk directly behind the man. It was the damned elevator exit, Thompson realized, located by some architectural fluke outside the subway station.

The man paused momentarily, then started across the street toward the station doors. Thompson could see his face clearly. Behind the thin moustache, it was lumpy and colorless, with thick lips and eyes hidden behind narrows slits of puffy flesh. An ex-boxer's face, or an ex-con's. It looked both stupid and dangerous.

Thompson was aware of someone behind him. He started, then turned to look up into the inquiring stare of a portly black man in a neat, carefully tailored Metro uniform. He was asking Thompson if there was some problem. "No, I . . . I just dropped something. It's okay."

The attendant turned away, and Thompson, holding himself in a low crouch, took off at top speed back down the now-empty escalator, jumping four steps at a time. He reached the bottom of the vast moving staircase in seconds and scrambled through the tunnel to the nearest train platform.

The platform was deserted, and Thompson was forced to wait. He paced along the empty ramp, his eyes shifting back and forth between the tunnel from the escalator and the dark tunnel where the next train would appear. He prayed the man would take the wrong turn at the bottom of the escalator and head for the other platform.

Finally a train arrived. Thompson squeezed into it the moment the door started to open, nearly bowling over an older woman laden with shopping bags. She screamed at him in a shrill voice as he hurried to grab a seat and sink down out of sight.

The train remained in the station, its doors open. Thompson, feeling dazed, held his breath and counted the seconds off, willing the doors to shut, but the train was in no rush. Girls from a Catholic school, in green knee socks and brown corduroy skirts, boarded and sat across from him, giggling and making faces.

Thompson saw him again through the open door. He was running down the escalator from the other platform. He sprinted across the twenty feet from the escalator to the train and boarded it several cars up from Thompson. Only then did the doors close and the train begin to move.

Thompson studied the map on the wall over the car windows. He was on a train headed back in the direction he had come—Foggy Bottom, Farragut West, McPherson Square, Metro Center. The Blue Line's itinerary then took it to Federal Triangle, Smithsonian, L'Enfant Plaza, and on through Washington all the way to New Carrollton in the far reaches of the Maryland suburbs.

With a sickening sensation Thompson realized that if he had not, through sheer idiotic luck, discovered the man tailing him, he would have led him directly to the apartment in Rosslyn, his supposed hideout. Just as easy as that.

Thompson thought of movie and television chase scenes, and all the chase scenes he had read or edited. How complacent and critical he had been! How he had demanded they be fast, novel, violent, ingenious, and end with a spectacular twist! Now the real thing had caught up with him, and it was altogether too exciting, and he was too immobilized by fear to think of anything clever. His brain fed him one message only: run like hell. Leave the train and find a crowd and lose him.

He decided to get out at the Smithsonian stop. It was a part of the city he was familiar with, and it sounded safe. Institutional and safe.

Just as the door began to close, Thompson jumped from his seat and squeezed out, ran across the platform, turned right, and dashed toward the exit marked "The Mall." He bounded up a short escalator, sprinted across the mezzanine to the exit turnstile, and then remembered that he no longer had the fare card needed to get through. The exit turnstile in Rosslyn had swallowed it.

No time to agonize. He scrambled over the turnstile and ran up another, longer escalator that deposited him in the sunlight at Jefferson Drive and Twelfth Street, just west of the Castle, the old turreted red-brick landmark building of the Smithsonian Institution.

With no destination in mind, he continued at a hard run onto the gravel walk of the Mall, parallel to Jefferson Drive, and headed east, directly toward the huge dome of the Capitol, looming in the sky nearly a mile away. He had a lot of company. The path was clogged with joggers chugging along among camera-burdened tourists and strolling government workers. But it was wide open, offering no place to hide, and people were staring at him as he pounded by.

His big, clunky attaché case bounced against his leg, impeding his progress. He thought about discarding it, but changed his mind and tucked it under his arm, like a football, and cut back past the Children's Carousel across to the south side of Jefferson Drive, running past the Arts and Industry Building, the Hirshhorn Museum, and down alongside the megalithic pile of glass and concrete of the National Air and Space Museum.

His breathing was reduced to ragged gasps. He would have to stop soon.

Halfway down the length of the museum, he slowed, his eyes on a crowd pouring off a tour bus and filing toward the museum entrance. He staggered through the line, sucking air into his bursting lungs, then turned and walked alongside it, insinuating himself gradually into the middle of the line. Faces glared at him, and people moved to avoid him, but he stuck with the crowd, and in a minute was inside the museum with them, standing next to the Apollo II command module and beneath Lindbergh's *Spirit of St. Louis*.

Heart pounding less furiously, his breathing back under control, Thompson moved furtively, staying in the densest parts of the crowds, and searched for a place to hide.

He followed a group onto an escalator to the second level (how many escalators had he ridden in the last hour? it seemed like a hundred) and ducked quickly in and out of several exhibits, his eyes scanning the throng for the tan suit.

He walked through Sea-Air Operations, World War II Aviation, Balloons and Airships, Air Traffic Control, and the Einstein Spacearium. In the World War I Aviation room he hesitated. It was dark and uncrowded—almost empty. Thompson moved across the airstrip behind a Fokker D-7, and decided that despite the dark corners the exhibit contained, there was no good place to conceal himself.

Across the airstrip he saw an exit and followed it out, back onto the mezzanine again, near the enormous Skylab exhibit. Another right turn off the mezzanine brought him into a new exhibition room, Appollo to the Moon. He darted around among a blur of displays of lunar rocks, life-size recreations of astronauts working on the moon, and giant Saturn rocket engines. Over the low hum of voices he heard the unmistakable Boston accent of President John F. Kennedy: "I believe that this nation should commit itself to achieving the goal, before this decade is out, of landing a man on the moon and returning him safely to earth. No single space project in this period will be more impressive to mankind, or mean more for the long-range exploration of space, and none will be so difficult or expensive to accomplish. . . ."

He was in a short, narrow corridor now, with a blank wall on his left, and a small open doorway on the right, the Space Flight Theater. He slipped in and found himself in a small three-walled room shaped like an upside-down pyramid with the top sliced off. The walls were carpeted and slanted back at an angle; overhead, three screens flashed a slide program. He stepped onto the low, tilted sill at the base of one wall and allowed his back to settle against the carpeting. The room was illuminated only faintly by the projector light reflected from the screens overhead. He welcomed it with a tremendous sigh of relief.

When his eyes had adjusted, Thompson noticed another man in the room—a short, thickly built figure with a large head and bushy hair. Was it his imagination, or did the shadowy form seem to be watching him? Had the man come in before him or after him? He wasn't sure. Thompson turned his eyes to the screens overhead and tried to lose himself in the slide show, a familiar series of photographs of astronauts in their bulky white space suits, lumbering awkwardly around the surface of the moon.

Out of the corner of his eye Thompson saw that the bushy-haired man was sliding surreptitiously along the wall, until he was now barely a yard away. A harmless middle-aged homosexual, working up to make a pass?

"Excuse me," the man said.

Thompson jumped, in spite of himself. The voice was low and hesitant, and Thompson turned for a better look. He saw a round, almost cherubic face, with blond hair and small eyes set close together under a pair of bushy blond brows. A comic, sad face.

"Pardon me for startling you, Mr. Thompson."

Thompson froze. The sound of his own name on this stranger's lips hit him like a whip. "Who the hell are you?"

The round face nodded nervously. "George Klimentov. I telephoned you yesterday at your office."

Thompson let himself breathe again. "What do you want?"

Klimentov's tone became whispering and conspiratorial, trying hard to ingratiate itself. "I would like to work out an arrangement with you."

Thompson remembered that his assistant, Kate, had taken a call from him. A Russian dissident with a book to sell, he had thought. But this man's accent was Harvard Yard.

"I'm very busy, Mr. Klimentov. Some other time."

Klimentov laughed. It was a nervous laugh, as if Thompson had told him a joke he didn't find amusing. Thompson felt the man's hand on his arm, pulling him closer to him.

"I know your connection with Roland," Klimentov whispered. His breath smelled bad, and Thompson instinctively pulled away.

"What are you talking about?"

"You know," he said.

"How did you find me here?"

"I followed the man who is following you."

Thompson swallowed hard. "The tan suit?"

Klimentov nodded.

"Where . . . where is he now?"

"Waiting for you. I believe in front of the museum."

"Who is he?"

Klimentov shook his head. "I don't know. But I know his kind. Very dangerous."

Thompson swore under his breath. "Thanks. What do you want?"

"We can help each other."

Three children burst into the room, and Klimentov stiffened against the wall, shocked by the sudden interruption. They watched the youngsters in silence as they swarmed around the small theater. Soon bored with the place, they departed as suddenly as they had come, and Klimentov started talking again.

"I worked for Allen Roland. Before, when he ran the agency, and again, recently, when I agreed to help him obtain material for his book. He paid me a research fee. A couple of months ago I uncovered unexpected material. He became very interested in it, and urged me to find more. He promised me a lot more money."

Klimentov caught his breath, licking his lips in agitation, and then continued on, his eyes darting frequently to the open doorway of the theater.

"The information I obtained for Roland two weeks ago was the most important yet, the most dramatic. He urged me to get more. Now I have more. It's shocking. Far worse than we suspected. But with Roland dead, I have no one to give it to."

Thompson listened, but found it hard to concentrate. Thoughts of the tan suit intruded. Klimentov went on, speaking his piece in a rush, as if he had memorized what he was going to say and was determined to get through it.

"I think they suspect me now. I may not have much time, so I want to make a deal. Information for money. With enough money I can leave the country. But you'll have to get it fast. Time is short."

Klimentov fumbled in a pocket of his suit coat and pulled out an envelope. He pushed it into Thompson's hand and squeezed Thompson's fingers around it. Klimentov's own hand was clammy with sweat.

Thompson felt suffocated. He wanted to shove the envelope in the man's mouth. "But I can't *do* anything for you!"

Klimentov raised a hand. "Please! You paid a million for Roland's memoirs. My information is worth more, and I'm asking for far less. The proposal is in the envelope. Meet me here tomorrow at ten in the morning."

He felt Klimentov grab his right hand and pump it up and down in a vigorous handshake, sealing a bargain Thompson had not agreed to.

"The man in the tan suit," Klimentov whispered. "You didn't lose him in the Metro because he's following you with a receiver."

"I don't understand."

"You have a miniature transmitter on you somewhere. He's following you with a receiver that picks up the signal you're transmitting. I watched him listening to it. He'll know when you leave here and follow you again."

Klimentov pointed at Thompson's attaché case. "It may be hidden in that case of yours. Find it and throw it away."

A large party of tourists invaded the tiny theater, and before Thompson could find out more, Klimentov had disappeared.

He stuffed Klimentov's envelope into his pants pocket, picked up the attaché case, and headed for the nearest men's room.

Locking himself inside a stall, he sat down on the toilet, opened the case, and began a frenzied search of its interior. He examined everything twice, but could find absolutely nothing that bore any resemblance to any kind of transmitter.

He made another exhaustive inch-by-inch examination, even looking for breaks in the case's stitching that might indicate something had been slipped into the lining. But he found nothing. Klimentov must just be wrong about the transmitter, he thought, or he was only guessing. The attaché case had not been out of Thompson's sight—barely out of his hands—since he had left Smith's house in Hanover early that morning. How could anyone have put a transmitter in it?

He went through it once more, paying particularly close attention to the items in his shaving kit.

And this time he found it. It was nestled in a small, flat tin of aspirin. The pills had been removed, and in their place sat a tiny black rectangular object, slightly smaller than the inside dimensions of the box. Thompson shut the tin and stuck it in his side pocket, shut the case again, and dug Klimentov's envelope out of his rear pocket. A small piece of yellow paper in the envelope contained one sentence, printed out in pencil: "Two hundred thousand dollars for Zodiac."

That was all. Zodiac again. The name in Roland's message. Klimentov wasn't giving him much time to help him, assuming he *could* help him. His demand for money just about ruled it out. Where was Thompson going to get two hundred thousand dollars? From Sam Marwick? He could see Marwick's expression now. Thompson flushed the paper down the toilet and threw the envelope in the paper-towel receptacle.

On his way out the south exit of the museum, Thompson intercepted another tour group, and as its members passed by on their way inside, he dropped the aspirin tin into a shopping bag carried on the arm of a very fat woman in tight pink slacks.

John Ellis, a retired dry-cleaning-store owner, and his wife, Sylvia, wandered into exhibit area 205. John saw the cut-away forward section of the Martin B-26B, and was suddenly happy as a child. It was the famous *Flak Bait*, donated to the museum after 202 bombing missions over Europe during World War II. During its twenty-one months of combat, it collected more than one thousand enemy hits, and was one of the few Marauders to come through the war still flying. John Ellis had flown in another B-26 in the same bomber squadron, and he remembered *Flak Bait* and the men who had flown her. His wife listened with good-natured indulgence as he launched into a description, already familiar to her, of his glorious days as a B-26 bombardier/navigator/nose-gunner in the U.S. Army Air Force.

John positively beamed when he saw the nose-gunner's station—his station—practically intact, just the way he remembered it: the cramped space in the exposed glass nose of the aircraft, crowded with cannon, ammo box, bomb sight, and nav equipment. Practically under the feet of the pilot and copilot, there was barely room left for the nose-gunner to squeeze into.

In the small jump seat, head and arms slumped over the machine gun that protruded through the tip of the huge Plexiglas cone that formed the nose of the airplane, crouched the portly figure of George Klimentov.

Sylvia pointed at him. "Why isn't that dummy dressed in a uniform, John?"

Ellis shook his head in puzzlement. Suddenly one of Klimentov's hands slipped from the machine gun's barrel and swung down heavily and hung twitching in midair.

Sylvia grabbed her husband's arm and screamed.

14

Friday night, October 26

Smith sat immobile at his desk, working the problem like a computer, examining and rejecting possibilities with lightning speed. For a minute he turned over the idea of simply putting through a call to the White House and explaining the situation directly to the President himself. Going to the top always appealed to him, especially when instant action was needed.

But this time it just wasn't practical. He didn't know this president as he had the five before him, and even assuming he could get to him, explaining why he was calling would be hard to make plausible. The days were gone when he could summon presidents to the phone and hear a bright "Tommy Smith, dammit! How's the master spy? We miss you down here in Washington, old boy! What can we do for you?"

Of course he still had friends in other places—CIA, FBI, DOS, DOD—the few who hadn't retired from government service. But they were encumbered by their bureaucracies and that would prevent them from acting quickly, if they could act at all. And there was the question of secrecy.

No, he had to act alone, without help. It was going to be like another mission, with no resources but one's own skill, training, and courage to rely on.

The odds this time seemed unusually steep. X, the enemy, was invisible and unknown. Thompson was incommunicado—or should be. And X, possessing superior strength and numbers, could not be stopped by Smith alone. Slowed down, perhaps, but not stopped.

Extract the location from me.

The phrase, staring up at him from his notepad, was a chilling one. Yet he felt it could be turned to his advantage. The knowledge that they were coming after him gave him some leverage. They could not expect that he had anticipated them. Surprise was now on his side. The problem was how to use it. He worried the phrase like a determined dog with a tough bone, turning it over and over, gnawing away at it.

Slow them down. Deflect them. With a trick. With a deception.

Why not?

If he had time.

For three hours Smith labored ferociously at his desk and typewriter, constructing out of paper and ink a fragile defense against the invisible legions of X. He replaced the page of the manuscript with the code on it with a new page, bearing an altered code. He then recreated the scribbled-on sheets of legal pad with the coded message worked out on them, reconstructing everything he had burned in the fireplace the night before.

When he was finished, he checked over his forgeries carefully. They duplicated the originals exactly, except for one crucial alteration, a word change that would not be contradicted by the eavesdropped conversation he and Thompson had carried on in the room.

"Zodiac file in cellar door . . ." had become "Zodiac file in parlor door." It was a subtle, almost flimsy ruse, but it stood a chance.

It was all he could do, in any case. He couldn't go into the field. He was too old for that. He would have to leave Thompson out there alone, a total amateur caught up in God knew what titanic political/diplomatic struggle. Alone, unprotected, innocent.

Why had Roland chosen to involve Thompson at all? Smith wondered. Roland must have known the odds were slim that Thompson could successfully carry on his investigation. And he must have known that he was exposing Thompson to great danger. But still he did it. Why?

Roland's enemies had always underestimated him. Smith would not make the same mistake. But if he had been Roland, he would have . . . done more. Somehow.

Well, Smith thought, perhaps Roland *had* done more. Who could tell? Perhaps Thompson was only a part of his counterattack. Perhaps he had reached others as well. Perhaps. Perhaps. It was useless to speculate.

At five o'clock he was finished. He crumpled up his forged documents, threw them in the wastebasket, and arranged his desk in a calculated state of disarray. He went up to the master bedroom on the second floor and from deep in the back of the walk-in closet, on a shelf buried under a pile of old sweaters, he retrieved a locked metal case and set it out on the bed. Several minutes of hunting through dresser drawers finally turned up the key for the case, and he unlocked it and withdrew the contents—a carefully oiled and wrapped Walther PPK/S, the pistol he had carried with him through World War II. A powerful weapon, and easy to conceal, it held seven .380-caliber bullets in its clip, and weighed only twenty-three ounces. He owed it his life on several occasions.

Working rapidly, Smith disassembled the weapon, wiped it clean of Cosmoline, reassembled it, tested its action, and decided it was restored to service. From a box of cartridges stored with the pistol, he loaded the clip and slapped it into place. It snapped into position through the hand grip with a reassuringly solid click, and he jacked the first round into the firing chamber and pushed the trigger release off the safety position.

Weapon in hand, Smith paced through the large house, unlocking the windows, the front door, the back door, and the cellar door, and then retreated upstairs to a small guest room in the back of the house.

He closed the door to the room, locked it, then pulled aside a large braided rug to reveal the black iron register set in the floor. Unused since the days when the house was heated by an old coal hot-air furnace, the louvers over the grille were stuck shut, so Smith yanked out the top part of the register completely, leaving in place only the grille. By lying flat on his stomach and resting his forehead on the back of his arms, Smith had a clear view of the area directly around his desk in the study below. He positioned the pistol on the floor beside him, and stretched out on his side next to the hole to wait.

The house grew dark at six, and Smith wondered if he had made a mistake by not turning on a light or two downstairs. He wanted to leave the impression that he was out, but he didn't want that to backfire by creating the impression of an ambush. He reassured himself that whoever was coming had no reason to suspect that Smith was waiting for him.

He had done all he could. The rest depended on a little luck.

The hours ticked by. A neighbor's dog barked for a while, a car blew its horn. Little else. The house remained still. Several times Smith dozed off, once for nearly half an hour, and he chastised himself for his lack of self-control. *Inexcusable. They'll arrive and I'll be snoring. Too old, too old for this kind of game.* Dim yellow light filtered through the closed lace curtain from the streetlight across Hanover Terrace, and Smith checked his wristwatch in its light. Just midnight.

A sound from the study below.

Smith raised his head a fraction of an inch from the floor and listened. A creaking on the house's ancient floorboards that even the heavy carpet couldn't completely muffle. Smith rolled over carefully until his face was over the register hole and peered down, his senses focused and alert.

The bright, narrow beam of a flashlight swept twice across the study, coming to rest the second time on the desk. A moment's hesitation, and then the invisible figure behind the flashlight approached the desk and shone the light slowly over the surface, examining the items there with great deliberation. The house was so still Smith could hear his own heart beating in his ears. He breathed in and out very slowly, shallowly, with his mouth open, determined to preserve the silence.

Smith watched the beam of the flashlight examine the notepad on the pile of manuscripts, then travel to the wastebasket. A hand reached into the wastebasket and carefully removed each wadded scrap of paper, flattening them out against a leg while the other hand trained the light on them. There were many pieces, and the process took a long time. Finally, near the bottom, the hand found something that interested it. The flashlight examined the scrap closely, and then the hand put it on the desk.

Smith could get little impression of the figure behind the flashlight. He was probably young, judging from the hand he could see in the beam of light. And tough. The hand's outside edge wore heavy calluses, indicating substantial karate training. And there was something else on the back of the hand—a smudge of dirt, perhaps, or a tattoo. He strained to make it out, but the intruder moved the hand too frequently for Smith to focus on it clearly.

He began reading the manuscript on the desk. Smith watched the flashlight move slowly down each page, then the hand turn the page and the light move down the next. The back of the hand came into view again, clearly illuminated by the flashlight beam. Smith squinted hard. A small circle inside an oval. Not an oval. More like the outline of a football.

An eye?

Smith held his breath.

Cyclops?

He knew about him from something Roland once let slip. The tattoo of the eye on the right hand. A contract assassin for the agency. Even with one eye, he was the best. But there had been some problem with him.

"He went feral," Roland had said, without explaining what he meant. "So we killed him." Smith remembered the words exactly, because he remembered wondering how they had done it. Roland hadn't volunteered any more, and Smith had known better than to ask.

He remembered, too, the incredible list of his scores that Roland, in that rare interlude of garrulousness, had confided to him. Roland, then just appointed DCI, had been too appalled to keep the information entirely to himself. It read like an international who's who—famous scientists, military brass, statesmen, businessmen, heads of state. Many of the victims were still widely believed to have died natural or accidental deaths. He was expert at disguising his kills.

From all this, Smith had deduced the explanation for Roland's decision to have him killed. The CIA had been losing agents at a rate of one a month when Roland took over, and he somehow put a quick stop to it. Had Cyclops been picking them off "free-lance" for another party? Smith thought it possible. It was the best reason for Roland to have killed someone whose services were otherwise so valuable to the agency.

Cyclops wasn't very dead, however. Unless another man had taken to wearing his tattoo.

Smith reached out in the dark and let his hand fall slowly onto the cold metal of the Walther on the floor beside him. He rested his fingers on it, but he did not move it. He watched Cyclops below him, now studying the manuscript page containing the overstruck letters of the code.

Cyclops. Eloquent testimony to the importance someone placed on Roland's file.

Cyclops, merciless and sadistic.

Cyclops, who would find him and kill him, once his work down below was complete.

Smith knew he must kill him first. Now. His fingers tightened around the Walther, already cocked, and moved it from the floor to the register, taking infinite care to place the pistol's muzzle soundlessly against the metal of the grille. He cautioned himself that he must not hurry. Cyclops would be there for a while yet. He must estimate the angle of the shot with all the care and precision possible. In the dark, that would take superhuman calculation.

Smith first satisfied himself that the muzzle end was unobstructed by the grille, studying it carefully in the faint light reflected upward from Cyclops' flashlight. Then he studied the angles, estimating exactly where Cyclops' head must be in relation to what he could actually see—a hand and part of an arm. Several times Cyclops shifted his position, causing Smith to recalculate.

How long it took, Smith had no idea, but the moment of truth finally arrived.

Commanding his nerves to relax, Smith gradually, firmly, increased pressure on the trigger.

He fired.

Three times in rapid succession, altering the angle of the barrel fractionally between each shot.

Three booms echoed out through the dark house, shattering the midnight stillness. When the ringing aftershocks had died, Smith listened for sounds from below. He heard none.

He lay there, panting now, the warm pistol still clutched in his hand, fearful of hearing something—the sound of footsteps on the stairs, the sound of a back door closing.

He eased himself carefully up into a sitting position and slid slowly across the floor until he was behind the bed. From the far side of the bed he could sit up, exposing only his head, and rest both hands, gripping the pistol across the mattress, facing the door.

For hours he heard nothing. Once he thought the floor below squeaked, but he couldn't be sure. Occasionally, familiar house sounds—the pump in the basement, the refrigerator in the kitchen—would startle him. The waiting became painful and the hours of tension drained his energy.

Was Cyclops dead?

Or was he waiting for Smith down there in the dark?

15

"It's the most frightening story I've ever heard," Harriet said. "I'd have been scared to death!" She was in the driver's seat of a borrowed Toyota Celica speeding westward through the dark Virginia countryside on Route 50. Thompson lay stretched out on the passenger side, his seat tilted back and his eyes closed.

"You were fantastically clever," she added, "outsmarting them the way you did." She sounded genuinely impressed, even a little awed.

Thompson shook his head. "I wish I could believe it. I was saved by the timely appearance of a middle-aged CIA employee. Whose own life, to hear him tell it, is now in *my* hands. What a mess!"

"Are you going to meet him tomorrow?"

"What can I tell him? I can't help him out. I've got my own neck to worry about."

Harriet looked at him intently. "We *have* to find out what he knows, after all."

Here we go again, Thompson thought. "No, we don't. I don't even *want* to know. If you want the information, you meet him."

"Jay!"

"He wants to trade information for money. Money I can't get for him. Naturally he's going to think what he has is worth a great deal. It's all he has to bargain with. But it might be no more than a few sordid details about something or someone we've never even heard of."

"Boy, you'd make a hotshot journalist," Harriet replied. "His information might be the key to everything, for all we know. It obviously ties in with Roland's note about the Zodiac file."

"Why do we always disagree?" Thompson asked.

"We don't always disagree!"

Thompson laughed.

"Well, you're just such a pessimist, that's why!" Harriet retorted. "You never think anything will work out!"

"I just want to be pleasantly surprised when it does."

"Silly."

Thompson cranked his seat back up and gazed out the window. Moonlit fields were zipping past at a dizzying rate of speed. Thompson stole a glance at the speedometer and saw that the needle was edging past 75.

"If you don't slow down, we'll be arrested for speeding—before we even get a chance to be nailed for breaking and entering."

"We've got to get there first."

Thompson shook his head. "You really are perverse. You tell me you'd be scared to death to go through what I went through today, but you can hardly wait to break into a dead man's house in the middle of the night and risk getting killed doing it."

"Don't you have *any* curiosity? Don't you want to know what that file contains?"

"I'm not sure that I do," Thompson muttered. "It's certain to get us into trouble."

"What are we in now?"

"We're still alive."

"Talk about perverse! Yesterday you were flying off to New Hampshire, hot on the trail of Zodiac. What happened?"

"I got scared," he replied.

Harriet fell silent and watched the road. He reached his hand across to her lap. "I like your blue corduroys," he said, trying to lighten the mood. "Let's forget Middleburg and stop at that motel you just passed."

He felt her stiffen slightly. "Work now, play later," she said.

Thompson studied her profile. The wisp of brown hair still curled untrained in front of one eye, and her chin appeared rounder from this angle. From the front it looked very strong, almost square, emphasizing the dramatic beauty of her face. From the side she seemed softer, more vulnerable.

"A personal question," he said, picking up on the phrase that had become a game between them.

"Okay."

"How come you're such a tease?"

"Am I?"

"Are you kidding? Three nights ago, you ask me to go to bed with you. A few passionate kisses later, you change your mind. And then you change your mind again. We *do* go to bed together. With our clothes on. The next time we meet—this morning—it's at a porno movie. Now I touch you and you go icy. How am I supposed to be reacting to all of this?"

"That's up to you, I guess." Her voice was flat.

"If you don't like me, don't flirt with me. I'm apt to take you seriously."

Harriet said nothing. Thompson ended the silence before it became too big to fill.

"How come you're not married? Or divorced? Or living with someone?" He blurted it out, surprised that he didn't know the answers to these questions already.

"Don't push me," Harriet said.

"I just want to understand you. You're always the one asking the questions. Now it's my turn."

Harriet's voice turned hostile. "What gives you the right to all these answers all of a sudden?"

Thompson sighed. "Forget it, then."

Harriet concentrated on her driving. A tense silence descended on them. Thompson feared that she would tell him she really didn't care for him. He felt cheated. He was lonely, she was an attractive woman, and they were thrown together in an exciting adventure. But he guessed she wasn't going to let herself be thrown any further. No doubt she had some terrific lover off getting shot at in some war zone for the *Times*.

"I'm sorry," she said. Her voice was so soft Thompson almost didn't hear. "I'll answer your questions."

"Are you in love with someone?"

She shook her head.

"Having an affair?"

"Four years ago."

"What happened?"

She shrugged. "We broke up."

"That's a long time ago. No one since then?"

"No."

"Not for lack of opportunity."

"No. Just turned off, I guess."

"What happened four years ago that turned you off?"

"It just didn't work. He cheated on me a lot and I . . ."

Thompson waited, but Harriet didn't finish the sentence. He could see she was struggling with herself, trying to decide whether or not to tell him more. He felt his stomach tense into a knot. He wanted to hear, but her reluctance made him apprehensive.

"I'm just all . . . mixed up," she said.

"About what?"

"Men. Sex."

"That doesn't sound so unusual."

"No." Harriet took a deep breath and then spoke in a rush. The words tumbled out, harsh, charged with emotion. "But it's been very hard for me. When I was twelve I had a bad experience. A friend of my father's raped me. It was really bad. He went to prison for it. Everybody in town knew what had happened. My mother and father were both so horrified. And they blamed me for it, I know. Secretly they thought that I had provoked it. And the social ostracism. It nearly killed my mother. I didn't go back to school for a year. We finally moved out of the state, to escape the shame.

"It was horrible. And I hated that man so much. I prayed every night that he would die. He's in an institution now—somewhere in Pennsylvania. As far as our family is concerned, he never existed. His name has not been uttered in our house in twenty years.

"It scared me. I dated a lot when I was in high school and college, but I never went to bed with anyone. I knew I wasn't normal. I made up for it by being a terrible flirt. I was determined to get every man's attention, just to prove to myself that I could. Then I'd hurt them before they could hurt me.

"I went to an analyst. She told me I was punishing everyone for what the man had done to me. I thought I left my problems behind when I moved to Washington, but I guess I didn't. I had a few affairs, but they were all miserable failures. . . ."

Thompson took his hand from her lap and rested it on her shoulder.

She glanced over at him. "Do you really want to hear all this?"

"Yes."

"Okay. The one four years ago was my last. He was a congressman, and he really attracted me. He had a great reputation as a lover, and I tried very hard to make the sex work, but it just didn't. And he didn't seem all that interested in helping me. He just turned his attentions elsewhere. I was very hurt. And failing with him convinced me that I would never succeed."

"So you gave up?"

Harriet shook her head. He couldn't read her expression in the dim light.

"I got involved with a woman."

Thompson could think of nothing to say. The opposite sex always overwhelmed him. It seemed to him sometimes as if they lived in an entirely different dimension, where everything was infinitely more complex and fragile.

"She was a friend from college," Harriet continued. "We had been very close. When my affair broke up, she was very sympathetic, very understanding. I didn't know that she was a lesbian. It happened so naturally. And it was . . . For the first time, sex worked. I was horrified with myself at first. Convinced that I was gay. I thought that that had been my problem all along.

"We stayed together for a while. She became really possessive and demanding, and even though I enjoyed the sex, I realized that I wasn't in love with her. I didn't have the kind of feelings toward her—or other women—that I still got about men. So one day I just stopped. We're not friends anymore, which is a shame.

"So here I am," she concluded. "Somewhere in limbo. Neither one thing nor another. Nowhere."

Thompson stared at the highway zipping past, digesting the story. Were he and Harriet now closer together or farther apart?

"I know it's not quite what you expected to hear," Harriet said, reading his thoughts. "But I'm tremendously relieved to have told you. I've never confessed all that to anyone."

A sign loomed in the darkness: Middleburg, 15 miles. Harriet, embarrassed, changed the subject.

"Have you figured out how they put that transmitter in your briefcase?"

Thompson cleared his throat. "It was in my room at the Hanover Inn all the while I was with Professor Smith. It must have been then."

"That would mean that one of them was already in Hanover."

"I'm afraid so. If, as you said, someone heard me tell you over the phone that I was going to Hanover, they could have been on the same plane."

"Do you think they did anything to Professor Smith?"

"I don't know. I tried to call him once before we left Rosslyn. No answer."

Harriet shuddered and Thompson decided not to pursue that line of thought. They would know soon enough—if someone beat them to the files.

The village of Middleburg, nestled in the hills of Virginia's hunt country, looked more like an Easthampton or a Newport than a small country town. Elegant, self-consciously rustic shops alternated with real-estate offices along both sides of the main street. Harriet turned right at the town's sole traffic light, onto Madison Street, past the Red Fox Tavern, an ancient four-story white-brick inn that exuded old money and gentility. Madison Street quickly metamorphosed into a narrow country lane that twisted its way alongside a brook past estates and horse farms, their acres of white fences sparkling dimly in the moonlight.

Roland's place was a brick farmhouse set back from the road, behind dense bushes of wild hedge and honeysuckle. Thompson checked the name on the mailbox to be certain they had the right house. The white letters spelling out *A. G. Roland* on the black mailbox looked like a larger version of his doorplate in Georgetown.

They drove until they found a dirt path about a hundred yards farther along the road, one that ran up through a wooded strip of land between two high stone walls marking the borders of a large field on either side. They parked the car in the narrow path, well out of sight of the road. Harriet switched off the ignition, and they sat for a moment listening to the tick of the cooling engine.

Thompson leaned across and kissed Harriet firmly on the mouth.

"Let's get it over with," he said.

He opened the trunk and removed a small canvas bag of Harriet's he had stocked with tools for the occasion, and then led the way over the stone wall, through a brief patch of trees and bushes, and across the field, through knee-high grass. Insects chirped; otherwise it was still. The woods around them presented a black silhouette against the blue-black of the sky and the hazy silver glow of the moon, three-quarters full.

"A gibbous moon," Thompson said, apropos of nothing.

Harriet looked at him and frowned as she fought to keep her balance on the uneven ground.

"When it's three-quarters full it's called a gibbous moon," he explained.

"By whom?"

"I don't know. People with a good vocabulary. Seems such an appropriate word, that's all. So spooky."

"Shush."

"Just trying to keep my courage up."

"You'll be whistling next."

They crossed over a low stone wall into Roland's backyard, a spacious lawn spread out beneath giant elms, its air laden with the fragrance of late-blooming clematis. The house sat shuttered and innocent, a two-story rectangular colonial with a long single-story wing extending from the back end. A barn, its double doors closed and padlocked, stood nearby. Everything appeared neat, undisturbed, and peaceful. Thompson dug a flashlight out of the bag and led Harriet around to the front of the house.

The front door, solid-looking with long black wrought-iron strap hinges and an old-fashioned wrought-iron handle in place of the usual doorknob, was locked by three locks, their shiny brass cylinders lined up in a row, one on top of the other. A notice was thumbtacked to the door at eye level, and Thompson held the light on it:

WARNING
This house under 24-hour surveillance
by law-enforcement personnel.

Trespassers will be arrested
and prosecuted.

Department of Justice
Federal Bureau of Investigation

Clarence Cookson, Director

Harriet was startled by it. "What does that mean?"

"It means the FBI has already searched the place. They must have put all those locks on the house."

They walked around the house several times, looking for a way in, but found none. The back door was similarly triple-locked, and all the windows had their wooden shutters pulled tight and locked from the inside. Thompson took from the bag a flat steel bar, purchased that afternoon at a hardware store in Alexandria, and tried to jimmy one of the shutters loose, without success.

"The damned things have bicycle chains running through them, and they're padlocked from the inside. It'll take forever to get one off. And then we'd still have to break the window. They really buttoned this place up."

For an hour they searched for a way in. They found none. Thompson sat down on the grass and draped his arms over his knees, thoroughly disgusted. "All we need to do is get into the cellar, dammit!" he said. "There *must* be a way!"

In frustration he heaved the metal bar at the house. It cartwheeled through the air, bounced off the side of the house, and then stuck, blade-first, in the wood of the cellar bulkhead door that protruded from the foundation wall at a shallow angle.

Thompson looked over at it, still quivering from its impact, gleaming faintly in the moonlight.

He jumped up.

"Of course," he cried. "The bulkhead! It's padlocked, but we can pry off the hinges!"

He pulled the bar out of the wood and inserted it near the top hinge, between the frame and the door. After several hard pries the screws began to pull out of the wood, fairly rotted as it was with damp and old age. With Harriet holding the flashlight, Thompson soon had the door off its hinges and folded back, revealing a narrow set of concrete steps beneath it that led into the cellar.

Harriet suddenly dropped the flashlight and shrieked.

Thompson spun around. "What the hell . . . ?"

Harriet was on the ground, scrambling for the light. "I'm sorry . . . it was a bat! It brushed right by my face when you opened that door!"

Thompson took the flashlight from her and led the way down the crumbling steps of the bulkhead. At the bottom he confronted another barrier—a low plank door with strap hinges, padlocked to a sturdy-looking frame.

"Now what?" Harriet said.

Thompson handed her the flashlight and asked her to retrieve the iron bar from above. "Maybe I can pry it loose."

While Harriet held the flashlight, he tried to lever the padlock plate out of the wood planking of the door. But the screws were deeply embedded and the wood unyielding. Repeatedly he jammed the bar behind the lock and pulled down with all his strength. His muscles trembled from the effort. Sweat poured down his neck and forehead, stinging his eyes. Minutes ticked by.

"It's breaking!" Harriet whispered.

A crack started in the wood behind the lock and creased down the entire length of the plank, splitting the inch-thick board from top to bottom. Several more strenuous attacks with the pry-bar pulled the remaining screws loose, and the padlock and its clasp fell free.

The door, composed of a double layer of planks nailed back to back, creaked open heavily on its rusted hinges. They ducked under the low lintel into a dank cellar studded with large wooden posts rising up out of a dirt floor to support the house's carrying timbers.

The huge beams created low headroom, forcing them to crouch.

"If you see a spider or a rat," Thompson said, taking the flashlight from Harriet's hand, "cover your mouth before you scream. We don't want to wake the neighbors."

"Shut up. It's not funny."

They edged their way cautiously around the cavelike interior, until they met a wall of fiberboard and chicken wire that enclosed a storage area at the far end. Retreating toward the middle of the cellar, they finally found the stairway that led up into the house. At the top of the stairs Thompson tried the door and found it open. He took a step into the room beyond and played the light around. The kitchen.

"Don't look any further," Harriet whispered. "The cellar door is right in your hand."

Thompson examined it with the flashlight and made an unpleasant discovery.

The door was constructed of three wide boards, three-quarters of an inch thick, held together by a Z-shaped configuration of narrower boards screwed to their backs. It was solid, not hollow, as Smith had predicted it would be.

"The professor flunks," Thompson said. "If there's anything in this door besides the wood it's made from, I'll be damned surprised."

Harriet agreed. "But maybe there's something small, like microfilm. It could be hidden in a small hole drilled out of the door from the bottom."

Thompson shook his head. "The message said a file."

"Well, there's only one letter difference between 'file' and 'film.' Roland might have made a mistake encoding it. Or Smith in decoding it."

"Maybe. But it takes time and a sophisticated lab to convert documents to microfilm. I don't think Roland would have done that. It would have complicated security."

They searched the entire house. No hollow-core doors anywhere. The rooms felt chilly and damp, and they huddled together as they took their search to the pantry behind the kitchen.

A booming crash froze them to the spot.

It came from the front of the house and reverberated through the old dwelling like an earthquake. Thompson switched off the flashlight, barely daring to breathe. He felt Harriet's nails digging into his arm.

"What in God's—?"

Thompson squeezed her hand. "Shhh!"

The first crash was followed seconds later by a series of thunderous blows that vibrated the floor and jangled the ceiling fixtures, as if a wrecking ball were battering the outside wall.

Thompson pulled Harriet back into the cellar and closed the door tightly behind them. More crashes, and then the loud, brittle cracks of splintering wood and shattering glass. He switched on the flashlight and they stumbled down the narrow steps. At the bottom, they halted.

"We'd better get out!" Harriet whispered.

"Not yet! The bulkhead door is on their side. They'll see us."

Thompson turned the flashlight off, and they stood shivering in the dark. Harriet still clutched his arm. He could feel his pulse beating in his ears.

Harriet's voice quivered. "Who *are* they?"

Thompson couldn't think of an answer.

The floor above them creaked heavily under the sudden weight of footsteps. The creaks continued, radiating invisibly along the floorboards, mixed with the muffled sounds of voices and slamming doors.

A minute pounded by. They listened to the noises overhead, mesmerized by a terror made all the greater by the realization that their worst fear was now a reality. The nemesis—whoever it was, whatever it wanted—had arrived.

A pause in the creaking. The voices stopped. Thompson held his breath, straining his ears to hear. Soft bumping sounds; then something like a tin can hit the floor and rolled for several feet.

A voice yelled "Let 'er rip!"

Thompson gritted his teeth and shut his eyes. A whining roar burst on them from above, a racketing blast of noise that seared the air and hammered against the eardrums. Harriet clutched Thompson's sweater and pressed her head against his chest.

"Chain saw!" Thompson cried, cupping his hand around her ear so she could hear his words.

The roar abruptly ceased, and in the ringing silence they heard the voices again.

"Goddammit all to hell! It ain't here nohow!"

The accent was southern—high-pitched for a man, and singsong.

A gruffer, flatter voice answered, "It's gotta be."

"Well, it's a goddamn trick, Hobey. You show me where's they's any file in the goddamn door!" The hysteria in the voice was genuine, and rising.

Thompson was baffled. They had sawed up a door somewhere in the house. But not the cellar door. How come? Someone had misled them. Smith?

The other voice hardened. "You wanna go back and say we couldn't find it? You wanna tell that to Farrell? That we couldn't find that file?"

"Goddammit, Hobey, it ain't my fault! What are we gonna do?"

After a pause the other voice replied, "We're gonna stay here and saw up every fuckin' door in this shack. We'll saw up the whole fuckin' house if we have to. But we ain't leaving here without that file!"

Thompson and Harriet started to grope their way toward the bulkhead, Thompson shading the flashlight beam with one hand. They were partway up the bulkhead steps when Thompson stopped. He grabbed Harriet by the wrist, overwhelmed by a sudden intuition.

"What's the matter?" Harriet whispered.

"I know where the file is!"

He retreated hastily down the steps, pulling Harriet behind him. From the canvas bag draped over her shoulder he fished out a screwdriver and motioned to her to follow him.

The chainsaw started up again, ripping through another door. The racket was ear-splitting, terrifying. The entire house trembled under the assault. The noise must be audible for a mile, Thompson thought. How long would it be before someone reported it to the police? They must hurry.

He led Harriet back to the storage enclosure at the far end of the cellar. It was a relatively recent addition, and the door into it, which he had glimpsed earlier, was a flat brown panel of plywood. He tapped it. It felt thin and lightweight.

"Hollow-core!" he whispered.

He reached down and twisted the knob, praying that it would not be locked. The knob turned easily and Thompson felt a shiver of elation as the door creaked open. To get at its bottom edge, he need only remove the door's two hinges. With Harriet holding the light, he applied the screwdriver to the first of the six screws that held the hinges in place.

The chain saw stopped, and they heard the men walking around again. They waited.

After a minute the machine roared to life again and started in on another door. Thompson went back to work with the screwdriver.

"Please hurry!" Harriet whispered.

The last screw removed, he yanked the door loose from the frame and quickly tipped it over on its side. Harriet shone the flashlight on the bottom edge.

"There it is!"

Two countersunk wood screws were visible at each end. Thompson set the screwdriver blade in the first. It turned easily, and when he had raised it half an inch, he yanked it the rest of the way out with his fingers.

He had started on the second screw when the chain saw stopped again. The floorboards groaned loudly and they could hear both voices upstairs cursing.

Suddenly the cellar door opened.

Harriet switched off the flashlight. They were out of sight of the cellar stairs, but they could not reach the bulkhead exit without passing directly in front of them.

A light came on—a dim bulb near the stairwell—and the aged steps at the top of the cellar landing squeaked under someone's heavy shoe. From back in the house a voice called out: "Where you going, Harley?"

"There might be some doors down here!"

Harley's reply sounded as if he were right next to them. Thompson squeezed Harriet's arm and pointed in the direction of the bulkhead. She started off, hurrying noiselessly across the bumpy dirt floor, Thompson close behind.

God, so close. So close!

He hesitated, looking back over his shoulder.

Steeling himself against the alarms going off in his brain, he turned back to the door to apply the screwdriver to the remaining screw, barely visible in the faint glow from the stairwell bulb. The man called Harley was still standing on the top landing, out of sight.

"You think they's any rats in this cellar, Hobey? I hate those suckers!"

"Whyn't you go down and find out, you fuckin' sissy!"

"I can hear somethin' squeaking."

"It's your fuckin' brain!"

"Yeah. It might be a rat, though. I hate those goddamn suckers!"

Thompson pulled the screw out at last and jammed the screwdriver tip underneath the wood strip and pried upward. The strip popped out and clattered to the earth.

"Goddammit, they's something down there, all right! I can hear it!"

Thompson strained frantically to squeeze his hand into the exposed slot in the bottom of the door. Finally, by flattening his fingers out, he was able to reach partway in. His hand felt nothing.

He pulled it out, grabbed the strip of wood lying in the dirt, and ran it quickly back and forth inside the slot. It moved freely through the door's hollow interior, encountering no obstacles. The slot was empty.

Thompson's disbelief was profound. He felt betrayed, tricked. He would have bet his life the file would be there. Maybe he *had* bet his life. He dropped the strip of wood and charged across the cellar toward the bulkhead.

Harley had overcome his hesitation and was descending the steps as Thompson passed beneath him. Harley's head and upper torso were still out of sight up the steep stairwell. Thompson caught a brief glimpse of cheap black shoes, shiny pants legs, and a hand thrust forward down the steps, gripping a pistol. Thompson feared he would burst from panic.

He saw the bulkhead opening, barely visible in the gloom, and dashed toward it.

His shoulder smashed against something. He reeled back from the jolt, gasping in pain. He had run into the edge of the bulkhead door, the one he had broken open to get in. He groped with his hand to find it again, and felt something light brush against his fingers, then bounce against his arm and fall soundlessly to the dirt floor. He moved to step around it, his senses screaming for him to bolt through the bulkhead and vanish into the safety of the night beyond.

Some impulse checked him, made him pause for the split second it took for him to bend down and run his hand rapidly around the dirt and find the thing that had just dropped there. His fingers felt it—a thick paper envelope, folded over several times into a long narrow strip, like a fan.

Thompson's blood raced. He squeezed the envelope in his hand and nearly yelled for joy. *It was the file!* He was sure of it!

In a flash he understood what had happened. There were *three* doors that qualified as the cellar door. The one he had just pried open and found empty must have been meant as a decoy. Roland had chosen to hide the file in the one least likely to be disturbed. He had simply folded it up and forced it between the two planks that formed the edge of the door. Breaking in, Thompson had widened the space by splitting the outside plank partway free of the inside one. When he hit the door going out, he jarred the file loose—right into his hands.

Harriet was waiting near the corner of the house, hiding behind a thick evergreen bush.

"I've got it! Across the field! Hurry!"

The moonlight illuminated their retreat over Roland's back lawn and through the meadow. Reaching the trees on the far side, they were plunged into the shadows again.

Harriet fell.

Thompson was over the stone wall before he realized that she was no longer with him. He looked around frantically, then climbed back over and ran out into the field to find her. She was on one knee, trying to stand. "Twisted my ankle."

He felt almost giddy from the adrenaline surging through him. He grabbed her arm, threw it around his neck, and pulled her to her feet.

With the other arm gripping her waist, he half-trotted, half-dragged her to the stone wall.

Christ, how was he going to get her over it?

Only one way. He lifted her up and set her on top. He looked back across the field. No one in sight. He scrambled over himself, pulled her down after him, and dragged her roughly through the screen of heavy bushes to the car.

Harriet's stoicism began to crumble. She whimpered in pain as he opened the car door and pushed her inside.

"I've sprained it, dammit!"

"Maybe not."

Thompson jumped into the driver's seat and slammed the door, instantly regretting the noise it made. He gripped the steering wheel and pressed his head back against the headrest.

"Let's go!" Harriet cried.

Thompson shook his head. "Not yet. They'll hear the engine start. We've got to wait until they start the chain saw."

"They know we're here!" Harriet was shaking violently, from pain and fear. Thompson wished he could reassure her.

"They didn't see us," he replied.

"But they must see the bulkhead door by now!"

"I don't know."

They heard yelling voices. Then a car engine starting, and a squeal of tires. The cones of light from its headlamps swung across the field, then down the driveway and out onto the road. The car turned left and barreled up the narrow road past them, grinding gears as it went.

Thompson fired the ignition, backed the Toyota down the dirt path as fast as he could without turning the lights on, swung it out onto the road, and crept off in the other direction, toward town. When he was safely around the first corner, he switched on the headlights and stepped on the accelerator.

"Watch for lights behind us," he said. "And pray you don't see any."

Harriet did, almost at once. The other car had already turned around and was speeding back after them, taking corners at reckless speeds. Thompson could see their headlights pop into sight in the rearview mirror whenever he hit a straight stretch. They seemed to be closing the gap fast. The Toyota, already hitting sixty-five, was barely holding on the very narrow road, which snaked up and down hills and around corners like a twisted telephone cord, and he didn't trust his driving ability to move it any faster.

"They're gaining on us," Harriet yelled.

"I know."

"What are we going to do?"

Thompson didn't know. His eyes flicked back and forth between the growing twin spots of light in the mirror and the surface of the road, twisting and bouncing under the Toyota.

Within a mile the other car had closed the distance to less than twenty feet. It was riding the Celica's tail now, a roaring beast of prey, tires squealing in unison with the Toyota around every corner.

Up a steep hill Thompson shifted down to second, and rammed the accelerator pedal flat against the floor. If there was any hope of gaining ground, it had to be on an uphill grade.

The Toyota's engine whined and protested, but climbed at seventy miles an hour, its tachometer needle hovering in the red zone, past 5500 rpm. At the crest of the hill the car behind them seemed to have lost ground. Thompson wondered what make it could be. A Mercedes? BMW? What could maneuver so well on this kind of road?

Harriet screamed.

Thompson looked past her out the windshield in time to see the yellow highway sign indicating a sharp turn. He had passed over the crest of the hill and was plunging down the other side, and he was into the curve before he could think about it, still in second gear, still at seventy miles an hour.

As soon as his foot left the accelerator, the low gear acted as a brake, seeming to seize the drive shaft with giant hands. Thompson tipped the steering wheel to the left, and felt the car tilt and the tires on the left side leave the road surface. He straightened slightly, staring at the dense stand of trees that loomed directly in the path of the car, then touched the brake and felt the rear end begin to slide. The vehicle was now moving sideways on two wheels toward the woods on the outside of the curve.

The car in pursuit had crested the rise a split second behind them, and had closed to within thirty feet when Thompson first saw the turn. The flash of Thompson's red brake light had a dramatic effect on the driver in the second car. He slammed on his brakes to avoid crashing into the Celica from behind.

Thompson watched the trees pan dizzyingly from left to right across the Celica's hood. When the car's rear end had slid far enough around to position the car parallel with the road past the curve, Thompson stomped his foot on the gas pedal.

The Celica shot forward on two wheels, like a stunt car, waggled on its side momentarily, came back to rest on all four tires, and screeched and bounded forward down the remainder of the hill, Thompson pumping the brakes to bring it under control.

The car in pursuit did not make it.

It skidded partway through the nearly ninety-degree downhill turn, then tipped up on its side, rolled over, and tumbled across the road and into the woods, bouncing like a toy.

It struck a giant tree trunk sideways at fifty miles an hour and wrapped its three thousand pounds of steel and plastic so completely around it that the left edges of the front and rear bumpers met on the back side of the tree.

From the bottom of the hill they heard the crash, and seconds later an explosion. They looked back up the hill. The wreck glowed brilliantly through the trees, a crackling funeral pyre of furiously burning metal. They could see the silhouettes of the two men inside, trapped in the yellow flames.

Too exhausted to talk, Thompson drove the entire distance back to Alexandria at forty miles an hour, Harriet weeping with relief at his side.

16

The telephone in the study rang, jarring Smith from the depths of his all-night vigil. He looked at his watch. Five in the morning. A faint gray had begun to lighten the sky beyond the oak tree outside the back bedroom window. Smith waited for the telephone to stop, but it kept on ringing—nine, ten, a dozen times.

He decided he must answer it. The time for waiting was over. He knew that Cyclops—if he was still alive—could not stay this long just to ambush him. Cyclops needed to act on the information recovered from Smith's wastebasket.

Smith rose slowly to his feet, stiff and aching from the hours sitting behind the bed, walked into the front bedroom, and picked up the receiver on the small white phone by the bed. He heard only a dial tone; then he remembered that it was on a separate line from the study phone. Stupid of me, he thought. Too tired to think straight.

The Walther gripped tightly in his right hand, he descended the stairs and walked slowly around to the back of the house and into the study.

No one—dead or alive—was in the room.

The telephone was still ringing. He looked around for signs of a struggle, signs of blood. There were none. Had last night really happened? Or was it a nightmare? Had he, at age seventy, begun to slip into a premature senility that confused events and time, reality and imagination?

Smith reached for the receiver and placed it tentatively against his ear. His throat felt constricted and full of phlegm. He cleared it loudly.

"Yes?"

"Professor Smith?" The voice was southwestern—Texas, Oklahoma.

"Yes."

"Nice try, professor."

Smith's hand squeezed the receiver, turning his knuckles white.

"Why are you calling?"

A sardonic laugh at the other end. "Remember Mahmoud Hamchari, professor?"

Smith did. Hamchari was a **PLO** terrorist, believed to have been assassinated by an Israeli hit team.

"That was *my* baby, professor. It was such a popular hit, I thought I'd give you an encore."

Smith sorted through the corners of his gigantic brain, trying to retrieve the details of that assassination. He heard a high-pitched note on the other end of the line, like a touch-tone signal, and suddenly he remembered how Hamchari had died.

"Good-bye, professor."

Smith threw the receiver away from him, kicked over the table holding the telephone, and dived backwards, seeking the protection of the desk. But too late.

The 20,000-cycle tone, emitted from a whistle like the harmonica bug, activated a micro-switch in a small plastic box hidden inside the base of the telephone. The switch closed a circuit that ignited a fuse and detonated a paper-wrapped package of nitroglycerin and ammonium nitrate.

A powerful explosion obliterated the telephone, hurling fragments of Bakelite out like the shrapnel of a bursting antiaircraft shell. The shock wave blew the furniture against the walls, tore the door from its hinges, and boomed through the windows, popping the glass like soap bubbles. A millisecond behind the blast, a lush black-and-red flower of smoke and fire blossomed in the room and consumed it, igniting the wallpaper and the spines of hundreds of books, and curling the framed degrees on the walls into cinders.

Professor Smith died instantly.

17

Saturday afternoon, October 27

The Chameleon sat on a bench in the zoological gardens of the Villa Borghese, reading a copy of the *Osservatore Romano* and smoking Cuban cigarillos. At precisely two o'clock, he folded his newspaper, brushed the flecks of ash from his white suit, and strolled through the park down the broad Viale delle Belle Arti, past the Galleria Borghese and the National Museum of Villa Giulia, and out the park's northwest corner.

From the Via Flaminia he walked across the Ponte del Risorgimento to the Piazza Monte Grappa on Rome's west bank and continued on from the piazza, enjoying the midafternoon sun along the Viale Mazzini and admiring the beautiful faces of the young women hurrying back from lunch to their shops and offices.

When his gold watch said two-thirty, he was standing directly in front of a small photography store on the Via Podgora, a short side street off the Via Monte Zebio. He double-checked the address, then walked inside and politely summoned the clerk standing with arms folded in the rear of the store.

"*Si, signore?*"

"*Buon giorno.* I wish to see the proprietor, Signore Anginotto."

The clerk nodded, his expression neither warm nor hostile. "I am Signore Anginotto."

The Chameleon opened his eyes wide and smiled. "Ah, you are surprisingly young, *signore!*"

Anginotto shrugged, not moved by the flattery. He was thin, short, and pale, but he was not young.

"What can I do for you, *signore?*"

The Chameleon hesitated for a second, assessing Anginotto, then made up his mind to continue. "I am here to take delivery on the rebuilt movie camera."

The Chameleon drew a cream-colored calling card from his waistcoat pocket and presented it to Anginotto. The storekeeper glanced at it, maintaining his deadpan expression. It contained the briefest amount of information: "A. Sierra, Argentine Films, S.A."

Anginotto permitted himself a slight nod. "This way, please, Signore Sierra."

The Chameleon followed the proprietor into a small room at the back of the shop, cluttered with camera equipment, ledgers, and shelves of chemicals. Anginotto unlocked a door on the far wall of this room and led the Chameleon down a narrow staircase to a long, low-ceilinged basement that extended the entire length of the building.

The cellar was a workshop. A wide wooden bench dominated the room, piled with sophisticated equipment and thousands of camera parts. One bench against a wall contained a metal lathe; another, in the middle of the room, was crowded with various kinds of hammers, wrenches, screwdrivers, and pliers.

Anginotto unlocked a steel cabinet crammed into a corner and pulled out a cardboard box. He cleared a space for the box on the center bench, opened it, and withdrew its contents.

The camera was an Arriflex 16S, a sixteen-millimeter professional model of the highest quality. The Chameleon examined it minutely, questioning Anginotto closely on a dozen matters.

Satisfied at last that the device met his needs, the Chameleon retrieved a large packet from his inside jacket pocket. "Please tell me how much I owe you, *signore.*"

Anginotto smiled, avoiding the Chameleon's eyes. His price was high, and it embarrassed him. But he was a unique craftsman; his work was unavailable elsewhere.

"Seventy-five million lire, *signore.*"

Without a murmur of dissent the Chameleon removed from the packet a stack of million-lire notes, counted out seventy-five of them, and placed them on the workbench.

Anginotto picked up the thick stack of bills without counting it, carried it immediately to a safe in the back of the room, and locked it up. His coffers so suddenly and dramatically swelled, Anginotto became expansive and offered the Chameleon a glass of cognac to seal their transaction. They drank to each other's health and long life, and Anginotto complimented him on the fluency of his Italian.

The Chameleon picked up the camera case and prepared to depart. At the outer door of the shop, he pointed down to it with his free hand and flashed Anginotto a broad grin.

"Very 'James Bond,' eh?"

Anginotto looked puzzled, then understood. "Oh yes, *signore*. Very 'James Bond.' "

18

Saturday morning, October 27

Thompson turned the eight-by-eleven manila envelope over in his lap and examined it. It bore absolutely no markings except for a few smudges of dirt.

"Open it, for God's sake," Harriet said. "After our close calls tonight, I don't want to end up dying of curiosity."

Thompson inserted a finger in one end under the glued flap, sawed it open, and extracted a thin stack of papers.

They were sitting at a small round table in the dining alcove of Herb Franklin's apartment in Rosslyn. A fixture with an imitation Tiffany shade hung low over the table, casting a pool of light in the center, and Thompson had to tilt the pages at an angle to eliminate the glare from the bulb. He counted them first. The stack was only seven pages thick.

The first two pages were photocopies of cables:

TO COS MEXICO DF   TRANSMISSION 3.14.84
FROM DDO LANGLEY
NODIS
PLEASE SUPPLY BACKGROUNDERS FOR NAMES

BELOW. ALL ARE MEXICAN NATIONALS WITH
ILLEGAL-ALIEN STATUS HERE. REQUEST INFOR-
MATION SOONEST.
CARLOS REYES, MEXICO DF
PEDRO RODRIGUEZ, MEXICO DF
FERNANDO RINCON, MEXICO DF
FELIPE HERNANDEZ, MONTERREY
DOMINGO SOLONA, MONTERREY
JOSE SOLONA, MONTERREY
JUAN VALDOSTA, VERACRUZ
ALBERTO ORTEGA, SALTILLO
JESUS ECHEVERIA, CIUDAD MADERO
ARMANDO VALDEZ, NUEVO LAREDO
LUIS COLON, GUADALAJARA
RAFAEL ESCOBAR, SAN LUIS POTOSI
REPEAT, REQUEST INFORMATION SOONEST,
                                    REGARDS,

TO DDO LANGLEY   TRANSMISSION 3.20.84
FROM COS MEXICO DF
NODIS
THIS IS SUMMARY OF INFORMATION RE-
QUESTED RE MEXICAN NATIONALS. DETAILS
ON WAY BY POUCH. ALL COME FROM POVERTY
BACKGROUNDS. NONE HAS MORE THAN
GRADE-SCHOOL EDUCATION. NONE HAS POLIT-
ICAL AFFILIATIONS OF ANY KIND, INCLUDING
CP. ALL HAVE CRIMINAL RECORDS: CARLOS
REYES, ARMED ROBBERY, ASSAULT, RAPE. PE-
DRO RODRIGUEZ, ARMED ROBBERY. FERNANDO
RINCON, BURGLARY, ASSAULT. FELIPE HERNAN-
DEZ, MANSLAUGHTER. DOMINGO SOLONA,
ARMED ROBBERY. JOSE SOLONA, ARMED ROBBE-
RY. JUAN VALDOSTA, MURDER. ALBERTO ORTE-
GA, MURDER, RAPE. JESUS ECHEVERIA, GRAND
LARCENY, FORGERY. ARMANDO VALDEZ,
ARMED ROBBERY. LUIS COLON, KIDNAPPING.
THERE IS NO TRACE AT ALL OF A RAFAEL ESCO-
BAR IN SAN LUIS POTOSI. WILL CONTINUE
SEARCH.
                                    REGARDS,

"So far," Thompson said, "it looks like we risked our lives for the wrong file." He handed the cables to Harriet and began reading the third page, a handwritten note in pencil, with no indication of either the sender or the recipient:

> This will come as a surprise to you. Joseph Madero, aka Cyclops, is not dead. I have just learned that he was seen this past May hiding out at a lodge in the Petén jungle, north of Guatemala City. I have this secondhand from Peter Mallory, formerly with us, now with the Secret Service, attached to the Veep's entourage. Vice-President Beecher visited this lodge on a hunting trip recently, and Mallory spotted Cyclops there. He didn't speak to him or give any sign that he recognized him, but he's positive that's who he saw. Madero seemed to be running the lodge, and claimed to be a retired real-estate broker from Austin, according to conversations Mallory overheard. Cyclops was in good shape physically, Mallory said, except that he was drinking a lot.
>
> The plan to eliminate him four years ago backfired because he found out about it and bought off the assassin. That was Little Boy, the Turk, you remember. He's dead now, in case they never told you. Drowned in the Florida Keys.
>
> Cyclops is no longer at the lodge in the Petén. He left there in July, on a secret assignment. He was hired through John Graves, from Boston, who does free-lance work for the agency now. I'm trying to find out what the mission is, but things are especially tight around here. Everyone is suspicious of everyone else.
>
> I'll have to be careful as hell from now on. I think I'm being watched.

The fourth page was another, shorter note, written in the same hand:

> Graves hired Cyclops for something code-named "Zodiac." It has no clearance classification because officially it doesn't exist. It is led by four men who use the code names Aquarius, Scorpio, Gemini, and Capricorn. Beyond that I only know that the leader of the group is the one they call Capricorn.
>
> Zodiac is developing fast. I should have more soon on its objectives and on the identity of the four men.

"It's getting better," Thompson said, handing Harriet the two pages with the handwritten notes.

The fifth piece of paper was a photocopy of a page apparently torn from a memo pad. The borders of the smaller piece of memo paper were visible on the copy, and the memo itself was handwritten, probably in ball-point:

> Capricorn wants domestic site for Zodiac training.
> Check with Gemini?

Thompson borrowed back the two pages he had passed on to Harriet and compared the handwriting. They were entirely different.

"This memo-pad writer sounds like someone who's actually in on the plot," he said. "Someone must have stolen these pages from his pad."

The sixth page was another copy from the memo pad, containing an even briefer note in the same hand:

> Zodiac 10/30

The seventh and final page was a photocopy of a map, probably from an atlas, Thompson judged, because the right side of the page, instead of showing a margin, ran off the page into what looked like a gutter. It was a detailed map of several townships in an unidentified area. Two towns, called Canaan and Burnham, were located entirely within the confines of the map. Around them lay portions of several others—Northfield, Greenfield, Hebron, Wentworth, Francestown, and Lebanon.

The last town, Lebanon, was familiar to him, but at first he couldn't tell why. Finally he remembered. It was the town just south of Hanover, where the airport was located. He had flown out of there only two days ago.

The map was a portion of the state of New Hampshire.

A thick black line encompassed a large, roughly rectangular area in the middle of the map. Its boundaries included large pieces of the real estate of five towns, and judging from the scale, the area looked to be about nine miles long on its north-south axis, and about five miles across. Save for the locations of half a dozen peaks and several large ponds and brooks, the space inside the black line was almost blank. No villages, no roads, no landmarks. It gave the impression of being either unexplored or inaccessible, like the *terra incognita* of a medieval map.

Someone had drawn an X inside a box in the northeast corner of the empty space and written "Zodiac" beside it. The writing appeared to have been made on the copy, not on the original.

Thompson pushed the map across the table to Harriet and sank back in his chair, shaking his head in bewilderment.

"Jesus. It all sounds ominous as hell. The 'Zodiac' conspiracy. Men code-named Capricorn, Gemini, Scorpio, and Aquarius. Some exotic character from a Central American jungle called Cyclops. But what the hell is it all about? There's hardly any *real* information here at all."

Harriet was studying the map. "I know what this is!" she said, suddenly excited. "It's a place called Halloween Park. It's a private hunting preserve in New Hampshire, owned by a group of businessmen."

Thompson glanced at her in surprise. "How in the world did you know that?"

"Because," she explained, "Senator MacNair is a member. He's the dirty old man we saw with his girls in the Old Ebbitt the other night. I found out about the park doing the story on him. He invited President Mills there for a hunting vacation at the end of the 1980 election campaign. It was a perfect retreat because the park is completely fenced in. It made it easy for the Secret Service to protect him—and impossible for the media to get at him."

Thompson took the page back and looked at it again. "It covers an enormous area. It must be a hell of a long fence."

"It is. The owners are rich men. They can afford a lot of fence. And the fence, as I understand it, isn't just to keep out the riffraff, but to keep the wild animals in. It's stocked with all sorts of exotic game—wild boar, moose, wild turkey, elk—everything but unicorns and dragons."

"And now they've added Zodiac," Thompson replied.

Harriet looked as puzzled as Thompson. "Do you think Roland knew what Zodiac was?"

"He must at least have had a general idea. Otherwise he wouldn't have been so desperate to stop it."

Harriet nodded. "That makes sense. Any ideas?"

Thompson tipped his chair onto its back legs and thrust his hands into his pants pockets. "A first wild guess would be that a disreputable bunch of astrologers has hired a dozen Mexican outlaws to train for some terrible deed in a park in New Hampshire. A plot only G. K. Chesterton could have imagined."

"The CIA," Harriet said, her face intent. "It *must* be. The cables back and forth from Mexico."

Thompson shook his head. "Maybe. But you can read it the other way, too. The CIA may have stumbled across the Zodiac business and started investigating it on its own. That's what it is, after all, an intelligence-gathering—"

Harriet cut him off impatiently. "But what about this long note about this Cyclops character? That's from a CIA source too!"

Thompson realized that they were falling into an odd kind of writer-editor relationship. She did the guesswork, and he edited.

"Yeah, I think you're right," he said. "In fact, it probably comes from Klimentov. He told me he was doing research for Roland. These two pages about Cyclops and the Zodiac code names must be his reports. But again, they can be read either way. Either he's spying on something going on within the agency or he's spying on something going on outside it. There's no way to tell."

"An assassination plot?"

Thompson stared at her. "Against whom?"

"The President."

"Mills?" Thompson considered it. "Well, there are a lot of Mexicans who hate him. But I can't see Roland trying to stop that. He'd have wanted to supply the weapons."

Harriet admitted it was just a guess. "But it has to be something of that magnitude. Klimentov must know. You'll have to find out from him when you see him tomorrow."

Thompson nodded. "Yeah. I'll do what I can. But I won't have the money he wants."

"Promise him a big book contract."

Thompson gritted his teeth. "You really have a terrible sense of humor."

"I'm serious," she declared. "Lie to him! And while you're working on Klimentov, I'm going to find out who John Graves is. He's the best lead the file's given us. It's the only real name we've got."

Thompson nodded, suddenly aware of his extreme fatigue. His eyes felt full of gravel, his throat raw. Two hair-raising chases in one day, after thirty-six years of mundane middle-class diversions, had left him on the edge of a catatonic exhaustion. He feared one more moment's exertion might kill him.

"Remember your promise, Harriet. We're taking everything over to the FBI tomorrow. As soon as I meet with Klimentov."

"I remember." Harriet sounded annoyed.

"We're in over our heads," he said, suspecting that she still resisted the idea of going to the FBI. "Tonight ought to have proved that to you."

"We're still alive."

"We're lucky." Thompson saw again the silhouettes in the burning automobile.

He gathered up the seven pages of the file, stacked them together neatly, and slid them back into the manila envelope. Its contents had already cost several lives, he thought. Having it in his possession was like owning something with a curse on it. The code names danced through his head. Capricorn. Scorpio. Gemini. Aquarius. What kind of people would choose signs of the zodiac for code names? The military? CIA? FBI? Foreign agents? Terrorists? Crazies?

He stood up and stretched, looking at the swell of Harriet's breasts as she leaned against the back of the chair. Sleeping with her curled up beside him seemed suddenly like the most intense pleasure on earth.

"A personal question," he muttered, his voice cracking with fatigue. "Are you staying here tonight?"

Harriet looked up at him with an expression of mock impatience. "Do you think I'm going home by myself at five o'clock in the morning? With a sprained ankle?"

"You hang around me like this, kid, and you'll only get in trouble." He meant it as a joke, but he was afraid it was true. If he were brave, if he had any of the makings of a hero at all, he would send her away, make her stay clear of him. Instead they would sleep together again, like brother and sister, on Franklin's double bed. It was too late and he was too tired for sex, anyway. Not that he had any choice in the matter.

He turned off the living-room lights and they walked toward the bedroom. He still had the file in his hand, and he wondered if he should hide it or take it to bed. He finally compromised and shoved it between the box spring and the mattress.

"What's the date today?" Harriet asked.

Thompson looked at his calendar watch. "October twenty-seventh. Why?"

"I just realized. We *do* know something important about Zodiac."

"What's that?"

"It's going to happen in three days."

Thompson stared at her, astonished. "How do we know that?"

"Isn't that what 'Zodiac ten/thirty' means?"

19

Two men walked slowly along the edge of the surf, which advanced and retreated across the sand in long, lazy patterns. The older and taller of the two, John Graves, was in his late fifties, and possessed a mane of white hair and a tanned, barrel-chested frame that appeared still robust and muscular in a jogging suit. He walked with an easy gait, his chin out and his eyes fixed on the horizon. The smaller, younger man, dressed in street clothes, stayed a half-pace behind him at his side, and directed his eyes downward, toward the sand. He was in his early forties—pale-skinned, thickset, and short-legged, with close-cropped hair and small features. In marked contrast to the older man's casual stroll, he appeared awkward and nervous, his leather-soled shoes slipping on the sand. He waited for Graves to speak.

The beach formed a crescent-shaped cove, and it was entirely deserted, because John Graves owned the beachfront for a thousand feet in both directions. His weekend house, a multilevel glass-and-wood palace, stood on the rise of land behind the beach, commanding a panoramic view of the mouth of Long Island Sound and the eastern tip of Long Island, far to the south.

Farrell, the younger man, glanced up at the house briefly. He could see Graves's wife there, sunning herself on a deck that extended out from the second story. A voluptuous redhead at least three decades younger than Graves, she wore a green bathrobe and a wide-brimmed hat to shield herself from the fall breeze. Farrell could also see one of Graves's private guards, in customary white ducks and blue shirt, patrolling the perimeter of the garden below.

Farrell was choked with anxiety. Graves had summoned him to Fisher's Island without warning. Indeed, one of Graves's lackeys had pulled him from his bed in Alexandria and hustled him, aboard Graves's Lear jet, to Graves's private airstrip in under an hour.

Once there, Graves had kept him waiting in a downstairs hallway for an hour and a half, and now he was giving him the silent treatment.

Graves wanted him to sweat, and he was sweating.

They reached the far end of the beach, where further progress on foot was blocked by a Cyclone fence and a massive rock jetty that ran forty or fifty feet out into the water. Graves stopped and focused his eyes skyward on an osprey wheeling slowly over the waters off the jetty. Farrell followed his gaze. The large bird traced a tightening circle high above the surface, its wings riding the air currents with effortless ease. As they watched, the bird braked in midair, its wings beating to hold it aloft, and craned its neck downward to search beneath the waves far below.

"Watch this," Graves said.

Abruptly the osprey folded its wings and dropped toward the ocean, talons thrust forward beneath its beak, a blur of concentrated fury straining toward the water. It hit with a high, narrow splash, and disappeared completely beneath the whitecaps.

Seconds later the bird broke the surface and struggled to become airborne. The magnificent five-foot-long wings burst free of the water in a rainbow of spray, and beat against the air. Clutched firmly in both claws was the prize—a huge fish.

The osprey gained altitude slowly and diminished from view over the island, its prey riding beneath it like an oversize pontoon.

Graves shook his head and smiled, more to himself than to Farrell. "I've watched that osprey fish off this jetty for years. There are only three pairs left on the island. DDT almost wiped them out in the sixties. But a few hung on, and now they're making a comeback. He survived. He's a tough bastard, and he rarely misses on the hunt. I've seen him pull bigger fish out of the water than that one."

Graves's mouth became stern again. He turned and looked down at Farrell with a rheumy, accusatory stare that Farrell particularly despised.

"There's a lesson there, Farrell," he said.

"Yes, sir."

Farrell thought to himself that the goddamn bird was probably a female, and felt like asking Graves how he knew it was the same bird he'd been seeing all these years. But he didn't. He kept his mouth shut.

"Now, tell me what went wrong," Graves said. "And don't leave out anything."

Farrell described the break-in at the house in Middleburg, the discovery of the empty hollow-core door in the cellar, and the car chase. In the crash that followed, only Harley Curtis had survived, and he was badly burned. Farrell had obtained the story from Curtis at his hospital bedside.

"Is his account reliable?" Graves demanded.

"Yes, sir."

"How do you know?"

"Well, I recruited and trained him."

Graves snorted. "At least he's not a Cuban. Those goddamned Cubans you recruited last year couldn't pour piss from a boot if the directions were on the heel."

"They were Hondurans, sir."

"Same difference."

"Yes, sir."

"What happened to the tail you put on Thompson? He should have known Thompson was going to Middleburg. And you could have trapped him there."

"That was Boxer. We put a hitchhiker on him, but Boxer claims that somehow the guy found out about it and removed it. He lost him at the Air and Space Museum."

Graves's exasperation was immense. "I don't believe it," he muttered, "I don't fucking believe it."

Farrell dug into his jacket pocket and produced a cassette tape. "You can listen for yourself. I taped the stories of both of them—Boxer and Curtis—for the record."

Graves stared at him, incredulous. His bushy white eyebrows knitted angrily over his ruddy face. "For the record?"

"Yes, sir."

Graves snatched the tape from Farrell's hand and heaved it with all his strength in a sidearm throw out into the ocean. It sailed on the air for a distance, bounced off the surface of a wave like a skipping stone, then sank.

Farrell looked up and met Graves's eyes. Sometimes his hatred of Graves burned so strongly he was sure Graves must feel it. Only his fear was stronger than the hate. He waited for Graves to explain.

"We don't keep things for the record, Farrell! There are no records, and there is no record-keeping. You can't afford to forget that ever again!"

"No, sir."

"Where are these two jokers—Boxer and Curtis?"

"In Alexandria."

"Who did you tell them they were working for?"

"The FBI."

"Good. Now get rid of them. Immediately."

Farrell bit his lip. "Terminate them?"

"No, no, no! They don't know anything! Put them in storage somewhere. Send them to South America! We might use them again sometime."

"They have families. They were mercenaries before—"

Graves cut Farrell off with an impatient wave of his arm. "I don't want to hear their life histories! If they have families, send the goddamn families with them. The client will pay. Just get them out of sight, before they embarrass us—or worse!"

Graves's voice was turning strident, its whiskey rumble becoming a rasp scraping across the grain of Farrell's self-respect. Farrell could feel the blood rising in his neck.

"Now, Farrell," Graves continued, "let's review this comedy of errors of the past few days. We're trying to stop a leak, a leak our client says will have grim consequences if it gets out. But instead of stopping it, we're leaving a trail of blood all over the East Coast, and so far we still haven't plugged the leak. The chief reason seems to be a book editor who I would have guessed to be about as dangerous as a one-legged man in an ass-kicking contest. Yet somehow he's beaten us to Roland's file and disappeared with it!"

"Yes, sir."

"Get Cyclops on him!"

"Yes, sir, I planned to."

"And find out what this friend of his, this Mitchell—find out what she knows. She must know where Thompson is hiding."

Farrell cleared his throat. "She's a reporter. We have to be careful—"

Graves shot Farrell the intimidating glare again. "I know she's a reporter, for Chrissakes! Do it any way you have to do it! That's what I hired you for. I don't care who the fuck she is!"

Farrell nodded. They had walked the length of the beach twice, and Graves now led them toward the path up the hill to his house.

"Listen, Farrell." Graves's tone of voice had shifted and become less hectoring, almost benign. "I'm not a very likable man—I know that. It's not that important to me. I've always been more interested in getting things done, and getting them done the way I wanted them done. And I've found out in life that getting things done and being well-liked just don't happen to go together. That's a trade-off I've been able to live with. But it doesn't mean that I have no feelings. I'm not a monster, Farrell."

Farrell felt embarrassed. He hated this kind of sentimental self-justifying, and coming from Graves, it made him doubly uncomfortable.

Graves went on: "I hate these killings as much as you do. But this is no time for us to get moral or squeamish or fainthearted. We've got to get this job done. We've got to succeed for them, regardless of the price, because this is one client we can't disappoint. If we fail, they'll eat us alive. You and me both, and I'm not exaggerating."

"Yes, sir."

"I don't know whether it's all for a good cause or not, but as far as we're concerned, it doesn't make a dime's worth of difference. Because we're not in a position to ask questions. We're fighting for our own lives. And success in putting the cap on this business is our only defense."

"I understand."

Farrell knew that Graves was lying to him. Graves's own ass was on the line, and he cared more about the reputation of his service and the big money it was bringing in than he did about rubbing out a few civilians. And Farrell was already smart enough to know that the only cause worth worrying about was Number One. That's what Graves was worrying about, and that's what Farrell would worry about.

"All we have to do," Graves continued, "is to recover that file and remove anyone who knows its contents."

"I understand."

They were nearing the outer gate of Graves's compound, and two of Graves's guards came forward to open it.

"We have to plug the leak fast," Graves added. "We don't have much time."

"I understand." Farrell lowered his eyes to the crushed rock of the path leading around behind the big house to the airstrip, where the Lear jet sat waiting, a dazzling gleam of aluminum in the midday sun.

"Three days at the most," Graves said, his voice noticeably strained with tension. "That's a direct order from the client. Seventy-two hours. After that, it will be too late."

20

Thompson struggled to control his panic. He looked out the living-room window at the figure on the sidewalk below. From nine floors up, he had an unobstructed view of three blocks of Queen Street. It was a bright, sunny day, with a strong breeze that imparted an almost supernatural clarity to the air, rendering in sharp detail objects a great distance away.

A clock chimed eleven-thirty. Thompson had first noticed the man below at nine o'clock—two and a half hours ago. He was wearing a light brown hat and a brown Norfolk jacket, and for the past half-hour he had been leaning against the fender of a parked car directly across the street from the apartment building, smoking and watching the residents of the building come and go.

A block farther on, Thompson saw the Celica he had parked there last night. No one had disturbed it. The sun bounced off the back window and the cream-white paint with an intensity almost painful to the eyes.

The time for the meeting with Klimentov had passed.

Klimentov might wait, of course, but he couldn't wait for hours, Thompson knew. Eventually he would realize that Thompson was not coming, and he would depart, taking his secrets with him, unconverted into the cash with which he had hoped to finance a fugitive future. Thompson didn't feel sorry for him. He felt sorry for himself.

And for Smith.

Who was dead.

An hour ago he had finally reached someone in Hanover—a secretary in the dean's office. *He died early this morning. A fire in his house. I'm very sorry. Were you a friend of his?*

Remorse burned through Thompson like acid. He had killed Smith. By his carelessness. His stupidity. He had tried to call him only once the night before to warn him to be careful. That was all.

He must get out now, he thought. Get the file to the FBI before more people died. And he must call Harriet at the *Times* immediately. Warn her. Get her police protection. He had procrastinated long enough.

Thompson felt around under the mattress for the file. It wasn't there.

He was unable to believe it. He tried to think it through, think of an explanation. Perhaps he hadn't put the file there? He had been so tired. Perhaps he just thought he had put it there. Or dreamed it. But where was it?

His bafflement gave way to rage. He ripped the bed apart. It was not there. He turned the apartment upside down—dumped out the contents of drawers and file cabinets, pulled everything from the closets, scattering Herb Franklin's possessions across the floor.

The file was gone.

He halted his frantic search and stood in the middle of a pile of loose papers on the living-room carpet, panting to get his breath.

How could anyone have taken it? No one could have the stealth to break into the apartment and steal it while he was there. Not from under his sleeping body. Or could they?

He called the *Times*. Harriet was not there. He reached her bureau chief. She had been there earlier but left, he said. No, she was not on an assignment. No, he did not know where she could be reached. Yes, he'd leave a message for her to return the call.

"It's urgent!" Thompson said.

"Yeah, isn't it always," the bureau chief replied, and hung up.

He called Harriet's apartment. He let the phone ring a long time before giving up.

A malignant suspicion was forming. He tried to suppress it, push it out of his mind, but it kept popping in again, unbidden, teasing him with its paranoid logic.

He allowed it to stay, finally, and began to examine his situation in the light of its radical premise.

Harriet had taken the file.

It was crazy, but it fit. She had the motive, she had the opportunity. The wheels in his panicked head began spinning, transporting his suspicions to their ultimate conclusion.

She was part of Zodiac.

He pounded his fists against his forehead. *It fit, dammit! It fit!*

Someone had waited for him in Hanover, and then killed Smith. Harriet had known he was going to Hanover.

Someone had spotted him outside the porno theater in Washington and tailed him through the Metro to the Air and Space Museum. Harriet had known he would meet her at that theater.

And Harriet had insisted they go after the file. And two thugs had arrived at Middleburg at almost the same time. A trap that didn't work?

He had insisted on going to the FBI. She had resisted.

And now she had taken the file.

And now someone down on Queen Street was waiting for him to emerge from Herb Franklin's apartment. And Harriet was the only one who knew he was hiding there.

And now she had disappeared.

She was the enemy. It was the simplest explanation. It fit the facts with a remarkable consistency, free of complication or contradiction. It didn't fit the emotions of those events, but those must have been only his emotions. She had even used those touching revelations about her past as a weapon to keep her distance from him.

She had deceived him totally. He had been completely taken in—by her wit, by her eyes, by that seductive curl of hair. My God, he wondered, was there no bottom to his innocence? What chance did he have, when he had been so trusting, so stupidly complacent?

Like a myopic child he had stumbled right into the middle of a battlefield. They could have killed him several times over. But instead they had used him, suckered him into fetching and delivering Roland's file into their hands.

He groaned aloud. All that remained now was for them to get rid of him. He could not outthink them. He lacked the experience, the nerve, the cunning, the resourcefulness. He should give up, surrender himself to the thug down in the street waiting for him. How easy it would be—like a mouse relaxing in a cat's jaw, knowing that further struggle is useless.

Thompson's sense of helplessness gave way gradually to a profound bitterness. The unknown forces behind her might seem omnipotent, but he had no such fear of Harriet. Her betrayal gave him something tangible to avenge.

If he could not escape this deadly army of ghosts, then he would run in the only direction left. Right at them. And the hell with the consequences. What did he have to lose?

An hour later Thompson pulled open the bedroom closet door with its full-length mirror and studied himself. He was draped in a worn, wrinkled blue suit, shiny at seat and elbows and spotted with stains on the lapels and the knees. Underneath the suit he had strapped a bath towel around his waist to add another six inches of girth and make the suit a tight but realistic fit. Herb Franklin was about his height, but a good bit fatter. Thompson was small-boned and slender, and the additional inches around the middle altered his appearance dramatically, making him not just fatter, but older—his thin face, neck, and wrists appearing fragile and withered in the capacious suit.

To further promote the aged look, Thompson had colored his hair and eyebrows white with flour from the kitchen, drawn some wrinkles around his eyes with a felt-tip pen, and stuffed pieces of foam rubber cut from the cushion of one of Franklin's Danish Modern dining chairs between his lower cheeks and gum to accentuate his jowls.

Up close in the mirror the total effect looked almost clownlike, the work of an incompetent theatrical makeup artist, but if he had any luck left at all, no one was going to get as close to him as the mirror.

He practiced walking like an old man, bent over at the waist, but the stoop just didn't look right. It seemed exaggerated, likely to attract attention. Finally he hit it. A slow waddle, back straight, stomach thrust forward, arms moving carefully at the side as if for balance.

From a distance it would work. He only had to make it to the Toyota, parked a block away.

He pulled an old leather suitcase from the bedroom closet, stuffed it with several changes of Franklin's underwear and socks, two sweaters, and two sport shirts a couple of sizes too big in the neck.

He stood, hand on the doorknob, and took one last glance at the apartment behind him. From this instant on, he told himself, he must focus his attention totally on the moment at hand. Forget yesterday, forget tomorrow, forget what might have been. An evil momentum was thrusting him toward a fatal finish and there was no one to help him.

21

Harriet had been walking for nearly an hour. She was in the farthest reaches of the cemetery, well off the tourmobile route that shuttled the busloads of tourists around among Arlington's famous gravesites. The path she was following ended at the monument of a long-forgotten World War I admiral, set under a canopy of tall elm trees and surrounded by a wide circle of hedges.

She raised her sunglasses up over her forehead and looked around. No one in sight. The sky was a pastel blue and the air felt crisp and magnificent. Ironic, she thought. It should be gloomy and overcast. She clutched the envelope in her arms and walked quickly around behind the monument.

He was sitting on the wide slab of gray marble that formed the monument's base. He looked up quickly, smiled, and motioned for her to join him.

"I'm sorry to drag you out here," Harriet said. "I wouldn't have if it wasn't important."

He nodded. He was middle-aged and expensively dressed in a bright paisley tie and a suit artfully tailored to hide the fat around his middle.

His hair, red and thinning, was cut long over the ears, giving his pink face, with its pointed nose and chin, a disarmingly pixyish look. His name was Archibald Truley. Arch to his friends. He was the CIA's chief of counterintelligence, the third-most-powerful man in the agency.

He raised his posterior a couple of inches from the marble and patted the spot next to him. Harriet sat down.

"Always good to see you, my dear. You're the only woman who can make my blood race—even a little. Makes me wish I had been born to be a family man."

Harriet smiled. "You'd have found it excruciatingly boring, I think."

Truley nodded and stared off into the distance. "I suppose you're right. But as I get on in years, I think of children sometimes." He squeezed Harriet's hand and laughed. "Don't let me get into my lonely old queer routine. I know you're not here for that. It's just that I always feel so close to you. There's hardly anyone I know anymore who I can talk to honestly."

Harriet kissed him lightly on the cheek. She had interviewed him several years ago for a series on the intelligence community, and they had became friends right away. He soon developed into one of her most important news sources. Aside from his agency connection, he traveled in the highest social, political, and diplomatic circles. He had given Harriet many invaluable pieces of information.

"Arch, listen," she began. "I called you because I'm onto a story that's getting out of hand. I can't tell you all the details right now, but believe me when I tell you it has me scared to death."

Truley stared at her in frank surprise. "I never thought I'd hear Harriet Mitchell say she was afraid of something. Let's hear it."

Harriet hesitated, then thrust the envelope into Truley's hands. "Read what's inside. It won't take you but a minute."

Truley looked at the envelope for a few seconds, turned it over, opened the flap, and drew out the thin stack of pages. Harriet pulled her sunglasses back down over her eyes and walked a few yards away from the monument, to give him a chance to concentrate on the documents. And to make certain no one was watching them.

Truley looked up at her several minutes later and nodded his head. She walked back to the base of the monument and stood in front of him.

"Where the hell did you get these?" His voice was an angry whisper. It startled her.

"They belonged to Allen Roland."

Truley shoveled them back into the envelope with a nervous hand and closed the flap. "I see," he said.

"Do they mean anything to you?"

Truley rubbed his pink chin and stared into space. "Yes and no. I've never heard of Zodiac. Or the other code names. And I pride myself on *knowing* these things."

"What about the Mexicans? The cables?"

Truley nodded. "Tommy Karamakis was DDO at Langley in 1983. He sent the cable to Mexico."

"Where is he now? Can I reach him?"

Truley shook his head. "He died in a boating accident off the Florida coast."

Harriet sat down beside him. "What about the COS—the chief-of-station in Mexico City?"

"I'm thinking. It must have been Dave Campbell—David Page Campbell. He's retired. Lives in the Canary Islands, I think."

"That's something."

"Not much, I'm afraid. If you reached him, his contract with the agency would forbid him sharing any information about the cable. It's classified NODIS. That means 'no distribution.' This was an ultra-top-secret exchange."

"What about John Graves?"

"He's head of a private security service, headquartered in Boston. He does work for the agency occasionally. He's a tough bastard with an evil reputation. The agency uses him for dirty work—stuff the operations people want done stateside but can't afford to get caught at. Graves has a huge force of goons working for him. Ex-cons, a lot of them. He's a modern-day warlord, with his own private army. If you're thinking of talking to him—or confronting him with any of this—you'd better be damned careful."

"What about Cyclops?"

Truley pressed his palms together and let his chin fall to his chest. "Yes. I thought he was dead, too. He's an assassin. A very good one. Ruthless. Crazy, probably. I thought Roland had gotten rid of him. The man seems to lead a charmed life." He pushed the envelope back into Harriet's lap. "Is this why Roland died?"

Harriet nodded. "And others, too. Now our lives are threatened."

"Our lives?"

Harriet explained Jay Thompson's involvement. "Arch, I think Zodiac is connected to the election."

"What makes you think that?"

The date. Ten/thirty. That's one week before the election. And that park in New Hampshire. I think the President's going to be there then. There must be a plot against him."

Truley took Harriet's hand and held it in both of his. "Listen to me, Harriet. Get out of this. Right now."

Harriet pretended not to hear him. "Do you know George Klimentov?" she asked.

Truley's pink face faded to white. He stood up and brushed the front of his double-breasted suit jacket, preparing to leave.

"George Klimentov?" Harriet repeated.

"He's dead, Harriet."

She swallowed. "My God! When?"

"Yesterday. The metropolitan police dragged him out of some display in the Air and Space Museum. Very macabre business. Killed with a poison dart."

Harriet stood up. "That's awful! He was going to give Jay information about Zodiac!"

Truley seemed genuinely alarmed now. He was moving his arms in agitation, anxious to terminate the conversation. "Harriet, I've told you all I can. If I find out more, I'll try to help, but I warn you, you ought to get straight out of it!"

Harriet clutched his sleeve. "You're not telling me something, Arch. Please!"

Truley shook his head. "That's all I can tell you!"

"What about the notes? The 'Zodiac ten/thirty' and 'Capricorn wants domestic site for Zodiac.' Who wrote them? Do you have any idea? Anything?"

Truley pushed her hand away. "I must go now. I'll get in touch."

"Arch!"

Truley started to walk back around the monument to the path on the other side. He turned and looked at Harriet for one last time. "I recognized the handwriting," he said.

"Whose is it?"

Truley shook his head and looked away. "I can't tell you that. Sorry."

"What are you going to do about it?"

"I don't know. Probably nothing. Nothing I can do."

Truley was gone.

Harriet stood by the monument for several minutes, collecting her thoughts. She had gone to her best source, and found out nothing. Except that someone else had been killed.

She looked at her watch. Almost one o'clock. She'd better call Jay. She expected that he would be furious with her for taking the file, but she was ready with apologies and explanations. There was a reception in the evening at the Turkish embassy that she had to cover. Shapiro, the bureau chief, had bullied her into it, in exchange for letting her stay on the Roland story. It was a meaningless social event. Perhaps she could take Jay with her. It would get their minds off Zodiac for a few hours.

Leaving the cemetery by Southgate Road, Harriet walked several blocks in the direction of the Pentagon until she found a public phone.

She dialed Franklin's number and let the phone ring twice, hung up, then rang back—their prearranged signal. But Thompson didn't answer. She waited five minutes and repeated the procedure. Still no answer. She checked the number with information, then made one last attempt.

No answer.

Was he so angry that he refused to pick up the phone?

Harriet hurried to the Pentagon Metro station and rode the two stops to Rosslyn, resigned by this time to going to the embassy reception without him. But she must at least see him first, to make sure that he was okay.

The apartment door was locked. A note had been taped to it. She pulled it off and unfolded it.

Harriet. Thanks for everything. Jay.

Back on the street again, she saw that the Toyota she had borrowed from Freddie Coyle for the trip to Middleburg was also gone.

She didn't know whether to be furious or frightened. How could he abandon her, just like that? Right in the middle of the most important, dangerous . . .

He was crazy to do this, she thought. Where could he have gone? He needed her to help him. He really did need her more than he knew.

Or was it the other way around?

22

John Graves's stomach was killing him.

All the way across on the ferry from Fisher's Island to New London, and down the Connecticut Turnpike into New York City, he dampened the burning pain with periodic gulps of Maalox, and made busywork for himself on his telephone in the back of the limousine. Now, as the Lincoln sped down the FDR Drive into Manhattan, he could think of no more calls to make, and he sat uncomfortably, trying to brace his nerves for the coming ordeal.

Graves's ulcers were a carefully guarded secret. Friends, associates, and enemies alike believed him to be forged out of a substance akin to steel. It was an impression he had worked to cultivate. A reputation for invincibility was the best edge a businessman could have. He had learned that the hard way, fighting his way up from Boston's Irish ghetto of Chelsea, where he spent most of his teens as a petty thief. In his twenties he graduated to muscle jobs for local hoodlums and loan sharks, and later into organizing goon squads for strikebreaking on the Boston docks. His talent for organizing was noticed but not appreciated by the local syndicate; after several close brushes with death, Graves began to reconsider his goals.

He decided to become, if not exactly law-abiding, at least legitimate, and he turned his talents to the creation of a security-guard service, enlisting many of his old associates in crime into the work. By the time he was thirty-five, he had made himself a multimillionaire.

Graves Security, Inc., now controlled a ten-thousand-man force whose specialties included assignments from simple bodyguard and plant-security work to sophisticated industrial espionage, strikebreaking, sabotage, and propaganda. When accountants and lawyers weren't enough, corporations and individuals of wealth and power turned to John Graves.

The qualities that enabled Graves to prevail in such enterprises were pugnacity, steady nerves, and a will so ruthless that he was the envy of many of the entrepreneurs whose paths he crossed.

But this afternoon Graves was uncharacteristically nervous. He wished that he had never agreed to accept the contract for Zodiac's security. He felt he had made a fundamental error in taking on something he could not completely control. The big money—two and a half million—had seduced him into a treacherous situation, involving him and his company in serious criminal acts. And more criminal acts would have to be committed if Zodiac's secrecy were to be preserved.

Too late to back out now. He would have to see it through.

Graves's chauffeur and bodyguard, an ex-con named Mojo, maneuvered the heavy vehicle off the drive onto the Forty-ninth Street exit by the UN Building, and proceeded rapidly across town to the entrance of 30 Rockefeller Plaza. Mojo jumped out, pulled open the rear door for Graves, and looked at him inquiringly.

Graves nodded. "Wait for me by the skating rink. I don't know how long this is going to take. Call the suite at the Sherry Netherland. I'll stay in town tonight. We'll go back to the island in the morning."

Graves, in a perfectly pressed pearl-gray banker's suit, was sweating profusely as he stepped into the private elevator at the back of the building. He mopped his face with a handkerchief and stared at the elevator control panel. It showed no floor buttons at all; as Graves waited, the doors slid closed and the elevator began its ascent to the top floor, seventy stories up.

The door opened soundlessly and Graves stepped out into a small reception area lined with luxurious black-walnut paneling and Japanese watercolors. Light from recessed fixtures along the walls left the center of the room rather dark and gloomy. Graves stepped across the chocolate-colored carpeting and sat down in one of two beige sofas that faced each other across a bronze-and-glass coffee table. The surface of the table was empty—no ashtrays, magazines, or plants—and the room itself contained nothing more than the watercolors, the sofas, and the table. Except for the elevator bay, the room did not even appear to have a door.

Graves sat and waited, knowing that he was being watched through a monitor in the wall. He affected all the nonchalance he could muster, but as the wait dragged on, his composure began to crumble, and he dabbed at his forehead with the handkerchief.

A female voice addressed him from a speaker hidden in the ceiling: "You may come in now, Mr. Graves."

One of the walnut panels slid back to reveal a suite of offices on the other side. Graves stepped through and glanced around to get his bearings. The door slid back into position behind him and clicked shut. A thin middle-aged woman, the unlikely owner of the voice he had just heard, sat behind a desk in the anteroom of the suite.

She nodded at him, unsmiling. "You may join the general. It will be just the two of you today."

She pointed a finger in the direction of the door at the extreme right of the suite. Graves walked to the door and opened it, thinking of the many subtle ways these people employed to intimidate him. In offices all over the city, secretaries would jump to his slightest wish, and heads of corporations would meet him in their lobbies. These people let him know what they thought of him—another flunky hired to do a job.

The room beyond was a light and airy dining room, with windows on two sides that commanded a magnificent view of the Hudson River and the Palisades on the west, and the lower half of Manhattan on the south. The rows of vertical louvers on the window blinds facing south had been tilted to deflect the direct rays of the sun, which poured in on the tall plants and luxurious furnishings with an intensity that seemed far stronger than at street level. A portable bar had been set up under one window, and the sunlight bounced off the multicolored bottles and sparkling crystal so brightly it made Graves squint. The setting was deceptively festive, as if the occasion called for a celebration of some kind.

General William Ward, director of the CIA, was sitting in a big leather armchair pulled up to the dining table, reading through a thick stack of reports and idly swirling a tall glass of Perrier water with one hand.

"Ah, Graves, so there you are."

Ward did not get up, but simply held out a limp hand to be shaken, then motioned Graves to a chair. Graves had met Ward in person only once before, in the same suite of offices. From then on he had been dealt with through an intermediary close to Ward. He had taken an instant dislike to the man. He found him condescending and phony, with a changeable, volatile temperament.

But the dislike went deeper than mannerisms. Ward was a third-generation descendent of a patrician New York family, a career Army officer with a West Point degree. The military career did not redeem Ward in Graves's eyes, because it had been spent in military intelligence, well behind the lines. Ward had never proved himself under fire, and Graves suspected he was a coward. He had had a gentleman's career, a series of sinecures arranged by social and political pull—like his present post as DCI, secured by huge family donations to the presidential campaign of John Douglas Mills in 1980. Graves had fought all his life to gain his power; Ward had been able to buy his.

Ward waved a hand in the direction of the bar. "Fix something for yourself, Graves."

Graves did—a double shot of sour-mash whiskey. As he poured it, he studied Ward out of the corner of his eye, anxious to assess his mood. Ward was a small, wiry man of about fifty-five—a "banty rooster" they'd have called him in Graves's old neighborhood—with red hair, close-cropped in a military cut, and a toothbrush mustache, the hallmark, Graves knew, of a fussy, overly authoritarian personality. His suit was a close-fitting Edwardian cut, a strange cross between a uniform and a hunting outfit.

"I don't drink, myself, during the day," Ward said. "I find it lowers the old efficiency. Can't think clearly with booze in the snoot. But I suppose you've been under a lot of pressure lately."

Graves nodded, refusing to be goaded.

"Well, that's what you're here about," Ward said. "No sense kidding around. Let's have a status report."

Graves told Ward what Farrell had told him that morning on the beach at Fisher's Island. He retailed the disasters without apology.

Ward listened, a tight grin on his face, as if to say, I'm not a bit surprised. When Graves had finished, Ward looked directly at him, holding eye contact until it had become a threatening stare.

"What became of Thompson?" Ward asked.

"He evaded our surveillance in Rosslyn."

"You mean he got away?"

"I have twenty men looking for him. They'll find him."

Ward shook his head and took a sip of the Perrier. "You'll find him when? You better make it a hundred men. We don't have much time."

Graves started to object, then thought better of it. Twenty men were already ten too many, he knew. You don't conduct secret manhunts as if you were the National Guard on maneuvers. He'd better at least spell that out.

"That'll increase our security problems, General."

"I'm aware of that! But if we don't have both Thompson and the file—and an early assessment of the damage he's done—in a couple of days, then security won't mean a damn thing. We'll be in trouble."

Graves answered back with a shot in the dark: "Maybe the file doesn't have anything in it."

Ward's grin broadened. "That would get you off the hook nicely, wouldn't it." He sipped his Perrier. "In fact, you may be right. But Roland had men still loyal to him in the agency. I cleaned most of them out, but some inevitably were missed. Even though I've compartmentalized Zodiac so it involves the fewest possible number—and all of them of unquestioned loyalty—he may have pieced together enough from the odd bit here and there. It's been done. Spies talk to each other. That bastard Klimentov undoubtedly leaked something important to him. We have to assume he knew something. How much he knew, we'll know when you get that damned file."

Graves nodded.

Ward swirled his Perrier again, with an elaborate deliberation that turned it into an insult. Graves would have loved nothing more than knocking the glass from his hand.

"What are you doing about Harriet Mitchell?" Ward demanded.

"We're following her. She'll lead us to Thompson again."

"Will she?"

"It's likely."

The grin again. "Did it ever occur to you, Graves, that she could *also* know the contents of the file?"

Graves hesitated. It hadn't occurred to him.

"Of course. But we need Thompson in any case. She's our way to him. We can round her up anytime."

Ward slammed the glass of Perrier down, sending the ice cubes and the sparkling water splashing out across the table.

"Then why in *hell* don't you catch her and squeeze it out of her!"

Ward's face was scarlet, the veins in his forehead pulsing. Graves had never seen such an explosive burst of temper in a man. Ward stared at the empty glass in his hand for a split second, then hurled it at Graves's face. Graves ducked, and the glass hit the paneled wall behind him and shattered.

Ward rose to his feet. "You stupid bastard! Get her and find out from her where Thompson is! Immediately!"

Graves would have killed any other man for less. His stomach was on fire, and he clenched and unclenched his fists. Someday he *would* kill him. If he promised himself that, he could sit on his emotions for the present, and humor this strutting little martinet. Self-preservation before pride.

Ward picked up another glass from the bar, and forsaking the Perrier, dumped a healthy three inches of bourbon into it. "You think you're under pressure!" He was still yelling. "*I'm under pressure!* You can't imagine! Zodiac is less than *three days away!*" He returned to his chair, took a slug of the whiskey, and calmed himself. Graves sat immobile, not trusting himself to speak. When Ward had control over himself again, he continued, his voice shaky, but several decibels lower. Graves thought he saw tears in the corners of his eyes.

"Capricorn left the security arrangements up to me! You're *my* responsibility! I should have used men from the agency for this. They'd have plugged the leak by now. But I wanted to keep them out of it. I needed the agency people for Zodiac!"

It sounded to Graves as if Ward was preparing his defense before Capricorn.

"Don't forget, I'm already using your best man. Cyclops."

Ward's voice started to rise again. "And don't *you* forget that compared to those idiots of yours, Cyclops has performed miracles. Miracles! *He* got Roland! *He* got Feldman! *He* got the files and manuscript from the publisher! *He* searched Thompson's and Mitchell's apartments! *He* got Smith! *He* got Klimentov! He did it *all!* What have your stumblebums done? Nothing!"

Graves sighed and covered his eyes with his hand. He finished off the whiskey in the glass and stood up to leave. "The hell with lunch. I've obviously got work to do."

Ward stood, too. "That's the smartest thing I've heard you say today."

As Graves started toward the door, Ward's mood suddenly changed. "John!"

Graves turned to look at him. He was cringing over the table, the glass of whiskey cradled in his hands. Graves thought he looked demented.

"I can stall Capricorn until tomorrow. Please give me something to tell him by then! Please!"

Graves stared at him, then walked from the room without answering.

III
The Trap

23

Harriet didn't even know where the Turkish embassy was located, so she was surprised when she saw it. It occupied a magnificent mansion on the southwest corner of Twenty-third and Sheridan Circle, opulent even by the standards of Embassy Row.

Once past the guards at the outer door and the line of servants in the vestibule, Harriet searched the ornate reception room for familiar faces, and couldn't find many. Members of the media were nowhere in evidence, and few of the powerful were on hand. Harriet recognized a smattering of congressmen and senators, a few ambassadors, and almost no one from the White House staff. The vast bulk of the several hundred guests swirling through the embassy's front salons was composed of that plentiful substance known as Bureaucracy—low level staffers from the departments and agencies, junior-grade Pentagon officers, embassy personnel, congressional staff members, and an unknown number of Washington lawyers and lobbyists.

With Thompson, this might have been fun, she thought. Well, the hell with him. She felt in a reckless mood. She snatched a glass of champagne from a passing tray and tipped its contents down her throat.

A line was forming to greet the new ambassador and his wife, and Harriet joined it. The ambassador, Mr. Ibrahim Fawzi, small and dark-haired, stood stiffly in his formal tails and sash. He bowed to Harriet when her turn in the reception line finally came, and shook her hand, his mustache twitching comically.

His wife, standing beside him with her feet planted slightly apart, as if she were afraid someone might try to bowl her over, was bigger and taller, with shrewd fiery black eyes, thick brows, and a full mouth made fuller with bright red lipstick. She wore a pungent musklike perfume, and her floor-length gown was intricately patterned and richly colored— a jarring backdrop for the panoply of accessories that accompanied it. She was dazzling and outrageous—a Gypsy queen, blatantly earthy and sexual.

She favored Harriet with an enormous smile and a hard hand squeeze, and said something in heavily accented English that Harriet could not understand. Harriet smiled back, congratulated her, and wished her a pleasant stay in Washington, wincing inwardly when she thought how Washington society would savage this naive and primitive original. She moved to a corner of the room, dug out her cassette recorder from her purse, and started to make notes. She liked the ambassador and his wife immediately, so she decided to strike the first social blows for their side.

Several glasses of champagne later, Harriet had finished her notetaking and was trying to escape from the counsel-general of Oman, who had taken to following her around the room. She had just about decided to sneak out and go home when a bustle and murmur of excitement near the front entrance caught her attention. Both the crowd and the noise level in the room seemed to drain from the fringes and collect near the doorway, and a small wedge of serious-faced men appeared, pushing through the press of bodies with determination. Harriet caught a glimpse of a motor-cycle helmet and several pairs of dark glasses and guessed at once that the Vice-President had arrived.

Vice-President Raymond Beecher was a tall man, and his face was visible above the crowd as he emerged through the doorway, big smile flashing around the hall like a searchlight. His mane of graying hair was brushed across his forehead in a schoolboy fashion that emphasized his good looks and artfully hid the forehead's low, sloping contours. His jaw was large, and his chin strong, with a cleft in the middle that excited his many female admirers. His movie-star appearance was softened by his eyes, which were not the cunning eyes of the politician, but large, limpid, and blue, with long lashes. His lips seemed a trifle too large, and he had a habit of posing them in a slightly parted manner that hinted of the sybarite.

At forty-eight, Beecher did not have a very distinguished career behind him. Before Mills picked him as his running mate, he had served three terms as a Republican congressman from upstate New York, and had been divorced by his wife, the daughter of a rich Saratoga Springs family. He compiled a poor record in the House, both for attendance and for not doing his homework. Washington insiders considered him intelligent but lazy, without real ambition. "Born to be a vice-president," one pundit cracked after the election of 1980. Beecher's strengths were his glibness, his good looks, and his charm. His appeal to the female voters had been an enormous help to Mills, whom women generally distrusted.

Beecher was a celebrity more than a politician. He seemed to have plenty of time free for television appearances, because even for the vice-presidency, a position notoriously short on responsible duties, Beecher was underemployed. His function was that of a public-relations man, pouring on the charm and the explanations for the administration whenever and wherever it was useful. It suited him, and he was good at it.

Harriet watched, amused, as Beecher worked the room. He was brought across first to be introduced to the new ambassador and his wife, and after a brief exchange of pleasantries he was escorted by one of his aides and two members of the embassy staff around to meet the other guests. It was the standard, polished VIP performance. He would shake a lot of hands, make a point of addressing everyone by his first name; then, after one complete circuit of the place, his minions would close ranks around him and he would be out the door amid a chorus of last-minute greetings and good-byes. Last to arrive, first to leave.

Harriet saw the entourage moving in her direction. She tried to slip out of the way, but she found herself hemmed in by the crowd and positioned directly in Beecher's path. He finished shaking someone's hand, looked up with a bored expression, and moved several steps closer. Harriet fought to push free from the crush of bodies clustered around him. She elbowed her way a few feet backward, but the next time his gaze swept past her position, his head stopped and his eyes widened. She had snagged his attention just as surely as if she had thrown out a line with a hook on it. She glared at him; he smiled back.

Beecher pushed himself in Harriet's direction. His aide, a pink-faced young man with a self-important manner, tried to shove Harriet out of the way and squeeze Beecher past to meet a distinguished-looking old man being pulled toward the Vice-President by one of the embassy staffers. But Beecher wouldn't let him. He held his ground, and fixing his eyes directly on Harriet, addressed the aide in a loud voice: "Now, hold on a minute, Stanley! I haven't met this obviously important person right here in front of me."

His aide, confused and hostile, turned to face Harriet. "Oh, yes," he muttered.

Harriet pushed her hand forward quickly, and Beecher took it.

"Harriet Mitchell, the New York *Times*," she said.

Beecher, holding her hand very firmly, didn't shake it, but instead pulled her closer to him, so that she found herself, thanks to his grip on her and the press of the crowd around him, suddenly squeezed against him, their faces inches apart.

"I've heard about you," he said, changing his tone from hearty to intimate. "I suppose I should run for my life."

"I was just going to say the same thing," Harriet replied.

Beecher arched his eyebrows. "Really?"

He had dropped his voice so low that no one near them could hear their conversation against the background party chatter. She felt giddy from the champagne and the warmth of the room, and to her dismay, she found herself fighting a crazy impulse to collapse into his arms. His large eyes were fixed on her, and she could feel their gaze all the way down to her knees.

"But I didn't know how beautiful you were," he said.

"Well, I'm glad you're having the chance to find out, Mr. Vice-President."

"Ray."

"Ray."

"So am I, Harriet."

"I'm covering this for the *Times*, Mr. Vice-President. Perhaps you'd like me to quote you on something?"

"Ray."

"Ray."

Beecher dropped her hand. "Always working, huh? Well, I will be leaving here in about five minutes, and I would be happy to give you a good quote then. Why don't you let me take you home?"

From the tone of his voice, it was clear he didn't expect her to refuse. Before she could reply, the aide interrupted and Beecher was being introduced to the Paraguayan vice-consul and his wife, and then some woman with a name Harriet didn't quite catch. She was young and pretty and eager to make an impression on Beecher. Political groupie, Harriet decided.

"Maybe you should take *her* home, Ray?" Harriet said. She could scarcely believe her own bitchiness.

Beecher laughed. "By God, I wish I could take both of you home, but I promised you first."

Harriet felt her face flushing as the other woman stared at her in naked awe. Harriet met the stare, trying to find the right facial muscles to convey her disinterest.

Beecher's arm was suddenly turning her around with him, and the girl slid out of view, to be replaced by three members of the Philippine delegation, including the ambassador. Beecher introduced Harriet to them, and she found herself making small talk with one of the ambassador's aides.

"You must find your public responsibilities very burdensome, too," he said politely, "being so close to the man who could one day become president."

"Well, I . . ."

Two photographers covering the reception were clicking away at her and Beecher, and it dawned on her that they had been taking pictures of them together every time Beecher was introduced to someone new. Well, of course, Harriet thought. Everyone liked to have a picture of himself shaking hands with the Veep. How many times had she been photographed with him? Five? Six?

Beecher completed the circuit of the room, and left, keeping a strong grip on Harriet, who decided there was nothing to be gained by protesting.

Outside the embassy, the motorcycle cop led the way, helmet and polished black boots gleaming in the streetlights, followed by Beecher's aide, and Beecher, with Harriet in tow, and two Secret Service agents bringing up the rear. A motorcycle and two chauffeured limousines were waiting at the curb. With practiced precision she and the Vice-President were ushered into the front limousine, the aide and the Secret Service agents piled into the rear one, and the cop kicked his motorcycle into life, flipped on a pair of flashing red lights near his handlebars, and led the procession off at a stately pace around Sheridan Circle.

Harriet felt drowsy, and suppressed an enormous yawn. "This is like a funeral!" she said. "Do you always travel this way?"

"I'm the Vice-President, Harriet," Beecher replied solemnly. He dropped his arm around her shoulder and pulled her across the backseat next to him.

"Well, that's your funeral, I guess." A dumb remark, she realized as soon as she said it. It made her giggle. The caravan turned onto Massachusetts Avenue and headed north. Beecher's hand insinuated itself onto her breast and caressed it lightly. She pushed it a few inches away with a weak nudge.

"You're taking me home, remember? I live in the other direction. Dupont Circle."

Beecher chuckled. Alone with her in the dark, luxurious backseat of the limousine, he seemed less boyish. "I *am* taking you home, Harriet," he replied. "To my home."

Harriet felt dizzy, but euphoric. "You're taking me to *your* home?"

"Yes."

"How come?"

"Well . . . we can relax there, have a drink . . . and you can ask me anything you want."

"I can?"

"I promise."

Beecher squeezed her shoulder. "Does that sound like fun?"

Harriet sighed. The vice-presidential hand reappeared on her breast, and she left it there.

The caravan picked up speed through Rock Creek Park, and was soon winding up the drive of the Naval Observatory to the Vice-President's mansion. As the tires crunched to a stop before the rambling old Victorian house, Harriet started laughing to herself, a tipsy sort of laugh, full of some private delight.

"What's so funny?" Beecher asked.

"You haven't changed a bit, have you?"

24

Jay Thompson drove into Burnham, New Hampshire, at about midnight. He had been on the road from Alexandria almost continuously for eight hours, making only one stop for gasoline, food, and a trip to a men's room to rid himself of his vaudeville disguise.

The village of Burnham, situated in a sparsely populated central region of the state, barely existed as a town. If it had not been for the sign announcing its location, Thompson would have missed it completely. The only local businesses in sight—a gas station and a general store—had long since closed for the day, and there were no signs of life anywhere. The few houses along the road were dark, and no cars had passed in nearly half an hour.

Several miles north of town on Route 10 he saw a spluttering neon sign announcing the Sleepy Oaks Motel, and pulled the Toyota into the narrow gravel driveway next to the office. The establishment consisted of one long single-story wood-frame building, containing about eight units, set in an unlandscaped area close to the edge of the highway. Stark and depressing.

It was the only motel he had seen near town, and it obviously had vacancies. One other car was parked in the drive. The owner's?

Thompson waited inside the tiny office, taking in the decor. The walls were a dark imitation wood paneling covered with little discount-store plaques: "The Buck Stops Here" and "In God We Trust. All Others Pay Cash." A small counter with a cash register on it was crowded into one end of the office, and behind the counter there was a door, slightly ajar. From the room beyond, Thompson could see the flickering blue light and hear the murmur of a television set. It was many cuts below his last accommodation, the Hay-Adams in Washington. It didn't seem possible that he had been there only a week ago.

He hit the bell on the counter a couple of times and a small-framed, balding man in his late forties eventually appeared in the doorway, wearing a white undershirt and wiping the sleep from his eyes. His movements and expressions conveyed boredom and defeat.

"Sorry, fella. I guess I was dozin' off back there." His voice was flat, with a pronounced Yankee twang. "We don't get many guests this time of year."

Thompson was surprised. "I thought the fall foliage season was a big tourist attraction up here."

The owner made a vague, dismissing gesture with his hand. "Well, we don't get many guests *anytime* of the year would be closer to the truth. Ever since that interstate extension was finished in seventy-six."

Thompson nodded sympathetically. The man passed the guest register across to him and handed him a ball-point pen. Thompson hesitated, then signed it "Allen Roland, Washington, D.C."

The man glanced at it, then looked up at Thompson. "Well, Mr. Roland, if you drove all the way from Washington today, you must be tuckered out. I got a nice room for you—number one, first door down. Hell, I got eight nice rooms for you. You could take your pick."

"Number one will be fine."

The owner took a key off the hook on the wall behind him and handed it to Thompson. "I'll have to ask you for the night's rent in advance. You understand, Mr. Roland . . ."

Thompson said that he didn't mind a bit, and drew out his wallet. After he had paid, the man introduced himself as Elmer Stark, and chatted on for several minutes about the weather and the price of gasoline. Then Stark asked him if he would like to have a drink with him before he retired, and Thompson accepted.

"The wife is out tonight," he said, ushering Thompson into the room in back. "So I'm just sitting around having a few pops for myself, watching the boob tube. Welcome your company. 'Course, I know you must be tired, so you probably won't want to stay but for a minute, I can understand that. This place back here is a goddurned mess, I'm sorry to say, but we had to let the cleaning lady go, what with business bein' so slow."

Thompson could smell alcohol on Elmer Stark's breath; the man was lonely and bored and wanted to talk. Thompson saw that he might take advantage of that.

The room behind the counter appeared to be the Stark living room. It was small, about ten by ten, and congested with cheap maple furniture and a thick layer of dust. Elmer Stark motioned Thompson to the sofa, and brought him a whiskey with water and ice, and a refill for himself. He dropped into an old easy chair with a threadbare blanket thrown over it and started talking, complaining about his son, about the motel business, the town of Burnham, the state of New Hampshire, and the world in general.

Stark had not bothered to turn down the TV set, so it blabbed on, dim black-and-white reruns and loud late-night commercials hawking the local stores and local merchandise.

Thompson pretended to be interested, but when Stark returned from a trip to the bathroom, he grabbed the conversational lead. "Tell me about this Halloween Park," he said.

Stark looked over at him, his drink halfway to his mouth. The blood drained from his face, turning his alcoholic ruddy tan into chalk.

"How did you hear about that place?" The emphasis was on the "that."

Thompson shrugged. "Well, it's where the President went hunting once, I understand. The newspapers covered the event, and I guess I read about it then. I hear it's a big place. Must be the most important thing in a town of this size."

The atmosphere in the room had altered noticeably. Elmer Stark became all at once cagey and suspicious, and a subtle strain of hostility crept into his voice.

"Most important thing? Well, I don't know about that. I don't hardly ever hear anything about it, from one year to the next. What business did you say you was in?"

Thompson told him he was a staff writer for the *National Geographic*.

"We're doing a piece on game preserves in a future issue, and I'm supposed to check this one out. I hear it's loaded with exotic animals."

Stark seemed to be struggling with himself, deciding whether or not to talk. But having an audience and something to tell it that it wanted to hear was too powerful a pleasure to be denied. Stark fixed himself another drink of whiskey and sat down on the sofa next to Thompson.

"I'll tell you one thing, straight off," he said in an exaggeratedly conspiratorial voice. "The fellas that own that park sure are publicity-shy. You ain't the first reporter who's come around here asking questions and getting nowhere, I can tell you that."

Thompson waved his hand, dismissing Stark's remark. "Oh, it's all settled between the park owners and the magazine. They're taking me on a tour through the place tomorrow."

Stark appeared to be impressed by the news. "I'll be damned," he said. "You'll be the first. They don't like anybody even coming *near* to that place anymore."

Stark took a deep draft from his glass and exhaled with a low burp. "They always was pretty fussy about who got in, you unnerstan'. Had to be a member an' all that. I was in there many times during the early seventies, though. I was working for Johnny Upton then, cutting lumber. The park used to make their taxes by selling off pulp wood and saw timber. The damn place is as big as several towns, and it's got the durndest wild pigs in there—boars, they call 'em—that could kill a man. Some of them is over four hundred pounds, and they're escaping all the time. The fence goes a foot or so underground and runs all the way around the whole park—that's thirty miles, I'm told—but those pigs still bust through. We had a couple near here last year. Killed one of the neighbor's dogs—a big German shepherd."

"I understand Senator MacNair is a member."

Stark nodded vigorously. "Oh, yeah. He's a big shot around this neck of the woods. And he's sure to belong to anything that likes to keep other folks out."

Stark rose unsteadily and headed toward a cupboard behind the television set. "Years ago *Yankee* magazine did an article on that place. They say in there the place used to be called Hallowell Park, after the original owner, back in the 1800's. But it was always such a spooky place—you know, kind of mysterious-like—so that folks started callin' it Halloween

Park, and it stuck. They say a number of our past presidents came to hunt there. I've got that article around here somewhere."

Stark rooted around in the cupboard for a long time. Thompson suggested that he fetch it for him tomorrow, but Stark had warmed to the subject, and like most drunks, had lost all sense of time. His main concern was to keep Thompson's company.

He eventually emerged with the copy of the magazine and dropped it onto Thompson's lap. "It's all in there," he mumbled. "You can read all about it right in there. I'm glad I saved it. You never know when it'll come in handy . . . for something . . ."

Thompson watched Stark fall asleep. It happened in mid-sentence. His head inched forward, his mouth fell open, and within seconds he was breathing deeply and slowly, his sad face looking troubled even in repose. Thompson removed the drink from his hand, turned off the TV set, and sat down to look at the article. Entitled "Thirty-Thousand Acres Inside a Fence!", it began, "Although there's little publicity about it, Halloween Park is still going strong. . . ."

A door in the kitchen suddenly slammed shut, and moments later a woman appeared in the doorway. She was about thirty years old, and was wearing a white blouse, unbuttoned halfway, and a pair of blue jeans that fit her so tightly that the mid-seam running between her legs separated the lips of her pudenda into twin bulges. Her dark blond hair was disheveled and her lipstick smeared, and she teetered momentarily and steadied herself with one hand on the doorframe. The other hand was holding a cigarette between thumb and forefinger, the flame end cupped in the palm, the way a cowboy might hold it.

She looked both hostile and lewd. "Who the hell are you?" she asked.

25

Vice-President Beecher led Harriet to a small sitting room upstairs, off the main bedroom, and mixed drinks from a portable bar next to the sofa that faced the fireplace. Being suddenly alone with him, after four years, brought a flood of memories rushing back. Unhappy memories, mostly.

"I see you still drink these things," he said, handing her a wine spritzer and sitting on the sofa beside her.

"You introduced me to them, as I recall."

"I don't remember that." Beecher slipped one arm along the back of the sofa cusions behind Harriet's head and let his fingers rest in her hair.

"A party at the Gardners' in Georgetown, four years ago," she said. "I was a green reporter just assigned to the Washington bureau, you were a third-term congressman. We argued about the hostage crisis in Iran. I was for apologizing to the Iranians; you wanted a naval blockade."

Beecher smiled and shook his head. "We hit it off right from the start."

"Then you asked me out to dinner and got mad at me because I wouldn't go to bed with you."

"*That* I remember. It took me weeks to get you into bed. I became obsessed with the idea."

Harriet remembered the tremendous tension she had felt. "I was afraid to sleep with you. You'd been with so many other women I was sure I'd be a big disappointment."

Beecher nodded and placed a hand on Harriet's knee. "And by the time I did get you into bed, I was already in love with you. So your strategy worked brilliantly."

"It wasn't a strategy, Ray." Harriet pulled his hand free and placed it on the sofa.

Beecher laughed. Harriet watched the self-conscious flash of his perfect white teeth and remembered how that laugh had always disturbed her. A laugh that listened to itself laughing. Yet she had been crazy about him four years ago. Crazy. That was the word. What was it that had made him so appealing? Even then she could dissect his personality into a hundred small characteristics—and find fault with half of them. Had she been that naive four years ago? That easily impressed? Perhaps, she thought, but somehow the whole of Raymond Beecher had seemed greater than the sum of his parts. She used to think he was the sexiest man she had ever known.

Was that why she had fallen for him? Thinking he was the cure for her problems?

"I always found you irresistible," Beecher said, as if following her thoughts. "A bitch, in many ways, to tell you the honest truth, but irresistible nonetheless."

"Thanks!"

Beecher's remark infuriated her. She remembered similar remarks from the past. She had forgotten how sexist he was.

She took a deep drink of the spritzer. On top of the champagne she knew it was going to give her a splitting headache. But she had wanted to get drunk tonight from the moment she had first arrived at the embassy. This makes the second time this week, she thought. She really had to cut it out. She pressed the cool side of the tumbler against her cheek for a moment, and noticed the discreet gold decoration on the glass.

"I didn't know vice-presidents had their own seal," she said.

Beecher ignored the dig and raised his own seal-decorated glass to his lips. The tension between them was strong. Harriet felt hot and uncomfortable, and Beecher seemed to be nervous, on edge about something.

"Well, how do you like it?" Harriet asked. "Being vice-president?"

Beecher opened a hand and held it out, palm upward. Harriet noticed that it trembled slightly. "I don't know if anyone ever *liked* being vice-president. But still . . ." Beecher forced a laugh. "Good hours, easy work. Great fringe benefits."

"Well, you don't *look* very happy."

Beecher said nothing.

"What will you do next year?"

"What do you mean?" Beecher's face registered alarm.

"After you and Mills lose the election?"

Beecher sighed and leaned back against the sofa. "You media types. You're all so damned sure we're going to lose."

"Oh, come on, Ray. The polls are predicting a solid Conway victory. You have to admit it looks pretty grim."

"It *looks* grim. The polls have been wrong before."

"By ten percent?"

"It's five percent. And there are nine days of campaigning left. We're going to surprise you."

"I've had my fill of unpleasant surprises recently."

"John Mills is a great president. You'll appreciate that someday."

Harriet thought Beecher's voice lacked conviction. "He's been a disaster. You don't have to defend him to me."

"Like most political reporters, you don't understand a damned thing about leadership."

"I think I liked you better when you were a congressman."

Beecher turned his head to look directly at her. "Not enough to marry me, apparently."

"That was four years ago. I had my own career to pursue. And journalism and congressional wifism just don't mix." Harriet picked up her drink and took another deep swallow. "Anyway, you know it was more than my journalism career that kept me from marrying you."

"Refresh my mind."

"Do I have to?"

"No."

"Well, I will. It had something to do with a pushy teenager named Sally Armstrong. You remember—big tits, small waist, round heels."

"I'd forgotten how possessive you were. And she was not a teenager. She was twenty-three years old."

"She must have been retarded, then. To screw you in your office during lunch hour. I walked in on the two of you, remember? And when the word got around that I was seeing you, I began to learn that everyone I knew had slept with you! Every time we went to a party or dinner, some broad would pull me aside and want to compare notes on you. It was humiliating! Somehow it didn't augur well for marriage."

"That's ridiculous!"

"And I know you're still busy running the score up. I wish I could tell you the number of women I've heard 'confess' to having sex with you. Even if half of them are lying, you'd still be pretty busy. I'm embarrassed these days even to admit I ever went out with you."

Beecher's face darkened in anger. "You were frigid, Harriet. What was I supposed to do?"

"Frigid?" she shot back. "I thought that term went out with 'hubba hubba.' You were insensitive and selfish!"

"Okay. Let's not talk about the good old days. There's no point being bitter about things that happened over four years ago."

"I'm not bitter," Harriet mumbled. She felt bitter.

Beecher walked over to the window on the far end of the room. He pulled back the heavy drape and stared out into the darkness of the Naval Observatory park.

"Why didn't you come to me for help?" he asked.

"Who said I needed help?"

Beecher turned and looked at her over his shoulder. "I can read the New York *Times*, Harriet. I know you've been following the story of Roland's suicide. And I know there's something . . . fishy connected with it."

"Like what?"

Beecher didn't answer. He let the drape fall back into place and returned to the sofa, looking thoughtful.

"We both need help," he said.

Harriet studied him. His face betrayed some serious inner preoccupation. His eyes seemed unfocused and the corners of his mouth strained and tight. It was uncharacteristic of him, Harriet thought. She could never recall his facial muscles displaying anything more profound than an occasional petulance. Now he appeared genuinely disturbed.

"What are you talking about?" she asked.

"You're caught up in something that's way over your head."

She wondered how deep Beecher's concept of trouble really went. Was there some scandal he was trying to hide, or did he really know something about Zodiac? She had to be careful. "Tell me about it."

"Look," Beecher said, an edge of exasperation in his voice. "I want to help you. Don't make it any harder than it is already. I know that you and some book editor from New York were involved in helping Allen Roland write his memoirs. I know that Roland was up to something peculiar, and I know that you and that editor have stumbled across dangerous information. Information that some people are desperate to lay their hands on."

Harriet was surprised that he knew so much. "How are you going to help me?"

"I can offer you Secret Service protection. Until we get to the bottom of this."

"We?"

"Yes, 'we.' I said I needed some help, too." Beecher lowered his gaze and spoke almost in a whisper. "I'm doing this for the President," he said. "A secret investigation, outside of the normal channels. President Mills can't trust the normal channels these days. He's very worried. He suspects the existence of a conspiracy—a plot directed at the presidency itself."

That confirmed Harriet's own suspicions. But she decided it best to feign ignorance until she at least found out how much Beecher really knew. She had learned never to trust politicians with information, and never to believe them when they gave you any. If she was going to get anything useful, she knew she'd have to play Beecher like a fish, dangling Zodiac in front of him until she got his information first.

She shrugged. "Maybe the President's just afraid the Democrats know something about him that will finish him off just before the election. Or maybe he's just looking for scapegoats. He's going to have to blame his defeat on someone."

Beecher ran a hand nervously through his hair. "I'm well aware of your opinion of the President. But I'm not talking about anything as trivial as a scandal."

Harriet prodded him some more. "What else could he be worried about? Russian spies? War with Mexico?"

"The President fears a possible threat to the country from some quarter," Beecher replied. "It could be foreign, he's not sure. All I know is that he's damned worried. He believes Allen Roland knew something about this threat and purposely neglected to tell him about it."

"Why would he have done that?"

Beecher sighed impatiently. "Roland hated the President because Mills fired him as DCI. He wanted revenge. Everybody in Washington knew he was looking for a chance to get even. It looks now as if he picked the wrong chance. The information Roland was hiding cost him his life. Had he come forward with it, the President probably could have protected him. At least, that's what the President thinks. And now you and that editor are starting to repeat Roland's mistake."

Harriet shivered. Beecher was beginning to find the target. "What am *I* supposed to do?" she asked.

Beecher shrugged. "Simple," he said. "Tell me what you know."

Whatever she said, she realized, might have consequences she could not control. For herself, and for Thompson. Once Beecher knew the contents of the file, he would tell the President, and she would be drawn onto a widening battlefield. How much was Beecher's protection really worth? She couldn't live forever like a prisoner, locked up in a house surrounded by Secret Service agents. Still, she needed help. He could provide it. She'd have to gamble. "Protecting me isn't enough," she replied.

"What else do you want?"

"Help me find Jay Thompson."

Beecher frowned. "Where is he?"

"If I knew that, Ray, I wouldn't need you to help find him."

"Of course. What happened?"

Harriet told him about Thompson's disappearance from the apartment in Rosslyn. "He was mad at me for something I did. He took a friend's car we had borrowed and left."

"When did this happen?"

"Sometime today. I haven't told my friend that the car is missing. I was hoping he might still return. Now I'm worried that something's happened to him."

Beecher pushed himself slowly to his feet and walked again to the window overlooking the park. He seemed agitated, Harriet thought. As if he expected to see intruders on the grounds. She seemed to be making everybody nervous these days, she thought. Thompson. Arch Truley.

"The Secret Service can't look for him. It'll have to involve the FBI.

They'll have to put out a bulletin to state and local police. Maybe the best cover for this would be simply to report the car stolen. If he's picked up, we can have him released into FBI custody, and they can then turn him over to us."

"That sounds reasonable. But the police will have to understand that it's urgent. Not just any old stolen car."

Beecher continued to stare out the window, one foot resting on the radiator cover. "Are you in love with him?" he asked abruptly.

She looked across at him. His face was partially hidden. "Why?"

"I don't know. Maybe I'm a little jealous, that's all. You don't have to answer it." Beecher's voice sounded strained.

Harriet bit her lip. The question had unexpectedly jolted her. "I thought I was going to be," she began. "Now . . . I guess I don't know."

Beecher returned to the sofa and refilled their glasses. "Do we have a deal, then?" he asked.

"Can I trust you?"

"What do you mean?"

"Just that. Once I tell you what I know, I'll be vulnerable."

Beecher nodded. "I understand that. That's why I'm offering you my protection. And agreeing to help find Thompson. You may have crucial information. Neither President Mills nor I is interested in publicity about this, for God's sake! It's pretty ironic for you, a reporter, to sit here worrying that we might leak something!"

Harriet smiled. "All right. I hope you can make some sense out of it all."

She gave Beecher a detailed description of the contents of the file—the CIA cables about the Mexicans, the curious notes about Zodiac, the map of Halloween Park, the memo about a man called Cyclops, the four code names—Capricorn, Gemini, Scorpio, Aquarius. She left out Klimentov, Truley, and the trip to Middleburg.

Beecher listened intently, his face growing whiter with each fresh detail. "How the hell did you get this file?"

"I'd rather not say, just yet."

"Where is it?"

"Home."

"We'd better get it. You can go over in the morning, with a Secret Service agent, to pick it up. I have some campaign stops to make in Roanoke and Richmond. I'll be back in the afternoon. I'll want to take it straight to the President."

Harriet didn't like that idea. Without the file, she would have no leverage. The President could do what he wanted.

"Why should I give him the file?" she said. "It may have nothing to do with him."

Beecher's exasperation began to show. "Harriet, are you going to defy the President on a matter of national security?"

"That's a pretty heavy-handed threat."

"Be reasonable, for God's sake! We need your cooperation. You can see the position I'm in. If I withheld this from the President and it turned out to be vital, he'd . . . I don't know what he'd do. Have me tried for treason, probably. And I wouldn't blame him. Anyway, I'd think you'd be grateful to have the President on your side."

Harriet shook her head. "You're not talking about the same president. The one I'm thinking of won't give a damn what happens to me or Jay Thompson. His only concern is getting reelected. If he can use this to help him in some way, he will. And Jay Thompson and I will still be in as much trouble as we're in now. People have been killed! Allen Roland, Max Feldman, others. I'm afraid Mills might do something stupid."

"I've offered you protection. What more do you want?"

"I want to know what the President knows about this. And what you know. I think you know something but won't tell me."

Beecher hesitated.

Harriet studied his face. "Well . . . ?"

"It's out of my hands," he said. "It'll be up to the President to decide if he wants to take you into his confidence. I'll show him the file, explain your situation—and Thompson's—and pass on your request. That's the best I can do."

Harriet drained off the spritzer and slumped back against the sofa. She wanted another drink, but resisted the impulse. Any more of the stuff, and she would pass out. "I'll think about it," she answered.

She wanted to forget about the damned file, about Thompson, about everything. She wanted not to give a damn. Would Beecher expect her to go to bed with him? Should she? Curiously, she half felt like it. It must be all the booze, she thought. Or the anger at Thompson—for leaving her, and for leaving her to cope with this crisis by herself.

But Beecher's earlier flirtatious mood had totally evaporated. He seemed distant and preoccupied, struggling with something.

"What's the matter?" she asked him.

Beecher smiled wanly. "I'm under a lot of pressure. Everything's suddenly coming to a head. The election, now this Zodiac business. The

President's been treating me fairly brutally lately. That's why I've got to perform for him in this investigation. To put it bluntly, my ass is on the line."

"Well, he can't fire you."

"No . . ."

Harriet pushed herself up from the sofa, and Beecher stood up beside her. They faced each other awkwardly in the middle of the room.

"I'd better go to bed, Ray."

"Of course. I'll show you your room."

He led her across the upstairs hallway to a door at the far end. It was perverse of her, she knew, but she felt a little hurt that he showed no interest in getting her to bed with him. What was bothering him? Their past failures together? . . . Thompson? . . . Zodiac?

"I'll have to be up for a while," he said. "I'd better get going on Thompson."

"What do you mean?"

"Finding him."

"Of course."

"I need a description of the car."

Harriet described it to him, and told him the license number.

"I'd better write it down right now," he said.

Harriet nodded sleepily. Beecher was staring at her.

"What's the *matter*, Ray?" she whispered.

Beecher rubbed a hand against his forehead, as if he had a headache. "I don't know," he muttered. "All the pressure. I'm nervous all the time. The things going on make me nervous. Sorry."

"Good night."

"Good night."

The Vice-President turned away and walked quickly out of sight through the door to the sitting room. Harriet switched on the light and stared at the old four-poster bed in the guest room, complete with a canopy.

They make me nervous, too, she thought.

26

Saturday night, October 27

The Chameleon examined the customs area at JFK's International Arrivals Building with a practiced eye. Six inspectors were on duty, processing the handful of passengers from Alitalia's Rome-New York flight with lazy, late-night irritation.

A station to his immediate left had one customer—a very well-dressed woman angrily stuffing her belongings back into her bags. The fat, gray-faced inspector had just finished giving her the treatment, pawing through the contents of her expensive luggage with the thoroughness of a lingerie fetishist, smugly enjoying his power. The Chameleon walked to his station, playing the percentages. Customs inspectors rarely pulled apart two victims in a row, even when business was slow.

He smiled conspiratorially at the inspector and tilted his head in the direction of the departing woman as he hoisted his own luggage on to the low bench.

The inspector was not in a chummy mood. He stared at the Chameleon and at the two pieces of luggage with hard eyes. "Open 'em up," he snapped.

The Chameleon nodded and cracked open the snaps of the large

Samsonite suitcase. The inspector jabbed among the clothes with his fingers and quickly lost interest. The Chameleon closed the case, watching the inspector out of the corner of his eye.

"The other one," he demanded.

The Chameleon slid the camera case with its artfully scratched and dirtied "Argentine Films, S.A." sticker in front of him and snapped open the four metal clasps that held the cover in place. He did this very deliberately, working on the inspector's impatience. He placed the cover on the counter and both men looked in at the camera, resting snugly in the plush-lined interior of the case.

"New?"

The Chameleon shook his head.

"You have papers for it?"

The Chameleon opened the Samsonite suitcase again and fished among his clothes for the customs declaration. He handed the inspector the papers and waited. The inspector flipped through them, looking bored. They indicated that the camera had been purchased in France in 1979, and declared at customs two weeks ago in Buenos Aires. Perfect forgeries, the Chameleon knew.

The inspector handed the papers back and asked to see his passport. Is he just a troublemaker, the Chameleon wondered, or is he really fishing for something? He pulled the phony Argentine passport from his breast pocket and handed it across, along with the freshly stamped entry visa.

The inspector glanced at the name, Arturo Sierra, checked it against a list of his own he kept on a clipboard, and handed it back. He pointed to the camera. "Take it out, please."

The Chameleon pulled it from its case and laid it gently alongside.

"Open it."

The Chameleon affected not to understand.

"Open the camera!" The inspector made opening gestures with his fat red hands.

"Ahhh!" The Chameleon nodded vigorously and snapped open the door on the side of the Arriflex, exposing the film-loading bay. The inspector bent down and peered inside, careful not to touch anything, as if he feared leaving fingerprints.

He nodded curtly and the Chameleon shut the camera and returned it to its case. He picked up the cover and started to drop it into place, when the inspector stopped him.

"What's in those?" he asked, pointing to the two film cans stored in a separate compartment next to the camera.

"Film."

"Open them."

The Chameleon's mouth widened in shock. If he opened them, he explained in broken English, he would ruin the film. He had just finished shooting an important story in Rome, for Argentinian television.

The inspector was unmoved.

The Chameleon made a fuss, first in Spanish, then in his halting English. He demanded to speak to the inspector's boss. The inspector refused. Several other travelers, waiting in line behind him, grew impatient and moved to other stations. If Señor Sierra refused to open them, the inspector said at last, he would be forced to confiscate them and hold them until their fate could be decided by a higher customs official.

Finally, in a fit of feigned anger, the Chameleon pulled the cans out of the case, yanked off their lids, and slammed them down in front of the inspector's nose. The inspector looked down. Two thick rolls of sixteen-millimeter film. He nodded, his face deadpan, and motioned the Chameleon to pack them back in the case.

"*Destruido!*" the Chameleon cried, waving his hands. "*Destruido!*"

The inspector nodded, a smirk on his lips.

Standing out in the chilly October night air at a taxi stand several minutes later, the Chameleon felt the perspiration cooling on his face.

Too close, he muttered to himself. Just too damned close!

27

Sunday morning, October 28

Thompson stood up and placed the magazine carefully on the arm of the sofa, transfixed momentarily by the lubricious apparition in the doorway.

"Who the hell are you?" she repeated. "The baby-sitter?"

"A paying customer, as a matter of fact."

The woman took a couple of steps into the room, smiling sardonically. "No kidding? Why'd you pick a fleabag like this? There's a Holiday Inn over in Claremont."

Thompson grinned and shrugged his shoulders. "I like the ambience of the Sleepy Oaks better."

It took her a few seconds to absorb the remark. Then she affected a laugh. "That's good! Ambience. Yeah, we got a lot of that."

Thompson held out his hand, feeling foolishly formal. "I'm Jay Thompson," he said, remembering too late that he was Allen Roland to the man on the sofa.

She looked him up and down, ignoring his hand. She wasn't exactly drunk, he decided, but she couldn't be counted among the sober, either. "Pleased to meet you, or whatever I'm supposed to say. I'm *Mrs.* Stark, as you might have guessed by now. Married to that sorry bastard on the couch. My friends, the few I got left, call me Barbara."

"Well, I'm just on my way out, Mrs. Stark . . . Barbara." Thompson nodded good night and started for the door out to the front office.

Mrs. Stark moved across to block his path. "Hey, not so fast! Why don't you stay and have a little . . . nightcap?"

She punched her cigarette out in a small ashtray on top of the TV set and pushed up close to him, to give him a good view of the deep valley between her breasts, bobbing loose beneath her blouse. Thompson found the sight remarkably stirring. She seemed oddly out of place here, like an actress cast in the role of frustrated smalltown wife—convincing, but a little too good for the part.

"I better not," Thompson replied, without conviction. "I've had a few already."

A taunting laugh from Mrs. Stark. "So've I, sweetheart. And I'm gonna have a few more before the night is over. The staff and management of the Sleepy Oaks want to make sure you enjoy your stay!"

She was suddenly leaning against him, one hand on his waist and the other rubbing teasingly against his fly. "We don't want to let all the *ambience* go to waste."

Thompson rested a palm tentatively on her buttocks. They felt muscular.

"You're a good-looking guy," she whispered, "and I feel like raising hell. I'll get the bottle and we'll go to number eight, in the back. Nobody can hear us down there."

Thompson thought about it. He wasn't sure if this meant his luck was getting better or worse. He thought of Harriet with a mixture of regret and fury, then followed Barbara out the door. What harm could it do? Elmer Stark wouldn't wake up for hours. He slipped his arm around her and slid his hand up under her breast and felt the weight of it bobbing in his palm. Having sex with a drunk wasn't exactly his idea of paradise, but it might be the best way to something more important, he realized. Information. If anyone in town knew what went on in Halloween Park, it was probably Barbara Stark.

Room number eight was a twelve-by-twelve box painted pea green, with a lumpy double bed, cheap dresser, two chairs, mirror, and a beat-up TV set. Once inside, with the door locked, Barbara didn't waste any time. She yanked off her blouse unceremoniously, popped open the buttons on her jeans, and peeled them off as if she were racing for the shower. Thompson was surprised to see neither bra nor underpants. Barbara was ten or fifteen pounds overweight—most of the excess stacked around the wide curves of her stomach and hips—but she was firm and blessed with remarkably white, unblemished skin, beautiful even in the room's bad overhead light.

Before Thompson had reached the second button on his shirt, Barbara was kneeling in front of him, fumbling for his zipper. "I want to get laid so bad I can taste it," she muttered.

She zipped his fly open with clumsy haste, fished out his still-limp penis, and popped it into her mouth.

As soon as she had him hard, she fell back on the bed and spread her legs apart. "Put it in me. Hurry up! Fuck me!"

The first coupling was frantic. Barbara exploded in a shuddering orgasm almost as soon as he had slipped inside, causing him to come himself within seconds, despite the alcohol that diluted his bloodstream.

He had barely recovered when she set to work teasing another erection out of him. His very fatigue let him relax and give himself up totally to her skill and enthusiasm, and she soon had him harder than ever, his penis pulsing almost painfully from the flick of her tongue and the caress of her fingers.

The second orgasm took much longer. When it was over, Thompson collapsed on his back in a pool of perspiration and drifted immediately into a kind of stupor, somewhere between waking and sleeping. He was vaguely aware of her beside him, smoking cigarettes and sipping whiskey from the bathroom glass, indulging in a long introspective monologue of which he caught only bits:

"I'll admit you're not the first man I've done this with. . . . And not only men, either. . . . Sometimes I feel guilty about it, cheating on Elmer and all, but it doesn't last long. Next day or the day after, I'm ready to go again. I get so horny, sometimes I think I'll go crazy if I don't get laid. And playing with myself isn't enough. I do that too, anyway, practically every day. I sneak into one of the empty rooms during the day with a vibrator and a mirror and watch myself get off. One night I got it on with a young couple in this same room. Boy, was that a trip! They were swingers—belonged to some kind of regular group, and they wanted me to join. The stories they told! They said we could rent the whole motel out for regular weekend parties for their group. Boy, was I hot for that idea! And this fleabag could have made some money for a change."

"Why didn't you?"

Barbara looked at him as if he were crazy. "Are you kidding? Elmer Stark letting orgies go on in his motel—with his wife as the star attraction?"

"He probably knows what you do."

"He probably *suspects*, but he doesn't really *know*. And he doesn't want to know. Besides, I don't want to flaunt it. He's okay, really. I wouldn't hurt him on purpose." Barbara got up and started searching the floor near the bed for her clothes. "It's six o'clock," she said. "I've got to get my ass to bed before Elmer wakes up. I wish I could keep you here for a whole week of this, but . . ."

She buttoned up her blouse and struggled to pull her blue jeans up past her hips. "You come stay here again and we'll have a ball. I have this girlfriend, Betty Ann, who's been dying to do a threesome with me sometime. You'd be great for that. She'd love you, too. You're just her type. The three of us could have a real orgy back here."

Thompson realized it was too late to sleep. The booze and strenuous sex had left him weak and jangled, barely able to see straight, but she was busy planning an orgy for them. An indefatigable spirit. He had completely forgotten to ask her what she knew about Halloween Park.

"Listen, Barbara. I've got to buy some hunting clothes. What's the nearest place around?"

She yanked her jeans past her hips with a mighty tug.

"That'd be Sears in Claremont," she replied. "Or the sports store— what's it called?—Hal's, I think. Hal's Sports. There's an Army and Navy in Claremont, too. But today's Sunday. They'll all be closed. What are you hunting this time of year?"

"I'm doing a magazine story on Halloween Park. Thought I should dress for the occasion."

"You're going into Halloween Park?" Her voice was guarded.

"Yes."

"That's unusual."

"Why's that?"

Barbara avoided his eyes, peering instead down over her breasts, trying to line up the button with the buttonhole on her jeans.

"Because nobody is ever allowed in there, except the members. So I think you're lying."

Thompson sat up. He had to choose his words carefully. He didn't want to scare her off. "Well, it's true, I don't actually have an invitation. But your husband told me a lot about it, and it sounded like such a fascinating place, I thought I'd try to interest the park in my doing an article on it for my magazine—"

Barbara cut him off, her tone hostile. "What did Elmer tell you?"

Thompson recalled Stark's comments as best he could remember them.

She laughed. "He didn't tell you very much."

"What did he leave out?"

"Who said he left anything out?"

Thompson saw that she was taunting him. He jumped up from the bed and grabbed her by the wrist. "What did he leave out?"

She tried to twist her arm away. He squeezed harder.

"Hey! What the hell are you doing, you prick! Let go of me!"

"Answer my question. I need to know."

"Fuck you! Who the hell do you think you are?"

"Never mind. Just take my word for it, I need to know!"

"*Why* do you need to know?" she cried.

"You don't want to know why. You don't want to know anything about it."

Barbara pulled herself away as if she were afraid he might throw her down. She found her cigarettes and lit one. Sitting on the edge of the mattress, hung-over, her hair disheveled, she looked pathetic.

Thompson found the bottle of whiskey and poured the remaining inch out into one of the glasses. He drank half of it and then handed it to her. She cradled it in her hand tentatively and stared at him.

"I need to know, Barbara. My life depends on it."

She rubbed the back of her hand across her nose and sniffled. "The owners hired a new management to run the place about a year ago," she began. "The owners are a bunch of rich old farts who keep to themselves, but the new managers . . . well, nobody really knows who they are. There's just one man there running the place that anybody ever talks to, and nobody sees him very often."

"What's so different about the new management?"

"Different? Barbara shook her head. "I don't know. But they sure do like their privacy. There've been rumors about strange things going on inside the park. But nobody around here really knows anything. Nobody gets inside anymore. The people who used to work in there were all replaced."

"What kind of rumors?"

Barbara stabbed her cigarette out angrily. "About six months ago a kid named Billy Beaulieu got inside the park and they shot him."

"How the hell did that happen?"

"Nobody knows. Billy used to sneak in the park all the time before the new people came. The old management didn't care, or probably didn't even know. The place is so big you could wander around in there for years without anyone ever seeing you. Anyway, Billy knew a place in the woods where he could get through the fence. He told me about it. He loved to go in there because it was a big adventure for him, I guess, with all the wild animals. But he went in this May and they killed him. He was twelve. They claimed it was a hunting accident. They were all very sorry, blah, blah, blah, but Billy had no right to be in the park, and so on. They said one of the new employees mistook him for game."

"That was all? That was the end of it?"

"Yeah. They hushed it up. They let the guy go who shot him, and gave the family a bunch of money. But no investigation, no nothing. A hunting accident. The bastards!"

"Maybe it really was."

"I don't believe it, and nobody else does either. There's no animal in that park that looks like a twelve-year-old boy!"

"I don't know. A lot of people get shot in hunting accidents."

Barbara shook her head. "No. There's something spooky about that place, and you ask anybody in town and they'll say the same thing. If they say anything at all. The fact is, since Billy was killed, people don't talk about the park anymore. And they sure as hell don't try to get invitations to visit it!"

Thompson nodded. He felt like a fool. He had manhandled the poor woman only to find out nothing useful. Barbara picked up her pack of cigarettes and stood up.

"I'm sorry if I hurt your arm," he said.

"Yeah." She tried to laugh. "I've been roughed up a lot worse than that."

"Well, I'm sorry. I'm in some trouble, that's all."

Barbara nodded. "I figured. I knew you were lying to me. Guys like you don't stay in fleabags like this. You don't look like a traveling salesman, and I don't think you're a magazine writer, either."

"No."

Barbara headed for the door.

"Wait," Thompson said. She stopped and looked back at him.

"Tell me one thing."

"What?"

"Tell me how to find that hole in the fence—where Billy Beaulieu used to sneak through."

28

Sunday morning, October 28

Harriet awoke and instantly wished to sink back into sleep again. Her head pounded, her mouth felt dry, and her stomach seemed to be acting like a washing machine.

Reluctantly she opened her eyes. The room was still dark, and only after a moment of disoriented panic did she remember where she was. She rolled over and squinted at the clock on the bedside table. A quarter to seven. Early.

She slipped out of bed and groped her way to the bathroom. Beecher had left a note taped on the mirror of the large old Victorian medicine chest.

> Harriet:
> Have to be in Richmond by 8:30. Didn't want to disturb you. Have instructed one of the Secret Service agents to drive you back to your apartment to change, pick up clothes, etc. And of course to get *file*. Will see you back here this P.M.
>
> Ray

Harriet removed the note and tossed it in the wastebasket. She needed medication. Hangover and anxiety were ganging up on her, and the day had hardly begun. She pulled open the medicine-cabinet door and examined the rows of bottles and cans, remembering Beecher's old medicine chest in Georgetown, which had never contained anything more serious than a bottle of aspirin. She used to kid him about it.

Times had changed. The chest before her was loaded with drugs—prescription painkillers, sleeping pills, and tranquilizers of great variety and potency. Being vice-president was not all fun and games, apparently, even for a playboy like Beecher. Harriet checked the prescription dates on the bottles; none was more than six months old. Either he went through the pills very fast or his troubles were of recent onset. Or both.

Harriet found some five-milligram Valium and took one, along with three aspirin. She closed the cabinet and caught her face in the mirror—puffy eyes, pale and drawn face, hair a tangle. "You're a frightful mess, whoever you are," she muttered.

An hour later she was bathed, dressed, and walking along the pebbled drive in front of the vice-presidential mansion with a Secret Service agent named Jeff. Her legs were weak and rubbery, and she was yawning compulsively, but she felt better. Another bright, breezy autumn day had begun, and on the ride to her apartment at Dupont Circle, she left the window of the government sedan rolled down, gratefully breathing the fresh air.

The scene at her apartment did nothing to improve her mood. It had been ransacked again, even more thoroughly than the first time. Her eyes fell on the fifteen-hundred-dollar sofa from Sloan's, slashed open in a dozen places, and she bit back her tears.

Jeff muttered sympathetically and began trying to straighten things up. "I never saw anything like this," he said, picking up the remains of one of the sofa's cushions, its stuffing hanging out of it like entrails.

"Do you like it?" Harriet asked. "It's the latest decorating style. Modern Vandalized. Cost me a fortune."

She refused to let it unnerve her. *She* was in one piece, she reminded herself. The rest were just possessions. All replaceable, more or less. And insured. And at least this time she knew what the intruders were looking for. Even better, she knew that they hadn't found it.

But it was time for her to get moving. She found the telephone on the bedroom floor and pulled it into the bathroom. She closed the door, locked it, sat down on the toilet-seat cover, and dialed Bill Shapiro, the *Times* bureau chief. She supposed the phone was bugged again, but was past caring.

"Where the hell are you?" he exploded.

"I'm home. I—"

Shapiro cut her off, unable to restrain himself. "Well, goddammit, you're fired! You didn't file your story on the Turkish embassy last night! You didn't even call in! You're fired, and I mean it!"

Harriet sighed. Shapiro had a loud bark. "Now, calm down and listen to me, Bill. When you hear the whole story, you'll hate yourself for yelling at me."

It took all of Harriet's remaining reserves of self-possession not to scream at him. Shapiro lecturing her was too much to tolerate. He carried on for a few minutes more, and Harriet waited impatiently for him to run out of steam.

"The Turkish-embassy story wasn't very important," she finally got in.

"What's this?" he yelled. "Are you rating the news for me?"

"I'm sorry, Bill. When I explain it to you, you'll understand. Meanwhile, I need help!"

Harriet waited through another blast of invective, then lowered her voice, forcing Shapiro to lower his own in order to hear her. "I'm onto the story we talked about yesterday. I can't talk about it on the phone."

"Your story," he growled, "is probably the reason this office was broken into last night! Everyone's desk was ransacked! I'm sick about it!"

Harriet closed her eyes. Zodiac seemed to have her surrounded. "I'm sorry."

"The files are a shambles! I don't know *what*'s missing! We're going crazy trying to find anything! And now you want a favor!"

"I'm sorry. It's important."

"What do you want? Go ahead, make my life even more miserable!"

"I need to know the President's schedule for today and tomorrow."

Shapiro yelled at somebody to find the schedule, then fumed until his secretary came on the line and read out President Mills's itinerary:

"He'll be on *Air Force One* at seven this evening. Fly to Pease Air Force Base in New Hampshire, stay overnight at the governor's mansion in Concord, address a rally in Manchester at ten the next morning, have lunch with the governor and Senator MacNair at noon at a Rotary Club there, hold a news conference, address a group of local businessmen at three at the Holiday Inn, and at four he's flying by helicopter to Burnham, New Hampshire, to stay with Senator MacNair at his hunting lodge for a three-day vacation."

The secretary hung up and Shapiro snorted. "Mills must be the first president in modern times dumb enough to take a three-day vacation the week *before* the national election."

"Is there a press plane to New Hampshire?" Harriet asked.

"Isn't there always a press plane? Yes, there's a press plane. It leaves today at five."

Harriet took a deep breath. "Bill, you've got to put me on it."

"What are you talking about? We only get one seat."

"Take Fred Carlin off and put me on."

"You've lost your mind, as well as your job. I can't do that. You're not covering the President. Fred Carlin is. And don't give me any clever reasons. You just can't have it. Period!"

Harriet begged him. It was an emergency, she insisted.

"Can't Carlin cover whatever it is in New Hampshire for you?"

Harriet was firm. "No."

Shapiro began to weaken. "I see."

"Please. It's life or death. Literally."

Shapiro finally surrendered. "If it turns out that your story is anything less than the plans for World War III, you're in trouble here. And you can have Carlin's place for exactly two days. That's it!"

Harriet listened to the loud crash of the receiver at the other end. Back in the bedroom, she picked out a leather suitcase from among the debris and stuffed it with a small blanket, a pillow, and a stack of table linen lying nearby. Returning with the suitcase to the living room, she handed it to Jeff. "Would you take this down for me?" she asked. "I'll be ready in a minute."

"Yes, ma'am," he replied, a stolid smile on his face. "Sure you wouldn't like me to help straighten up a bit more?"

"The hell with it."

"Yes, ma'am." The agent took the case and headed for the door.

"And stop calling me ma'am, for God's sake!" she said to his back. "My name's Harriet!"

The agent turned by the door. "Well, no, ma'am, sorry. The Vice-President doesn't like us calling his . . . ladies by their first names."

Harriet gasped in delight. "Really!"

"That's correct, ma'am." Agent Jeff looked uncomfortable.

"How quaint!"

"Yes, ma'am. I guess so."

Harriet crossed her arms in front of her and tilted her hip, giving the agent a broad, flirtatious smile. "Do you know what the Vice-President used to be called—when he was in school?"

"No, ma'am."

"Baby-Bottom."

"Baby-Bottom?"

"Yes. Baby-Bottom Beecher. His cheeks were very rosy and he didn't start shaving until he was nineteen."

The agent looked perplexed for a second, unsure of how to react. Harriet watched him, smiling mischievously. Suddenly his granitic facial muscles cracked and he broke out into a fit of laughter. She could still hear him giggling a minute later while waiting for the elevator in the hallway. Let him enjoy himself, Harriet thought. He'll be in serious trouble before the day is out.

She returned to the bedroom, grabbed a blue rip-stop nylon overnight bag from the floor, stuffed it with slacks, sweaters, jeans, and underwear, retrieved her leather bag from the closet, satisfied herself that it still contained more or less its original contents, and walked back out into the living room. She peeked out the front door to make sure that the agent had gone down in the elevator, and then headed rapidly toward the back service stairs.

She knew she could not stay with Beecher. Hiding wasn't her style. If the President was as interested in the file as Beecher claimed he would be, then she would damned well take it to him herself. If Zodiac was as serious a matter as Harriet was now convinced it was, then she must not give away the tremendous leverage she possessed. She would go to the President and offer him a trade—the file in return for help in finding Thompson and for protecting both of them. The President was a Neanderthal and a chauvinist, but at least he was truly in a position to do something. All she had to do was convince him that it was in his own best interests to help her.

Harriet stopped next to the firehose on the landing one flight down the service stairs. The heavy canvas hose, coupled to a three-inch water line, was rolled up in a loose coil on its hanger against the wall, where it had hung, untouched, for years. Harriet grabbed the long brass nozzle attached to the end and hastily unscrewed it.

From inside the hose she plucked the rolled-up envelope containing Roland's precious file and stuffed it into her overnight bag.

Two more flights down brought her to the basement. She hurried out the basement door into a backyard that led into an alley, and then along the alley to a street a block away from Dupont Circle. She flagged a taxi as it pulled up to a stoplight and jumped in.

Next stop, New Hampshire.

29

Sunday morning, October 28

Thompson appraised himself in the bathroom mirror, measuring the effect wrought by some old clothes of Elmer's Barbara had found for him: a well-worn paint-splattered pair of chino workpants, a brown workshirt with a frayed collar, a cable-knit sweater with holes in the sleeves, and a visored cap to help hide his face and his expensive haircut.

The Italian dress shoes he had been wearing since Wednesday remained the only incongruous element. Even caked with dirt they looked suspiciously out of place. Elmer wore a size eleven, so his shoes were of no use.

He snapped shut the catches on Franklin's suitcase, put his wallet in the chinos, and picked up the car keys. The telephone rang. He hesitated, then picked it up.

Barbara was on the other end, calling from the front desk. "The cops are here," she whispered. "They're asking about the owner of the Toyota. I told them you were in room one. They're on their way over there right now, and they'll see you if you come out the door of number eight!"

"What should I do?"

"I'd like to know what the hell you've done!" Barbara's whisper was fierce, the tone admiring. "They're after you for more than adultery, that's for sure!"

"Yeah. Well, the car's stolen, in a manner of speaking. I'll explain it all to you someday."

"I hope so. But if I were you, I'd head out the bathroom window. It goes right out into the woods, and if you go straight back from the motel, you'll come out on Route Thirty-two in about ten minutes."

Thompson said thanks, but Barbara had already hung up. At the window he inched the drapes aside and looked out. He was astonished to see three state police cruisers, one positioned on each side of the Celica, and the third blocking the exit onto the highway. Troopers—about a dozen of them—milled around, looking awkward and self-conscious, like uninvited guests at a lawn party. He could hear somone pounding on a door in a distant part of the motel.

For a fugitive moment he thought of letting himself be arrested. They were only after him for stealing a car, something he could explain with the help of a good lawyer, and in the meantime he'd be taken into custody. Protective custody.

But it wouldn't help him much. He had no evidence to persuade them what he was up against, nothing but stories about people chasing after him for no explainable reason. He didn't even have that damned file anymore! They would lock him up and probably put him under psychiatric observation. Then what?

The bathroom window was a small double-hung model that opened easily, but it was situated high up on the wall, and Thompson was forced to stand on the toilet tank and squeeze himself out headfirst. He pushed himself halfway through, and hung there, momentarily unable to move farther. Around the other side of the building he could hear them pounding on the door to number eight. In desperation he pressed both hands against the outside wall and forced himself the rest of the way out the window.

As he fell through, he managed to double over in a somersault to avoid landing on his head. He rolled over an empty can, and it cut into his back so sharply he had to bite his hand to keep from crying out.

As Barbara had promised, the woods grew right up next to the back of the motel, and within seconds he was dodging through a thick stand of saplings and blackberry bushes, snagging his pants and shirt on their thorns as he pushed through.

He reached Route 32, gasping for breath, and stopped to rest just out of sight of the highway traffic. He needed to formulate a plan. According to Barbara's directions, Billy Beaulieu's hole in the park fence was only about three miles away. He could cover that on foot in forty-five minutes.

Only Barbara knew how he was dressed, and Elmer's description of him would likely not be very accurate, so the police could not recognize him on sight. Still, he was a stranger here, and cops had a sixth sense for spotting someone out of place.

It had grown cloudy since dawn, and the sky, now a heavy purple, threatened rain. A cold, gusty wind accompanied the overcast, and it bit uncomfortably through his thin sweater. He would have to hurry.

He covered a mile on Route 32 at a steady jog, encountering only one farmer in a pickup truck. It was barely past seven in the morning, and the countryside hadn't yet come fully awake. He found the town road just where Barbara had indicated, and moved along it at a slower pace, looking for a derelict barn.

Finally, he found it—an unmistakably abandoned and weathered hulk with a swaybacked ridgepole and bulging sides, about one good windstorm short of collapse.

Behind the barn he located the path—a faint, overgrown track that showed no signs of recent use. A small dog was sniffing around the barn, and when he saw Thompson he came running after him, sensing some adventure at hand. He was a beagle hound with no collar or tags, and a lame front leg that gave his trotting style a comic, swaying motion. Thompson tried repeatedly to shoo him back, but the dog wasn't to be denied. He would simply stop, wag his tail, and wait for Thompson to start forward again. Thompson gave up and let the dog follow him.

The trail twisted over a hill, through a deep valley, across a stream, and then wound through a dark pine forest whose towering trees grew in evenly spaced rows, planted that way thirty or more years before—for what reason, Thompson could not imagine.

The pines suddenly ended and gave way to what Thompson thought at first was a pasture, but on second look turned out to be a broad, continuous grassy swath, like a clearing for a power line, stretching in front of him in both directions. The strip was about fifty yards wide, he guessed, and divided down the middle by a tall fence.

The fence.

He didn't know quite what he had expected, but the fence surprised him. It stood about ten feet high, constructed of interlocking loops of heavy steel wire that formed a tight mesh. An additional three feet of height was gained in the form of a double barbed-wire barrier strung along the top and tilted out in both directions, like the arms of the letter Y. With the swath of no-man's-land on either side ot it, the fence needed only a few guard towers to complete the effect of the perimeter of a gigantic prisoner-of-war camp.

Thompson could not imagine any animal escaping through it. Or any man, either. He recalled that Elmer Stark had told him that the land had been cleared on both sides of the fence to prevent trees from blowing down across it and creating an opening that park animals might slip through. But the effect seemed more ominous.

The beagle took off across the grass and ran sniffing along the base of the steel-mesh barrier, excited by some exotic new scents.

Thompson hesitated, looking down the wide, cleared alley of field in both directions, half-expecting that the long fence might be patrolled; but finally he walked across to it. On the other side of it, and running parallel with it, Thompson saw a rutted dirt road, covered with fresh tire tracks. Beyond the road, in the park's interior, he saw only an impenetrable wilderness, mountainous to the north and flat to the south, with dark green stands of pine and hemlock mixed in a vast sea of hardwood trees, their bright autumn yellows and reds beginning to fade in the late-October weather.

He found no opening. Barbara had told him it was less than two hundred feet to the left along the fence from the end of the path. But she had never seen it herself. And if the perimeter was patrolled regularly, as the fresh tire tracks indicated, the hole might have been seen and patched. He thought of looking for one of the gates. According to Roland's map, the park contained seven of them, spaced at intervals around the thirty miles of fence. But he could be miles from the nearest gate. And it would be locked, anyway. As a last resort, he could try to scale the fence, but that seemed an almost impossible task.

The beagle was still with him, busy sniffing in the grass and weeds. Suddenly he began to bark. Thompson looked over at the animal, about fifty feet ahead of him, and watched him run back and forth along a rough, steeply pitched stretch of fence, then stop and put his head down, whining with excitement. When Thompson caught up with him, he saw what the fuss was about.

The mutt had found the hole. The ground was so uneven that it had been impossible to string the fence sections at a uniform depth under the surface, and here the bottom edge of the steel mesh was exposed, and a worn depression about a foot wide beneath it indicated that someone or something had slipped through it many times. The rocky gully made the gap under the fence invisible from the perimeter road inside, so it would have been missed by anyone looking from passing vehicles.

Thompson patted the dog gratefully, then slid under the steel mesh. Once through, he looked back at the dog, which was wagging its tail and eyeing him through the wire with a mournful expression.

Thompson tried to coax him through, but the dog wasn't having any of it. He clearly hated to see Thompson go on without him, but he had even stronger feelings against passing under that fence. Thompson finally left him and followed the perimeter road north, walking in the tall grass near the edge of the woods, so that he could duck out of sight if he heard a vehicle approaching. Less than half a mile along, another road branched off from the perimeter road and headed into the interior of the park. Thompson decided to follow it, and soon found himself walking through a gloomy forest of hemlock. They were remarkably tall trees— virgin, uncut timber, far older than the park. Sprinkles of rain danced in the air now, and a breeze moved through the boughs with a silky murmur. Except for an occasionally glimpsed bird overhead, he had yet to encounter any wildlife, familiar or exotic. The park, in fact, seemed mysteriously empty.

Thompson tried to recall in his mind's eye the exact spot on Roland's map where the X had been drawn. The park was roughly rectangular in shape, its nine-mile length lying on a north-south axis, and if one divided that rectangle into four smaller ones, the X lay in the northwest corner of the northeast rectangle. Thompson knew that he had entered the park on its east side, had walked north, and was now walking west. With luck, the road he was on—or the first one to branch off from it to the north—would take him into the area of the X.

Rumblings in his stomach reminded him that he was hungry. He looked at his watch and was surprised to see that it was nearly noon. He had been up and moving for six hours after a night empty of sleep. He felt surprisingly good, considering. Wonderful stuff, adrenaline.

A fork to the north appeared about half an hour later, and Thompson followed it. The wheel tracks in the dirt looked fresher here, and he counted that a promising sign. Much as he refused to admit it to himself, he was bumbling around without any real plan. He was operating on sheer instinct—a fugitive book editor roaming a wilderness park in search of an X on a map. It was all that he had left. He was trapped in a murderous riddle and his life had been narrowed to the stark proposition of finding the secret before it found him.

And the secret was here in the park. He was sure of it.

A sudden crashing in the heavy bushes near the road behind him made him whirl around. Seconds later the shrubbery parted and a large animal appeared twenty feet in front of him. It stopped dead in the middle of the road and turned its head in his direction. It stood about four feet high, the size of a small bear, with a massive upper body, balanced on four short legs. Coarse black hair stuck up along the ridge of its back, giving the beast the aspect of a gigantic, enraged dog. Its snout was long and massive, and two enormous curved tusks protruded out beneath its whiskery muzzle like the tines of the devil's pitchfork.

A Black Forest boar.

Thompson could scarcely believe its size. He guessed it must weigh between three and four hundred pounds. The beast made a snuffling noise, and turned to face him head-on, pawing the ground with a front hoof, like a bull about to charge. It fixed Thompson with its small eyes, and clacked its jaws open and shut a couple of times, as if challenging him to advance.

The movement of the beast's jaws gave Thompson a closer look at the tusks. There were two on each side of the mouth—a long one that grew up from the bottom jaw in a broad, backward curve; and a smaller, inner one, twisting upward out of the top jaw and scissoring against the bigger outer tusk, keeping it honed to a cutting edge. It was a creature out of a nightmare—armed, ugly, and dangerous. In India, Thompson had once read somewhere, they called it "the beast who can drink between tigers."

Thompson retreated a few steps, and the animal advanced, bristling, stamping its hooves on the dirt, emitting a guttural oink that sent icicles along Thompson's spine.

He dared not retreat farther, for fear of encouraging it. And turning his back on it to flee was out of the question. He stood and looked around for some weapon. He saw several rocks near the edge of the path, and moved sideways toward them, keeping his eyes on the boar.

The beast charged.

The sudden clack of hooves kicked up a cloud of dust behind them, and the creature became a blur of angry motion. Thompson turned to run, but the beast was on him in an instant.

The boar smashed brutally against his side, knocking him off his feet. As he fell, the animal hooked its head, and a tusk met his thigh, ripped through the pants leg, and cut into flesh.

Thompson writhed in the dirt and tried to scream, but the wind was knocked out of him. He rolled over several times, groaning, sucking air into his lungs, then lay still, stunned and overwhelmed, near the edge of blacking out.

The beast had stopped about ten feet away, and turned to face him again, heaving its ugly bulk and wagging its snout slowly from side to side. Thompson shook his head, trying to clear it. He forced himself to crawl across the path to the pile of rocks. He picked up the largest, a boulder that he could barely lift with both hands, and staggered to his feet with it.

The boar charged again.

Fear lent him the strength to raise the boulder over his head. There was no aiming it. He let it fall forward, pushing out hard with his arms, praying that his timing was accurate.

The rock struck the beast exactly between the ears. It let out a fearsome squeal of pain and its front legs buckled beneath it. It pitched over on its side and lay still.

Thompson hoisted the rock into the air again and dropped it on the boar's head, crushing its skull. He stumbled several paces away and sat down. He stared at the inert mound of bristly black hair, waiting to see if it would move again. It didn't. The animal's mouth was open, its tongue hanging out, and on one of its tusks Thompson saw his own blood.

The pain was making his eyes water. He wiped away the tears with a sleeve and examined his leg. The boar had ripped a jagged gash along his thigh, and blood was oozing heavily from it, soaking his pants and socks a dark, sticky red.

"Welcome to Halloween Park," he muttered.

30

A Ford Econoline van crept through the dust-choked back streets of Nuevo Laredo, dodging chickens and dogs. The driver, a native of the Texas panhandle, swore under his breath and used all his self-restraint to keep his fist off the horn and his foot off the gas pedal.

Eventually he found the alley he was looking for. It was a narrow dirt passageway leading into a small yard and terminating against a large warehouse door. The Texan maneuvered the vehicle around on the street and backed it up the alley until the tail end of the van was nearly touching the door. He tapped his horn once and waited.

A Mexican in clean workclothes appeared from a smaller door and came around to the driver's side of the van.

"What can I do for you, *amigo?*" His tone was unfriendly.

The Texan laughed. "I'm looking for the Aztec ruins. Maybe you could direct me to them?"

The Mexican stroked his chin, appraising the Texan through narrow eyes. "I'm very sorry, but there are no Aztec ruins around here. You have to go farther south."

The driver nodded. "Well, maybe in the meantime I could leave some of my equipment with you for safekeeping."

"We will take excellent care of it, *amigo*."

The Texan supposed it was a necessary precaution, but he found this code-word stuff a pain in the ass.

"That's great," he said. "Now, if you'll just hustle around and open up the back doors of this buggy and lift out those two crates, you'll find everything you ordered, and I'll be able to get back to Amarillo sometime before tomorrow morning."

The Mexican became suddenly businesslike. "Could I see a list of the inventory, please."

The Texan laughed again. "There ain't any damned list, *amigo*. You'll find it all there, don't you worry none. This ain't some half-assed Mes'can delivery service you're talkin' to, you know. You'll find your five gallons of tan paint, one dozen shirts, one dozen hats, one dozen pants, and one dozen machine guns. And there's a shit-load of ammo and some pretty little decals with instructions on how to apply them."

The Mexican grunted, and yelled to someone in the warehouse. The big door rolled up and two younger men appeared. On orders from the Mexican, they pulled open the rear doors of the van and hefted two wooden crates out of the back and into the warehouse. As soon as they had them out, the Mexican shut the van doors, and the Texan, who had not moved from behind his steering wheel, started the engine and retraced his route out of town, driving as fast as he dared.

31

John Graves stood alongside the Land Rover out on the grass of Halloween Park's small runway, shielding his eyes from the intermittent drops of rain. He and Ward had flown in together on a CIA craft an hour earlier. General Ward sat inside the Land Rover, the window partway down, smoking a cigarette and brushing the ashes nervously from his hunting pants.

"Well, we need the rain, General," Graves said, to break the tension.

"What the hell for?"

"It's been dry up here this fall."

"It can rain all the hell it wants to after the thirtieth."

Graves nodded, regretting his effort to be civilized. "What about the file?" he asked.

"They didn't find it," Ward replied harshly. "Aquarius must have fucked it up, somehow." He rolled down the window the rest of the way and leaned his face partway out. "Has Cyclops been briefed?"

"I talked to him before the plane left Washington. I told him the local police let Thompson get away."

"What did he say to that?"

"He laughed."

Ward shook his head. "He won't laugh when we tell him he has twenty-four hours to find Thompson."

"I've told him already. He said he'd have Thompson 'washed and hung out to dry'—those were his words—in half that time."

Ward snapped his cigarette butt with his forefinger and thumb toward the ground, barely missing Graves's shoe. Graves looked at him questioningly, wondering if he had done it on purpose.

"What makes him so sure, Graves?"

Graves cleared his throat and peered into the overcast again. "Well, he said he knew where Thompson was going."

Where's that?"

"He wouldn't tell me."

Ward stroked his mustache. "Arrogant bastard. I wonder why the hell we put up with him."

"He's your best, isn't he?" Graves replied, mocking Ward's earlier assertions.

Ward didn't answer. He was thinking about the special assignment he was going to give to Graves. He looked down at his lap, carefully studying the buttons on his safari jacket. "When this is over," he said, "I want you to get rid of him."

"Cyclops?" Graves was incredulous.

Ward nodded. "He's a loose cannon."

"Get rid of him? After all he's done? He's been invaluable! You said as much yourself!"

Ward smiled crookedly. "Well, that doesn't speak very well for your boys, does it, Graves?"

Graves clenched his fists, saying nothing.

"In any case," Ward continued, "we won't need him after this. He'll have served his function. Invaluable, as you say, but he'll have no place with us after Zodiac, and to let him go, knowing what he does, would be suicide for us."

Graves felt fear rising in his throat. "It'll be tricky. I'll have to get a special man for it."

"No." Ward was emphatic. "You do it yourself."

Graves stared at Ward, his craggy white eyebrows twitching in anger. "I'm not a hit man!"

Ward waved his hand impatiently. "Yes, yes, I know, John. This is different. Consider it an act of self-defense. You'll be ridding the world of a menace."

"Not on your life!" Graves cried. "There are professionals who get paid for hits. We'll hire a top man."

Ward tugged Graves by the sleeve. "Now, listen to me, John. You'll be close to him and he'll never suspect you. He won't be on his guard. You'll be able to do it easily, right here, while we're still in the park. We'll work out a little hunting accident."

Graves decided to let the matter drop for the moment, without actually agreeing to do it. He knew Ward was right. The man was too dangerous to be let go, and he, Graves, would have the best chance to kill him. But Graves had no stomach for cold-blooded murder, even for someone like Cyclops. He would have to think of a proxy Ward might accept.

"And anyway," Ward added, as if another reason was needed to seal the argument, "Roland ordered him terminated three years ago. He was afraid of him. He thought he was a double agent. Cyclops is irrational, psychotic. Most of the good hit men are."

You should talk, you son of a bitch, Graves thought to himself. "What happened?" he asked Ward.

Ward smiled. "A typical Roland fuck-up. Cyclops was warned, and the attempt backfired. I think he bought the hit man off, then killed him later. When I took over, I decided we could sever him from the agency, park him somewhere where he could do little harm until we decided what to do with him. But when Zodiac was threatened, we suddenly had a real need for him. It was natural for me to think to send you to collect him and put him to use plugging the leak. Especially since he's expendable."

Graves glanced up, hearing a faint rumble in the sky to the southeast, and in another minute the silver silhouette of a twin-engine Lear jet broke through the cloud cover and descended to the far edge of the small airstrip, coming to a stop at the edge of the woods on the opposite end of the runway.

The jet wheeled around and taxied to within twenty feet of the Land Rover. The pilot came out first, opening the door and dropping the small set of steps into place.

Ward was impatient. "Where's your passenger?" he yelled.

The pilot looked up but didn't answer him.

A few seconds later a figure appeared in the doorway, head bowed.

Ward and Graves watched as he stepped down gingerly onto the grass. He seemed to lose his balance for a second, as if drunk. His eyes were puffed nearly shut, and dried blood caked his shirtfront.

Ward gasped. "Truley! What are you doing here?"

Truley tried to say something, but his voice cracked and the words were unintelligible. Cyclops materialized behind him in the aircraft doorway.

"Ole Truley here found out all about us, General!" Cyclops said. "Ain't that a fact, Truley?"

Truley collapsed.

32

By late afternoon Thompson was thoroughly miserable. It had rained hard for nearly an hour, and his clothes clung to him like wet sheets, intensifying the chill from the wind. He was hungry and his leg throbbed. He had managed to stop the bleeding by ripping off the bottom half of the torn pants leg and tearing that into two pieces—one to fold over the wound as a pad to stanch the flow of blood, the other to tie around his leg to hold the pad in place. At first the bandage kept slipping off as he walked, but finally the clotted blood had dried it to his leg. Now the rain had loosened it again.

He sat on a rock beneath an oak tree by the dirt road and reviewed his situation. He had so little to go on. An X on a map. That was about it. That, and his instinct that he was doing the right thing by carrying the fight to the enemy's ground.

Zodiac. What did it mean? What the hell was he looking for?

A mysterious X. The mathematician's symbol for an unknown quantity. The X that marks the spot. He felt his mind beginning to drift. He knew that he had to start thinking about where he was going to spend the night. Staying in the park, with no food, no shelter, no protection from another boar attack was a dismal prospect. He had better try to get back to the motel, he decided. He could return to the park in the morning.

It was nearly five o'clock now. If he could travel eastward in a reasonably direct line, he could reach the fence in an hour, possibly less. Once at the fence, he would only have to walk along it until he came to the hole he had crawled through this morning. His only problem was determining which direction was east. The heavy cloud cover completely obscured the sun's location, and retracing his erratic, zigzag course through the park would be difficult. Still, there remained two hours until dark. He would have to try.

He stood up, and felt a sharp stab of pain in his thigh. The wound would start bleeding again when he walked, but he would have to suffer it. If he could find his way back to the motel, he could clean it and bandage it properly.

He followed a road he hoped led east, until it narrowed, becoming little more than a dirt path, and then split into two trails, forcing him to make a choice. It hardly mattered, he realized. He was thoroughly lost now anyway.

Some minutes later he stopped. The rain had eased, but the wind had picked up, moaning through the evergreen boughs. Something in that wind caught his attention, something that wasn't there before. He held his breath and strained to hear it again. It was borne on the air only intermittently, faint and uncertain, but audible nevertheless. It sounded like music.

He walked on farther and stopped to listen again. He was sure the sound was real now. It was coming from the left side of the trail, evanescent still, but clear. A distant car radio, perhaps? The melody sounded mournful, in a minor key.

The path seemed to be taking him closer to the source. He could hear it more clearly now. A man was singing to a guitar accompaniment. Mexican?

The trail ran straight for a long stretch, and at the top of a rise Thompson saw that it led into a field a short distance ahead. He approached the clearing cautiously, looking for some signs of activity.

Abruptly the music stopped.

When Thompson reached the edge of the clearing, he was astonished by its size. A field of many acres opened before him, surrounded on three sides by low, wooded hills. There were no signs of life, but the huge meadow was not empty. Sitting out in the tall grass about a hundred yards from where Thompson stood was a long concrete-block building, painted white. It contained two doorways and four windows on the side facing Thompson, but there were no doors in the doorframes, and no glass in the windows.

A crude roadway had been cut through the grass from the far edge of the field directly past the building to the edge of the woods near Thompson's path. Where the roadway passed the building, it was intercepted by a gate that stuck out at a right angle from the building. The gate consisted of two pairs of posts about fifteen feet apart, cradling a pole that lay across them at about waist height. It looked like a horse jump.

About a dozen rusted, derelict automobiles, missing windows, tires, and other parts, were lined up along the roadway on both sides of the barrier, and were facing toward it, as if they had stopped at an imaginary railway crossing to wait for a train to go by.

Even more bizarre were the dummies.

Each derelict automobile had one sitting behind the driver's seat, and many of the old cars contained several of them, stuck upright in both front and back seats. More dummies were propped standing by the wooden barrier, dressed in mismatched shirts and trousers. And three mannequins were positioned behind the raised trunk lid of one car, as if retrieving something from the trunk. All three wore dresses: one was a child, only about half the height of the others. For a disconcerting instant Thompson thought they might be real, but their frozen unnatural postures told him that they were not.

The tableau held Thompson transfixed. The music did not return; straining his senses to the utmost, he could still not pick up any sound or movement. Even the wind had stopped blowing. An eerie stillness prevailed. Thompson wanted to take a closer look, but he hesitated, searching for some rational explanation for this strange outdoor stage set in the middle of the New Hampshire wilderness.

Something broke the silence—the distant growl of an engine. Thompson scanned the far edges of the field, trying to locate it. Nothing. Then, out of the woods at the farthest corner appeared two blue Volkswagen minibuses, bumping slowly along, one behind the other. They made their way single file slowly across the field, staying several car-lengths apart, toward the makeshift barrier and the building.

Thompson ducked behind some bushes and crouched near the ground to watch. Both buses carried six passengers—live ones, not mannequins—

two in the front seat, two in the middle, two in the rear. All were men.

The vehicles approached the line of automobiles on one side of the barrier, pulled up carefully behind them, and stopped. For nearly a minute nothing happened. The twelve passengers sat motionless in the buses, as if waiting for an order, while the vehicles idled in neutral, the distinctive rusty putter of their air-cooled engines barely disturbing the silence of the huge meadow.

Abruptly, as if on a signal, both engines died, and the doors began to open. The men stepped out, almost warily, stretching their arms and legs and talking in low voices, as if they were taking a break after a long drive. They were short men, Thompson judged, and dressed in a variety of outfits—jeans and chinos, workboots and sneakers, sweaters and denim jackets, neckerchiefs, and a variety of hats, from simple visored caps similar to the one Thompson was wearing, to battered, workworn Stetsons. Several men sported black mustaches. Migrant laborers was the image that came to mind. What in hell were they doing?

They gravitated toward the rear of the second minibus and crowded together in a tight group around the back door. One man yanked it open and started handing each of the others something from the inside of the bus. Thompson relaxed. They must be workmen come to clean up the site.

The instant that thought crossed his mind, he was forced to choke it back. He watched with astonishment at the sequence of events that unfolded before him.

On a signal from one of them, all twelve men came running from behind the second minibus, brandishing machine guns and screaming at the top of their lungs. They rampaged among the derelict cars, spraying bullets through the doors and windows, the force of the exploding cartridges causing the mannequins inside to jump in a macabre imitation of live victims. Some of the attackers pulled car doors open, hauled dummies out onto the ground, and pumped bullets into them at point-blank range. The standing mannequins were literally mowed down, then kicked and stomped on. One man pulled out a knife, and on hands and knees jabbed it repeatedly into a mannequin, until its stuffing burst through the rips in the fabric.

Several of the men turned from the autos and began spraying the building with machine-gun fire, pumping round after round through the windows and doorways and across the outside wall. Chips of concrete block and concrete dust flew in all directions. The racket from the machine guns and the voices was intense, crashing against Thompson's eardrums until his insides seemed filled with noise and vibration. The attack was so real, so savage, that Thompson felt frozen to the spot, terrified. He was witnessing a massacre—against a collection of junkyard wrecks and cloth dummies.

One man, with a green canvas bag slung over his back, disappeared inside the building. Thompson kept his eyes on the doorway, and a moment later saw him reappear, yelling at the top of his voice.

"*Vámonos! Vámonos!*"

The firing ceased and the men dashed back toward the Volkswagens, piling inside in great haste and disarray, weapons still in hand. Doors slammed, engines coughed to life, and the two buses swung in a sharp U-turn together across the grass, back onto the makeshift roadway, and barreled off at high speed back toward the far side of the field.

They had not yet disappeared into the woods when an explosion buckled the walls of the building, lifting chunks of concrete and pieces of the roof into the air, smashing down on automobiles, and crashing through the trees over Thompson's head. Black smoke and flame billowed through the doorways and windows and rose in a dense cloud through the gaping wounds in the roof.

The blast of fire quickly died, leaving a pall of dense smoke enveloping the wreckage, through which Thompson could see small tongues of flame licking at the broken edges of exposed boards and roof rafters. One of the derelict autos was smoldering, its upholstery ignited by the gunfire. From another a mannequin hung headfirst out a back-door window, its plaster fingers lightly brushing the ground. Sprawled around the grass among the other cars, the broken bodies of the other mannequins lay in grotesque caricature of real corpses, their mutilated trunks and appendages ripped and separated and folded in impossible positions.

The attack was over.

For a long time Thompson lay hidden in the leaves behind the bushes, waiting for the ringing in his ears to subside, contemplating the meaning of what he had just witnessed. It was a rehearsal for something, he knew. A full-scale dry run for an attack on something, somewhere. On some *people* somewhere. But who? And where? And by whom? And to what possible end?

He had found the X on the map; of that he was certain. But the mystery had only deepened.

As dusk neared, Thompson ventured from his hiding place, satisfied that the men in the minibuses didn't plan to return. He followed the path through the grass across the field to where it disappeared into the woods on the far side. A short distance from the meadow he came upon a smaller clearing, occupied by three long mobile homes set tightly in a row beneath a stand of pine trees.

No one was around. Tire tracks in the dirt and grass indicated that the minibuses had stopped here and then moved on, following the road deeper into the woods. Thompson inspected the grounds and then tried the doors of the mobile homes. The first two were unlocked, and a quick look inside told him that they had been used as barracks, presumably by the men he had just seen out on the field. Mattresses were spread on the floors; Thompson counted a total of twelve. Empty drawers, some scattered clothing, and discarded food containers and beer bottles suggested that the occupants had just moved out, apparently in the time since Thompson had watched them perform their strange maneuvers on the field. He picked up a shirt lying on the floor next to one of the mattresses. It was of cheap white cotton, left behind because of a long tear in one sleeve. He looked at the label in the collar: "Los Caballeros, 52 Calle San Miguel, Mexico, D.F. Hecho en Mexico."

The third mobile home was locked. Thompson walked around it twice, looking for a way in, and then kicked at the front door hard with the heel of his shoe. On the third kick, the cheap lock gave way and the door banged open.

The interior—living room, bedroom, dining room, kitchen, bath—was cheaply furnished but tidy and clean, in marked contrast to the other two. A headquarters? The coffee table in the narrow living room was piled with copies of *Time, Newsweek, Business Week, Esquire, Playboy,* and several newspapers, including recent editions of *The Wall Street Journal, The New York Times,* the Manchester (N.H.) *Union Leader,* and the Washington *Star.* The kitchen refrigerator was stocked with frozen foods, orange juice, beer, and ice cream, the shelves filled with cans of soup, rice, potatoes, and other staples.

In the bedroom Thompson discovered a map of the park pinned to the back side of the door. It showed considerably more detail than he remembered from Roland's map. Two penciled-in squares indicated the location of the big field and the site of the mobile homes, almost dead center in the middle of the park. About half a mile north of them, an airstrip had also been penciled in, connected to the field by a roadway. The remainder of the map's markings showed the roadway system and the locations of the various private cabins, with their owners' names next to them: Eagle Point, Frank R. Connally; Sunrise, Jerome Stoddard; Deerslayer, Ralph Barkley; Wit's End, Stanley N. Whitney; Highground, Roger Hopkins; Wilderness, Gen. William Ward; Voyageur, Charles MacIntyre; and so forth. Senator MacNair's cabin was called Big Sky.

Thompson knew who William Ward was, and Charles MacIntyre was the governor of New Hampshire. The other names were not familiar. The map also showed the seven separate entrance gates of the park, spaced around the perimeter fence at roughly even intervals. Near the main gate stood a cluster of buildings—a main lodge, a game and forester's station, and a visitors' lodge. The map divided the park into zones, marked in red ink, and below the map a schedule was posted, indicating which zones were in use by which party on which days. "Connally and guests, Zone B, Aug. 10 thru 15" was a typical entry.

At the bottom of the schedule the following notice appeared: "All cabins in the park will be in use by Senator MacNair and his guests for the following dates: 10/27, 10/28, 10/29, 10/30.

Thompson stared at the last date. Ten/thirty. Today, he recalled, was October 28. Early evening. Zodiac's day would begin in thirty hours.

In the fading light of dusk, Thompson searched the trailer, but found nothing out of the ordinary. Exhausted and in pain, he took some time to clean and treat his leg wound with iodine from the medicine cabinet and make a clean bandage with a couple of strips ripped from the bed-sheets.

In the kitchen he opened three cans of tuna fish and devoured them all, washing the meal down with canned orange juice. Darkness was settling fast in the woods outside. He started to flick on a light switch and then thought better of it. He opened the refrigerator door. No light inside, but the refrigerator was still cold, so he assumed that the power had been recently shut off. That was reassuring. It meant no one intended to return, at least for tonight. He was safe. He could stay there, in relative comfort, and be on his way in the morning.

He glanced at the newspapers. The headlines on the Washington *Star* read: "POLLS SHOW CONWAY WIDENS LEAD." The subhead continued:

"Democratic contender holds six-percent margin over Mills, according to Gallup." A companion story next to it was slugged: "Mills says polls are wrong, remains confident of victory." Thompson flipped idly through the rest of the paper and stopped at page twelve, his eye caught by a photograph. "Highlight of the reception for the New Turkish ambassador," the caption beneath it read, "was the appearance of Washington's most eligible bachelor, Veep Raymond Beecher, in the company of beautiful New York *Times*person Harriet Mitchell."

Thompson studied the photograph, grainy and difficult to see in the weak light. He looked at Harriet's face, the strands of stray hair across her forehead, the reckless smile. Beecher's arm was wrapped tightly around her waist, his hand spread with insinuating familiarity across her stomach, pressing into the dress hard enough to create wrinkles in the cloth around his fingers. They seemed to be posing in the center of a large crush of people, smiling and pressing in on them from all sides. The festive mood was striking. It looked like a wedding picture.

Thompson ripped the page out, crumpled it in a tight ball, and threw it as hard as he could across the room. It traveled only a few feet and fell soundlessly onto the carpeting. He stood up, still in a fury, and kicked at it, but his wounded leg gave way beneath him and sent him crashing to the floor.

He lay where he fell, too dispirited to move. He could not recall ever feeling such intense loneliness and despair.

33

The Chameleon directed the cone of light onto the dial three feet in front of him. This is the last possible place, he told himself. The last remaining bit of unexamined territory. If the man had anything to hide, it had to be hidden here.

In less than fourteen hours the Chameleon had combed through every inch of Senator Albert MacNair's property. He had broken into his Senate offices and his house in Chevy Chase, and cased them from corner to corner, top to bottom. And now he had completed the same exhaustive search of the senator's country home in Peterborough, New Hampshire. So far, he had not found what he suspected the senator must have. He stood in the dark of the second-story bedroom listening for the possible step of the caretaker, aware that the success or failure of his search depended on what lay behind the small metal door before him. It was possible that the wall safe, which he had discovered hidden behind an old family oil portrait, contained nothing more remarkable than the personal papers of a man's life—property deeds, a will, life-insurance policy, stocks, bonds—in which case the whole tenuous edifice of the Chameleon's theory would come crashing down. And Madame Regine would prove to be a false prophet; or worse, a charlatan.

He palpated the cool metal of the dial with his thumb and forefinger, then cranked it slowly around to the right. It was an old, relatively unsophisticated safe, a model built by Mosler in the early 1950's. But like most wall safes, it had not been opened very often, and the pin tumblers showed no signs of wear. The dial moved too smoothly under the pressure of his fingers; he could not crack such a combination lock without hours of effort. And disturbing the safe by cruder methods, like drilling, was out of the question. He must see what lay within, but no one must ever know that he had.

He sat down on the edge of the bed, turned off the flashlight, and concentrated his mind on finding a solution. There was always a way. An entire life spent defying the odds had taught him that. Perhaps he could divine the combination. What would a superstitious man, a man who believed in astrology . . . ?

The Chameleon switched on the flashlight and returned to the safe, his heart pounding in sudden anticipation. Of course!

He spun the dial a couple of times, stopped it, then slowly advanced the pointer around to the right until it rested directly on the fifth mark from zero. From there he gave it a complete turn to the left until it rested on 28, then to the right again to the number 20. He took a deep breath and tugged lightly on the knob of the dial.

Nothing. It remained locked. He tried the combination again, thinking he might have made a mistake: right 5, left 28, right 20. The result was the same.

"Dammit!" he muttered. He had felt sure it would be right. He sat back down on the bed. In two hours it would be dawn; he must be away from the house within an hour to be safe. Defeat was creeping into his stomach.

Wait. Reverse it!

The Chameleon jumped up, twirled the dial, then brought the pointer to rest on 20, spun it back around to 28, then advanced it to 5.

The door clicked open.

He stepped back, stifling a laugh. It was just too damned funny for words. He had actually divined the right combination! How silly, how predictable people were. How wonderfully predictable! The senator had set the combination to his birthdate, May 28, 1920—5/28/20, and then reversed the order of the numbers.

The Chameleon pulled out the pile of documents and began sorting through them. The first several items contained no surprises—a property deed to the Peterborough house, some life-insurance policies, a packet of stock certificates, a will.

A buff envelope wrapped with a rubber band proved to contain a stack of pornographic photographs. They were yellowing and brittle with age, and looked very amateurish—Polaroid shots taken years ago in what looked to be somebody's office.

A birth certificate stated that Albert Alphonse MacNair had been born at Massachussetts General Hospital, at three o'clock in the morning of May 28, 1920.

A heavy brown envelope contained five Krugerrands and a small diamond.

A letter from MacNair's mother, dated January 2, 1936, contained eight pages of close handwriting explaining to her son why she had left his father and was not coming back.

The Chameleon reached the last item in the pile. It was a black folder, approximately eight by eleven inches, and half an inch thick. A legend was stamped on the cover in gold: "TOP SECRET ZODIAC."

"Jackpot!" Chameleon whispered. "Jackpot!"

He began to read.

34

Monday morning, October 29

Thompson woke up disoriented and cold. Dawn was at the windows and a strong wind drove rain against the trailer. He struggled to a sitting position, stupefied from his deep sleep, and blinked his eyes at his watch. Fifteen minutes past six. He had slept for nine hours. He was thankful no one had returned during the night.

He roused himself slowly from the floor and stretched his limbs carefully. The wound on his thigh was swollen and sore, and felt hot to the touch. The rest of his body ached profoundly.

With the power shut off, the faucets in the bathroom sink refused to supply water. He found a bottle of drinking water in the refrigerator and used that to splash on his face. He looked at himself in the small mirror on the medicine chest and frowned. His face was ghostly and wan, and the two days' growth of beard shadowing his jaw emphasized his unhealthy appearance. He ran his hands through his matted hair to make it lie more or less along its part, and returned to the living room to consider his next move. He stood in the middle of the narrow room, watching the light outside grow brighter. It was Monday morning, October 29. Zodiac minus one. What should he do? Get out of the park before someone saw him? Or try to find an explanation for the mock attack he had witnessed in the field yesterday?

Looking down, he noticed that the carpeting near the spot where he had slept was pulled up in a lump. He bent down to straighten it out, and discovered that it was cut into a flap about two feet square. Something caught his eyes in the exposed floor underneath, and he folded back the entire flap to have a better look. A small metal flush pull, like the handles used on cupboards aboard small boats, was set into the floor near the edge of the cut carpet.

A trapdoor.

Two hard tugs pulled it open, and Thompson, straining to see into the compartment below, reached down and fished around with both hands. The space was quite small—a foot deep at most and no wider than the door that covered it—and it contained a single item: a black folder with a spring binder, holding a sheaf of papers about half an inch thick.

The binder's glossy black cover carried a three-word legend stamped in gold leaf. Three words that jumped off the folder at him and burned into his brain.

He swallowed hard, placed the folder on the carpet in front of him, and stared at it. His heart was pounding in his chest so hard that he could hear it. The X on Roland's map had marked the spot exactly. This was ground zero. He had come to the end of Roland's treasure hunt, to the heart of the murderous mystery that was consuming his life.

He picked up the folder again, gingerly, as if it might magically disappear if he mishandled it. The gold letters swam into view again: "TOP SECRET ZODIAC."

He took a deep breath and opened the folder.

The first page repeated the legend on the cover, and beneath that, inside the borders of a red rectangle was typed the following:

> THESE PAGES ARE CHEMICALLY TREATED.
> ANY ATTEMPT TO COPY THEM BY ANY METHOD,
> SUCH AS PHOTOGRAPHY OR XEROGRAPHY,
> WILL CAUSE THE PRINT TO DISAPPEAR.

The second page contained a warning:

> EXDIS
> TOP SECRET

EYES ONLY
UNDER NO CIRCUMSTANCES ARE THE CONTENTS OF THIS DOCU-
MENT TO BE SHARED WITH ANYONE, OR THE EXISTENCE OF THIS
DOCUMENT TO BE ADMITTED TO ANYONE. YOU ARE RESPONSIBLE
FOR THE SAFEKEEPING OF THIS COPY. THIS COPY IS NUMBER 4 OF 5
COPIES.

The next page was the contents:

OBJECTIVE
PERSONNEL
WEAPONS
SUPPLIES
TIMETABLE
CONTINGENCIES
MAP OF TARGET

Thompson turned another page and read the short paragraph it contained:

OBJECTIVE

Operation Zodiac will be a hit-and-run attack, with panic and
disruption as its chief goal. Capture must be avoided at any cost.
Maximum damage must be inflicted on the target structure and
the uniformed personnel manning it within the time span of five
minutes. Innocent bystanders are to be spared if possible, but not
at the risk of capture or failure of the mission's goals.

Thompson skimmed quickly through the pages of the next three
sections. "Personnel" contained the names and biographies of twelve
Mexican males—the same names listed in the cable in Roland's file, he
believed. And probably the same twelve men he had watched in the field
yesterday. "Weapons" listed brands and serial numbers of machine guns,
and types and amounts of ammunition. "Supplies" detailed a long list of
items, ranging from clothing, personal possessions, and food to passports,
cash, identity papers, visas and reading matter. Listed also were two
secondhand VW minibuses and two 1983 Toyota Land Cruisers.
The section headed "Timetable," Thompson studied carefully:

10/28	1800 hrs	Embark NYC. Three rental cars.
	2300 hrs	Disperse to separate accommod. Two airport motels.
10/29	930 hrs	Gather Aero Mexico lounge, JFK.
	1030 hrs	Flight 320 JFK–Mont.
	1430 hrs	Private cars to San Antonio.
	1800 hrs	Overnight, Finca Hidalgo.
10/30	1400 hrs	Embark for transfer.
	1430 hrs	Transfer at Calle Tenente.
	1500 hrs	Depart for target.
	1515 hrs	Arrive at target.
	1520 hrs	Initiate assault.
	1525 hrs	Depart target.
	1540 hrs	Transfer Calle Tenente.
	1600 hrs	Return Finca Hidalgo.
	2200 hrs	Begin disperse south singly.

Thompson turned to the map. It was a street map, with the name of the area blacked out. It looked to be a small city; the street names were in Spanish. The north side of the town was bordered by a large river, but again, the river's name was blacked out on the map.

Thompson returned to the timetable and tried to decipher its cryptic schedule. The twelve men were flying an Aero Mexico flight from JFK at ten-thirty this morning to "Mont." What the hell was "Mont."? Montreal? Montana? Montego Bay? Whatever its name, it was three and a half hours from San Antonio, and San Antonio was in Texas, so perhaps the identity of "Mont." didn't really matter. And Finca Hidalgo must be in, or very close to, San Antonio. It could be a farm outside the city, judging by the name. But if their destination was a farm near San Antonio, why didn't they fly directly to San Antonio in the first place?

The only way it made sense, Thompson finally decided, was if San Antonio was in Mexico. It was a common-enough place name. There were probably dozens of San Antonios throughout Central and South America. And if San Antonio was in Mexico, that would explain why they weren't flying there. It probably didn't have an airport.

Thompson tried again. From a city whose first four letters are "Mont." they would go by automobile to a town called San Antonio, and then to a nearby farm, Finca Hidalgo, where they would spend the night. The following afternoon, they would drive half an hour to an unnamed city with a street called Calle Tenente. Thompson looked at the street map again. He traced his finger along a line drawn in pen on the map, indicating their route. It came into town from the south, headed north through the center of town, then detoured down a series of side streets and terminated at "X." He turned the map sideways to read the tiny print on the street. Calle Tenente.

The schedule gave them half an hour at Calle Tenente, and then headed them north again, until they reached the point on the map where the inked-in line terminated at an arrow at the edge of town, just across a bridge over a large river.

That was their target. Something on the north bank of the river. Thompson tried to put together the information in the folder with what he had seen yesterday afternoon on the field. An armed band of Mexicans was going to attack something somewhere in Mexico, something resembling what he had seen on the field. What in God's name could it be? And how could it be so important?

He pondered it for some time, going over the details of the timetable and picturing the derelict automobiles, the mannequins, the shell of a building, the strange wooden barrier.

What the hell could "Mont." stand for? If he knew that, he could figure out the identity of the city near the site of the attack. Why hadn't they spelled it out? It was maddening! If only he had an atlas! He tried to conjure up a map of Mexico in his mind, but most of it was blank. He saw Mexico City somewhere down south, Mérida out off the Yucatán peninsula, Acapulco on the west coast, Tijuana on the California border. He vaguely recalled that there was a big city on the Atlantic side as well. What was its name? Veracruz. No help.

He looked at the timetable yet again. "1030 hrs: Flight 320 JFK-Mont. 1430 hrs: Private cars to San Antonio." He felt he could safely assume that the mystery city of "Mont." was four hours from New York City. That meant northern Mexico, even if the flight was nonstop. And if Aeronaves flew there from New York, it had to be big.

When it finally hit him, he felt ashamed of himself. Well, geography was never one of his strong subjects.

Monterrey.

No wonder they hadn't bothered to spell it out. It was too obvious.

Three and a half hours from Monterrey would bring them to Finca Hidalgo. Another half-hour would bring them to the city near the target. Another fifteen minutes would bring them to the target itself. So from Monterrey to the target required about four hours and fifteen minutes by car. But in which direction?

East or west would probably run them into the ocean.

That left north or south.

Thompson tried to remember distances. He had once driven through Mexico south from Texas, following the Pan American Highway to Mexico City. Monterrey, as best he could recall, was about 150 miles from Laredo, Texas, at the border.

That was it. He looked at the map again. The river could be the Rio Grande! And the town near the target could be Nuevo Laredo, just south of the river. Four hours and a half from Monterrey. Just about right.

So the attack, he calculated, was aimed at something just across the river, on the north side. What could that be? What lay between Laredo, Texas, and Nuevo Laredo, Mexico, that could be so important?

The image of the derelict automobiles swam into his head again, and the mannequins, and the wooden gate, and it all fell into place with a sudden jolt.

The border. The stage set out on that field was a mock-up of a border post!

And tomorrow would be the real thing. That band of Mexicans would attack the American customs post at Laredo. Judging from the stated objective in the folder, and from the rehearsal he had seen, the assault was going to be brutal.

It made no sense, he thought. In fact, it seemed preposterous. Training a bunch of Mexican thugs in secret in New Hampshire, then shipping them back south of the border so they could attack a U.S. customs post? Why? Who would benefit from such an insane act? Even the CIA couldn't conceive of something that demented.

But of course it made sense to somebody, he realized. To four unknown conspirators code-named Capricorn, Scorpio, Gemini, and Aquarius. If he knew who they were, Thompson thought, he might know the purpose of the attack. And why they were so willing to kill to keep it a secret.

Now, at least, he was in a position to act. He could do something to save the lives of innocent people at the border tomorrow. With this folder in hand, he could get some fast attention. The FBI. The border patrol. The Texas Rangers. But he had to get out of the park first.

He heard a noise outside. It was a distant thud, like a door closing. It startled him. He listened carefully, but heard nothing more. His wristwatch said seven-thirty. Time to get out of here in any case, he thought. Before someone found him. It was a long way through the woods to the fence. With his bad leg, travel would be slow. He set the trapdoor back into place, folded the flap of carpet over it, and tucked the folder under his arm.

There it was again.

He caught his breath and listened. It sounded closer. Manmade. Definitely manmade. A car door? He'd better get moving.

He looked out the windows of the trailer. It was still raining, but it had tapered off to a drizzle. In the window by the kitchen alcove he thought he saw something move in the bushes. He strained his ears to pick up the faintest sound. The rain pattered lightly on the metal skin of the mobile home. Nothing more.

Was someone waiting for him outside? Hiding in ambush? He stood, waiting to hear something, watching for movement. Nothing. He was letting his imagination run wild. Still, he was crazy to stay in this potential trap another minute.

He slid the folder beneath his belt and buttoned his shirt over it to keep it dry.

A noise by the corner of the trailer made him freeze. It sounded like a bump — like someone bumping against the side. Dammit, it was probably a squirrel or a raccoon, he thought. They were always prowling around. He'd heard the same noise several times during the night. It was just that he was so jumpy.

He stood by the door, waiting for the sound again.

The hell with it, he told himself. He had to get going! He opened the door and took half a step outside, quickly looking to his right and left. Nothing around. Dead still. Just the light rain.

He closed the door quickly, and moving as fast as his sore leg would permit, he limped around to the back of the mobile home, toward the protective cover of a thick stand of pines. He felt a thrill of relief, being finally out and moving again.

Halfway past the end of the trailer an arm squeezed him around the neck from behind and pulled him over on his back, choking off his breath and turning the morning daylight and the green pines into a dancing sea of red.

35

Monday afternoon, October 29

Thompson surfaced from unconsciousness bound by the wrists and the ankles to a metal chair. The cord bit into his flesh. A violent headache surged across the back of his skull, and when he swallowed, he experienced a raw pain in his throat and neck that made him gag.

His captor sat across from him, legs crossed, one elbow resting on the Formica table in the trailer's dining alcove. He was sipping a bottle of beer and eating peanuts from a large jar, pouring out a few nuts into his hand, then shaking them slowly in his fist, as if he were rolling a pair of dice, before finally popping them into his mouth. His cowboy hat rested on the table next to the peanuts. Without it, his head looked small, narrow, emphasized by the hair combed straight back in the sixties style, thick on the top and cut close to the scalp on the sides. His face, neck, and arms were deeply tanned, and his hands were large and square.

A small tattoo was visible on the back of one hand—a circle inside an oval. It looked like the CBS television logo, Thompson thought. An eye.

His captor had not identified himself, but he didn't need to. The glass eye, the tattoo, made it plain that this was the mysterious Cyclops mentioned in Roland's file.

Thompson watched the movement of his arms as he swigged the beer and rattled the peanuts in his fist. The sleeves of his blue workshirt were rolled back, revealing a long, fresh scar on one forearm—a purplish strip of raised flesh that looked like a large welding seam.

Occasionally their eyes met. Thompson found it unnerving, looking at those eyes—one live one, a washed-out blue, darting restlessly back and forth, an eye from the jungle; and one dead one, cold as stone, focused on infinity.

Neither had spoken—Thompson because he did not trust his voice, his captor probably because he knew the silence would work on his imagination and magnify his fears.

If he turned his head slightly to the right, Thompson could see the trees beyond a small window. The rain had stopped and the sky was clearing. A cardinal, his red plumage dazzling in the bright sun, lit momentarily on a branch near the window, and Thompson turned his head away. The reminder of the innocent October day outside his prison was more than he wanted to think about.

Cyclops finished his beer and peanuts and introduced a new focus for Thompson's attention—a .38 service revolver. Cyclops drew it from a holster at his waist and began toying with it, snapping open the cylinder, loading each of its six chambers carefully with a bullet, snapping it back into place, spinning it slowly, then snapping it open and removing the cartridges and lining them up in a standing row on the table, like a rank of chess pawns.

He repeated the ritual several times. Thompson watched, fascinated, feeling dread trickle through him like a poison, paralyzing his will.

Cyclops studied the bullets, straightening them with a forefinger until he was satisfied that they were perfectly in line, then selected one and replaced it in the cylinder. He slapped the cylinder closed, spun it, then opened it and looked to see where the bullet had ended up. This ritual he also repeated, with a maddening deliberation, savoring every move with a quiet concentration that Thompson found unbearable.

Eventually Cyclops ended this torment and moved on to another. He spun the cylinder with its one bullet in one of its six chambers and brought the pistol up to his own temple. Thompson drew in his breath, not wanting to watch, unable to turn away. Slowly Cyclops increased the pressure on the trigger with his forefinger, and Thompson saw the cylinder begin its rotation into place, the hammer arch back, then snap forward.

A click.

Cyclops grinned and brought the pistol down from his temple and pointed it at Thompson's head.

Thompson could look directly down the small barrel, only four feet from his eyes. A round black hole in the end of a piece of metal pipe. Innocent, impersonal.

The deliberation with which Cyclops tormented him was pushing him toward nervous collapse. He searched for a place to transport his conscious mind, to hide it from awareness, to make it concentrate simply on the task of drawing breath, on living one second at a time.

Cyclops held the pistol on him for an eternity, until the desire to scream tore at his throat and he swallowed repeatedly and licked his lips, trying to bring the moisture to them that had fled to his palms and his neck, now soaked with perspiration.

The cylinder turned, the hammer struck.

"No . . ." he croaked.

Another click.

Thompson gasped, and fought down a powerful wave of nausea.

Cyclops repeated the ritual, bringing the pistol back up in front of Thompson's face, letting the barrel roam from eye to mouth to nose to cheek, as if hunting for the best target. Cyclops had pulled the trigger twice since spinning the cylinder, Thompson thought. The odds were getting short. Four chambers left. Three to one?

He will not kill me, Thompson told himself, chanting it inwardly like a prayer. *He will not kill me. He needs information from me. He needs to keep me alive.*

When Cyclops pulled the trigger again, Thompson's senses registered the explosion, the flash of red from the barrel in front of him, and the acrid smell of cordite. The bullet shot past his ear, splitting the air so close to his head that he felt the sting of its trajectory. The concussion of the blast slammed against his eardrums as if someone had clapped him violently over the ears. His self-control vanished. Tears streamed down his face, and his chest was racked by heavy, spastic sobs. Cyclops affected a look of disgust, returned the pistol to its holster, and walked outdoors, as if suddenly bored.

Thompson collapsed against the chair, letting his body go limp, and sucked in air. He trembled from head to foot, like someone with a malarial chill.

Cyclops returned to the trailer, zipping up his fly. "Gonna have to soften you up some," he said. The accent was southwestern, the voice low and scratchy, as if he had strained his vocal cords yelling at a football game.

Cyclops tugged at his wide leather belt and continued, "You're thinkin' that if you can just keep your mouth shut, I can't kill ya."

He walked over close to Thompson, thumbs in his belt loops, and stared out the window in back of Thompson's head.

"Let me tell you why that ain't gonna work. The next few hours is gonna be a nightmare for you, and before I'm finished takin' you apart, you're gonna be beggin' me to kill you."

Cyclops fastened his live eye on to Thompson's face, letting the message sink in. "Then you're gonna answer my questions, just to cut short the agony. Then I'm gonna kill you."

Cyclops gazed out the window again, his eye bright, as if he saw a beautiful vision.

"Put you out of your misery," he said. "Sometime tonight. And you're gonna thank me for it."

Cyclops stepped back from Thompson, raised his leg, and kicked the bottom of his boot into Thompson's face, sending him and the chair toppling to the floor. The chair back landed on his tied wrists, crushing them under the weight of his body, and he screamed in pain before he fainted.

When he came to, he was free of the chair, with his arms tied behind his back. He was being dragged out of the mobile home by Cyclops and another man, to a Volkswagen minibus—one of the beat-up blue vehicles he had seen full of Mexicans only the day before.

"We're gonna play another game now," Cyclops said, laughing at his private joke with a thin, mirthless cackle. "Beats Russian roulette *all* to hell!"

36

Monday afternoon, October 29

Harriet had barricaded herself in her motel room, waiting for the summons.

She was beginning to lose hope. Almost twenty-four hours had passed since the press plane had deposited her at the Manchester, New Hampshire, airport. And almost twenty hours since she had slipped one of President Mills's aides that note.

Had something gone wrong? she wondered. Had the aide failed to deliver the note to the President, even though she had made him swear that he would? It was hard to trust anyone in the present climate. Had the President somehow misread the note? Or failed to understand it? Its message was pretty unambiguous: "Mr. President," it said, "I have Allen Roland's file. Urgent I see you privately. I'm in room 334 at the Holiday Inn. Harriet Mitchell."

If the President hadn't understood the note, it would mean that Beecher had lied to her. Why would he do that?

It was three-thirty. According to his schedule, the President had already left Manchester for Halloween Park. Dammit! she thought. How much longer could she afford to wait? It was the afternoon of the twenty-ninth. She must see Mills. Or the whole trip to New Hampshire would accomplish nothing.

The telephone on the night table buzzed. The sound was feeble, but it sent Harriet springing from the bed as if bitten by a snake. "Hello?"

"Miss Harriet Mitchell?"

"Speaking!"

Harriet pressed a hand to her breast to quiet her heartbeat.

"The President will see you now."

A black Lincoln limousine driven by a Secret Service agent was waiting for her in front of the motel. It chauffeured her from downtown Manchester to Pease Air Force Base, where she was taken aboard a helicopter and flown northwest to Halloween Park, where the President, she was informed, would see her immediately.

She clutched the leather bag containing the file close to her side and watched the ground below as the helicopter swept in a long arc around toward the western interior of the state. The mixture of broad fields and woods gave way eventually to a carpet of solid forest draped over the spine of a long, low ridge of hills bright with color. A large rooftop, surrounded by several automobiles, came into view in a clearing, and just beyond it, a large meadow. The pilot, a suntanned, sandy-haired man with big ears and a wide grin, pointed toward the meadow, indicating that it was their destination.

The craft tipped forward and accelerated in a downward spiraling arc toward the clearing. Harriet could make out one large helicopter at the edge of the field, and a Land Rover parked in the middle, with two figures standing by it.

The helicopter swept in low, and for a moment seemed about to descend directly on top of the Land Rover. But the pilot edged the craft around in a tight circle and settled it down as gently as a falling leaf just thirty feet from the Land Rover.

The two men rushed up to the door on her side, pulled it open, and helped her to the ground. One man guided her arm, and the other took her bag from her and carried it to the Land Rover.

Harriet started to protest, anxious about letting the bag out of her hands even for a second, but the pilot had fired up the helicopter again, and the roar of the blades drowned out her voice. The one carrying her bag opened the rear door and tossed it carelessly inside, then came around to open the passenger-side door for her.

The other man maintained a firm grip on her elbow; he seemed almost to be pushing her along. The blast of turbulence from the helicopter blew against their backs and Harriet nearly lost her balance, only to be pulled upright by the strong hand on her arm.

She stepped up into the Land Rover, and he released her arm and trotted around to the driver's side. The other man, larger and older, slammed the door closed and climbed into the jump seat in the back.

The driver started the engine, popped the clutch, and stepped hard on the accelerator, propelling the vehicle forward with a neck-snapping jerk and sending it lurching across the grass field and bumping down a narrow dirt road.

"Boy," Harriet said, "when the President says jump, you guys really jump, don't you?"

There was no answer. Harriet stared at the driver. His eyes were fixed on the dirt track ahead of him, one hand squeezing the steering wheel, the other grasping the floor shift.

"I don't mean to seem pushy or arrogant" Harriet continued, "but when you pick up somebody for the President, aren't you supposed to show some identification, then politely introduce yourselves—you know, 'Welcome to Halloween Park, Miss Mitchell. My name is agent Jones. The President will see you at once.' Or 'The President will see you tomorrow morning.' Or 'The President has instructed me to tell you to go to hell.' Something like that."

She raised her eyebrows inquiringly in the driver's direction. Her attempts at humor made the large man in the jump seat behind her laugh. But it was a rude, unpleasant chuckle, and it made Harriet angry. She turned to address him just in time to see his big hand reach around her face and clamp itself firmly over her mouth and nose and jerk her head back violently against the seat. The handkerchief in his hand was soaked with a sweet-smelling liquid. Even before she could struggle, Harriet faded into unconsciousness.

IV
The Kill

37

Monday afternoon, October 29

They drove Thompson to the airstrip a short distance from the mobile home. Leon, a skinny, leathery-faced old man who sported a hunting knife in a holster on his hip, did the driving, while Cyclops sat in the back, his pistol shoved against Thompson's ribs. A large helicopter with "The United States of America" emblazoned across its side was parked on the near side of the field, guarded by two soldiers. Thompson wondered why it was in the park.

The car approached another craft, a sleek twin-engine executive jet bearing the legend "Graves Security Force" in black letters along its hull. A man waited for them at the bottom of the ramp by the doorway, while Thompson was hauled from the minibus and prodded up the steps in front of him.

He was the pilot, a fiftyish man with a brush mustache, a brown leather flight jacket, and a military manner. He didn't seem surprised to see Thompson brought in at gunpoint with his hands bound. He treated it with a peculiar sort of detached good humor, giving Thompson a friendly wink, as if the whole business was just a game.

Cyclops yanked the door closed and pulled down the handle that sealed it airtight. The plane's interior was arranged much like a small sitting room—four blue-upholstered swivel chairs anchored in a circle around a polished wood coffee table, another chair in front of a built-in desk against the forward bulkhead, and a sofa across the rear wall. The cabin appointments were luxurious—polished teaks and brass, elegant draperies, plush upholsteries—more like the fittings of a yacht than an airplane.

Thompson was ordered to sit close to the door; Cyclops sat opposite, his pistol still drawn, while Leon deposited himself in a small jump seat against the rear bulkhead.

The pilot grinned at Cyclops. "What's our flight plan, chief?" he asked.

Cyclops favored him with a malevolent one-eyed stare. "How big's this piece of jungle we're in?"

"Nine miles by five miles, more or less."

Cyclops nodded. "Let's just do a holding pattern around it. Make like you're stacked up over La Guardia."

The pilot touched his cap and headed toward the cockpit.

Within minutes the plane roared down the bumpy grass field and jumped into the air. It leveled off and settled into its "flight plan," circling clockwise around the park. The turbulence was strong, and at such low speed the ride was choppy. As the plane bucked and pitched its way around its invisible track, Cyclops recommenced playing with the revolver, spinning the cylinder indolently, giving no hint of what the plane ride was all about. Thompson wanted to speak, to cry out, to plead. But he held back. Cyclops seemed to have no interest now in talk.

Thompson was afraid of dying, but he was also afraid of the consequences of surviving. He feared that in trying to save himself, he might kill those parts of himself most worth saving. What might he do, after all, to preserve his life? Prostrate himself and beg for mercy? Tell Cyclops all he knew? Tell him lies to please him? Blame others? Harriet?

Cyclops turned to Leon, sitting quietly in the back. "Hey, old-timer! You ever do any skydiving?"

Leon touched his chest with his finger, surprised. "Me? Nah."

"You oughta try it."

Leon laughed and shook his head, showing his bad teeth. "Nah. Not me."

Cyclops mimicked his laugh. "Yeah, you. You oughta try it. Where are those chutes you packed aboard?"

Leon pointed to a bulkhead compartment behind him.

"Dig 'em out, Leon!" Cyclops gestured with his pistol toward the compartment. Leon pulled out what looked like an enormous nylon backpack and lugged it over to Cyclops' chair.

With uncharacteristic enthusiasm, Cyclops launched into a detailed lecture on the use of the parachute, insisting that Leon strap himself into the chute so Cyclops could demonstrate his points.

This must be for my benefit, Thompson thought. But why was he putting the old man through this torment? Was he going to make him jump?

Thompson's hands were tied, but his legs were free, and he yearned to strike back. Cyclops kept the pistol in his hand, but now he was ignoring Thompson, his attention focused on Leon and the parachute lesson. Thompson wished he dared knock the pistol loose. But he could not take on these two—and the pilot as well—with his hands tied. And where could he escape to? If he gained possession of the pistol, he would have to shoot Cyclops and Leon and then persuade the pilot at gunpoint to fly him to safety. He knew he could never do that.

He would have to be patient, watching the theater of humiliation being played out in front of him and trying not to dwell on where it might be leading. The terror of the morning's Russian roulette had passed, but it had left behind a residue of numb anxiety. The events of the past forty-eight hours had exhausted him, and as he sat there in the opulent cabin of a plane designed to ferry corporate executives around the country, the situation began to lose its reality. He watched the sunlight sweep around the windows of the plane as the craft continued its lurching, monotonous circuit of the park. It wasn't really possible, he thought, that this was happening to him.

Leon was now standing beside Cyclops' chair, wearing the parachute and listening with obvious anxiety as Cyclops demonstrated its operation. He looked ridiculous, like an overloaded pack animal, the bulky main and emergency chutes weighing him down from both front and back. The wide H-shaped harness strapped over his chest appeared several sizes too big, but Cyclops tightened it and pointed out the location of the rip cord.

"Now," Cyclops said. "This is as simple as picking your nose. I'll give it to you just like you was in jump school. You go out that door just like you was heading for a belly-flopper at the local swimming hole."

Cyclops demonstrated by bending forward, spreading his legs, and holding his arms out like a bird's wings. When Leon tried to imitate him, Cyclops jeered in disgust and pushed him with his boot into the floor.

"Now, stay right there!" he yelled. "Spread those fuckin' arms out! Now the legs—get those legs out! Head back!"

Leon strained to follow instructions, struggling and panting at the effort, trying to balance himself and his main chute on top of the small mound created by the emergency chute, strapped to his stomach. He kept tipping over to one side, and Cyclops with each fall kicked him in the ribs until he regained his balance.

"Okay," Cyclops went on, yelling like a drill sergeant, "that's your first count. That's how you go out the door! That's arch-thousand!

"Then look-thousand! You look for that fuckin' rip cord!

"Then reach-thousand! You grab that rip cord!

"Then pull-thousand! You pull that goddamn rip cord!

"Then look-thousand! You look back to see that that pilot chute is pulling out of that mother of a canopy. If it ain't . . ."

Cyclops pushed his foot against Leon's chute and rolled him over on his side. ". . . That's when you go for this sucker right here! That's the reserve chute—strapped to your skinny old gut!"

Cyclops grabbed Leon's hand and slapped it on to the handle of the reserve-chute rip cord. His pace was manic now, a sadistic burlesque of enthusiasm, pushing Leon into a panic.

"Now you pull that fuckin' rip cord!"

Leon started to pull it, and Cyclops stepped hard on his hand, arresting its movement. "No, you asshole! Don't pull it now!"

Leon winced from the pain and made a whimpering sound. "You *yelled* pull it!"

Cyclops yanked Leon back over on his stomach and put him through the drill again, making Leon yell out the count.

"Arch-thousand!

"Look-thousand!

"Reach-thousand!

"Pull-thousand!

"Look-thousand!"

When Leon had mastered the count, Cyclops walked over to the door near Thompson's seat. Still holding the pistol, he grabbed the door lever and pushed it up, breaking the air seal with the outside. The door cracked open with a whoosh, as air escaped the cabin to equalize with the outside pressure at fifteen thousand feet. Cyclops pulled the door back against the inside bulkhead. Thompson felt his ears pop and then the rush of cold air back into the cabin.

"Okay, Leon! Let's try it for real!"

Leon was sitting on the floor, recovering from his exertions. A look of sheer terror spread across his face; Thompson found it difficult to look at him. Cyclops stepped over to Leon, lifted him by the elbow to a standing position, and half-walked, half-dragged him to the door.

"There's nothin' to it, Leon! Be the biggest thrill in your miserable fuckin' life! Trust me on it! It's better than pussy, Leon! Swear to God!"

Leon's feet had given way beneath him, and he was now sitting in front of the door, with Cyclops' hand latched onto his backpack, trying to pull him to his feet again.

"Jesus, no! I can't do it! I can't do it!"

"Shit! Sure you can!"

"Honest I can't! I'm scared of heights!"

Cyclops seemed to relent for a moment. "You're a big disappointment to me," he said. "I thought you was gonna set a good example in front of our buddy, here. Show him what a real hard-ass tough sumbitch you are. And now you're turning into chickenshit, right in front of his eyes!"

Leon swallowed several times, trying to get his breath back. He looked pathetically grateful for the reprieve, but his eyes were transfixed by the doorway, gaping open directly before him, and his lined old face was as white as paint. Thompson turned his head away.

"Honest I can't," he gurgled.

"Sure you can, you old fucker!"

Cyclops' voice echoed with menace. Leon began to whimper again. *"Geronimo!"*

Cyclops yelled the word and gave Leon a violent shove that sent him toppling out the door. Thompson heard only a second's worth of scream, swallowed by the wind. Cyclops pressed his face to the edge of the doorframe, looking back toward the plane's wake, to spot the chute. In a few seconds he laughed.

"There, the dumb fucker did it!"

Cyclops crossed to the intercom on the forward bulkhead and flipped the On switch. "Captain! Take us up to twenty thousand!"

Thompson heard the pitch of the engines change and the faint growl of the hydraulic system as the pilot trimmed the ailerons and sent the jet surging into its climb. The cabin was quite cold now, and Thompson began to shiver.

With the elaborate deliberation that seemed to be his trademark, Cyclops pulled out another parachute from the bulkhead compartment and began strapping it on. Thompson felt an increased sensation of lightheadedness. The higher altitude was starving his brain of oxygen.

"Our turn to try a little jump, now," Cyclops said.

Thompson watched him attaching the harness to his waist. The pitch of the engines changed, and the plane leveled off. Twenty thousand feet. Four miles up. Higher than most of the world's mountains. Cyclops opened a compartment and pulled down an oxygen mask and held it to his face. Thompson stared, feeling disoriented and weak, his breathing increasingly labored. He sucked the thin air deep into his lungs and felt a momentary improvement. But thinking was becoming very slow, very difficult. Why didn't Cyclops give him some of that oxygen?

Cyclops had put his pistol back in his holster. He was talking to him, untying his hands. Thompson knew that was good, but he couldn't think what he should do. Maybe things were going to get better.

"Now, you see." Cyclops was grinning. "I'm gonna let you go. Ain't I a nice guy? Give you a fair chance to get away. Right out that same door."

Cyclops took a few more drafts from the oxygen mask, then put on a look of surprise. "Oh, shit! I forgot! Leon took your chute!"

Cyclops shook his head. "That's a shame," he said. Thompson nodded stupidly, agreeing with him. It was a shame.

"Well, shit. I tell you what," Cyclops said. "You just tell me who you told about that file you took from Roland's house. You tell me that and then maybe I'll give you my chute."

Thompson nodded. Why not? If that's all he wants, why not tell him? What harm could that do? Except he didn't see why he should have to jump.

"We got the file. Now all we need to know is who you told. I'm waiting right here to hear those names."

He stared at Thompson, studying him closely. Thompson was too groggy to answer him. He felt as if he had been given a shot of morphine. How could he have the file? Thompson wondered. Harriet must have given it to him. So he was right. Harriet was the enemy. She had betrayed him. He wanted to sleep. He didn't want to jump today at all. He just wanted to lie down on the floor. Cyclops squeezed his fingers into the base of Thompson's neck, causing pain to jolt him like an electric shock.

"Nobody," Thompson replied, his voice faint.

"Well, shit! I know better than that!" Cyclops replied.

"It's true," Thompson mumbled. "Nobody. Jus' me 'n Harriet."

Cyclops pulled Thompson by the hair, jerking his head back and forth and lifting him out of his seat. "Fuck! I thought I was gonna get some cooperation here!"

Thompson shook his head. He felt very dizzy.

"I guess you don't get Leon's chute after all," Cyclops continued. "A chute wouldn't do you any good, anyway. You wouldn't even know how to use the sucker! This way you won't have to bother your sissy little head with all that arch-thousand, look-thousand shit. Hell, no! For you it's just gonna be Geronimo!"

Cyclops came up behind Thompson and wrapped one arm tightly around his neck and the other one around his waist. Thompson tried to struggle, but he could barely stand. He couldn't think what he was supposed to do. Cyclops was pushing him toward the door. He could hear the blast of the engines and the wind, and feel the numbing cold.

"All you have to do," Cyclops was yelling in his ear, "is enjoy the fuckin' trip!"

Thompson dropped to his knees and groped for the edges of the doorway. His fingers found the steel lip that ran around the perimeter of the doorframe and squeezed it with all the strength he could muster. The panorama of the park, twenty thousand feet below, rotated slowly past.

Cyclops pounded on the back of his hands and broke his grip. Thompson clutched his hands to his chest and rolled over on his back. Cyclops loomed above him, reaching down to grab his arms. Thompson kicked upward with the toe of his shoe and smashed it into the assassin's groin.

Cyclops roared with pain and pressed his hand to his crotch. Wheezing like an asthmatic, he staggered back toward the oxygen mask.

Thompson watched him reach out unsteadily, trying to snatch it from where it dangled at the end of its hose, swinging back and forth with the lurches of the plane.

He must get oxygen too, Thompson thought. He grabbed the arm of the nearest chair and pulled himself onto his knees and finally to his feet. Cyclops, three steps away, still groped for the mask. Thompson lunged across the short distance before Cyclops was fully aware of his movements and grabbed the mask from the air, pulling it toward his own face.

Cyclops slashed out and struck Thompson with the edge of his palm between the neck and shoulder, sending Thompson crashing over sideways, still clutching the mask. The hose snapped free of its anchorage in the ceiling, and Thompson rolled over on his side, groaning from the blow and gasping from the enormous exertion he had made. He let go of the now-useless mask and tried to crawl toward the rear of the plane.

Waves of dizziness washed over him like a tide, threatening to pull him under. He fought it with everything in him, forcing his lungs to suck desperately at the thin air. He felt so numb and light-headed that he had lost a clear sense of the situation. Dim fear and a still-flickering purpose remained. His brain framed a simple message and sent it to every nerve in his body. *Stay in the plane. Stay in the plane.*

Cyclops flopped to his knees beside him, grabbed him by the belt, and started sliding him back in the direction of the open doorway. He saw Cyclops' face, contorted with exertion, the live eye bulging with his efforts to resist the bleeding away of consciousness.

Thompson's hands scrabbled for a hold—now the anchored metal leg of a chair, now the ungraspable strands of carpet pile, now the smooth surface of the wall near the open doorway. And each time Cyclops dragged him slowly past. He felt the chill roar of the wind again.

Cyclops was tugging with a spastic desperation at his pants and shirt, trying to advance him the last several feet. Thompson found his hands on the doorframe again, clutching it with a far weaker grip than a minute ago. The light around him seemed to be fading, as if evening had suddenly invaded the afternoon.

His head was through the doorway. He heard himself groaning. Something hard hit his fingers, forcing him to let go of the doorframe. A boot kicked his legs, kicked at the bottom of his shoes. Consciousness was fading. Specks of bright light were beginning to flash past his eyes. He screamed, but he could not hear his voice.

The wind was roaring in his ears, battering his clothes and face; the green, red, and yellow earth and blue sky were spinning past his eyes with a sickening rapidity; his arms and legs were pumping out, obeying the inborn infant reflex to reach for a hold. He was tumbling at a hundred miles an hour through the October afternoon.

38

Harriet could barely breathe.

Something in the air—the dust in the room or the pollens outside—had clogged her sinuses to the point where she could inhale just enough air through her nasal passages to avoid suffocation. Her hands were tied behind her back and her mouth was gagged with a rolled-up handkerchief held in place by a strip of cloth bound around ner neck.

She had been dumped on a narrow bed in a back room somewhere in a small lodge, and a heavy wool camp blanket, reeking of mildew, had been thrown on top of her. By shaking her head back and forth, she had been able to move the blanket free of her face and examine her surroundings. The room was a cubbyhole, its only furniture the bed, its only light filtered through a heavy curtain drawn across a small window.

Harriet tried to change her position, but found it impossible. Her wrists were bound together in back and tied to her ankles, which were pulled up behind her. The more she struggled, the more her lungs burned for lack of oxygen. Eventually she gave up and lay still on the bed, concentrating on getting her breathing back.

A door closed in the next room. She heard a chair scraping across the floor, and a muttered greeting. She lifted her head from the mattress to listen. Two men were talking. Their voices were muffled, but she could make out the words.

"Where is she?"

"In there."

"Ah."

"You want to talk to her?"

The other man laughed, and Harriet was jolted by the familiarity of the sound. That wheezing, salacious rumble could belong only to Senator Albert MacNair. "No, no, of course not," MacNair replied. "Can she hear us out here?"

"I don't know."

"You don't care?"

"I said I don't know. But it isn't going to matter, Senator."

She heard the senator clear his throat. "Is this the file?"

"That's it. The dumb broad had it in her bag."

"What's in it?"

"Not a hell of a lot, it turns out. But enough to explain a few things."

"Zodiac?"

"No details. The name and date appear, that's all. There's a map of the park, a couple of reports from someone giving our code names, and copies of a cable exchange between Langley and Mexico City on the recruits. That's it. Take a look for yourself. I'm bringing it to Capricorn tonight."

A silence followed, punctuated occasionally by the tap of a glass on a table and the faint flick of a turned page. Capricorn, she thought. According to Roland's file, he was Zodiac's leader. Did that mean that he was here in the park?

"How the hell did Roland get these documents?" Senator MacNair asked.

"I don't know. But I think he must have gotten some of them from Klimentov."

"Who's he?"

"He was a GS-13 at the agency. Counterintelligence. A Roland holdover. I should have fired him, but somehow he got overlooked. He's dead now."

It took Harriet a minute to make the connection. When she did, the shock was profound. William Ward! My God, she thought, no wonder

Arch Truley had seemed so alarmed when she had shown him the file. Something in it must have told him that his boss was involved.

MacNair and Ward. A U.S. senator and the director of the CIA. And there were two others, including Capricorn, their leader. So the conspiracy went to the very heart of Mills's administration. What in God's name could they be planning to do?

"What about the Zodiac team?"

"They're on their way, Senator."

"Laredo?"

"Laredo. And Harrison Conway's making a speech there just hours before."

Both men laughed. "That'll put a firecracker under his bandwagon," MacNair said.

"It's inspired. Leave it to Capricorn to think of that twist. The man's a genius."

They talked briefly about a boar hunt they were scheduled to go on the following morning, then fell silent. MacNair cleared his throat, then spoke in a quieter voice, which Harriet could barely hear.

"I'm nervous about all this."

"What the hell are you nervous about?" Ward asked. "We're home-free now! We have the file, and the leaks are all plugged. Mitchell's in the bag. And Cyclops is working over Thompson right now. We're pretty sure she didn't tell anyone but Truley about the file, and we don't think Thompson told anyone at all. But Cyclops will make sure."

Harriet shut her eyes. She felt she would drown in the turbulent wash of emotions. Anger. Fear. Guilt. Remorse. She had pushed Jay into this, against his own judgment. And she had taken the file, without telling him. A terrible mistake. What could he have imagined? It was probably because of her that they had been able to capture him. And now she had blindly tumbled right into their hands, and brought the file with her! What an idiot she had been, she thought bitterly.

MacNair was talking: "It just seems so damned dangerous! Messy. I keep asking myself if you've thought this all the way through."

"What do you mean?" Ward's voice was querulous, challenging.

"What are you going to *do* with them? You know . . . to keep them quiet."

Ward laughed. "We'll let Cyclops handle that. He's the disposal expert."

"It makes me queasy as hell. How the hell will you explain the disappearances?"

"What's this 'you' business, Senator? It's 'we,' isn't it?"

"I'm perfectly aware of my involvement," MacNair said. "What bothers me is what the rest of you are doing that may put *all* of us in jeopardy. The way things are going, I feel like a hostage to incompetence."

"Then let me set your mind at rest. We won't have to explain anything. Graves is going to eliminate Cyclops after this job. It's long overdue. Then everything will be hung on Cyclops. He takes the fall for it all. We arrange a hunting accident and we hang the whole business on his dead body. We'll have complete deniability. Legally it's a cinch."

"As a lawyer, I can tell you that nothing criminal is *ever* a cinch, particularly at this level. How does *his* disposal get explained away?"

The irritation in Ward's voice was sharp. "An assassination attempt against the President. Perfect cover. And given Cyclops' background, totally plausible. It'll never even be seriously questioned, let alone investigated."

Another silence, then MacNair's voice again: "I'm nervous about keeping her here."

Ward raised his voice, his tone sarcastic. "Where do you suggest we put her? In the President's bedroom? Just relax, for Christ's sake. This is no time for a case of nerves. She'll be out of here tonight."

"You realize that if we ever get caught . . ."

"Who's going to catch us? We're in a thirty-thousand-acre game preserve. With a fence around it patrolled by the Secret Service!"

Another silence; then MacNair again, sounding resigned. "I should have realized this might lead to killing. . . ."

"Just remember who's doing the dirty work, Senator. Not you. So let us do the worrying, too."

A scraping of a chair indicated MacNair was leaving.

"And what about this man Truley?" MacNair demanded, his voice suddenly loud. "The one Cyclops brought with him. He's as dangerous to us as Thompson or Mitchell."

"Hardly."

"What do you mean?"

"He's dead."

"Jesus! Another one."

"That's right. Truley found out about Zodiac through Mitchell. But one of Graves's men was following him and turned him over to Cyclops. No one will ever find his body in the park. Cyclops—"

"Stop!" MacNair roared. "I don't want to hear any more."

A door slammed.

Tears rolled from Harriet's eyes. God help me, she prayed. God help me.

39

Monday afternoon, October 29

Cyclops lay on the floor by the plane's open doorway, breathing hard and concentrating on his watch. He followed the sweep second hand around with his eye until it hit forty-five seconds. At that moment, he punched the hand back to zero and started it forward again.

Then he fell out the door.

Once away from the plane, he brought himself immediately into a "frog"—a relaxed, face-to-earth free-fall position, his legs bent back at the knees and his arms spread out and bent forward at the elbows, forming a shallow U. This suited his purposes better than the basic arch position, because his line of sight was directly down, and the reduced drag increased his rate of descent. At five seconds from the door he was falling at 84 miles per hour; at six seconds, 94; at seven, 100. At twelve seconds his speed leveled off at 125 miles per hour.

He adjusted his hands alongside his head, palms downward about a foot from each ear, then began to tilt his palms sideways until they were at a forty-five-degree angle with the earth. The slight deflection of air off the palms' surfaces caused him to begin to rotate slowly. Carefully he dipped the shoulder facing into the turn's direction, to increase the speed of his rotation, and scanned the woods and lake spread out below him.

About halfway through the rotation he spotted Thompson. He was below and directly in front of him, roughly two thousand feet away, Cyclops judged. He was tumbling out of control, cartwheeling through the sky in a spectacular Z.

Cyclops straightened his knees, bringing his legs into line with the trunk of his body, and stretched his arms against his side, causing his torso to slip downward and forward. Like a diving eagle closing on its prey, Cyclops screamed through the air, accelerating his velocity to almost 200 miles per hour. The wind tore at his face, causing his good eye to tear. He cursed himself for forgetting goggles. He risked his flight stability to wipe his eye and then modified his position by bending slightly at the waist, cupping his hands in front of his knees, and spreading his legs slightly. This gave his body more lift, causing his dive to flare out into a shallower angle. Using his hands, arms, and feet to alter the deflection of wind around his body, Cyclops controlled his speed and direction and slanted steadily downward and forward toward Thompson's cartwheeling form.

Sixty seconds from the airplane door, he had closed to within twenty feet of him. He was almost directly above him now, relieved to see that Thompson was falling well within the boundaries of the park. He could see the narrow strip of perimeter road snaking through the deep blanket of trees in a wide arc off to his right.

Suddenly he noticed that Thompson was changing his position.

His flailings had abruptly thrown him over onto his back, and he was now falling faceup, legs and arms pointed skyward. Cyclops flared into a frog position ten feet away, aligning himself carefully just above and behind Thompson so he could duplicate his velocity exactly. Thompson's new configuration was increasing his rate of descent dramatically. It was going to be close, Cyclops judged. Damn close.

Cyclops dropped down, closing the remaining ten feet that separated them. The sweep hand on his wristwatch had passed the first minute and was fifteen seconds into the second minute. Eight thousand feet from the ground, Cyclops estimated. Time to impact, forty seconds. He must pull at one thousand feet at the latest, and that would be coming up at 1:50 into the fall. Thirty-five seconds from now.

Thompson was looking up at him, fully conscious, eyes popped wide open, lips pulled back from clenched teeth. The phrase "contorted with terror" crossed Cyclops' mind. He was fascinated. The idea of being just feet away from a man who knew he was falling to his death thrilled him deeply. He wished he could go on watching; he wished he could take a photograph.

Alternately bending and straightening his knees, pulling his arms in and extending them, Cyclops inched down alongside Thompson until he could reach out and touch the bottom surface of Thompson's shoes. He had expected to get Thompson around the waist from the back, but that was no longer possible. He would have to improvise.

He reached down and grabbed Thompson's ankle with both hands and pulled it up toward him, causing Thompson to complete half a backloop, spinning until he was standing on his head in midair, then falling back over to the horizontal, facedown. As soon as Cyclops had him revolving, he let go of the ankle and grabbed Thompson around the waist, to guide him through the half-backloop, and to steady his own position, falling with him. The turn complete, he gripped Thompson from behind with both arms, one around the waist, the other around the chest. Thompson was flailing, but Cyclops maintained them in a stable position by maneuvering his legs.

The ground was close. A solid mattress of trees loomed below, closing in on his eye like the image in a zoom lens. He didn't like landing in the trees, but he had no choice about that. He moved his hand off Thompson's chest momentarily to check his watch: one minute, forty-nine seconds into the fall.

Time was up. He had never pulled this late.

Suddenly Cyclops lost control of their formation, and they began to tilt forward headfirst. He swore to himself. The pull was going to be a real son of a bitch now. But no time remained to correct their attitude.

Cyclops found the rip cord and snapped it out, then instantly wrapped his arms back around Thompson's waist and chest.

The pilot chute, spring-loaded into the top of the parachute container, popped out into the airstream and inflated. Acting like a wind anchor, it pulled the sleeved canopy out of the container behind it, followed by a spaghetti-like mass of suspension lines, unstowing rapidly from their rubber bands and unlocking the sleeve flap, allowing the sleeve to slide up and off the canopy. The small drag offered by the pilot chute and the canopy sleeve corrected their tilt slightly, but they were still tipped dangerously head down. The pilot chute pulled the sleeve completely free, exposing the canopy fully to the streaming air, which gathered rapidly under it and began to inflate it, from the apex downward, like a giant balloon. Instantly the canopy bellied out full, like the skirt of a cancan dancer, and bounced upward, inverting itself momentarily, jerking Cyclops and Thompson violently upright, snapping them in seconds from 125 miles an hour to fifteen. Cyclops braced himself to maintain his grip on Thompson, feeling as though his arms would yank from their sockets.

They steadied twenty feet above the treetops. Cyclops felt his skin erupt in perspiration. He had pulled with less than a fifth of a second's margin.

They floated down into the tops of a thick stand of pine trees, and slipped and bounced through, branches stabbing them from every side. Cyclops was pleased he had Thompson in front of him, to shield him from the worst of it.

The fall ended twenty feet from the ground. Cyclops looked up behind him. The chute had caught on a high branch. He tried to bounce up and down to break it free, but could manage to move it only a few inches. He would have to unfasten his harness and jump down.

But there was the problem of Thompson, now a deadweight in his arms. He would have to drop him, of course, but he wanted to make sure he had no chance of getting away. He moved the hand holding Thompson by the chest to Thompson's neck, and pressed hard on the nerve under his ear. He believed Thompson was already unconscious, but this would make certain.

He dropped Thompson to the ground, watched him hit, landing limp and unmoving in a bed of pine needles. Cyclops unbuckled his harness and swung free of it onto a heavy limb and started to climb down. Halfway to the ground, he saw Thompson stagger to his feet and in a lurching run scramble across the pine needles into a dense cover of evergreens and disappear from sight.

40

The room had been dark for several hours, except for the thin sliver of light beneath the door. Since Ward and MacNair had departed, Harriet had been fighting a losing battle with panic, wrestling with a seemingly unsolvable problem—how to get free.

For a long time she had struggled with the ropes binding her hands and feet, and succeeded only in making them tighter. Now she lay still and pushed her exhausted brain to tackle the problem again. But all her efforts came back to the same inescapable reality. She couldn't get out unless she could get untied, and she couldn't get untied unless someone untied her or she somehow cut the rope herself. Yet neither was possible.

Once, when she was ten years old, she had locked herself in a bedroom closet while playing hide-and-seek. The closet door had a slide bolt on the outside, and by using a piece of string she had devised a clever way to lock it from inside the closet, so it would appear to her cousin that she could not possibly be hiding inside.

Unable to find her, her cousin had eventually given up the game and left the house. Harriet had waited in the dark closet for nearly an hour, enjoying her cleverness, before it dawned on her that she could not get out by herself. She had yelled for help, but no one came.

Her aunt had finally found her, several hours later, crying and distraught. It was the first of many times that someone would tell her that she was too clever for her own good. At least then there were adults in the world, she thought, benevolent giants to step in and rescue you when your foolhardy adventures went astray.

No rescue this time. Either she got out of this dark closet by herself, or she didn't get out at all.

It was the wind, finally, that gave her an idea. The breeze had picked up outside, and rattled the window, an old double-hung wooden-frame model with six panes in each half—upper and lower. She wished she could smash it, break through the glass and push herself outside. It couldn't be done, of course. Suicidal, ridiculous. Even if she could succeed with such a stunt, she would only hurt herself, and she would still be as tied-up as ever. And the noise would only attract the attention of her captors.

But there was another possibility.

With great effort she raised her head and upper torso off the mattress and struggled to throw her body weight upward into a kneeling position—the only position possible, given the manner in which she was tied. After a dozen failures she succeeded, landing upright on her knees, and then letting herself tip back until her toes touched the bed behind her. It was brutally uncomfortable, but as long as she didn't lean too far forward, the position was reasonably stable.

Carefully, painfully, she walked her knees across the bed until they were pressed against the wall, directly under the windowsill, which met her at waist height.

A curtain was drawn over the window, but she counted that a help, since it would protect her head against the glass when it shattered. She studied the panes—six in the two rows in the bottom half of the window—and picked the one in the middle of the top row. She pressed her forehead against it, but the action pulled the rope around her ankles up and lifted her toes off the mattress. She steadied herself back on her toes again, and judged that she would just have to pitch herself forward against the pane. She cheered herself on, nerving herself for the blow. She knew she risked being overheard, but several hours of silence in the adjacent room had convinced her that no one was there.

She threw herself forward, driving her head toward the pane, and felt the bump of the wooden window frame strike her across the forehead. The blow knocked her off balance, back onto the mattress.

She struggled to her knees again, then pressed her forehead tentatively to the spot on the pane she wanted to hit—taking aim, in effect, intent on not smashing her head against the wood again.

An explosion of glass shards rewarded the second try. Harriet felt a tremendous surge of exhilaration and fell back down on the bed to rest.

Back up on her knees after a short respite, she edged toward the window to study the damage. A dim half-moon, slipping in and out of the clouds, bathed the trees and parking area outside in faint silver light. The pane was completely gone; barely a shard remained. It was an upsetting discovery, but she knew immediately what she had to do. She lined herself up with the next pane to the right, took its measure, and pitched her head into it.

When she got back on her knees this time, she found several pieces of jagged glass remaining in the frame. Perfect! Slowly she worked herself around on the bed until she was facing away from the broken window, and then walked her knees backward until the bottom of her feet pressed against the wall beneath the windowsill and she could grope with her fingers along the windowpane.

But she had miscalculated.

The panes she had broken were too high for her fingers to reach. She strained to twist her hands upward, but her fingers could not reach more than halfway up the lower row of panes, at least six inches below the broken panes in the row above.

She had to break a pane in the lower row, and it was going to be a lot harder to do. Don't give up now, she told herself. Don't give up now!

It took her four exhausting attempts. Each time, aiming her head low into the bottom middle pane, she misjudged it, missing the spot and hitting the wooden frame. She was sweating profusely now, even against the cold wind blowing in the broken panes, and her forehead ached as if with a migraine. But the fourth time it worked. After another brief rest on the mattress, she succeeded in getting her fingers against the pieces of broken glass sitting in the bottom groove.

The first piece she was able to pull loose seemed ideal for her purposes. It was large, easy to hold, and jagged enough to cut rope. But she dropped it, and listened to it clatter to the floor between the bed and the wall, completely out of reach.

272 /   VERNON TOM HYMAN

Harriet looked into the heart of despair. The hopelessness of her predicament was beginning to reach her. She would never escape. She would die. They would kill her without a qualm. She was just one more obstacle to be swept aside, one more troublemaker to be silenced.

Her strength was ebbing. She could barely resist succumbing to the urge to fall back on the bed. It took all her effort now just to breathe, drawing air painfully through her nose, her body trembling from her exertions. She prayed for the strength to continue, to try one more time.

Her fingers found the windowpane again, and she cut two of them on the jagged edge of the glass. Ignoring the blood trickling down her wrists, she pulled another piece of glass free and collapsed onto the bed sideways, concentrating on the single, vital task of maintaining the precious object in her grasp.

She rested again, and then gradually, remaining on her side on the mattress, she worked the shard of glass into position in one hand and twisted her wrist down until the shard's edge encountered the rope tied between her ankles and her wrists.

The rope was nylon, not hemp. After minutes of sawing, she ran her fingers along the rope and could feel only small scratches on the cord's surface. She tried exerting more pressure, pulling against the rope with her ankles to make it as taut as possible, to hold it more firmly against the cutting edge of the glass. A dozen times she dropped the shard and a dozen times she scrabbled blindly around on the mattress with her fingers to find it again, cutting herself repeatedly.

When it happened, it caught her by surprise. She was pushing her legs downward, moving them back and forth to increase the sawing motion, impervious to the terrible pain it inflicted on her wrists. Suddenly the rope snapped, and her legs shot out straight, sending a jolt of intense cramps down her thighs and the back of her knees, bent so long at a ninety-degree angle.

She lay still, letting the cramps subside. A thrill of hope came flooding back. Maybe it was possible. Maybe she really could escape after all. Cutting the cord that still bound her wrists was going to be difficult, but she had cut the cord once. She could do it again. She had a chance.

The door burst open.

Images, sensations, crowded in on her faster than she could sort them out.

The door slammed closed and a dark shadow loomed behind a blinding beam of light and advanced toward the bed. Harriet blinked her eyes against the intense brightness and felt her hair twisted and pulled, yanking her upright from the bed. She saw a hand place a flashlight on the mattress, then move toward her face. The hand smashed against her cheeks, ears, and jaw again and again, a barrage of stunning blows that seemed to explode inside her head.

The slaps stopped, and in the ringing silence the hand ripped the gag brutally from her mouth.

Her heart raced furiously, and she wanted to scream, but couldn't. Something inside her pressed against her chest with a terrible pounding weight, forcing spastic sobs and gasping noises from her throat. She felt as if she were drowning, choking on air.

Her head and body were a firestorm of panic of a kind she had never before imagined. She was in the midst of a severe trauma, unable to control her reactions, unable to breathe, to speak, to act.

The slapping hand now moved to the front of her blouse. It clawed at the top button for a firm grip, then ripped the blouse wide open down to her waist. She watched the hand grab the bra next, and jerk it off with one hard pull that broke the straps around her back and shoulders.

The intense pain on her hair suddenly eased, as the intruder released his hold and turned away from her momentarily.

She fell on her back onto the mattresss, writhing convulsively, alarmed by the terrible pounding inside her chest.

She saw the beam of the flashlight follow the baseboard along the wall farthest from the bed. When it came to a wall socket, it stopped, and the other hand plugged in a lamp cord.

No light came on, however.

The intruder stood up and returned to the bed, shining the flashlight in her eyes again, and then resting it upright on the floor, so that its beam shone across his features, exaggerating them into a sinister caricature of a face. She knew whose face it was, although she had never seen it. It was the face of Cyclops.

She saw two hands, extended in front of him, clad in rubber gloves. The lamp cord's wires had been separated, and each hand held one end, pinched between thumb and forefinger, the last several inches of which were stripped of their insulation.

Cyclops spoke, the planes of his face forming grotesque shapes of light and shadow, one eye sparkling like agate.

"I'm gonna ask you a question, cunt. I ask it, you answer it, right off.

Don't hesitate. I don't have any time to fuck around with you. You got that?"

Harriet tried to say "No," but nothing came out. She spoke into a soundless void.

"Who knows about the file!"

Harriet shook her head, her eyes fastened with dread to the raw ends of the lamp cord, now held close above her face.

"No . . . nobody," she gasped.

The rubber-clad hands moved rapidly down toward her, bearing the live wires of the cord—one against her throat, pressing the wire to her jugular; the other pressed into the nipple of her breast.

She burned with a pain that drummed through every nerve passage of her body—a jolt that seemed as if it were melting her bones.

She found the strength to scream. It came out in halting waves, between sharp intakes of breath, fighting the pressure against the throat.

She screamed and screamed and screamed.

41

Monday night, October 29

The Chameleon sat near the motel window in his underpants, to catch whatever breeze the Texas night had to offer. He could have turned on the air conditioner, but he preferred the warm desert air. It possessed a mysterious and not unpleasant smell in the evening, like the bittersweet scent of dry eucalyptus. It brought him memories of home, of his Egyptian childhood. Not many happy memories. His entire family was dispossessed and murdered by King Farouk's soldiers. Only he escaped into exile—an orphan at the age of ten.

The wretched Farouk. His name still tasted bitter after fifty years. It had been his desire for revenge, to kill the man who had dishonored and destroyed his family, that had forged in his heart an assassin's will, that had shaped his future as a political killer.

Better than most, the Chameleon understood the true nature of power. Once its victim, he had spent his life as its instrument. He was on familiar terms with the dragons that lived in the shadows of every palace, chieftain's hut, government house, and executive mansion. The dragons that compromised the high-minded and destroyed the weak; that corrupted and devoured; the beasts that transformed the ambitious into villains and murderers.

The Chameleon lifted the camera case onto the bed, opened it carefully, and removed the Arriflex 16S from the plush-lined interior. He checked the lens turret, then attached the shoulder pod—a brace to steady the instrument on the shoulder while shooting—to the mount at the camera's base.

Resting the pod securely on his shoulder, he aimed the camera out the window, peeped through the eyepiece, and adjusted the viewfinder until the streetlight several blocks away came into perfect focus. The magnification was ten-power, and it required a rock-steady hand to keep the image from bouncing.

He removed the camera from his shoulder, turned it around, and examined the twelve-inch boom that ran from the camera's front head forward over the lens turret. The boom's purpose was to support the matte box, a square frame hung in front of the lens on the end of a collapsible black bellows, used to hold filters and provide shade against reflections.

This boom served another purpose.

The Chameleon inserted a fingernail behind the tiny lip of a plug at the end of the boom and popped it out. Inside, the boom was hollow, expertly machined into a foot-long .22-caliber rifle chamber.

He rested the camera on the bed and turned his attention to the handle on the camera's case—a thickly padded six-inch-long grip attached to the case with a leather strap. He sliced off the padding from the handle with a penknife and held the bared core up to the light. It was a bluish-black rectangle of machine-tooled steel with a round opening in one end and a large slot cut out of one side. The breechblock and firing mechanism.

He opened the side door of the camera housing, slid the metal block snugly up against the back opening of the rifle barrel, and locked it into place. He marveled at the perfection of Anginotto's craftsmanship. The pieces fit with a solid, reassuring precision.

From inside the camera housing he fished out the male plug end of a set of wires and connected them to a terminal provided at the back of the breechblock. The wires converted the normal trigger and firing-pin mechanism into an electronically controlled device. To fire the weapon, he need only press the film-advance motor button on the camera grip.

Last came the ammunition clip. He dug out a can of talcum powder from his suitcase, removed its top, and extracted the clip from the powder with a pair of tweezers. After cleaning the clip thoroughly with his shaving brush, he counted out twenty bullets from a box of shells purchased earlier in the day and pressed them one at a time into the clip.

He snapped the clip into place in the bottom of the breechblock, closed the camera and hoisted it once more onto his shoulder.

He pressed his eye again to the rubber cup of the eyepiece. The viewfinder had been converted into an ingenious through-the-lens telescopic sight, complete with cross hairs and corrected for parallax.

He had tested the weapon in Italy, two days ago, driving out to a remote area near Ostia and firing it at a target he had crayoned on a rock. It worked.

The Chameleon packed the camera away and prepared for bed. It was late and he needed sleep. He must stockpile his energies for the task ahead.

He thought of the conspirators—Capricorn, Gemini, Scorpio, Aquarius.

He knew them all now. It had taken him only a few hours of research to find them, after Madame Regine's tip about Senator MacNair. With MacNair as the known part of the puzzle, the rest had been a straightforward process of elimination.

Senator Albert MacNair. Born, May 28, 1920. Sun sign: Gemini. The coincidence of his birth sign turning out to be one of the four code names in Roland's letter to him was too great to ignore. Especially given MacNair's own weakness for astrology. That left Scorpio, Capricorn, and Aquarius to be uncovered.

The Chameleon compiled a list of about a hundred names—members of Congress, the Cabinet, the executive, the military, big business, people with ties to MacNair. Their birthdays he collected from a library copy of *Who's Who.*

He quickly narrowed the original list down to a couple of dozen names. Then to six. Finally to three: a Capricorn, a Scorpio, an Aquarius.

He realized that the names could be wrong. It was possible. He had absolutely no proof. But given the nature of the Zodiac plan, logic told him his names were the right ones. They fit the puzzle too closely to be doubted: They all knew each other very well. They all held positions of power. They all shared a point of view. And a motive. And they all stood to gain by Zodiac's success.

And together they possessed the unique means to achieve their ends—
and get away with it.

The Chameleon could not catch them, nor could he bring them to
justice. He could not even expose them. He had neither the proof nor the
power.

He could only try to stop Zodiac. Try to destroy their plan.

He sat up in bed and swallowed the painkiller pills. They were a
necessity for him now. Without them sleep would never come.

This would be his last mission, he realized. The odds against him were
formidable. Most likely he would be killed. But he knew he would die
soon anyway. Better to die an instrument of justice, an instrument of
revenge. That was his destiny. It was what Allen Roland had unknow-
ingly saved him for when he rescued him from his own well-deserved
death on the Grande Corniche those many years ago.

He only regretted that he could not take on Capricorn, their leader,
face to face. But that was foolish daydreaming. That was beyond the
realm of an assassin's ambition. A tin-pot African dictator, an Eastern
potentate, an Arab strongman, a South American generalissimo, a Com-
munist-party boss, traitors and spies on all levels. These, yes. But not the
President of the United States.

42

The windows of Timberlake, the main lodge at Halloween Park, blazed with light. The rambling two-story structure, modeled after a Bavarian hunting lodge, with carved woodwork, balconies, cathedral ceilings, and stone fireplaces dressed with the trophy heads of boar and deer from the park, was the temporary seat of the government of the United States of America.

Secret Service and military vehicles filled the parking areas around the lodge, and special electronic communications equipment and telephone lines cluttered the grounds and hallways, guarded and fussed over by a small battalion of men from the Signal Corps and the Secret Service.

In a second-floor sitting room, closed off from the rest of the lodge and guarded, President John Douglas Mills sat at a thick oak trestle table eating a late dinner. With him at the table were Senator Albert MacNair, General William Ward, and John Graves.

Graves, anxious to ingratiate himself with the President, was boasting of the prowess of the park's newly acquired "catch dog," a fearless brute trained in Yugoslavia specifically to hunt boar. According to Graves, the dog—a Rhodesian Ridgeback—was capable of tracking a wild boar and holding it at bay almost indefinitely.

Mills was losing interest in Graves's talk. He cut in on him to order the waiter to clear the table, and Graves quickly shut up. The dessert dishes were removed and the waiter serving them disappeared for the night, leaving behind an urn of hot coffee and a well-stocked bar.

An awkward silence settled on the table. President Mills ran a hand over his bald head, a habitual gesture of his, and drained off the remains of a glass of Nuits St. Georges burgundy.

He looked around at the other three men at the table, thinking about their weaknesses. Their strengths were important, of course, but he knew that it was through their weaknesses that he controlled them. He looked for signs of fear, excessive nervousness, possible disloyalty. His main concern now, at the eleventh hour, was that none of them lose his nerve.

The President tilted his head toward MacNair. Among intimates President Mills dropped his corny, down-home Texas facade totally, and commanded those around him with the blunt authority of a ship's captain.

"What's your horoscope say for tomorrow, Senator?" he asked.

MacNair grunted uncomfortably, and sipped his glass of bourbon.

President Mills turned to Graves, the relative stranger in the group. "The senator here," Mills said, "takes his astrology seriously. Doesn't like me to kid about it. Maybe he's right. That's how Zodiac got its code name, after all. And how we got ours. It was the senator's idea, and the rest of us decided to indulge him. Maybe we thought it would bring us a measure of luck."

The President's tone bordered on sarcasm. He was edgy, and had consumed just enough alcohol to uncover some traces of belligerence.

"I'm Capricorn," he continued. "That's my sun sign. And Ward here is Scorpio, and the senator is Gemini. Makes the whole operation sound spooky as hell, doesn't it?"

Graves nodded and forced a laugh.

"When's your birthday, Mr. Graves?"

"September tenth, Mr. President."

Mills turned to MacNair. "What do you say, Senator? Do we have a code name left over for Mr. Graves? He's earned it, don't you think?"

MacNair snorted, annoyed at the ribbing. "You're a Virgo, Mr. Graves," he muttered.

The President laughed. "Virgo! Sounds a bit effeminate, doesn't it? Almost as bad as Aquarius. He's the fourth member of our little club, Mr. Graves. Aquarius. We left him home. He hates to hunt, so we didn't invite him. He'd probably only shoot himself in the foot, anyway."

No one thought the remark funny. This time even Graves refused to laugh. MacNair and Ward looked off into the middle distance. Mills sighed. He needed to let off steam, but he could see that he wasn't going to be popular teasing anybody tonight.

"Well," the President said, "if you won't tell me your horoscope, Senator, tell me how your ticker's doing." MacNair had a history of heart trouble.

"My ticker's been fine," MacNair answered. "But *I'm* a nervous wreck!"

Everybody laughed, and the tension in the room was momentarily dispelled. The President stepped over to the bar and made himself a Scotch and soda.

"It's been a tough week," he admitted. "For all of us."

He clinked a handful of ice into his glass and then turned on the radio next to the bar and found a station playing mood music. "Just in case the help is listening at the door," he said.

When he returned to his chair, he bore a look of serious concentration. His eyes finally rested on Graves.

"Where do we stand now, Mr. Graves? Is it airtight?"

Graves nodded quickly. "No leaks, Mr. President. Thompson and Mitchell are both here in the park."

The President lifted an eyebrow. "And . . . ?"

"And Cyclops—one of our men—has determined that they didn't spread any information about Zodiac."

"What about Truley?"

"He was the only one they told."

"He'd better be," Mills muttered. No one commented on Truley's brutal end, but Mills suspected it was on their minds.

"I know how Mitchell got here," Mills continued, "but what the hell was Thompson doing in the park?"

Ward cut in: "We caught him coming out of one of the trailers."

"He found a copy of the Zodiac plan there," Graves added.

The President's face grew dark. "Whose copy?"

Ward blushed.

The President sighed. No point in chastising him now. He turned back to Graves. "So that's it, then?"

"Yes, sir. He'll take care of them tonight."

Mills nodded. The others studied their drinks. He'd better face the issue with them head-on, he decided. "I know you've all been upset by some of the things that have had to be done to protect Zodiac in the last few days," he said. "And I can't say that I blame you. I haven't been sleeping so well myself."

The President paused. He realized that he had to take away their guilt. It was the guilt that was undermining their tranquillity.

"This is no time to get squeamish, gentlemen," he continued. "When the stakes are high, the game gets rough. And we've had some bad luck. If it hadn't been for Allen Roland and his foolish bitterness toward me, this would all have gone off without any problems. But a few innocent people have gotten in the way and they have suffered as a result. A few have been hurt. That's true. I regret that. I regret it deeply."

The President sipped his drink and focused his eyes against the far wall. The others sat watching him. Only Ward smoked, lighting one cigarette after another. People had been more than hurt, the President knew. They had been killed. And he *did* regret it. He wished it hadn't happened. He wished it hadn't been necessary. But he did not feel guilt about it. Innocent people died in war. This was an equivalent situation. For those few who died, millions of people would be spared future catastrophes. It was a matter now simply of riding out the present situation. In a few months, a few years, it would all be remembered quite differently. The winners wrote the history books, after all.

"We're coming through nicely," Mills continued. "Yesterday we were within an inch of having to abort the whole mission. Today, things are much improved. The leaks are plugged, and the Zodiac team is on its way. We're back on schedule. We'll all rest easier tomorrow, of course, when the worst is over . . ."

The President rubbed a hand over his forehead. "Anyway, no need to lecture you fellows. We've just got to hold tight for a few more hours."

Mills rose to mix another drink. He reflected that he had consumed a good amount of alcohol—far more than normal for him—and yet he remained depressingly sober. When he returned to his chair he was subdued.

MacNair cleared his throat. "History is on your side, Mr. President. No doubt about that. Zodiac will focus attention on Mexico's record of hostility against the United States. The country will support you. A president's popularity is always highest during an international crisis."

MacNair always preceded a complaint with flattery. Mills looked at him expectantly.

"Let's assume everything goes as planned tomorrow," MacNair continued. "God knows, we're due for a little luck. But what about the next day? What happens on October 31? And the day after that? I'm worried. With all the secrecy that we've had to maintain, have we been able to do adequate contingency planning?"

Mills nodded. "Let General Ward answer that. He's been up to his ears in contingency planning for weeks."

Ward glanced at MacNair, a certain contempt evident in his expression.

"On October 31," he said, rattling the words off as if he had memorized them, "we heavily reinforce every post along the border. San Diego to Brownsville. Each day thereafter there will be a rapid buildup and deployment of forces. All three services will be mobilized immediately. The reserves will be called up. Portions of the Seventh Fleet, now on station in the Pacific and in dock at Hawaii and San Francisco, will steam to Mexico's west coastal cities of Mazatlán, Manzanilla, Acapulco, and Tapachula. Portions of the Atlantic Fleet, on station at sea and berthed at Norfolk, Virginia, will proceed to the east coast cities of Matamoros, Tampico, Veracruz, and Mérida. Within forty-eight hours all ports will have been mined by carrier-based and land-based planes. Within seventy-two hours a complete naval blockade will be in place. . . . All air bases near the border will be on full alert—Tinker in Oklahoma City, Biggs and Bliss in El Paso, Randolph and Lackland in San Antonio, Cannon in New Mexico, Carswell in Fort Worth, and Laredo Air Force Base in Laredo . . . Two hundred thousand troops will be moved near the border and Marine landing parties will be loaded on ships offshore at six points along the Mexican coast. The 82nd and 101st Airborne will be stationed at Lackland and March Air Force Base in California, and put on battle alert—"

MacNair cut Ward off: "Mexico will complain to high hell to the UN and the OAS and everyone else!"

The President nodded. "Yes. But the die will be cast. They'll be powerless to act effectively against us, and nobody else can come to their rescue. I'll admit it sounds as if we're overdoing it, but we want to act fast and decisively to get the crisis behind us as swiftly as possible. It'll all be over and settled before they'll even be able to get the Security Council in session at the UN. And patriotic sentiment in this country will soar."

MacNair nodded. A silence fell. The implications of the mighty juggernaut to be mobilized against Mexico left them all a little staggered.

MacNair pressed his inquiries further: "What happens after that? How the hell is the confrontation going to resolve itself so quickly, as you suggest?"

Ward's face turned red again. He felt MacNair was doing this just to embarrass him personally. The President cut in: "We'll resolve it completely in our favor. We'll win without having to fire a shot. The enormous pressure of our military presence, particularly our blockade, will bring Mexico to her senses in a very short time. If it doesn't, we're going to install a friendly regime in there to take its place. One that will do business with us."

MacNair looked shocked. "Where is this friendly regime going to come from?"

Ward interrupted angrily, "What the hell do you think we do all day at Central Intelligence? We have our man in Mexico! Carrera! He's a general in the Army. And the Army is loyal to him. He's a natural leader with a lot of support from responsible elements in Mexico. He's solid and he's pro-American! It's all set."

MacNair nodded, obviously not anxious to hear more.

The President could read MacNair's mind. The senator's sense of fair play and propriety were outraged, but he was too far compromised to make a fuss about it. At heart the senator was a coward. Corrupt and venal to the bone, and terrified that he might be found out.

The President felt no such burden. Zodiac was a necessary tactic to force Mexico into a more cooperative relationship with the United States. Or more accurately, with the Mills administration. It was a worthwhile goal, and Mills was willing to take the risks involved. But he was not deluding himself. The real reason for Zodiac lay beyond Mexico. The real reason was to ensure that Harrison Conway never became president of the United States. In Mills's mind, that would be a greater disaster for the country than anything Mexico might do. Of course, keeping Conway out of the Oval Office meant keeping himself in. Well, he never claimed to be a humble man. He knew his policies were right for the country. He knew that the country needed him. Zodiac was a harsh but necessary demonstration to convince the country of that fact. It wasn't moral. But it would work. And in the long run the country would admire him for it. He was convinced of it.

Mexico would be punished, too. But that was only a bonus of Zodiac, a salutary side benefit. It was Harrison Conway that Mills was going to punish—for his bankrupt liberal philosophy, his naive assumptions of superiority in matters of domestic and foreign affairs. And for the terrible threat he posed to John Douglas Mills.

The President's mood was darkening. Thinking about Conway did that to him. Conway had made Mills an unpopular president. Because of Conway, he had become a misunderstood man with the electorate. His achievements had been belittled and his reputation had been slandered.

"What's the matter with this country that it can't understand what I'm trying to do for it?" Mills directed his remark at Graves, as if he were accusing him of America's shortcomings. Graves shook his head.

"That immigration bill," the President continued, "was an act of courage. Of statesmanship! Of course it was unpopular. Most great achievements are! We were faced with a staggering human problem. The border states were being flooded with millions of poor, uneducated aliens, unskilled, unable to speak English. Unable to defend themselves from exploitation, from peonage!"

The President rubbed his head and frowned. "Something had to be done, gentlemen, and so we engineered Operation Clean Sweep. We had the guts to do it, and we did it. And despite what my critics claim, it was a humanitarian program! We're no longer an empty country with a boundless frontier. It's 1984. Our resources are limited. We can no longer support the world's unemployed population. The welfare of American citizens has to come first! . . . Now, you'd think everybody in this country would applaud what I did. But instead, instead . . ."

The President's voice changed from one of aggrieved innocence to malice. "Instead, huge crowds applaud Harrison Conway when he calls me a racist!"

Mills took a drink and calmed himself. He realized that he was making the others uncomfortable, but he needed to unburden himself.

"Well, this is one racist who's not going to let a third-rate international power like Mexico push us around. We can't affort it. Gas is three dollars a gallon at the pump. We don't have a friend in the Middle East except Egypt and Israel, and neither of them have oil to export. Saudi Arabia is threatening to cut production a million barrels a day this spring. Liberia, our second biggest supplier, is threatening to cut our supply if we don't boycott South Africa. The world has become a tough and hostile place for America, gentlemen. The line has to be drawn somewhere. And Mexico is the place. We're not going to let those thieves cheat us out of our rightful share of their oil. We're not going to let Mexico bring us to our knees! . . . And that's exactly what'll happen if Conway becomes president. The country will be ass-deep in a depression, and they'll be electing illegal immigrants to Congress! It'll be a disaster! A goddamned disaster!"

Mills rested his head in his hands. The others sat in stunned silence.

"I'm sorry," he muttered. "I've had a little too much of the bottle. We better all get to bed. We've got a big day tomorrow."

Slowly Ward, Graves, and MacNair stood up from the table, stretched, said good night, and filed out the door. Downstairs a government car waited to drive them the short quarter of a mile to their lodge.

The President sat alone for a minute, nursing his drink. The radio near the bar was playing a song Mills remembered that had been popular back in the sixties, when he was a young congressman from Texas, still married to his first wife. It made him feel maudlin.

The President turned off the radio, mixed himself another drink, and took it with him to his bedroom. He looked at his wristwatch. Past midnight. The thirtieth of October had begun. In a few hours the Zodiac team would start moving north toward its objective.

An objective that amounted to no more than a smokescreen. Zodiac's real mission—its true purpose—was known only to three men. Himself, General Ward, and one of the twelve Mexicans.

God help me, he thought. I am not a moral man.

43

Tuesday morning, October 30

He was gone.

Harriet breathed more evenly now, profound exhaustion dulling the excesses of pain and terror she had endured, leaving her in a state near insensibility. Sleep beckoned seductively, offering oblivion, but she could not surrender to it.

He would return soon, she feared, to continue his tortures until he was satisfied there was nothing more she could tell him. Then he would kill her. They had made that his responsibility. Find out what she knows, then kill her. Desperation prodded her to try to make one last attempt at escape. Her mind and body felt violated past repair. She had nothing more to lose.

Miraculously, Cyclops had noticed neither the broken panes of glass behind the curtain nor the severed length of rope behind her back. And he had not replaced the gag.

She struggled painfully to her knees again. It was easier now, with the rope between her wrists and ankles cut, but her muscles ached with an unbearable soreness, making each movement an agony. But she knew now how she could cut herself free.

She knelt sideways to the window, adjusting her position until she was able to raise her bound wrists up behind her and into one of the broken panes in the window's bottom row. Some jagged pieces of glass still remained in the bottom groove of the frame, and she concentrated on bringing the rope tied between her wrists into contact with it. She cut her hands several times before she could line her wrists up to straddle the glass's edge and begin a sawing motion that would drag the rope across the cutting edge.

She worked with a concentrated fury, past caring about the blood running down her hands. When the rope snapped and she felt the pressure on her wrists slacken, she collapsed back onto the bed, weak with relief.

With her hands free, she untied the rope at her ankles, conscious that he might return at any second.

She peered through the keyhole in the door, holding her breath. What little of the other room she could see was empty. But when she tried to pull the door open, she discovered that it was locked.

She was too close; she had worked too hard to fail now. Cutting the rope had given her new hope. The possibility of having it dashed sent a new wave of anxiety sweeping through her. He must not catch me now, she vowed, he must not!

She tried the window, discovered that it was not locked, and slowly slid the bottom half upward. It was counterbalanced with lead sash weights hidden in the frame, and they squeaked and bumped as the window rose. She prayed no one was close enough to hear.

The screen attached to the outside of the window was a further obstacle, but she was able to push it out, catch it before it fell to the ground, and pull it back inside.

She squeezed through the bottom opening of the window, pulled her legs out, and balanced for a brief moment on the sill, trying to see the ground below. It was invisible, lost in the shadow of the lodge and the nearby trees. No matter. The dangers of a fall twenty feet or so into the pitch dark seemed barely worth considering. She jumped.

The earth met her with brutal suddenness, hitting her on her forearms and stomach, knocking the wind out of her, and sending a jolt of pain through her elbows. An inch-thick layer of pine needles saved her from more serious injury.

She lay on the ground for several minutes, to get her breath back. She looked around carefully, hoping that she had not attracted any attention.

The fall had deposited her about ten feet from the back side of the lodge, on a gentle bank that sloped directly away from the building into a pine forest, and as soon as she was able to move, she crept over to the nearest tree and slid around behind it.

Head propped against the tree, Harriet sat and contemplated her next move. She was fiercely anxious to get away from the lodge, but plunging off into the woods in the dark would not get her very far very fast. If they discovered her disappearance anytime soon, they could hunt her down easily.

A parking lot was visible around the corner of the lodge. Taking care to stay under the deep shadows of the pines, Harriet edged toward the lot and studied the vehicles in it. She counted eight. Five or six nondescript sedans—U.S. government interagency motor pool, she guessed, used by the Secret Service; two vans of uncertain purpose; and one fairly beat-up Land Rover—probably the same one those two thugs had used to meet her at the airstrip.

There was her answer, of course. Steal a car.

She had heard someone drive away earlier, she remembered, so starting up another car now might not attract suspicion. She might get away with it. At least no one was guarding the lot. Secret Service agents were sure to be posted at the park exits, though. And maybe on the park roads. Incredibly risky.

She ducked down and hurried across the space between the trees and the lot and ran behind the first sedan to get out of the light shining from the lodge's front entrance. She crept around to the driver's side, opened the door, and slid behind the wheel. Through the windshield she could see most of the front of the lodge. No one was in sight.

Harriet reached down for the ignition and made an unpleasant discovery. No key.

What now? She sat and thought about it for thirty seconds. Why would they bother to remove the keys? Car theft was surely rare in Halloween Park. She slipped out of the sedan, leaving the driver's door ajar, and crept over to the next one. She opened the door and felt for the ignition. No key.

Her pulse pounding, Harriet went down the line, leaving a row of open car doors, looking for an ignition with a key in it.

The last vehicle was the Land Rover. Its door squeaked open loudly, and Harriet caught her breath. But the key was there!

Behind the wheel, she considered the best way to conduct an escape. It seemed to boil down to a choice between a desperate, high-speed break-out—which every nerve in her body screamed for her to take—and a slow-speed deception, which meant starting the vehicle up slowly, and driving away slowly, pretending to be part of the night's regular activity. She knew that was the better option, but she expected that her self-control might disintegrate in the middle of it.

She took a deep breath and twisted the key in the ignition. Her hand shook so badly she could barely keep it on the key, and in her anxiety she pumped the gas pedal and flooded the engine. It took a dozen more sanity-threatening attempts before the engine coughed to life.

In low gear she maneuvered through the parking lot, past the line of motor-pool sedans, and out the exit, a narrow dirt drive that she realized was leading her around to the right, directly toward the front of the lodge.

She drove by at five miles an hour, holding her breath and keeping her head fixed firmly ahead. Out of the corner of one eye she suddenly noticed two men. They were standing in front of the wide stone terrace, talking—one with a foot resting on the first step, the other standing bent forward in a listening pose. They stood about thirty feet away, and as she passed near them, they both turned their heads.

She felt the tension along the instep of her foot, so badly did she crave to press down on the accelerator. Her throat went dry. She had only one chance to do the right thing, and she had to do it now.

She honked the Land Rover's horn and waved her hand at them. Not a big wave, just a stiff lift of the forearm in a casual masculine salute. The men waved back and looked away.

Her heart thundered in her chest as if it were trying to break loose, and perspiration beaded on her forehead. She wiped it off and concentrated on the road.

It seemed to lead nowhere. She drove along an increasingly narrow path, plunging deeper into the wilderness. Beyond the headlamps, illuminating the rough tracks of the road, the wall of trees rose up on both sides and joined in an arch overhead, a vaulted passage through a desolate nighttime world. She saw nothing ahead, and the rearview mirror was black.

The road forked. She took the less-traveled path and drove on as fast as she dared. A mile further the path became much bumpier, and branches scraped against the sides of the cab. The dirt path had disintegrated into little more than a set of old tire tracks. She jockeyed the vehicle forward until finally even the tracks disappeared and she could drive no farther. There was no room to turn around. She tried the reverse gear, but the Land Rover's backup lights were not working. She was stuck. She turned off the ignition and sat to wait for daylight.

For the first time she noticed the CB radio bolted under the dashboard. She lifted the hand microphone from its cradle on the side of the set and flicked on the power switch. A small dial glowed green, and a dull hum sounded from the speaker. She identified the channel selector and began turning it, watching the numbers on the dial change. She went around the dial twice, but beyond the buzz and static, heard nothing. Not surprising, she thought, at this hour.

She tried again, speaking into the mike with a tentative "Hello?"

Nothing.

Then she realized that she had to key the mike—press down the button on the side of the microphone. She tried again.

On Channel 7 a sudden burst of voice through the speaker made her jump. "Come on, breaker!"

She pressed the mike button, her voice quavering with excitement. "Hello! Hello!"

"Four-ten roger, beaver. What's your handle?"

"Who is this?"

"The handle is Macho Red, chickadee! What's your handle and what are ya wrapped in?"

Harriet stared disbelievingly at the microphone, then pressed the key to reply. "I'm sorry, but I don't understand you. Just listen to me!"

"Let's have your handle, superskirt! What's your call sign? Are you on your training wheels?"

The voice had a distinct New Hampshire accent, twangy and humorous, and it sounded eager to chat.

"Listen, Macho Red . . ."

"Ole Macho's a gear-jammer, sweet thing! I'm walking a nine-banger bulldog bottle-popper down Route Eighty-nine, for that Manchester town! If you got a dress for sale, I don't have time for a nap trap, but I can make a ten-one-hundred! Where's your twenty at?"

"This is Harriet Mitchell, whoever you are, and I'm in a place called Halloween Park!"

"Whooeee! Halloween Park! I'd sure like to put an eyeball on ya, highway princess, but I know you ain't in no Halloween Park!"

It was like talking to a foreigner. Harriet got a grip on herself.

"Listen! This is an emergency! I don't know anything about this damned radio I'm talking to you on, and I don't have time to learn! This is an emergency and I need desperately for you to just listen to me—in English!"

The voice at the other end sounded dubious. "A ten-thirty-three?"

"If that spells emergency, yes!"

"You need a teddy bear?"

"Teddy bear?"

"Yeah. A smokie. A boogie man. A fudge cycle!"

"No, I don't need any of those things! I need for you to listen to me very carefully and do what I ask!"

"That's a ten-four!"

"Stop it!" Harriet yelled.

Macho Red's tone became defensive. "I'm just tryin' to tell ya that I hear ya!"

"Good! Then pull your rig off to the side of the road, dig out a pencil and a piece of paper. I'm going to dictate a message to you that you must relay for me, and I want you to get it down exactly right!"

"Jesus! Are you pulling my leg, lady?"

"Are you a patriotic man, Macho Red?"

"You're damn right I am!"

"Then please do this for me. You'll be doing your country a great service, I promise you. But we don't have much time. Do you read me, Macho Red?"

"Yes, ma'am, I read you, loud and clear."

Harriet smiled. "That's a big ten-four!" she said.

44

A tickling sensation along his skin brought Thompson's eyes open. A large brown spider was slowly walking across the back of his hand. He brushed it off and closed his eyes again.

A sound penetrated, bringing him further awake. It was rhythmic and so hollow that he imagined it must be his own pulse beating in his ears. It became louder, closer, and then it faded. A helicopter? He opened his eyes again.

He was lying on his side, underneath the roots of an oak tree blown partway over by some past storm. A small hollow had been ripped open beneath the trunk, just large enough for Thompson to have curled up inside during the night. He felt profoundly chilled, and his chest was racked by waves of uncontrolled trembling.

Moving in slow motion against the stiffness and pain in his leg, he crawled toward a patch of sunlight a few feet away.

The night beneath the tree had been a haunted experience, an exhausted sleep beset by nightmares and disturbed by the cold and the howling of the wind through the forest. A last bad dream still clung like a cobweb to the fringes of his consciousness.

He pulled his aching frame up onto a rock warmed by the early rays of the sun and examined himself. The borrowed workclothes were caked with dirt, and every part of him—arms, legs, face, head—bore deep scratches. His leg wound was swollen and hard and the skin had turned a deep purple-black in a wide margin around the tear. The entire area was inflamed and felt hot to his touch.

As long as he could walk, he told himself, that was all that mattered.

He stood cautiously and began flexing his limbs to work the worst of the soreness out. The beating sound returned, much louder than before. A helicopter passed directly overhead, its rotor blades blowing the leaves from the tops of the trees. Thompson pressed himself against the trunk of a tree and waited, motionless, until the sound had faded. The hell with the soreness, he decided. He'd better get moving. He set off as fast as his body would allow, stumbling in a half-trot, half-walk toward the east, in the direction of the morning sun.

He stayed clear of the dirt roads, where he might be spotted, and moved in a straight line through the rough terrain and heavy undergrowth. It took him almost an hour to reach the fence. He paused at the edge of the woods behind a heavy stand of birch saplings and surveyed the swath of field between him and the perimeter road. Far to the right, his eyes caught sight of a gray sedan just appearing over the rise. He watched it pass, fifty feet away. There were three men inside.

A few minutes later another gray vehicle materialized from the same direction, also with three men inside.

Later a third came by. A small seal of some kind was visible on the driver's door, with gold lettering beneath. Thompson strained to read it, but it was too far away.

A fourth car drove by, then a helicopter. It appeared suddenly over the horizon, a giant bird of prey beating along crabwise through the air, following the line of the fence. Was it the same one he had seen earlier?

They must be looking for him. It seemed crazy—so many people—but they must all be part of the conspiracy. Cyclops, Leon, the Mexicans—and now all these cars and helicopters full of men. Where did it all end? What power was he up against, that could mobilize such resources?

He had to get through that fence. It was his only chance. But that meant searching for the hole he had come in through, and that would take time. Time the cars and helicopters weren't going to give him.

He would have to wait until dark and try the fence then. Meanwhile, he would have to find a place to hide. He must find some water, too; he felt dehydrated, unable to swallow. That stream he had crossed—he could find that again.

He turned from the fence and stalked back through the woods, heedless of his direction, his mind racing in a fever of incoherent fantasies of escape and revenge. Something dark and troubling inside his head was trying to get out.

You're not thinking straight, he told himself. But he didn't care. His senses felt keen, and the pain in his body no longer concerned him. He felt the exhilaration from the adrenaline pumping through him, just as yesterday, when he was running through the pines to escape from Cyclops. He had charged off, he remembered, impervious to obstacles, leaping through the dense growth like a deer chased by hounds. He had felt possessed of Herculean strength, numb to pain, unstoppable.

But why had Cyclops let him go? He remembered the field, and the big helicopter, and then he remembered he was running through the pines, at dusk. Why did Cyclops take him into the woods and let him go?

Did he escape?

Maybe. He couldn't remember.

Thompson came upon an abandoned barn, the skeletal remains of a long-forgotten farm. The cellarhole of what had once been the farmhouse lay nearby, its stone chimney standing in the woods like a monolith of some forgotten civilization.

Thompson walked around to the barn's doorway, debating with himself whether the barn would make a safe place to hide. Its doors had fallen away, and the grass was firmly entrenched between the flat, workworn stone blocks that once served as the doorway's threshold. A hayloft extended halfway out from the back of the interior, suspended over the main floor like the balcony of a theater and commanding a view of the open doorway.

Thompson froze.

A man was standing in the hayloft, looking down at him.

He turned and fled from the entrance, but then he stopped a short distance away, as the details of the image he had seen resolved more accurately in his mind's eye. He crept back cautiously and peered through the doorway again. The man was still in the hayloft, but he wasn't exactly standing in it. He was suspended just above it. His arms hung down loose at his sides and his head was bent forward, his neck caught and twisted in the suspension lines of a parachute. Light from the morning sun poured through the wide cracks in the barn siding, laying yellow zebra stripes across his face and his khaki workclothes.

The man had landed on the roof, and the rotten shingles and roofboards had given way under the impact and dropped him through, tangling him in the suspension lines when the parachute canopy caught on the broken roof rafters and refused to fall through after him.

The apparition caused Thompson's head to pound violently.

The parachute.

He began to feel light-headed.

The parachute.

It was speaking to him, telling him to remember.

Leon.

It was Leon.

Leon who took his parachute.

God, it was coming back to him, full force.

He was falling. A long time falling.

Death on the way.

Thompson dropped to his knees and vomited, gagging repeatedly on the dark stream of phlegm his empty stomach pumped onto the ground beneath him.

45

Tuesday morning, October 30

Jason Spellman, a reporter on the *Times* metropolitan desk, put his container of coffee and cinnamon doughnut, his ritual breakfast, down on his desk and glanced at the clock on the wall on the far side of the city room. Eight o'clock on the nose. The earliest he had been at his desk in weeks.

The big room was nearly deserted, except for Fred Vickery, two desks over, winding up his night shift.

"Anything on the wire?" Jason asked. "The Second Coming? The end of the world?"

Vickery, a veteran with a streak of cynicism deep even for a journalist, shook his head. "Nah. Had a good crank call, though."

"Yeah?" Jason pretended interest.

"Yeah. A guy named Walt Tompkins called from Burnham, New Hampshire. Says he drives a truck for Pepsi-Cola."

Spellman was half-listening, spreading out the bulldog edition of the *Times* on his desk and scanning the front page for his byline.

"So?"

"So he said somebody was going to 'stage a border incident'—those were his words—at Laredo, Texas, sometime today."

Spellman shook his head, still reading the newspaper. "What did he expect us to do, run a six-column head on it?"

Vickery shook his head. "No, he wanted us to stop it. Alert the border patrol. Said the future of the country might be at stake."

Spellman smiled. "How *about* that. What did you say?"

"I told him there were two dozen border incidents down there every day, and what made his so special? Well, it turned out he didn't know, he was just passing the information along."

Spellman looked up at Vickery, a grin on his face. "Jesus, Fred, I thought you said you had a *good* crank call."

"There's more," Vickery snapped.

"More?"

"That's what I said. Being an experienced journalist, I remembered to ask him what his source was. Are you listening to me?"

"Yeah, yeah. You asked him his source."

Vickery maintained his deadpan expression. "Harriet Mitchell told him."

Spellman's head popped up from the paper. "Say that again?"

"He said he got a call from her at six o'clock this morning on his CB radio. Gave him this number to call. Real urgent, he said."

Spellman rubbed his chin and stared off into the middle distance. "What's Mitchell doing talking on a CB radio in New Hampshire? Isn't she supposed to be in Washington?"

"You're asking me?"

"Well, why the hell didn't she just call in herself?"

"He said she told him she was lost in the woods."

"Incredible. What are you going to do about it?"

"Do about it? Where's your sense of humor, lad? I'm not going to do a goddamned thing about it. It's a prank!"

"I guess so. Pretty weird prank, though."

Vickery tidied up his desk, and stood up to put on his sport coat. "Well, what can I tell you. They're pretty weird up there in New Hampshire."

Several times during the morning Spellman thought about it. It didn't make any sense, but that was exactly what bothered him. He was tempted to put a call through to the border patrol at Laredo, just to alert them to the possibility of something unusual. Just in case. And he thought of calling the Washington bureau to find out where Harriet Mitchell was.

But at ten o'clock the mayor called an emergency press conference on the city water shortage, and Spellman rushed off to cover it. By noontime he had forgotten all about Vickery's call.

46

Thompson heard the helicopter again.

He staggered to his feet, and half-limping, half-running, scrambled across the small pasture near the barn and dived into the screen of heavy bushes that bordered the clearing.

The helicopter appeared over the barn and circled it slowly. The sun pouring through the Plexiglas dome of the cockpit showed one man inside at the controls, wearing a cowboy hat. Even at such a distance, Thompson had little doubt as to his identity.

The craft dropped lower and hovered directly over the barn, like a giant honeybee after pollen, then moved off a short distance and hovered again. Thompson knew the pilot was examining the parachute canopy, plainly visible where it had caught on the broken roof rafters. He watched, motionless beneath his leafy camouflage, and prayed that Cyclops would not decide to land.

After several more slow circuits of the barn, the helicopter climbed in a wide sweeping arc, dipped its nose northward, and clattered out of sight over the treetops.

Thompson realized that hiding in the barn was out of the question. Someone would return to investigate the parachute.

Where, then?

If he could find a hiding place in the surrounding woods, within easy reach of the barn, that would be best, he thought. He needed the building as a point of reference to help him reach the fence as fast as possible. As soon as darkness fell, he could return to the barn, then follow the dirt road eastward from the barn to the fence.

He looked into the woods behind him. A few feet from where he lay he saw the contours of a dry streambed that curled out from under the trees and into what was now a mudhole in the middle of the pasture. He stepped down into the streambed and followed it deeper into the woods, to see where it might take him. The bed was narrow, the steep banks on each side overgrown with thick clusters of gray birch and beech saplings that stretched out over the path and forced Thompson to crouch down in order to avoid their branches.

The streambed meandered through the forest and then gently up the middle of a shallow ravine between two small hills. Some small puddles remained from the showers of two days ago, but most of the bed was dry and firm underfoot.

In several stretches, where the bottom was still muddy, hoof prints were visible. Thompson bent down for a closer look. They were of a peculiar shape, like the head of a large pair of pliers or a lobster's claw. He remembered the biblical cloven hoof, and supposed that they must be boar tracks.

Sensing the possibility of a hideout in a steep hilly area on his left, Thompson climbed out of the streambed and scrambled up the incline onto a small, well-hidden ledge. From it he could look back over the trees and see the barn and its pasture to the south.

Beneath the ledge the rock formed a small shallow cave big enough to squeeze into. Thompson had not noticed it climbing up, because it was hidden behind the branches of several trees that had fallen across its mouth.

The ledge made an ideal lookout. He could lie there and rest, and wait for dark. If Cyclops picked this area to search for him, he would be able to see him coming and slip around into the cave underneath the ledge.

But still he worried that that little bit of advance warning might not be enough. If he were spotted, he was finished. It was as simple as that. He needed to do something more to protect himself. But what? He was totally unarmed and helpless. And he might be trapped in the park for days.

He remembered the hunting knife strapped to Leon's waist. At least it was a weapon, and it gave him an idea. He might be able to use it to fashion an even better weapon. It was a farfetched scheme, but if Cyclops cornered him, it would give him a fighting chance.

Thompson returned to the barn and climbed up into the hayloft. Leon still hung there, eyes open, an expression of surprise frozen on his wrinkled face. His corpse stank of feces. Fighting a powerful revulsion, Thompson extracted the hunting knife from Leon's belt, cut the suspension lines twisted around his neck, unfastened the parachute harness straps, and let him drop to the floor.

Thompson cut several long pieces of suspension line from the parachute and rolled them into a coil around his shoulder. He fastened Leon's knife holster to his own belt and slipped the knife into it. Satisfied that he had everything he needed, he retreated to the streambed, his mind working furiously on the details of his plan.

Walking along the streambed, he examined the saplings that bordered it until he located a young birch tree, about twenty-five feet high, growing on the bank near the edge of the path. He decided it suited his purpose and he proceeded to cut it down. He worked with a concentrated fury, mindless of all distractions—pain, hunger, thirst, cumulative exhaustion. The tree was about four inches thick at the base, and it required strenuous hacking with the knife before he was finally able to cut through it.

As soon as he had the tree down, he lopped off the top few feet, stripped the remainder of its branches, and put it aside. Then he picked out two small beech saplings and cut them up into a dozen half-inch-thick foot-long stakes, each sharpened at one end to a long, tapered point, whittled as fine at the tip as he could manage.

He cut a series of parallel slits about three inches apart through the smaller end of the birch tree, extending to within two feet of the tip. Into the slits he forced the beech stakes, until all twelve of them were lined up to form a three-foot-long rake of bristling wooden spikes.

Thompson carried the birch pole to a point just past a sharp bend in the streambed, where it deepened into a narrow knee-high trench, just before the short detour up to his hideout. He studied the trees along the banks on either side, and finally picked two substantial saplings growing close together about ten feet off the path.

He wedged the trunk end of the birch pole between these two trees and adjusted it until it stuck out at a right angle across the path, so the row of stakes was positioned waist-high across the entire width of the streambed. Using a length of the rope cut from the parachute lines, he lashed the birch pole securely to both trees.

The problem of constructing a workable trip release stumped him for some time. His knowledge of the device, called a "pig-stabber" by the tribesmen in the Philippines who first used it, was limited to what he could remember of it from a book on bushcraft he had edited nearly ten years ago. The details of the trip release were just too complicated to be recalled after all this time. In any event, the release required thin cord or wire, and he had neither.

He finally devised a simple, direct release that he would have to trigger himself. He tied one end of another length of parachute line to the middle of an extra foot-long stake, and the other end to the tip of the birch pole, and then bent the pole around as far as his strength would permit, pulling it clear of the path, until it was arched back like a giant bow from the two trees that anchored its base.

Sweating from the effort, Thompson pulled the line attached to the pole's tip behind the trunk of a nearby sapling and then continued pulling the line back parallel with the path for about ten feet. There he pushed the stake tied to the end of the line through the crotch of another small tree and turned it so that it rested against the two arms of the Y, held in place firmly by the tension of the bent pole.

He decided he had better test it.

He slapped the end of the stake with his hand, knocking it out of its position. It slipped swiftly through the crotch, releasing the tension on the pole. The pole whistled around through the air, snapping across the streambed path like a cracked bullwhip. The explosive, violent power of it made Thompson gasp. It was better than he had hoped.

He cocked the pig-stabber again, pulling the line through the same tree crotch and setting the stake carefully in position across the two branches of the Y.

With this weapon guarding the approach to his hideout, he would feel more secure. It had the disadvantage of requiring that he be nearby to activate it, but there was an important advantage, as well. It wouldn't be tripped accidentally by an animal or an unintended victim.

He doubted that he would have to use it, in any case.

He climbed back up the hill to his ledge, sat with his back against the rock, and waited for the day to pass.

47

Tuesday morning, October 30

The President stood in front of the full-length mirror and admired his hunting outfit: a checked red-and-black-wool Maine Guide shirt; a pair of heavy-duty tan field pants with a poplin-lined double seat and green nylon duck facing sewn down the front of the legs; and a quail coat with corduroy-lined collar and cuffs, pivot sleeves, and large rubberized game pockets with side entrances.

He was eager to start the morning's hunt. He had slept poorly, as he had for many nights of late, dreaming of blood and burning cities, and he needed to lose himself in the vigorous activity of the chase. Today was to be a fateful day. A historic day. He had willed it. But patient waiting was not his style. He wanted to hurry the day onward, to stampede it.

General Ward, sitting in an easy chair in a corner of the President's bedroom, looked up from his pad and pencil.

"I get twenty-eight, altogether," he said.

President Mills nodded. "Including the Mexicans?"

"Yes."

"That's a lot."

Ward agreed. "Well, there's four Secret Service men, seven people in the agency, and the rest work for Graves."

The President hefted the big .44-40 Navy Arms Henry carbine lying on the table next to him and swung it up into firing position, watching himself in the mirror.

"We've got to take damned good care of these people," he said. "Not just for this year and next, but for the rest of their lives. We've got to watch them, make sure they stay happy."

Ward nodded. "Most of them know only little pieces."

"It doesn't matter. It has to be airtight. Look what happened with those 'little pieces' Roland picked up."

"I'll make sure."

Mills nodded. "Good. Get on your hunting clothes, General, and let's get out after those boar. When all hell breaks loose on the Mexican border, I want to be slogging through the boondocks, miles from the nearest reporter."

Ward left, tucking the pad and pencil into the side patch pocket of his jacket. One of Mills's aides appeared in the doorway. "There's a Mr. Joseph Madero waiting out here to see you, Mr. President."

Mills was puzzled. "Who's he?"

"One of Graves's men, sir. General Ward requested that he accompany you on your hunt this morning. He'll be responsible for the catch dog."

"What does he want?"

"He said he had information he wished to give you in private."

Mills sighed deeply. A faint alarm was going off in the back of his head.

"All right. Send him in."

The President picked up a clean white rag and began polishing the barrel of the big carbine with it. A man appeared at the door, touching the brim of his cowboy hat with his finger in salutation. Mills noticed the glass eye at once and realized, with an unexpected chill, that Madero was the man called Cyclops. He had never seen him, but he knew his history well enough. Ward had extolled his virtues at length to persuade him to use him for Zodiac. And Mills had received daily reports on his work since. Allowing him a private audience was not very smart, Mills thought. Kings do not meet with assassins. What could he want?

"Come in, Madero! Close the door and have a seat. Can we get you something to drink? Coffee?" Mills's voice was suddenly booming with heartiness, as if he were addressing a crowded hall rather than one man. The convivial facade was a contrived tactic—the words meant to flatter, the tone to intimidate.

Cyclops ignored Mills's offer of a seat and walked instead over to the gun cabinet against the far wall. He fingered several of the rifles idly, like a shopper killing time. His manner irritated the President, and Mills suspected that for some reason it was meant to.

"You hunt much, Mr. Madero?"

"Some."

The President cleared his throat. "Those are some of my big guns, there. That's a Savage lever-action three-oh-eight there on the end, and a Winchester Ninety-four Frontiersman next to it—a real beauty! Limited edition. See, it's got a silver-plated forend tip and a silver medallion in the stock."

Cyclops nodded, surveying the rack skeptically. Mills wondered if the man knew anything at all about rifles. If he did, he should realize that he was looking at part of one of the best gun collections in the world.

"There's a Heckler and Koch Seven-seventy Sporter there, with the delayed roller lock system," the President continued. "That Dubiel there in the middle is one of my favorites. It's chambered for four-fifty-eight, with a Canjar trigger and the best wood stock you ever saw on a rifle. I think my Golden Eagle is in that case, too; and the Harrington and Richardson three-oh-one."

Mills affected to study the row of rifles from his chair. "Yeah, there it is, right next to the Mannlicher Model M with the scope."

Cyclops pulled down the rifle from the far end of the rack and turned it over in his hands slowly.

"Now you've just put your fingers on the best rifle in the house, Madero. Champlin Firearms Classic. Had it made to order and chambered for three-fifty-seven Magnum. It set me back five thousand dollars. One of a kind, though. And powerful as hell. It'll stop Cape buffalo and elephant."

Cyclops brought the rifle up to his shoulder and squinted down the iron sights, craning his head awkwardly to line them up with his good left eye.

"What are you going to use it on here?" he asked.

The President felt suddenly on the defensive. "Just the thing for those European boar," he answered.

Cyclops replaced the rifle in the cabinet. "Kind of a big bullet, I'd say."

Mills nodded. "Yeah. Well, big bore for a big boar, eh?" He forced out a laugh. Cyclops didn't smile. "What caliber would *you* recommend, Mr. Madero?" The President's tone was polite.

"Winchester two-seventy or thirty-thirty."

Mills smiled and shook his head, a hint of condescension in his expression. "I doubt they'd stop these boar. These beasts are big and mean."

Cyclops grinned crookedly and looked directly at the President for the first time since entering the room, freezing his attention with his one-eyed gaze. "You may be right, there, Mr. President," he said. "But I blew out the brains of a three-hundred-pound African dictator last year with nothin' but a little ole two-forty-caliber. They said he was mean, too."

President Mills frowned and rubbed the rag vigorously against the carbine.

Cyclops continued, " 'Course, you wouldn't own the kind of weapon I use. Mine is made out of lightweight titanium alloy and breaks down into five pieces that fit into a clarinet case. One of a kind."

Mills dropped the rag on the table and opened the rifle's breach. "Don't talk about that kind of thing in front of me, Mr. Madero. I know all about your record. That's why we brought you into this."

Cyclops emitted a brief laugh. Mills felt the conversation was taking an ominous turn, and looked for a way to divert it into a safer channel.

"I understand you're quite a marksman," he said, pumping conviviality into his voice. "When this is all over you'll have to come and hunt with us on my ranch. Hell, I'll bet you grew up shooting rats and rattlesnakes out on the prairie, just like I did. My daddy taught me to shoot a twenty-two when I was just six."

Cyclops sat down in the chair across from the President and leaned back. Mills watched him closely. He saw great tension in the man's overly careful, self-conscious movements. Beneath his outward calm, he seemed to be under great stress. Mills wondered at the possible cause. Sometimes just being in the presence of the President did that to people, but he didn't think that was Cyclops' problem.

"I didn't have a daddy to teach me how to shoot."

"I'm sorry to hear that."

Cyclops laughed and slapped his knee lightly. A calculated gesture, Mills thought.

"Well, I *had* a daddy," he continued. "I just never saw him. He ran away before I was born. So I grew up without him, in the rat-assed part of town where they did all the shooting late at night in the bars and whorehouses." He sat forward.

"Never saw my old lady much, either, come to think of it. When my daddy ditched her, she went right into the fuck business to put food on the table. Did real well, too. Ran the best whorehouse in Texas."

The President cleared his throat.

"She got in some trouble and somebody killed her," Cyclops went on. "Some say it was my daddy arranged it. She was blackmailing him, they said, so he had to shut her up."

The President had had enough of this. "Come to the point, Mr. Madero. What do you want from me?"

Cyclops laughed. "Want? Hell, I just want to show you that ole Cyclops knows how to take care of himself."

"What is that supposed to mean?"

"Now that I've done your dirty work, you folks are looking at me and seeing a liability. Too much blood on my hands, maybe. Dangerous killer, not to be trusted. You know what I'm talking about."

"I *don't* know what you're talking about, Mr. Madero. You were chosen because you were a professional who knew how to do his job and how to keep his mouth shut about it afterward. You'll have all the protection you need from us, I can promise you."

Cyclops sneered. "Your promises aren't worth shit!"

"Don't talk to me that way," the President warned.

Cyclops ignored the reprimand. "Graves and Ward have already planned to kill me—today. That's why Ward wants me along on this hunt. I squeezed that information out of the Mitchell cunt, if you need my source. She overheard Ward telling it to MacNair."

"But they can't. I never authorized it!"

"Maybe not. But you damned well are gonna *un*authorize it!"

The President said nothing.

"You're a tough sumbitch to beat, Mr. President, but you ain't beating me. Ole Cyclops is leaving this park with his ass in one piece."

"What are you talking about?"

"I'm talking about an *hombre* named Rafael Escobar."

"You're talking nonsense."

"Am I? I saw that list of Mes'cans in Roland's file. Eleven of them are just bums who've spent most of their lives in the slammer. Easy to bribe, easy to disclaim, easy to get rid of. But not Escobar. He's something else. He's a hit man. I've never met him, but I know him. I know his style, I know some of his hits. We assassins form a fraternity of sorts, Mr. President. Just like any other profession."

"I fail to see your point, Madero."

"Just this, Mr. President. What would Zodiac—a simple in-and-out raid, needing no finesse, no skill—want with the likes of Rafael Escobar? And why would a honcho of his talent fuck around with a dumb mob action? The answer I come up with shocks even me. . . . The answer is that this President is a honcho who doesn't take any chances. You never really were sold—for certain—that Zodiac would rope in that election for you. And that's what you want—a sure thing. Something dead solid. No second-place finishes for ole John Mills. Nossir!"

Mills's eyes flashed. "You're talking dangerous nonsense!"

". . . So the best way to make sure you win that election, to make absolutely fuckin' *positive*, is to knock off your opponent! . . . And what better way to do it than under the smoke of this attack, which happens to coincide—right to the rat-assed minute—with the visit of Harrison Conway to the Laredo customhouse!"

Cyclops shook his head in admiration. "Pretty fuckin' ingenious, when you think about it. And it should be an easy shot for Escobar. He's been known to pick off a target from five hundred yards in a thunderstorm."

President Mills's eyes flashed again, his jaw worked—opening and closing several times without any sound coming out. He squeezed the carbine, slippery now from the sweat of his palms. "This is reckless talk, Mr. Madero."

"If that's a threat, I ain't real worried."

"Why is that?"

"Because my premature death will leave some embarrassing loose ends hangin' around."

"Loose ends?"

"Thompson and Mitchell."

"What about them?"

"They're still alive."

President Mills swallowed hard. He could anticipate what must be coming, and his mind raced ahead, searching for the measure that might defeat this sudden new menace. "Why?" he asked Cyclops.

"They're my protection. They're still in the park, but I'm not going to kill them until you call off Graves and Ward. And in case one of you thinks you might scrape up the guts to do it yourself, I should warn you that they're both well hidden. It'll take you a hell of a while to find them."

President Mills nodded. He worked the lever of the carbine back and forth to vent his fury—and his fear.

Cyclops stood up, grinning to himself, and walked back over to the gun cabinet to pick out a rifle for the hunt. "I know what you're thinkin', you ole bastard. You're thinking you'll outsmart me somehow, and nail me yet."

Cyclops pulled down the Mannlicher from the gun cabinet and cracked open the breech and sighted through the barrel, admiring the perfection of it. He picked up a box of shells from the tray beneath the rack and began feeding them into the chamber.

"It's funny," Cyclops said. "When I was a young boy back in Galveston, I used to have this dream. I dreamed that my daddy came back one day and took me hunting with him. Out after mule deer or whitetail somewhere in the hills of east Texas on a beautiful fall day. I used to tell the johns about this dream, and they used to laugh like hell. Well, I guess they were right. This is probably as close to that dream as I'm ever gonna get. Too bad you ain't my daddy. You're a mean-enough sumbitch, by God!"

Cyclops laughed at the thought of it.

Mills's head was in a turmoil. He would have to settle this, somehow, before the day was over. Before anyone left the park.

48

A battered yellow bus bumped along the dirt road from Jarita to Nuevo Laredo at high speed, trailing a plume of dust in its wake. The midday sun had grown intense, evaporating the scant traces of moisture from the air, and the breeze blowing through the open windows of the bus felt hot and dry on the skin. Its twelve passenger rode in silence, oblivious of the dust and heat, their minds fixed on their mission.

On the outskirts of Nuevo Laredo the bus turned off the main route and followed a winding series of unpaved side streets until it reached the small warehouse.

A single beep of the horn made the warehouse door rise, and the bus disappeared inside.

Five miles away, across the border, another bus was stalled in the streets of downtown Laredo. The driver had rammed it into the back end of a taxi, which had stopped suddenly to avoid hitting an ice-cream vendor's pushcart. The bus had crunched into the taxi's rear end, propelled it forward into the pushcart, knocking the cart on its side and breaking the peddler's leg.

For over an hour the crowd on the bus—which included Governor Conway, his wife, his press secretary, his campaign manager, and his running mate—took turns arguing with the police to clear up the matter so the bus could move on. The press, following in its own bus, gleefully filmed the whole affair, while a crowd gathered to watch.

When Conway's party had finally given the police the required information, the driver of the bus discovered that the bus itself—a gleaming VistaCruiser rented from Greyhound—had suffered damage to its front end and was not drivable.

While candidate Conway napped in air-conditioned comfort inside the VistaCruiser, his aides scrambled desperately to find another bus to complete the day's schedule. One was located at last, and Alice Porter, in charge of the candidate's schedule, was biting her nails and glancing nervously out the big tinted front windshield, waiting for it to arrive. It was two-forty-five in the afternoon, and she kept revising the timetable in her head every fifteen minutes. She had already been forced to cancel two appearances, and she wanted to cancel the candidate's three-o'clock speech at the Laredo customs house, but Conway had vetoed her. If the damned backup bus wasn't there by three, she decided, she would *insist* they cancel the customs house and start for San Antonio. A big rally was scheduled at the Alamo at five o'clock.

At two-forty-five precisely the warehouse door opened again and two Toyota Land Cruisers, painted tan and bearing Mexico's national coat of arms on the side doors—a golden eagle perched on a mound with cactus plants, holding a green snake in its beak—emerged and turned slowly up the alley toward the main street of Nuevo Laredo. The six men in each jeep were dressed in the khaki uniforms of the Mexican Army, and the drivers of the jeeps wore captain's bars on their epaulets.

Each man's lap cradled a Valmet M71S assault rifle, and under the rear seat of the lead vehicle sat a canvas bag containing twenty-five pounds of high-explosive *plastique*.

49

Thompson heard the vehicles, whining in low gear along the road. He stood up on the rock outcropping on top of his hideout and looked to the south toward the barn and the pasture, shading the sun from his eyes with his hands.

A jeep appeared and stopped next to the barn. Thompson counted five men. Four got out. Three of them, carrying rifles in the crooks of their arms, conferred near the hood of the jeep, while the fourth, armed with a shorter weapon that looked like a submachine gun, stood a discreet distance away, as if guarding the others. The fifth man, who appeared to be wearing a uniform with an officer's cap, remained in the jeep, an attaché case resting on his lap.

A few minutes later a second jeep arrived, carrying two more men. They both retrieved rifles from the back of the vehicle and walked over to join the others. Four of the six appeared to Thompson to be middle-aged, judging by their shapes and movements. The uniformed man sitting in the jeep he could not judge. The man with the submachine gun was slim and tall, and looked to be much younger. He took up a position away from the group that gave him a clear view down both directions of the roadway. Thompson could see a small rectangular two-way radio bulging at his waist, with its stubby "rubber-duck" antenna sticking out the top.

The seventh member of the party wore a cowboy hat. Cyclops.

He had supposed that Cyclops would hunt for him alone. Who were these others? They looked like a bunch of rich businessmen on a weekend hunting trip. Was it just a coincidence they had picked this area? Or had Cyclops spotted him from the helicopter? He couldn't believe he had.

The conference at the hood of the jeep lasted for several minutes, until finally Cyclops walked back to the second jeep and opened the rear door.

Thompson's heart skipped. A large ginger-colored dog hopped out onto the ground and trotted eagerly over to join the group.

The hunters loaded their rifles and started across the pasture. The dog bounded off ahead of them, racing across the field in a broad zigzag pattern, his nose in the tall grass.

Soon the party was out of sight, their heads disappearing below the edges of the treetops as they crossed the pasture. The tall man with the submachine gun and the uniformed man in the jeep remained behind.

Perhaps it *was* just a hunting party, Thompson thought. He remembered the notice on the wall near the map in the mobile home—the guests of Senator MacNair had the run of the park for several days. It could be a group out hunting boar. And wouldn't that explain the dog? Wouldn't dogs be used to track boar? Thompson didn't know, but it seemed plausible.

Still, why was Cyclops with them?

He thought about the streambed, and the boar tracks he had seen, and suddenly his heart sank. He had left his own tracks in the streambed as well. If the dog led them to it, following the scent of the boar, they would almost surely notice his footprints.

He cursed his carelessness. He could have easily taken a branch and swept the trail behind him. But he had never even thought about footprints, he had been too busy constructing his pig-stabber.

For a while Thompson heard nothing. A couple of crows had spotted the hunters earlier in the pasture and were still cawing over the treetops, warning the neighborhood of their presence.

Thompson decided, since he could no longer see the hunters, that he would be safer in the cave under the outcrop. He stepped carefully down the rocky side and under the windfall back into the small opening in the rock. It was a very shallow cave, but no one would find him here even if they took the trouble to climb up to the outcrop.

He started worrying again about the footprints. He stepped out a distance in front of the mouth of the cave to check, fearful that he might have left evidence of his presence in the leaves and dirt.

He gasped.

The dog was standing just below him, twenty feet away, staring at him intently. Its tail was rigid, and a low growl rumbled from its throat.

Thompson waited, not daring to move, watching to see what the dog would do. The growl became more pronounced, the lips curled up the sides of it muzzle, baring back teeth. Ears back, eyes still fixed on Thompson, it inched its way closer, one soft step at a time.

He expected it to bark, but it didn't. He held absolutely still, hoping it might lose interest. It crept closer, seemingly intent on stealing up on him. Thompson rested a hand on the knife holster. The movement caused the dog to stop and cock its head in surprise. The animal's concentration on him was unnerving. He must prevent it from giving away his location.

The dog began to angle to the right, keeping about ten feet distant. Thompson turned slowly, to remain facing it. It continued to circle, edging between him and the mouth of the cave he had just crawled out of. He swallowed at the implication. The dog was cutting him off from his hiding place, blocking his retreat.

A diabolical beast, he thought. The normal hunting dog would have stood fifty feet away and barked its head off.

A rock. He could brain it with a heavy rock. It had worked against the boar. If he missed, and the dog charged him, he would still have his knife as a second line of defense. He had never used a knife in his life, and he didn't relish a contest with those jaws.

The dog stood now directly in front of the mouth of the cave, and began inching toward him again. It was less than eight feet away, Thompson judged. He glanced around him. The dog's eyes seemed to follow his, as if guessing his intention. A rock as big as a fist lay three feet behind him on his right.

He lunged for it, grabbed it, and raised it over his head. The dog charged him instantly. Thompson threw the rock and missed. The dog dived toward his legs. He kicked, and the animal's teeth snagged his trousers and pulled him off his feet. He slammed into the ground on his back, one hand landing on another rock. He picked it up and in a continuous motion hurled it against the dog's head. Stunned, the dog released its grip on his pants long enough for him to jump to his feet. He plunged down the hill toward the streambed, crashing through bushes, tripping over roots.

The dog was behind him, barking loudly now, flushing him in the direction of the hunters.

His feet were suddenly in the streambed. He looked back and saw the dog loping down the slope toward him.

Someone whistled. The dog stopped and barked louder than ever. Thompson started running along the streambed, away from the direction of the whistle, looking frantically for the pig-stabber. Which way? He stopped, paralyzed with indecision. He looked back along the trail toward the field, afraid that he had already passed it. He saw Cyclops emerge, running. Strung out in single file came the others, some distance behind him.

Thompson turned and ran the other way, casting his eyes along the left side of the path, looking for the trip release. But the trees all looked the same.

He rounded a corner and stopped, knowing for certain that he had passed it. Desperately he searched among the dozens of small trees for the fork of branches with the stake across it. Had it been accidentally tripped? Cyclops was already turning the corner twenty feet behind him, his boots crunching over the twigs and leaves. The dog jumped into the path ahead of him, to block his escape.

Thompson saw the stake at last, two steps behind him, resting undisturbed across the fork in the tree's trunk, just as he had left it. He lunged toward the tree, reaching for the stake with both hands.

Cyclops was grinning, his teeth visible through the shadow his cowboy hat cast across his face. He was holding his rifle in one hand, as if he intended to fire from the hip.

Thompson felt aware of every inch of flesh on his body, and what a large target it was. He slapped the stake with the heel of his hand, twisting it from its horizontal position upward a few inches, and watched the end slip past the branches of the fork and the parachute line snatch the stake through.

He dropped to the ground, arms forward, burying the side of his face in the sand and leaves. He saw Cyclops hit the ground a fraction of a second after him. Ten feet behind Cyclops, the next hunter came into view.

Cyclops had raised his head and was pushing his rifle around in front of him, preparing to fire from a prone position.

Nothing had happened!

Thompson looked in the direction of the fork in the tree. The stake was gone.

But it had traveled only a foot, catching itself in the branches of another tree. Thompson could see it—suspended vertically, precariously, in midair, like a magician's wand—one end resting against the side of a thick branch, the other end pressed against a smaller branch. The pressure was bending the smaller branch at an increasingly extreme angle, but the stake was not moving.

He heard Cyclops yelling at the top of his voice: "Get down! Get down!"

Thompson could see a hunter behind him, stopped by Cyclops' side, his rifle still cradled in the crook of his arm.

It was a familiar face. Who? Fragments swirled through Thompson's brain. He remembered the man with the submachine gun and the two-way radio waiting by the jeeps. And the man in uniform with the attaché case. The big helicopter at the airstrip. *United States of America.* The gray sedans patrolling the fence, the helicopters overhead. Friends of Senator MacNair. I know that park, Harriet had said. The President goes hunting there. *The President.*

"Get down!"

President Mills moved his big carbine into firing position, aimed at Thompson's head. Cyclops' Mannlicher boomed from the ground, and a bullet slapped into the earth in front of Thompson, throwing up a thick spray of dirt across his face. Another round hit the dog, standing over him. It yelped and flopped to the earth, whining piteously.

The President still had not fired. He appeared confused, uncertain of his target.

Thompson wanted to cry out, to explain that this was all a terrible mistake. The President of the United States must not let him die! He was not guilty of anything. This was monstrous. He wanted to live!

He watched the muzzle end of the President's rifle dip downward and away from him, until it pointed squarely at the small of Cyclops' back. The President's finger was on the trigger and his eyes were on Cyclops' head, less than six feet in front of him. Cyclops, still sprawled out flat, was aiming along the ground for another shot at Thompson. Thompson prayed for the President to pull the trigger.

His eye caught a slight movement in the trees alongside the path. The stake had begun to slide slowly along the weaker branch, bent now to the breaking point.

It snapped, and the stake shot free.

He heard a low-pitched whistling directly over his head, like a bull-whip cutting through the air.

Thompson saw President Mills throw his arms skyward, flinging the rifle over his head, and open his mouth in a roar of pain unlike anything he had ever heard before. It filled the air, vibrating in his ears like an explosion. The pig-stabber struck Mills directly in the stomach, driving two of the sharpened stakes deeply through the red-and-black-checked hunting shirt and sweeping the President from the path until his back slammed against a small white birch tree.

Mills slumped forward over the pole, pressing it to the ground, and landed on his hands and knees. His bellow rapidly tapered off to a low, suffocating moan. Blood gushed from his stomach, running down his arms and legs and soaking into the sand.

Thompson was transfixed, unable to raise himself from the earth. Cyclops was sitting up, turned around looking at the President. The other three men stood down the trail, not moving, as if caught in a mine field.

The President's arms gave out and he collapsed forward completely, driving the stakes the remainder of their length into his stomach. The moaning stopped.

Thompson felt the crush of doom.

His shattered mind groped to encompass the enormity of the event, the apocalyptic horror of it. He had killed the President. An accident, but he had done it. The sky did not open up. Thunder did not strike him down. But he would never escape the consequences.

Still he craved to live. That was all his brain would allow him to contemplate. Not even so long as until tomorrow. Such an immense span of time seemed past imagining. Just until dark. Just until sleep. Just for as long as he could resist. Eternity was in the next minute.

Thompson willed himself to rise. He struggled to one knee, to one foot, both feet, feeling hip-deep in molasses. He forced his legs to pump beneath him, willing them to move, but unable to feel them beneath him at all.

Gunfire.

Nothing hit him. He was still moving, running across the ground now like a startled deer, numb to every sensation but fear.

The streambed led up a shallow hill and over rough, broken terrain beyond the area he had reconnoitered earlier, then out into a wide, soggy marsh, where boars' hoofprints crisscrossed one another in the soft dirt in a dozen directions. Then the streambed broadened out and disappeared.

Thompson kept moving, picking the path of least resistance through the bushes and low-hanging branches.

A steep rock ledge loomed directly ahead. It was a nearly vertical barrier, an unbroken wall of stone thirty feet high, stretching out in both directions as far as he could see. It blocked his escape, and rather than run alongside it, he elected to scale it. He saw a chimneylike opening in the rock face that ran three-quarters of the way to the top along a steep diagonal line. Adrenaline pumping, he squeezed into it and began scrambling up, grabbing sharp edges of rock for handholds, oblivious of the lacerations.

Near the top of the chimney he stopped to catch his breath and consider his next move. He heard a crashing below him, and squeezed himself as far back into the crevice as he could, crouching down to gain the further cover of a squat scrub pine growing out of a crack in the rock near him.

He saw Cyclops emerge into the marshy area, face bent to the ground, searching for footprints.

Thompson watched helplessly as Cyclops worked his way forward, heading for the base of the cliff, directly below him.

Ten feet away, Cyclops lost the footprints, and peered down along the length of the rock wall, swiveling his head back and forth several times in each direction. Thompson waited for him to look up, praying he wouldn't, knowing he would.

A rifle shot rang out, exploding in a burst of chips off the rock face inches from Cyclops' head. Cyclops fell instantly to his stomach. Thompson looked back through the woods and saw one of the other men from the hunting party, down on one knee with his rifle in firing position, zeroing in for another shot.

Cyclops was suddenly on his feet, running.

Events happened in a blur. Three black boars, excited by the gunfire, rose out of the marsh grass between Cyclops and the other hunter, grunting and thrashing angrily. Mistaking their movement for Cyclops, the kneeling man fired wildly into the mass of moving animals. Cyclops ran in a slanting line toward the man's right side, dashing from tree to tree, closing in on him. The kneeling man corrected his aim and pumped a steady blaze of shots at Cyclops. The noise racketed through the forest, sending birds up in all directions and putting the boars into a frenzy. Is he trying to save me? Thompson wondered. Who is he?

Abruptly the shots stopped and Cyclops lunged from his cover, closing to within less than a dozen yards of him. As the hunter struggled desperately to reload his rifle, Cyclops shot him twice in the chest. He dropped over backward from the force of the shots without making a sound, the shells flying from his hand and scattering on the ground behind him.

"Graves!"

The shout came from a distance. Thompson looked back through the woods again and saw another member of the party, back where the streambed first broadened into the marsh. He was craning his head in agitation, trying to see through the bushes. Thompson recognized the man by his thin mustache. General William Ward.

"Graves!" he cried again. "What happened?"

No answer.

"Graves! Did you get him? There was a tinge of panic in his voice.

"Yeah, I got him!" Cyclops shouted, taunting him.

Silence.

Thompson watched Ward react. He seemed to shrivel, recognizing Cyclops' voice. Cyclops was already crawling toward him through the marsh grass, moving like a deadly snake. The boars seemed to have vanished.

Ward made no effort to use his rifle. He held it at his side, while he bent forward, trying to spot Cyclops through the bushes.

A wounded boar emerged from beneath a big hemlock. It was a huge beast, the size of the one that had wounded Thompson earlier. Crazed with pain, it smashed into bushes and trees, thrashing its tusks at anything in its path.

Ward heard it coming in his direction and broke into a clumsy run. Cyclops saw him the instant he turned. He stood up, raised the rifle to his eye, and took very deliberate aim. He seemed to be content to let whole seconds pass, to let the distance widen, the difficulty of the shot increase.

One shot did it.

The back of Ward's head exploded, and he dropped in mid-stride like a marionette with its strings cut.

The carnage below complete, Cyclops turned at once toward the rock face and Thompson, trapped against it, thirty feet up, with nowhere to go.

Senator MacNair felt nearly paralyzed with shock. He watched the others disappear from sight up the path; then, moving as if in a dream, he bent over the President's inert form and looked for signs of life. Mills lay on his stomach in the streambed; MacNair saw the widening stain of blood in the sand around him.

The President's face was turned on its side, and the senator crouched down on his hands and knees until he was close to his ear.

"I'm going to get help, Mr. President!"

The President's eyes fluttered open, and he reached up with a hand and grasped MacNair's shirtfront, pulling him down closer to his mouth. MacNair recoiled, and tried to push the President's hand away, but his grip was surprisingly strong.

"Stop Zodiac," he whispered.

"We will, don't worry!" MacNair replied, barely able to hear him. "We must get you help first!"

The President closed his eyes and pulled MacNair closer. "No. Stop Zodiac. . . . Conway . . ."

"Yes, Mr. President!"

"Still time . . . Conway . . ."

"What about him, Mr. President?"

Mills's face looked gray and dead, the color of modeling clay. He had lost a tremendous quantity of blood. MacNair saw the pole bent beneath him, and the row of sharpened stakes protruding from it on each side of the President's body. It sickened him.

"Next president . . ." Mills mumbled. "Conway . . . should be Conway."

MacNair made a determined effort to pry Mills's fingers free of his shirt. "You'll be all right, John. Don't talk!"

"Tell Aquarius . . . stop Zodiac."

"I understand, John. Don't talk any more!" MacNair didn't understand at all.

President Mills's hand fell from the senator's shirt by itself, and the President closed his eyes.

MacNair lumbered back along the streambed, gasping from the exertion. He reached the edge of the pasture and saw a Secret Service agent calmly leaning on the hood of one of the jeeps, smoking a cigarette. He yelled at him and then collapsed on the ground, too exhausted to stand.

The agent came at a run, brushed past MacNair's crumped form, and headed down the streambed. He didn't need any explanations; he knew instinctively that the President was in trouble.

MacNair sat propped up on his hands and sucked oxygen into his lungs, terrified of a heart attack. After a few minutes he remembered to look at his wristwatch. Three o'clock, exactly. Too late to stop Zodiac. Too late for everything.

50

Tuesday afternoon, October 30

The tan Toyota Land Cruisers drove through the checkpoint on the Mexican side with a wave-through and a salute from the Mexican border guards, and approached the broad new plaza on the United States side of the river.

Carlos, the driver of the first jeep, realized that something was wrong as soon as they reached the midpoint of the bridge and could see the U.S. customs installation. The southbound lanes on the left were empty of traffic, while the northbound lanes were jammed with vehicles, backed up for nearly a quarter of a mile from the customs checkpoint. Carlos swore and pulled the jeep up into the lane farthest to the left, behind a rusted-out vintage 1955 Chevrolet Bel Air.

Several children were jumping in the Chevy's backseat, making the car's rear end bounce up and down. The father, a middle-aged Mexican with a red bandanna around his head, was standing outside the car. When Carlos stopped, he approached the jeep, saluting Carlos' uniform.

"*Buenos días, capitán!*"

"What's going on?" Carlos demanded.

"The Americans are having a party."

Carlos looked ahead and saw the crowd gathered in the customs yard on the U.S. side. The faint squawk of a loudspeaker, mounted on top of a bus, reached his ears.

"It's the American presidential nominee," the man explained. "The Democrat, Señor Conway. They stopped letting cars go through until he finishes his speech."

The man's wife was having trouble with the children. She leaned out the car window and yelled at him to come back and restore order.

"*Un momentito!*" he answered.

"Abolardo!" She was not to be put off. "*Ven aquí!*"

He shrugged at Carlos, smiled helplessly, and ran back to the car.

Carlos was stunned. They had no information about a political rally. He picked up the small two-way radio on the seat and informed Fernando, the driver of the second jeep, what was causing the delay.

They decided to wait.

Carlos fixed his eyes on the Chevrolet, watching the father reaching into the nest of children romping in the back, trying to slap them into submission. The futility of his efforts angered Carlos. He wasn't in a mood for domestic drama. In the rearview mirror he could see that the line of cars had built behind the jeeps eight or nine deep, and was still growing.

Ahead he saw something else.

Border-patrol officers from the U.S. side were walking down along the lines of waiting cars, inspecting papers. No doubt they intended it to save time when the border reopened. But the Zodiac plan did not call for waiting to be asked for papers. The plan called for them to drive straight into the customs yard. No one had anticipated a traffic jam.

He stroked the ends of his mustache with thumb and forefinger and watched the customs inspectors work their way toward the jeeps. He estimated one of them would reach him in about five minutes. They would have to improvise.

The Chameleon watched the crowd below from his vantage point on the flat roof of the customs building, three stories up. He was perched on the low parapet on the building's south end, which gave him an excellent view of the plaza, the bridge over the Rio Grande, and the customs yard. The yard was separated from the plaza by a Cyclone fence, interrupted in one place by a two-lane gateway, covered by a low shed roof, like a toll booth on a throughway.

The yard was jammed with people, clustered around the campaign bus of the Democratic candidate, Harrison Conway. The bus was parked alongside a high wooden platform constructed for the occasion. Conway stood on the platform now, a good seven feet above the crowd, surrounded by a knot of local Democratic-party functionaries and several of his staff. The crowd was noisy and still growing, the back fringes of it already pressing against the chain-link fence and filling the two southbound exit lanes of the checkpoint gate. The Chameleon had counted it a lucky stroke when he had learned that Conway was making a speech there. It made his disguise as a press photographer a natural. But now Conway's presence worried him. The dense crowd that had come to hear him would severely limit the Chameleon's field of fire and his mobility. Conway and his crowd would obviously be in Zodiac's way if the terrorists really intended to blow up the customs building. The odds for disaster were multiplying.

Conway's presence—in this exact place at this exact time—was an incredible coincidence, the Chameleon thought. Too incredible to be an accident.

He eased the Arriflex to a more comfortable position on his shoulder and gazed southward down the wide plaza. Traffic in the northbound lanes was backed up double file all the way to the bridge, and still growing. He consulted his watch. Three-twenty-five.

Where was Zodiac?

The Chameleon pressed his eye to the camera viewfinder and panned the telescopic sight slowly down along the line of vehicles. At nearly four hundred yards the crosshairs picked up two Toyota jeeps, arranged single-file in the inside lane. Both were painted tan, and the left fender of the first jeep carried a Mexican flag, the right fender a two-star general's flag. Such arrogance, the Chameleon thought. Such treacherous arrogance!

The Chameleon watched the Toyotas turn out of the line of cars and swing over into the empty southbound lanes. The first jeep knocked over two of the orange markers set out to divide the north and south lanes, and the second followed through the opened space. Both headed north, creeping directly toward the customs building. He followed them with the viewfinder, counting six men in each vehicle. They swung in a wide arc when they were within fifty feet of the checkpoint gates, and began backing up the remaining distance. He saw the glint of machine-gun barrels in the windows.

The jeeps' back doors swung open. The Chameleon counted five guns in each jeep—four sticking out the back, one out the passenger-side window. Ten guns in all. He had expected them to disperse, but they seemed prepared to fire from inside the jeeps.

Thirty feet from the back fringes of the crowd, the Toyotas slowed to a stop. The Chameleon looked down into the huge throng clustered around Conway's platform. Its attention was focused entirely on the candidate, speaking over a pair of loudspeakers mounted on top of the bus. The breeze was blowing the words eastward, and the Chameleon could not hear them over the cheering of the crowd. No one in the customs yard seemed aware of the jeeps.

The Chameleon turned his gaze back to the open rear doorways of the jeeps. The Mexicans inside were crouched down and tensed, ready for the order to fire. He raised the viewfinder to his eye and let the cross hairs drift across the huddled uniforms, his mind swiftly plotting the order of actions he must take.

"Hey, you!"

The Chameleon turned in the direction of the shout. A man in gray slacks and an open-neck shirt was approaching him, his shoes crunching noisily across the gravel on the roof. He held a service revolver in his hand, trained directly on the Chameleon's stomach.

Cyclops could have killed him immediately and been done with it. Thompson knew that. But the deep streak of sadism that shaped Cyclops' character preferred that he prolong his victim's agony. He pointed the rifle at Thompson, a grin splitting his face, and let the muzzle play back and forth across Thompson's exposed form, the same way he had tormented him with the pistol in the mobile home.

When he had extracted sufficient satisfaction from that exercise, he turned to another game. He fired a round just over Thompson's head that brought a cascade of rock chips raining down on top of him.

A sudden disturbance caused Cyclops to turn around. Thompson saw the wounded boar charge out of the bushes at the far end of the marsh. It advanced with a diabolic fury, bucking its head, bellowing with a high-pitched, unearthly scream.

Cyclops dropped to one knee and fired at it, point-blank. The shot seemed to strike the beast directly in the chest, but it kept coming, its legs kicking up clods of dirt, its tusks sawing the air. Before Cyclops could jump out of the way, it struck him, knocking him over backward and trampling him underfoot. Still clutching his rifle, Cyclops rolled over several times to escape the pounding hooves, then rose quickly to his knees to fire again. The animal turned, like a matador's bull, and charged again, smashing into Cyclops head-on, hooking its tusks in search of flesh. Cyclops threw up both arms to protect his face, then rolled over on his stomach, writhing in pain. The beast, blood glistening on its shaggy black hide, slipped down on its front knees, balanced there for a moment, snorting and gasping for air, and then toppled over on its side and lay still.

Cyclops pushed himself slowly to his feet, holding one hand over his face, feeling the ground around him for his rifle, finding it.

He staggered toward the rock cliff again, his hand still on his face, blood oozing from between his fingers. He reached the foot of the cliff and began feeling his way along it, until he was standing directly below Thompson. Holding his rifle in one hand, he began climbing the rock chimney, feeling for handholds, pulling himself steadily upward. Thompson watched, transfixed.

With his free hand now scrabbling at the rock surface, Cyclops' face became visible. Blood was gushing from it, running down his cheek and neck and joining the broad stains of blood from the boar on his shirt and pants. Even his hair was soaked with gore.

He tilted his face upward, looking directly at Thompson for the first time since the boar had attacked him.

One eye stared up, cold and blank. The glass one. Where the good eye had been, Thompson saw only an empty socket running with blood.

Cyclops was blind.

Painstakingly he groped his way up the face of the rock, until he stood barely ten feet below Thompson's precarious perch. He rested against the rock and brought the rifle around under his chest, clutching it tightly, taking extreme care not to lose his grip on it.

"You can't escape!" he said.

His voice vibrated with rage.

"Gonna kill ya!"

Thompson looked for the hundredth time at the expanse of rock above him. There was absolutely nowhere to go. Nor could he squeeze out of the slot he was in without stepping off the narrow ledge supporting him. Cyclops had brought the rifle up in front of him, resting his elbows against the rock, maneuvering the weapon into firing position. It was uncanny how he sensed exactly where Thompson was, although Thompson had not made the slightest sound.

"Fuckin' amateur! Gonna kill ya! Gonna skin you like a rabbit, and dump your guts on the ground!"

The rifle barrel was homing in on Thompson's chest, as if it had an eye of its own. The tip of the barrel was so close he could almost reach down and touch it.

There were no choices left. After everything, Thompson could not just let himself be killed.

He pulled the knife from its sheath, gripped it hard in his right hand, and studied Cyclops' position below him. He was nearly perpendicular, leaning tight against the cliff to keep from falling over backward, the toes of his boots holding a difficult purchase on a small lip of rock. Two yards separated the top of Cyclops' head and the bottom of Thompson's shoes.

Thompson leaped from the cliff.

Both heels landed squarely on Cyclops' shoulders, knocking him off the rock face, with Thompson on top of him.

They landed thirty feet below in a bed of hard earth and sharp rocks, Thompson's fall broken by Cyclops' body.

With the wind knocked out of him, Thompson struggled to roll to one side. Cyclops, still miraculously conscious, caught him with a hand, and Thompson felt the man swarming on top of him, panting and muttering in a deranged voice. His muscular hands found Thompson's neck and closed quickly around it, pinning him to the earth. He could no longer breathe. The pressure around his throat was crushing, overwhelming.

The man in the gray slacks beckoned the Chameleon forward with his free hand. The absurdity of it, the Chameleon thought. A Secret Service agent, assigned to the Conway party, zealously performing his duties.

"What the hell are you doin' on the roof?" he demanded. "Nobody on the roof!"

The Chameleon nodded. He stole a glance at the jeeps below. No one had moved. The Mexicans on the back were still waiting for the order to fire.

The Secret Service agent reached the Chameleon's side and gripped his arm. "When I say get off the roof, goddammit, I mean get off the roof!"

"I'm sorry," the Chameleon answered, trying to control his voice. "I'm a press photographer."

A sudden roar from the crowd below, responding to Conway's exhortations over the loudspeakers, drowned out his words.

"Nobody on the goddamned roof!" the agent repeated, yelling it into the Chameleon's ear.

The Chameleon grasped the camera pod tightly with his left hand to hold the Arriflex on his shoulder and smashed the fist of his right directly into the man's Adam's apple. The agent gagged and slipped sideways, his elbow striking the top surface of the parapet wall at the roof's edge. The Chameleon pinned the hand holding the pistol to the parapet, while the agent clutched his throat, gasping for air like a beached fish. The Chameleon's brain was reeling. What a mess he'd made of it now!

The agent grabbed his arm with his free hand and tried to break the grip on his wrist. The Chameleon squeezed with all his strength, trying to force the pistol loose, but he knew he was outmatched, trying to hold the camera on his shoulder.

The agent kicked him a stunning blow in the shins, sending a shock of pain up through his leg and into his stomach. He pressed harder with his free hand, and tried to trip the man's feet, debating furiously with himself. Should he just kill him?

The agent jerked his arm free, and unintentionally squeezed the pistol's trigger, sending a shot wild into the air. The Chameleon felt the camera slipping from his shoulder, and reached up to save it. Free of him now, the agent hit him on the jaw with the pistol butt. The Chameleon clung desperately to the Arriflex, the inside of his head ringing from the blow. Only the pain in his jaw prevented him from passing out. He clasped his hand to his cheek and felt the bone below his ear grate against itself where it had broken.

Through the film of pain he saw the agent's mouth opening in the next instant and watched the top of his head disintegrate in an extraordinary explosion of flesh and bone. The man flopped like a bag of sand down across the flat top of the parapet. The Chameleon began to duck, and then felt something slap his shoulder and spin him around.

Grimly he clung to the camera and scrambled forward on his knees to the edge of the parapet. One of the Mexicans had opened fire on them, probably in response to the agent's accidental shot. Those at the back edge of the crowd in the customs yard had heard the racket of the machine gun, and they began to press inward, away from the checkpoint lanes, screaming. Panic spread through the throng like a shockwave, and soon the entire crowd was pressing against the wooden platform and the big VistaCruiser. The bus was rocking visibly, and the dignitaries on the platform scrambled to get off before the surge of the crowd collapsed it. Conway's voice boomed over the loudspeakers, begging for calm.

After the short burst of fire at the roof, the Mexicans had stopped. They seemed mesmerized by the panic inside the yard, and had not yet opened fire on the crowd. After a delay of nearly half a minute, the driver's door of the jeep on the right burst open and one Mexican leaped out, brandishing a machine gun at waist level and pointing at the crowd, exhorting the others to open fire.

The Chameleon settled the Arriflex deliberately on his shoulder, and pressed his eye to the viewfinder, steeling his body to ignore the pain searing through his shoulder and the side of his head. The crosshairs fell on the Mexican outside the jeep, dividing his body into four sections. The Chameleon could hear his *"Tiren! Tiren!"* clearly over the welling groans and shouts coming from the crowd as he pressed the film-start button on the side of the camera. He barely heard the shot, but he saw the man go down. He counted "One" out loud.

In rapid progression he moved the crosshairs from right to left, letting the center point rest for the briefest fraction of a second on the upper torso of a target before it moved on to the next.

Two. Three. Four.

Five. Six. Seven. Eight.

Reaching the extreme left side of the second jeep, he swung the Arriflex slowly back to the right, panning the open backs of both vehicles. Three bodies lay in a tangle in the first jeep, four in the second. Eight dead or dying. He picked another man off in the first jeep as he tried to crawl out over the bodies of the others.

Nine.

The two Mexicans who had been sitting in the passenger-side seats had climbed out and taken up positions by the front-right fenders of their vehicles, shielding themselves from the Chameleon's line of fire. The driver of the second jeep was still at the wheel. The Chameleon watched, too weak to duck out of the way, as a spray of bullets splattered against the wall just below him, gouging out pieces of concrete. The driver of the second jeep panicked and started the vehicle, slamming it into first gear and popping the clutch. It lurched forward, knocking down the man firing from the protection of the right fender, and ran directly over him with both front and rear tires.

Ten.

The jeep shot across the plaza, careening wildly from side to side, the driver fighting to bring it under control. The Chameleon aimed for the gas tank under the rear doors. He missed. And the range was getting more difficult every millisecond.

He aimed for a rear tire and believed that he hit it, but it had no effect on the speed or direction of the jeep. But at the widened distance the angles had changed so that the driver's head, previously hidden by the back edge of the jeep's roof, was now coming into view through the open rear door.

The Chameleon decided to try for one last good shot, using the back of the jeep's front seat to frame his target. Part of him was aware of terrible screaming, coming from the customs yard below him on the left. He heard a series of loud cracks that sounded as if the platform by the bus had finally given way.

He pressed the button and watched the jeep veer abruptly to the left. The head disappeared below the seat back, and he watched in horror as the jeep picked up speed and headed directly for the lines of waiting cars in the northbound lanes. It struck an old Chevrolet broadside and slammed it sideways into the car beside it in the outside lane, collapsing both of them against the reinforced-concrete piers at the edge of the plaza. The Chevrolet burst into flames, engulfing the jeep and six other cars near it. People were now fleeing their automobiles all along the line and running back toward the bridge or out into the empty half of the plaza.

Eleven.

Meanwhile, the last survivor of the attack team had driven the remaining jeep up against the south wall of the customs building, so that the Chameleon could see only its roof and hood, directly below him. The man inside was effectively hidden from the Arriflex. The Chameleon considered firing through the roof, and hoping for a lucky hit, but he had lost count of the rounds, and dared not waste another shot. He examined his shoulder for the first time since he had been hit. It was bleeding copiously, the blood staining shirt, pants, and shoes and puddling on the tar surface of the roof where he knelt. His entire left side was numb.

He looked back in the other direction toward the customs yard. One corner of the platform had collapsed and the bus behind it was rocking back and forth from the surge of the crowd. Conway was still visible, standing near the platform's back edge, holding on to a two-by-four railing, waving his free arm—either to quiet the crowd or to signal for help, it was impossible to tell. The microphone stand had slid off the platform, and Conway's voice was lost in the roaring swell of noise.

The Chameleon looked back around at the jeep against the wall beneath him. The twelfth man had still not emerged. The Chameleon expected him to make a dash for freedom—in the jeep or on foot. Had the man lost his nerve?

No!

Suddenly he knew. The jeep below was empty. His concentration had been off the vehicle for half a minute while he was shooting at the one escaping down the plaza.

He looked back at the crowd trapped in the yard. It milled in panic, the hysteria feeding on itself, the terrified throng unaware that the gunfire had ceased. At the far end, hands and feet were attacking the Cyclone fence and it was starting to give way.

Then he saw him.

He was working his way through the middle of the crowd.

The Chameleon raised the Arriflex and found him in the telescopic sight. Magnified tenfold, the Mexican's face filled the lens. He was shoving forward violently, the tip of the machine gun's barrel jutting up in front of him. The people around him paid no attention. He was just another body in the milling mob.

He had pushed to within twenty feet of the platform, where Conway still stood, clinging to the back railing. A suicide mission! The Chameleon kept the crosshairs on him, praying somebody would wrestle the gun from his grasp. But nobody realized what he was going to do!

The Mexican was near the edge of the platform now. The Chameleon panned the sight around. Where was the damned Secret Service? He found two on the platform with Conway, fighting to keep their balance. The others were somewhere in the crowd, struggling fruitlessly to push it back from the platform.

Nobody saw the Mexican.

The Chameleon tried to keep the crosshairs on the killer's neck, but the frenzied movements of the crowd made that impossible.

The Chameleon saw the tip of the gun barrel again. It had moved from the vertical to a forty-five-degree angle. The Mexican was trying to line it up on Conway, fifteen feet away. One burst of bullets, and Conway would be ripped apart.

The Chameleon knew he had to risk it. It was almost an impossible shot. Only the Mexican's head was visible, and then only for split seconds. He'd have one chance. He had to hit the brain.

He forced his arms and his fingers and his eye to hold rock-steady. The crosshairs showed the side of a face—the wrong one. Hold it! *Please, please, get out of the way!*

There! The Mexican's head emerged from behind a woman's huge Afro hairdo.

Now! He pressed the film-advance button.

The head disappeared. Had he hit him? The crowd seemed unaffected. He swung the sight to Conway. He was still there, clinging to the railing. He searched the crowd along the front of the platform. The Secret Service was still pushing people back.

Had he hit him? He still couldn't tell. It was maddening! He strained to see among the swirling kaleidoscope of faces. Before he found the answer, the box of explosives in the jeep below, set to a timing device by that twelfth Mexican, Rafael Escobar, ignited. The jeep blew apart with an earth-shaking concussion. The shockwave collapsed the south wall of the customs building in a roar of flying concrete, metal, and flame.

The Chameleon pitched on his face away from the parapet, the camera flying from his grasp. The surface of the roof was breaking apart, buckling as if struck by an earthquake.

He rose to his knees. The effort made him dizzy. He looked across the fifty feet of roof to the bulkhead door guarding the exit stairs. It looked a mile away. Hopeless. He heard sirens somewhere, added to the cries of the crowd and the roar of flames searing the parapet behind him. He pushed himself up and staggered toward the bulkhead in a spastic, stiff-kneed clamber, driven by willpower and desperation, his brain screaming at him: Too far! Too far!

Thompson realized that the knife was still in his right hand, invisible to the blind man at his throat. He plunged it with all his waning strength into Cyclops' side, and felt it penetrate with remarkable ease—seven inches of blade sliding through fabric, flesh, muscle. The pressure on his throat relaxed momentarily, then became more powerful then ever, pressing into his windpipe with viselike force.

Thompson yanked the knife free and plunged it in again, until the strength melted from his arm and it could no longer obey his brain's frantic directions. His vision blurred, then grew dark.

When his eyes opened again, Cyclops lay on top of him, his head against his chest, his arms along the side of Thompson's head. The palpable odor and feel of blood was everywhere, sticky and congealing around his arms and legs, trickling warmly over his neck.

He wanted to lie there. He felt so everlastingly tired. The earth was soft, the blood warm, and he wanted to sleep.

With tremendous effort he rolled Cyclops' corpse away from him and pushed himself to a sitting position. His throat and lungs felt scorched, making every breath a contest with pain.

He struggled to his feet, picked up Cyclops' rifle, and stumbled blindly into the woods, thinking one thought.

East.

East to the fence.

One foot in front of the other.

East to the fence.

He heard the helicopters. They seemed to be in the air everywhere— buzzards after carrion.

He knew he should wait until dark. But he could not last the night.

He rested near the no-man's-land along the inside of the fence, watching for traffic on the perimeter road.

No cars came by.

The day was turning colder. Thompson walked out onto the perimeter road and started north, looking for the hole in the fence. The only way out. The only way home.

He heard a car approaching from behind him, and he turned to face it, dropping to one knee on the crown of the road and steadying the rifle in his hands. He fumbled with it, slamming the bolt back and forth, trying to get the feel of it.

The vehicle slowed, but continued to move toward him. Thompson took careful aim along the small, unfamiliar iron sights, and lined them up with the windshield on the driver's side. If he got this one, it would be his third kill, he thought. Third kill of the day. Third kill of his life.

The vehicle was still advancing, but more slowly. It seemed it would never reach him. Close enough, Thompson decided.

He fired.

A shot boomed out, far wide of its target.

The vehicle was slowing down. He sat back in the roadway and waited, hoping for a better shot.

The jeep stopped fifty feet away and someone jumped out and began running toward him. He aimed the rifle carefully and pulled the trigger. Nothing happened. The figure ducked down, then came running again. He pulled the trigger a second time. Still nothing. Again, nothing. The weapon was empty. They could kill him now.

Someone was bending over him, taking the rifle away. He looked up into the face. A woman. Alone.

He was hallucinating, he feared.

"You?"

"My God," she said. "You look barely alive!"

He didn't understand. He was too tired to think it through. "Why did they send you?"

She dropped to her knees and wrapped her arms around him. "Nobody sent me," she said, her voice breaking. "We've got to find a way out!"

Thompson shook his head. "You're not one of them?" he whispered.

"Of course not." Harriet was pulling him to his feet. "We've got to hurry!"

She helped him into the Land Rover, then jumped behind the steering wheel and slammed the shift into gear.

"I'd have shot you," he said. "If I had the bullet."

She nodded. She was crying. He tried to say more, but his throat constricted around the words and nothing came out. He felt incredibly light-headed, overwhelmed. Seeing her tears made him begin to weep as well.

A half-mile farther on he recognized a landmark. This was the place, he knew. He tugged her arm and pointed toward the fence. Before she could bring the jeep to a stop he had opened the door and stumbled out. She switched off the ignition and ran after him.

Going through the hole in the fence seemed to take a long time.

Through the woods, he remembered the way. It was very hard, walking. He wanted to stop, but she kept him going, held him up. She talked to him but he didn't listen. The outside world felt very distant. He watched the leaves. A strong wind out of the northwest was blowing them off the maples and ashes in clouds, filling the air. His mind drifted with them.

He saw the motel at last and pointed to it. She nodded, smiling sadly.

Inside the motel room the bed looked infinitely beautiful. He collapsed on top of the spread and fell asleep.

51

Saturday night, November 3

Early on the morning of October 31 Harriet had put Thompson into a rented car and driven to New York City.

For three days they hid from the world in his apartment. Harriet found a doctor in the building to treat his leg. She ordered groceries and cooked. The days ran rapidly together, day into evening, night into morning, indistinguishable one from the next. They slept, ate, drank, and slept again. The telephone stayed unplugged, the doorbell unanswered. Insulated from the outside, they watched the public unfolding of the events of October 30 on television.

Tonight, for the first time, they made love.

Harriet initiated it. Thompson awoke in the late evening, stirred by a luxurious excitement, feeling the weight of soft breasts pressing into his chest, and wet tears falling on his cheek. Incredibly, he discovered that he was hard and deep inside her, and on the verge of exploding. He pulled her tight against him, still disbelieving, afraid a sudden movement might dissolve the intense pleasure into a dream.

"I'm sorry I took so long," she whispered.

"It's all right."

"Be patient with me."

"Yes."

Harriet raised herself to a sitting position and leaned forward. In the dim glow of the clock radio he could see the shadowy curves of her breasts and shoulders. Her hair sheltered her face in darkness. He ran his hands down over the mounds of her buttocks, lifting her slightly and then pressing her back down against him. She was very wet and he slid in and out of her with an exquisitely smooth slipperiness. She took up the motion on her own, inching herself slowly up and then slowly lowering herself again. The sensation bordered on pain.

Harriet continued the ecstatic slow-motion exercise, holding Thompson on the edge of orgasm for a long time. Finally she increased the pace of her movements, then pressed down against him in a sudden intense convulsion of pleasure. A long trembling moan escaped her lips. He grabbed her waist and thrust himself back and forth rapidly and exploded inside her with dizzying pent-up force. She gasped and shuddered and collapsed on top of him.

She was weeping unashamedly, "The first time," she said. "Oh, my God!"

They were aroused seemingly past satiation, and they continued on for hours more, stopping and beginning again a dozen times, whispering, giggling, crying, riding through a forest of sensual delight.

And drifted at last into a profound sleep.

Thompson sensed it before he heard it, crashing through the membrane of sleep, becoming part of his nightmare, then destroying it, bombarding it with decibels until it shattered into a million fragments of dust and drifted invisibly away, leaving only a black void and the terrible ringing.

Harriet's face was close to his ear, her hand shaking his shoulder.

"The door!" she was whispering fiercely. "Someone at the door!"

Sensations trickled back, one at a time. The feel of Harriet's fingers on his shoulder, squeezing hard. The dim, familiar outlines of the bedroom, illuminated by a clock dial. And still the ringing. It cut through everything, harsh and punishing, attacking the walls, the night, his sleep.

"What time?" he asked, pushing himself upright, his mouth slack with fatigue.

"Three-thirty!"

They scrambled unsteadily from the bed, grabbing for bathrobes, and made their way toward the vestibule past the living room. Thompson slapped clumsily at the light switch, and the room's sudden brilliance forced him to shut his eyes. The ringing went on.

Thompson found the Talk button on the intercom connected to the downstairs lobby door, and after a moment's confusion, pressed it.

"Who is it!"

He pressed the Listen button and waited for an answer. Nothing. But the damned ringing went on! Thompson punched the button in mounting fury, screaming for the unknown prankster to stop.

"It's the buzzer *here!*" Harriet shouted over his cries. "The door right here!"

He understood. Who? Who could have gotten in? Who in the building would ring his buzzer in the dead of night? He took the step to the door and peered into the small peephole. The entire corridor was visible, reduced and distorted by the peephole's fish-eye lens. An old man was there, a hand on the buzzer, the other bracing the doorjamb for support. His face was hidden in shadow.

"Who is it?" Harriet's voice quavered.

"I don't know."

"Tell him to stop!"

"What do you want?" Thompson yelled.

No reply. He yelled again. Harriet came to the door and looked out the peephole.

"He's sick," she said.

"Sick, all right," Thompson muttered.

"No. He looks hurt!"

The ringing went on, the caller refusing to remove his hand from the buzzer, refusing to speak. No one had come into the corridor to investigate the noise. The other apartment on the floor was empty. Thompson knocked the chain out of its slot, flipped the bolt on the Segal lock, and yanked open the door.

The Chameleon dropped his hand from the buzzer and stepped immediately inside. Thompson backed away; Harriet retreated to the doorway by the living room. His chin was pressing on his chest, and he stepped stiff-legged, like a drunk struggling to stay upright. His face was leather-skinned and smooth, almost mahogany in color, and drained of blood. The face of a mummy. His eyes, closed almost to slits, wrinkled in their corners, and the lips parted in a painful half-smile. A long-fingered hand reached out toward Thompson for a handshake. Thompson took it, baffled beyond reply. It trembled, hot and papery, in his uncertain clasp.

"He's sick!" Harriet said again, coming toward him to investigate.

"Thank you," he whispered, and then collapsed against Thompson and began to slip downward along his chest. Thompson caught him under his arms and fell with him to the floor.

52

Monday afternoon, November 5

Thompson sat in a small anteroom near the Oval Office, waiting for his summons. Every ten minutes a tall, thin, dark-haired woman in her forties would appear in the doorway, smile, and apologize for the delay. Otherwise he was left entirely alone, among six empty upholstered armchairs, several bare side tables, and a massive three-screen television set that squatted against the wall across from the chairs. Thompson remembered that the set was a legacy from Lyndon Johnson, who had a compulsion for watching the evening news on all three networks simultaneously. The set was on now, its volume turned down, each screen flashing silent color images, like a display in a department store.

Otherwise, it was oddly still. Occasionally figures passed by the open doorway, their footsteps deadened by the deep carpeting. That was all. The Oval Office, the vortex of a major national crisis, lay but a dozen feet away on the other side of the wall, yet it seemed as if nothing was happening. Where were all the others, Thompson wondered, who must also be waiting to see the President? Segregated in another room somewhere? The stillness seemed to loom in the air, portentous and electric. He was in the eye at the center of the storm.

He breathed deeply to steady his nerves, and examined his suit for the hundredth time. It was the same suit he had worn the day he had discovered Allen Roland hanging from the ceiling of his study in Georgetown, thirteen days ago. Maybe he should retire the suit after today, he thought, the way baseball teams retire the numbers of their great players.

His leg felt stiff and sore, but today, for the first time, he was able to walk without much pain. He had been able to abandon the cumbersome crutch for a wooden cane, which he rather liked. His other injuries—the assorted bruises and lacerations that covered almost half the surface of his body—were healing rapidly. Fully dressed, all that showed were a deep cut across his forehead and a scattering of scratches around the neck.

The psychological damage probably cut deeper, but at the moment he felt strong and full of purpose, in charge of his life as never before. Marwick had promoted him to vice-president and publisher, making him an officer of the company and substantially increasing his income. And he was in love with Harriet.

She was working nonstop to complete her series of articles on the Zodiac conspiracy for the *Times*, and Thompson knew she was going to win a Pulitzer for it. And he was going to give her a whopping advance for a book on the subject.

But the specter of Halloween Park, still fresh and raw in their memories, dominated their personal lives like a palpable evil spirit, lurking in the shadows of their thoughts, waiting each night to invade their sleep. It would take a long time to exorcise it.

And his battles with the law, concerning his own actions in the park, were yet to come.

Thompson watched the silent images on the three screens of the console. All three of the networks were covering the same event—the funeral of President John Douglas Mills. After lying in state for four days in the Capitol Rotunda, he was taken home to Lubbock, Texas, to be buried. The ceremonies had begun at ten in the morning. Leaders from around the world were in attendance—it was the biggest such gathering since Marshal Tito's funeral in 1980—but to Thompson it appeared to be a hastily arranged and undignified affair. There was, for example, a morning parade of floats down Lubbock's Main Street, featuring tableaux of the President's great moments in office. No one, he reflected, had attempted the most powerful tableau—the moment of his death. Because no one yet knew how it had happened.

Not since November 1963 had a nation together watched so much television news. The reporting had been continuous since Tuesday. And even today the funeral ceremonies were interrupted constantly by taped interviews and news updates on the still-unfolding story of the events of October 30. Today the three networks were also providing spot coverage of another funeral—that of CIA Director William Ward. At the request of the general's widow, he was being buried at Arlington National Cemetery, with full military honors.

John Graves had been buried on Friday in a private ceremony in Bristol, Connecticut, his hometown. The press had not been invited.

Senator Albert MacNair had taken his own life in his home in Peterborough, New Hampshire, on Thursday, November 1, by putting a shotgun in his mouth. His funeral was scheduled for tomorrow.

There had been no ceremony at all for Joseph Madero, the man called Cyclops. His body was being held at the city morgue in Manchester, New Hampshire, awaiting the location of his next of kin.

Autopsies had been performed on all the bodies found in Halloween Park. It had been determined that John Graves and William Ward had died as a result of wounds received from a Mannlicher Model M hunting rifle. Joseph Madero had died from multiple stab wounds in the side. Both the rifle and the knife had been recovered. The President had died from multiple punctures caused by a wood-and-rope animal trap, described in one newspaper as a "Philippine pig-stabber." Official federal and state investigations and hundreds of laboratory tests were under way.

The killings at the Laredo customs station were also under federal and state investigation. Twelve Mexican nationals, posing as soldiers, had died there, as well as two women in the crowd around Conway's bus and a family of five Mexicans in the lane of northbound traffic. Dozens of others had been seriously injured. In the rubble of the south wall of the customs building, searchers had uncovered another body, that of a Secret Service agent assigned to the Conway campaign. No one had yet been able to offer a coherent explanation of what had happened, or why.

The Mexican government was investigating the incident at Laredo as well, and had asked the United Nations and the Organization of American States to condemn the United States for warlike acts against its citizens. The State Department was considering offering an apology and a promise of restitution, once the details of the incident were sorted out.

344   /   VERNON TOM HYMAN

Presidential candidate Harrison Conway, who had received a superficial head wound when the platform in the customs yard collapsed, was back on the campaign, wearing a white bandage on his head. He had called for President Beecher and the Congress to set up immediately a commision of distinguished national figures to investigate the bizarre tragedies. It seemed a foregone conclusion that they would.

Meanwhile, wild stories were circulating in the press to explain the mysterious incidents—journalists, commentators, pundits, and politicians vying with one another for the scenario that best fit the scarce details so far available.

The only thing that was clear in the turmoil and confusion was that the country was in for years of committee investigations, blue-ribbon panels, Senate and House hearings, charges and countercharges by high government officials, and a river of books and articles by journalists, historians, psychiatrists, politicians, and assassination buffs.

The screen on the far left of the console dissolved to frame a reporter standing on the White House lawn, the columns of the north portico in the background. Thompson stepped over to the set and turned up the volume:

"This is Win Peterson at the White House. Tonight, at eight o'clock eastern time, President Raymond Beecher will address the nation from the Oval Office. A major speech has been expected from the new President ever since his swearing-in six days ago, and there has already been much speculation on the possible contents of the address. Whether or not it will contain any new revelations concerning the events at Halloween Park and Laredo, place names that have already, in the space of these last few tumultuous days, gained household status around the world . . ."

A thickset, sandy-haired man materialized in the doorway to the anteroom, the tall woman hovering behind him. He looked back over his shoulder at her, and when she nodded, he walked directly over to Thompson's chair, blocking his view of the television screen.

"Please stand, Mr. Thompson."

Thompson pushed himself up slowly out of the chair, looking over at the tall woman with a puzzled expression. The man placed his hands under Thompson's arms and ran them rapidly down his sides, then patted him hard on the chest, shoulder blades, stomach, and small of the back. Without a pause he opened Thompson's suit jacket, snaked his hands around his waist, then knelt and felt around the ankles, the inside thighs, and the crotch. Finished, he stepped back and regarded Thompson critically, like a bad piece of sculpture. "Are you carrying any weapons or recording devices, Mr. Thompson?"

Thompson stared at him in disbelief. He had already been subjected to a thorough search and interrogation at the outside gate by four guards before he was even allowed into the West Wing. The Secret Service was under tremendous pressure, of course, since its failure to protect President Mills and his party from the massacre in Halloween Park. Criticism of the agency was harsh and widespread, and a major shake-up was inevitable. What would he do, Thompson wondered, if he knew that he had President Mills's assassin right in his grasp, right here in the White House?

"Didn't you find it?"

"Where is it?" the agent demanded, his voice flooded with menace.

"I'm just kidding."

"Don't."

The agent turned on the heels of his wingtips and marched from the room. The tall woman remained behind, an embarrassed smile bending her pressed lips.

"The President will see you now, Mr. Thompson," she said.

The Oval Office was larger than Thompson had imagined, and he had imagined it large. The curved walls, the high ceilings, the intensity of the sunlight filtering through the tall bay of windows behind the President's desk lent the room a dramatic quality that took Thompson's breath away. The President stood exactly in its center, framed by the set of three glass-paned French doors that opened onto the colonnade and the rose garden. He was poised like a model, his polished shoes resting on the big presidential seal woven into the tapestry of the blue rug, one hand thrust casually into a pants pocket. He looked tall, handsome, distinguished—and strong. Thompson thought of the history the room had seen and he trembled inwardly at what lay ahead, wondering if he had the courage to see it through.

As they shook hands, Thompson saw that at closer range Beecher appeared haggard, the big-toothed, confident grin and shock of white hair dissolving into a gray-fleshed, wrinkled face, eyes red-rimmed with fatigue.

He motioned Thompson to the set of sofas that faced each other near the far end of the oval from the President's desk. Thompson sank down into one of them; the President sat on a hard-backed chair near the sofa's corner. Thompson supposed Beecher meant this as a way of putting him at his ease, to take as much of the strain out of the occasion as possible. Or to put him off his guard.

"Thank you for coming, Mr. Thompson."

"My pleasure, Mr. President."

Beecher cleared his throat and looked around the room. Thompson realized that its ambience was nearly as unfamiliar to Beecher as it was to him. Beecher was still in awe of it, still in awe of himself as the country's chief executive.

"I had also hoped to talk with Miss Mitchell today," he began, "but I understand that . . . ah . . . she will not be available for another day or so."

Thompson nodded. At first Harriet had wanted to come with him, but he had convinced her that it would be safer for him to see Beecher alone.

"I think we should clear the air first, Jay, if I may call you that?"

"Yes. Of course."

"I expect that you are aware that Harriet and I . . . ah . . . once were involved with each other. . . ." Beecher was having a very hard time getting his words out.

Thompson managed a strained smile. "Yes, I am, Mr. President."

"Well . . . good. I just wanted to assure you that . . . I want you to know that . . . that's all very much in the past, we . . . Although, I think, I'm bound to say . . . Harriet's a wonderful, remarkable woman. Very beautiful, too. You're lucky. . . ."

Beecher let his words trail off, never having properly organized any sincere sentiment in his mind. Thompson suspected he was burying his real feelings in the confused verbiage. Feelings of what? Jealousy? Anger? Guilt?

Beecher ventured onto safer ground. "I'm giving a major address to the nation tonight." He waved his hand toward the pile of television equipment by the door, awaiting the technicians who would set it up later in the day.

"I don't have to tell you," he continued, his voice grave, "that the country is in trauma. Suspicions of the most outlandish variety are coming from the mouths and pens of normally responsible people. It's much worse than the Kennedy assassination in 1963, because of the bizarre circumstances, and because no credible suspect—or even credible motive—has been found. Just this morning the head of the Joint Chiefs of Staff was in here, telling me that he had evidence that the Russians were responsible. Last night it was the new deputy director of the CIA. He told me it was the work of Iranian terrorists. According to him, there are hundreds of Iranians in New Hampshire—enrolled in colleges there. He thinks a group of them, working for the new Iranian regime, hid in the park and ambushed the President. These are the kinds of things I'm hearing. Insane stories, making everyone nervous and distrustful. And on top of all that, we have the Laredo incident. So-called responsible people here are urging we go to war with Mexico!"

Beecher stood up and paced the room, walking first to the French doors, then to his desk, where he watched the play of lights flashing incoming calls on his console telephone.

"I have to reassure the nation tonight that we're on top of events. I want to debunk the worst of the scaremongers and get the country's mood turned away from its obsessive preoccupation with this tragedy, getting it thinking positively again." The President paused, casting his eyes along the wide expanse of blue carpet between them. He didn't sound entirely convinced he could do it.

He must be wondering, Thompson thought, about his tenure as President. Remarkably, a network television news poll, taken during the last twenty-four hours, had indicated a big swing in the electorate toward Beecher, now the Republican party's standard-bearer, thanks to a hastily convened special GOP convention. Much of the swing was no doubt the direct result of an outpouring of sympathy for Beecher's sudden responsibilities, and a widely felt desire to back the new President in a crisis— almost the same situation, ironically, that Mills had intended to manufacture for himself with Operation Zodiac.

Beecher now stood an even chance of winning the election tomorrow. He must know, Thompson thought, that his speech this evening could decide the matter.

"One of the things I'll be telling the nation tonight," he continued, "is that I have directed the Attorney General to head a special criminal investigation to expedite and complete the process of gathering evidence in the Halloween Park and Laredo incidents. I expect you'll assist them in this in every way possible."

"I'll do what I can, Mr. President."

"Good."

Beecher leaned against the desk. A stack of documents was arranged in a neat pile on one corner of it, and Beecher removed the top one and began thumbing through it.

"More than anyone else, you must know what happened at Halloween Park," he said. "Before the committees and subcommittees and grand juries get to you, I need to have your version of the events of that day. You are in a precarious situation, legally. In return for your cooperation, I'll help you to the extent I can."

Thompson waited until Beecher lifted his eyes from the page he was reading. "I'm not aware that I've broken any laws," he lied. "Unless the government intends to prosecute me for trespassing on private property."

Beecher didn't answer immediately, but instead continued turning the pages of the document. Finally he looked across at Thompson, his expression cold. "I believe trespassing is a matter for the local sheriff. I had more serious offenses in mind."

Thompson felt a chill creep over him. He fixed his gaze on the tall bay of windows behind Beecher's desk. The white gauze curtaining had been pulled aside and the inches-thick bulletproof glass was refracting the late-afternoon sunlight like a prism, illuminating the edges of the windowpanes in a bright rainbow of colors.

Beecher closed the folder in his hand and tapped its cover with a finger. "Some of the forensic and laboratory tests from Halloween Park are already here. The results are beginning to surprise me. Your fingerprints, for example, Mr. Thompson, have been found on the Mannlicher rifle responsible for the deaths of both John Graves and William Ward. And your fingerprints have also been found on the knife identified as the weapon used to kill Joseph Madero."

Thompson clenched his jaws and stared at Beecher. Beecher dropped the folder back onto the pile. "That's incredible enough," he continued, "but even more incredible is the finding of your fingerprints all over the device that killed President Mills."

Thompson cleared his throat. Beecher was sitting on the corner of the long, ornate desk, hands in his pockets, a humorless grin on his face. The distance that separated them unnerved Thompson, made him feel isolated and vulnerable, unable to fight back. He raised his voice, feeling the anger in it.

"There are explanations, Mr. President, which will become clear in the course of the investigations. You'll also find Cyclops' fingerprints on the rifle that killed Graves and Ward. And probably President Mills's as well, since he owned the gun. I'm sure that's all there in your report, too. As for the pig-stabber, you just invented that. There's no forensic laboratory in the world that can lift accurate fingerprints from wood."

Beecher raised an eyebrow. "You checked?"

"I checked."

Beecher stood in front of the desk now, his arms folded across his chest. "That still leaves the knife, the one that killed Cyclops."

Thompson nodded. "I know. I used it. I killed Cyclops in self-defense."

"And who else?"

"Cyclops killed everyone else."

"Including the President?"

Thompson hesitated. "That was an accident."

Beecher walked slowly over to the French doors and looked out into the rose garden. "You'd better hire yourself a hell of a good lawyer."

President Beecher had backed him into a corner far more effectively that he had anticipated, Thompson realized. The lab reports had shocked him, even though the Chameleon had warned him to expect it. The tentacles of the great bureaucracy were already reaching out, attaching their suckers to his body, preparing to bleed him to death by degrees, to accomplish legally what even a gang of killers had been unable to do. The irony was not lost on him. He should be a national hero. Instead, he might end up fighting to stay out of prison.

"I'll make a deal with you," Thompson said.

President Beecher wrinkled his forehead. "You'll make a *deal* with me? What are you talking about?"

"I'll tell you exactly what happened at Halloween Park and Laredo. If you throw the election."

The statement was greeted by a long silence. Beecher looked at him as if he had blasphemed. He seemed to be sifting through possible ways to respond. Thompson felt terrified. He had taken the irrevocable step. There was no turning back now.

Finally Beecher laughed. It came out as a sarcastic explosion of sounds. A sneer. "Even assuming I'd do something so ridiculous," he said, "what sort of deal is that?"

"For you, an excellent one. You might avoid impeachment and prison."

Beecher's face grew white. "Have you lost your senses?"

Beecher's shocked innocence angered Thompson. "You tricked Harriet into telling you the contents of Roland's file and where she kept it. You pretended you were helping her, when in fact you were luring her into a trap. You arranged to steal the file from her apartment when she was still with you. And you extracted from her a description of the car I had taken. You guessed I would head for Halloween Park, so you alerted the others and they pressed the local police into tracking me to that motel. No doubt they had orders to turn me over to someone fronting for Zodiac. Cyclops, probably."

"You've concocted a bizarre fantasy." Beecher's voice was calm.

"I don't think so, Mr. President. I'll admit I have no proof. But the circumstantial evidence is compelling. Most compelling of all is the fact of the date of your birth—February 3."

Beecher shook his head, appearing perplexed.

"You're an Aquarius. Harriet and I should have figured it out earlier, but we were too busy being hunted down by Zodiac's murder squad. When it was explained to us, it was obvious. Code names drawn from the signs of the Zodiac, picked to match your birthdates."

Beecher dropped his arms from his chest and took several steps toward Thompson, then stopped, as if he had seen a snake under the sofa. "You're talking vicious nonsense! Who told you this?"

"The man who stopped the attack at Laredo. A professional. You don't know who he is, and I have no intention of telling you. With all Zodiac's efforts to kill me and Harriet, you never guessed there was another, far more skillful man on your tail. You underestimated Allen Roland's resourcefulness."

Beecher's composure began to crack, his voice suddenly harsh and strident. "Are you trying to implicate me in some conspiracy?"

"Yes. You're Zodiac's missing fourth member. Once our friend had those code names from Roland, he suspected that one of the conspirators had a weakness for astrology. He checked his suspicions with a famous astrologer in Paris, and she gave him the name of Senator Albert MacNair. He broke into MacNair's house and found the plans for Zodiac. The rest was easy. He knew MacNair was a Gemini. All he needed to do was identify the other three. He simply checked a library copy of *Who's Who* for birthdates of prominent political figures tied closely to MacNair. He quickly narrowed it down to President Mills, a Capricorn, CIA Director Ward, a Scorpio, and you, an Aquarius. It was too incredible a coincidence to be accidental."

Thompson felt adrenaline surging through him, making him tremble. And there was no outlet for it. No fight or flight. Just words. It had been easier to kill Cyclops.

"It's still hard for me to believe it," he continued. "Still hard for me to accept that any man could be so enamored of the vice-presidency that he would let innocent people die just to hang on to it. . . ."

Thompson let the words penetrate, hoping they would sting Beecher into incriminating himself. The President was leaning against his desk again, hands resting behind him on the desktop, his eyes focused in the distance. He seemed not to be listening.

"And out of all the violence," Thompson continued, "out of the collapse of Zodiac, you emerge as President, with a good shot at winning tomorrow's election. With your co-conspirators all dead, you're the sole beneficiary of the plot. Ironic, isn't it?"

Thompson felt the force of his own words so intensely he barely realized when he stopped that the President was not answering him. The silence continued until it became a subtle force of inertia, making the breaking of it more difficult as it grew in strength.

Finally Beecher spoke. His voice was tight, choking back emotions at which Thompson could only guess: "The presidency is a very powerful office."

Thompson waited for him to continue, but he did not elaborate.

"That's what your predecessor thought," Thompson said. "He overstepped himself."

Beecher nodded. "I understand your outrage, Mr. Thompson. But your own ordeal has totally twisted your thinking. Matters are not so neatly black and white as you would have them. The world is not divided into good and bad."

"Everyone has rationalizations for his acts."

The President began to lose his temper. "You're trying some kind of ill-conceived bluff with me, and you're getting yourself in very deep trouble. Do you think that you're invulnerable to prosecution? I can have you arrested for what you've said in this office!"

"But you won't. The details of Halloween Park will come out no matter what, and I'll have to face them. You can't affect that one way or the other."

"You are a dangerously naive and stupid man!" Beecher said.

"We'll see who's dumber, Mr. President, you or me. I didn't expect I'd get a confession from you. I came to offer some advice. You'd better consider it. Tomorrow's New York *Times* will carry the first of Harriet's articles on this crisis. The information in it will be explosive, to say the least. She'll reveal to the world for the first time the story of the Zodiac conspiracy. Everything. From Allen Roland's murder to President Mills's attempt to have Conway assassinated during the confusion of the attack on the Laredo customs station."

Beecher's eyes widened in shock. "What!"

Thompson smiled. Beecher had finally given himself away. "He didn't tell you about that part of the plan, did he? He must have been afraid that you'd back out if you knew what his real intentions were."

Beecher was not intimidated. "It's a fairy tale. I don't believe it. And Harriet should have assembled her story a little sooner. Tomorrow is election day. Those who read the *Times* tomorrow morning will vote against me anyway. I expect to lose New York State."

Thompson shook his head. "You seem to forget. The next day's *Times* is on the streets of New York City by ten-thirty the night before. That means an hour and a half after your speech tonight the major networks will have the story—in time for the eleven-o'clock news. And the wire services will send it out to their member papers in time for tomorrow's editions in every state in the Union. The country will go to the polls tomorrow stunned by the revelations of gross criminal behavior in Mills's administration. Your name will be omitted, because we don't have the proof against you that we have against Mills, Ward, MacNair, and others. But the guilt by association will cost you the election. That's why we're offering you the chance to exit gracefully tonight, in your speech. You'll beat the *Times* by an hour and half, and save yourself much grief. All you have to do is insert a paragraph in the speech declaring that you feel the true story surrounding President Mills's death will inevitably compromise your administration. Urge the country to vote for Conway. That's all. If you do that, you stand a chance of escaping implication in Zodiac. Maybe no proof against you will ever be found. I'm sure you've been careful to cover your involvement. But if you win the election, you will be under the cloud of Zodiac, you will be unable to govern, and the chances of your eventual exposure as a part of the conspiracy will be far greater. You might end up in prison."

Beecher stared at Thompson. A fine bead of sweat had popped out on his brow just below the thatch of white hair. "I have reasons for everything I've done!" he shouted. "I could explain them and make you understand. I could explain how it's possible to be part of something without having a choice about it, without being in a position to control the acts of others. But I don't have to explain anything to you!"

Thompson's fear was giving way to contempt. "If you mean you weren't calling the shots, I know that already. Of the four, your behavior was the most cowardly. The most contemptible. You set up an old girlfriend for murder, then you stayed away from the action, just in case anything went wrong. And you almost crawled out untouched. Almost."

Beecher moved back across the office slowly, as if he hoped he would never reach the other side. He stopped by the desk and fixed his eyes on the telephone console. He caressed the receiver lightly with his hand.

"I fully intend to win tomorrow's election, Mr. Thompson," he whispered. "And even if I do not, I will be in this office until late January. Your future, I daresay, is not so promising."

Beecher looked around the room as if he had momentarily forgotten who he was, what he was doing here. He seemed to be staring back at Thompson, but the focus of his eyes fell past, on the wall behind him.

". . . not promising at all."

The tall dark-haired woman reappeared, nodding primly. "Mr. President, your next appointment. . . ."

Beecher snapped out of his reverie and smiled brightly at the woman. "Ah, Agnes. Of course! Mr. Thompson was just leaving!"

Thompson stood and wondered whether or not to shake hands, just to preserve the semblance of normality. Beecher seemed uninterested, so Thompson nodded at Agnes and walked from the room. He caught a last look over his shoulder before turning the corner in the outer vestibule. Beecher was standing in the center of the room again, on the presidential seal, in much the same pose as when Thompson had first walked into the Oval Office. Cheerful light flooded the room from the windows behind him, casting his silhouette in sharp relief against them. Thompson could not understand why, but he felt an overpowering urge to cry.

Back out on the sidewalk by Lafayette Park he was thoughtful, awed by the legendary dimensions of his own actions. Implausible, at the least. He was bringing down his second President in six days.

Thompson walked into the small park, strolling aimlessly, following an erratic course of reversed directions, retraced steps, and sudden tangents. It took him almost twenty minutes to locate the tail President Beecher had put on him, a slender man wearing a narrow-brimmed hat and a shapeless black raincoat. He was the only one. Thompson ran across the street to the taxi stand in front of the Hay-Adams and jumped into a waiting cab. As it moved into the flow of traffic, heading west on H Street, Thompson slumped back and let his head fall against Harriet's shoulder.

"Thank God that's over," he muttered.

"Will he do it?" she asked.

"I'm not sure. We'll have to wait until tonight, I guess."

"We can't."

"We can't?"

Harriet reached into her capacious leather sack and drew out two airline tickets. "We'll read about it later," she said. "These are taking us all the way to a Greek island. I've packed bathing suits, toothbrushes, and passports."

Thompson jumped upright. "Greek island? Tonight?"

"Assam has given us the run of his cottage for as long as we like. He said it's the most beautiful place on earth."

"Assam? Who the hell is Assam?"

"The Chameleon. I finally wormed his real name out of him."

Thompson nodded. "Well, you would. Where's he now?"

"He said he had an appointment to keep in Geneva. He'll join us on the island in a week."

Thompson slid his hand along Harriet's thigh and rested it on her knee. It sounded right. A temporary escape to a sunny paradise, thousands of miles away. With a beautiful woman whom he loved. That was the best ending you could get in the real world. The rest—the aftermath of Zodiac—would be faced another day.

Harriet folded her hand around his and squeezed it. "A personal question?" she asked.

"Okay."

"Am I as good in bed as that Barbara woman from the motel?"

Thompson looked the picture of shocked innocence. "What are you talking about?"

Harriet laughed. "Oh, come on! I saw the way she doted and fussed over you when we staggered into that motel. Like a long-lost lover! She practically elbowed me right out of the way!"

Thompson shut his eyes and shook his head. "I can't believe you're talking about this now. Where's your sense of priorities?"

"Right where it's supposed to be. You're evading the question."

Thompson smiled. "You're right."

"Well?"

He patted her knee. "You'd kill me if I said you were only a close second, wouldn't you?"

Harriet smiled and touched her lips to his ear. "Not at all. I'd just say I needed a few more weeks of practice."

Thompson nodded in mock solemnity. "That's the spirit."

EPILOGUE

Two days after Jay and Harriet's arrival on the island of Ios, Demetrios brought them a copy of the *International Herald Tribune*. Raymond Beecher's speech that night had contained no hint of concession. On election day, Harriet's report in the *Times* had caused a national sensation. By the time the polls closed in California, the story had seeped across the continent. Harrison Conway, trailing Beecher in a close race, won California and took the election to become the forty-first President of the United States.

Demetrios also brought them a letter:

My dear Harriet and Jay,

Enclosed you will find a document which you must bring to a Mr. A. Papagopolis, my lawyer in the village. Demetrios will know where he lives. The document is in Greek, but I will spare you the mystery of its contents. It is an addition to my will, deeding the cottage on Ios to you both jointly. Care for it, and spend as many days of your lives there as you can find to spend. The locals claim Hercules once visited Ios, so you can see that it is a fitting place for heroes, which of course both of you are.

I will be required to spend the next few days in a hospital in

Switzerland. They will take very good care of me, but I do not expect to be released. Think of me when you look out on the Aegean Sea. It was my brief connection with eternity.

Assam (the Chameleon)